Tour of Deception

by

Dennis Broderick

Best Wishes,

Dennis Broderick

In memory of the fallen heroes
who died saving others
and the legacies they left behind

CAST OF CHARACTERS

AMERICANS

Peter Craft—operative, CIA; professional golfer

Jennifer Wilkins (aka Victoria Beach)—operative, CIA; business-media manager

Jason Vaughn—senior operative, CIA

Jack Wilson—senior scientist, CIA

Catherine (Kate) Walker—director, CIA

Callie—greens-keeper; childhood friend of Peter Craft

Amanda Craft—mother of Peter Craft; daughter of Bill Craft

Bill Craft—deceased military intelligence expert, Naval Intelligence; grandfather of Peter Craft; father of Amanda Craft

Pete Sullivan—deceased New York City firefighter, father of Peter Craft, Amanda Craft's fiancé, brother of John Sullivan

Clifford Beaumont—director, Directorate of Clandestine Services; CIA

Dr. Emily Page—psychiatrist, CIA

Ms. Kim—technician, CIA

Gul—director of Iranian Operations, CIA

Mr. Tagami—motorcycle expert, CIA

Jefferson—Peter Craft's caddy played by Jason Vaughn in disguise

Charlotte Bates—newspaper report; worked as intern for Peter Craft's mother

Kekoa Kalani—senior operative, special operations expert, CIA; mentor of Peter Craft

John Conrad—security officer, CIA

Zachary—high school football teammate of Peter Craft

Chris Davis—childhood friend and football teammate of Peter Craft

Doreen—hospital administrator; girlfriend of Chris Davis

Maj. Frank Young— soldier; person manning CIA watch station

Taylor King— professional golfer

Tiger Woods—professional golfer

Rory McIlroy—professional golfer

Joe Miller—childhood football teammate of Peter Craft

Maurice—fashion designer; friend of Daria Turani

Anna—glamor magazine staff, administrative assistant to Daria Turani

John Sullivan—New York City firefighter, the uncle of Peter Craft, younger brother of Pete Sullivan

Ms. Morgan—convenience store employee in Kitty Hawk, NC

IRANIAN

Kamran Turani—professional golfer; son of Amir Turani

Daria Turani—glamor magazine owner; daughter of Amir Turani; sister of Kamran Turani; niece of General Farzad Shirazi

Amir Turani—founder of financial investment firm; father of Daria and Kamran Turani; bother-in-law of General Farzad Shirazi

Farzad Shirazi—general, Iran Quds Force; uncle of Daria and Kamran Turani; bother-in-law of Amir Turani

Malek Asadi—chief executive officer of Hamedan Chemie; al-Qaeda leader

Gilani—Islamic cleric; father of Ali

Ali—small business owner; son of Gilani

Ahmad Reza—security officer, Iran Quds Force

Moein Tehrani (aka Vahid Salehi)—rogue operative, Iranian Ministry of Intelligence; golf course maintenance worker

Javid—soldier, Iran Quds Force, direct report to Ahmad Reza

Rahimi—President of the Iran

OTHERS

Kai Peng—Cyber Golf Champion

Luke—classmate of Malek Asadi known for bullying other children

Azzam Baahir—founder of financial investment firm based in Saudi Arabia

Sara Baahir—daughter of Azzam Baahir

Jeremy West—retired operative, British Intelligence; owner of small boat fleet; boyfriend of Amanda Craft

Erwin Klein—German intelligence officer played by Peter Craft in disguise

Christopher Reed—reporter for British tabloid magazine

Bartholomew Higgins—host of a British sport news program

Martin McKinney—leader of Scottish running group

Lenard McKnight—caddy at St. Andrews

Amid—taxi driver

Bandar—Saudi Minister of the Interior

Zahra—equestrian, horse trainer and stable manager; daughter of the Saudi Minister of Finance

Mr. Preston Jackson—British actor

PROLOGUE

CHARLESTON, SC

Wrapped in a white blanket and wearing a blue knit cap, the red-faced 9 lb. 8 oz. baby boy slept soundly in the bassinet by the side of the bed. Although a difficult delivery, the child was never in danger; the topnotch medical staff made sure of that. The new mother struggled to stay awake, weakened from the long, laborious birth. Now in a semi-conscious state assisted by a strong sedative, she placed one hand lightly on the baby's back, feeling him breath as air moved in and out of his tiny body.

Catherine looked through the window into the morning light, emotionally drained from hours at the hospital. She said a prayer of thanks, still in awe of witnessing her best friend Amanda give birth to the precious baby boy. The joy she felt for her friend was dampened by the concern that the child would grow up without his father. She and Amanda had first met years earlier while attending gymnastic summer camp and became best friends at college, coping with life's challenges as they transitioned from teenagers to young adults. Now, Catherine worked in Naval Intelligence as an intern. Her boss, Amanda's father, sat on the corner of the bed in his wrinkled suit and day-old beard, studying his grandson's features.

Worried about her friend's emotional state, Catherine hoped that Amanda could put the death of the boy's father behind for the sake of the child. At that moment, staring through the window as if looking into the future, Catherine Walker made a silent declaration *that she would not rest until every last one of them was dead.*

"Sir, it's time to go," Catherine whispered to Amanda's father, trying to not wake mother and baby. In twenty minutes, Bill Craft was scheduled to give a critical intelligence briefing to the United States Central Command. She knew there was only one thing important enough for him to entrust his family's well being to another... *killing al-Qaeda in the mountains of Afghanistan.*

Dennis Broderick   vii

CHAPTER 1

U.S. CAPITOL BUILDING
WASHINGTON, D.C.

The hammering of the chairman's gavel called to order the closed session of the U.S. Intelligence Committee. Alarmed by Iran being chosen to host a major golf tournament, the elite committee peered down from the grand oak bench with contempt at the middle-aged woman in the center of the room. Wearing an elegant business suit with reading glasses positioned to hold back her shoulder length brown hair, the woman sitting in the "hot seat" waited patiently to give another intelligence update.

Catherine Walker, the Director of the Central Intelligence Agency, expected to take fire from both sides of the aisle. When it was her time to speak, she confidently addressed the committee, thanking the members for their diligent oversight of the nation's intelligence mission. The Director's forceful presence far eclipsed her petite, feminine stature. A career officer, Walker's steadfast commitment to national intelligence gave her the willpower not to bend to political pressures. She believed it was the CIA's duty to give unvarnished fact-based intelligence to the elected officials, regardless of their political affiliations.

On Capitol Hill Walker was both respected and feared. Some respected her as a strong-minded woman who could get things done within the Agency's old boy network. Others feared her for having firsthand knowledge of U.S. Intelligence operations. The insiders knew Walker led the design of systems that now collected information on everybody, foreign and domestic—calls, messages, purchases, travel, and anything else one might imagine. Nothing was off limits anymore. If pushed, she had the power to expose congressional backroom deals, and that scared the hell out of Washington politicians.

For decades Iran had been considered a high priority national security threat. However, faced with an imminent Israeli attack and crippling economic sanctions, newly elected moderate leaders dismantled the nation's nuclear weapons program and opened trade with Western nations.

Enamored by positive political change in Iran, the committee disregarded the CIA's objection and redirected intelligence assets towards China.

After giving the update, Walker concluded her assessment by saying, "Although no actionable threat is known at this time… *significant uncertainty remains.*"

As usual, political posturing dominated the hearing. The President's pro-business allies pushed for assurances that Americans attending the high profile golf event in Iran would be safe. The opposition twisted information in a way that might weaken the President's reelection campaign. Unsatisfied with the inconclusive assessment, committee members took turns scolding the Director for not being sufficiently definitive in her assessment.

The committee chairman tossed the Director a softball question, "What's behind the Middle East's new interest in the game of golf?"

Annoyed by the elementary question, Walker responded, "It's the combination of geopolitical change and golf market expansion enabled by technology advancements."

Unhappy with the terse response, the chairman asked, "Please elaborate?"

Why don't you just read the analysis provided in the read-ahead package? She thought, and then proceeded to explain, "From a geopolitical perspective, unfettered access to information via social media dispelled government propaganda that golf was a Western elitist sport reserved for the wealthy. People could see for themselves that professional golf offered opportunities to all ranks in life, with some of the best players coming from the poorest countries. Middle East nations that once demonized golf now embrace it as a tool to keep the youth occupied, redirecting their energies away from rebellious activities. With regard to golf market expansion, people in large cities can now experience competitive golf by playing in networked simulators. In addition, golf courses can now be built in water scarce desert areas with synthetic materials. Together, these factors have fueled a global fight for market share and Tehran is unclaimed territory."

The Senator from Virginia asked, "Why didn't the CIA stop the selection of Iran as a Major tournament host?"

"Respectfully Senator, international organizations do not ask the CIA's permission before making business decisions," she responded.

Tired of listening to the Director's golf tutorial, the pro-business

Senator from Texas demanded specific examples of where uncertainty still remained.

From memory, Walker rattled off the names of al-Qaeda operatives whose whereabouts had been unknown for many years, emphasizing it was plausible these operatives could have found sanctuary in Iran.

When the Senator from California insinuated that not knowing the whereabouts of al-Qaeda leaders was a dereliction of duty, Walker responded, "National security is a shared responsibility. You and your colleagues have cut the Intelligence budget, redirected resources away from Iran, and now are unhappy with intelligence you receive. Must I remind you, there are consequences to your actions?"

"Ms. Walker, do you need help doing your job?" the California Senator asked indignantly.

The CIA Director stood up and lifted the tall stack of new regulations with both hands as high as her 5'4" height would allow, and looking with fiery eyes at the irreverent man, slammed the papers on the table.

"Senator, if you and your colleagues really want to help," she said, ready to depart the room, "Then you could start by repealing these inept laws that require my people to fight using a complex set of rules... *enemies that have no rules.*"

HAMEDAN, IRAN

With his forehead pressed against the carpet, Asadi asked the great prophet Mohammad give him the strength to deliver a crippling blow to Western infidels, those decrepit people that dared denigrate the sacred lands of Islam. He fervently recited passages from the Holy Qur'an, thankful that decades of waiting would soon end. He looked up at the replica of Mohammad's sword on the wall and pledged, *soon all would know Allah's power to enact vengeance upon the earth.*

When Asadi was five, a grassroots religious rebellion began in the streets of Tehran with the intention of overthrowing the Shah's secular government. His father, employed by the ousted party, moved the family to London to escape the retaliation of Islamic extremists. The displaced child spent his early years in a small shop with his parents who refurbished antique furniture, a skill they learned in Iran. His parents believed their stay in Britain to be temporary. They thought that Iran's citizens would rebel against the regime of the Ayatollah Khomeini but that did not happen. Now, they longed for the day when it would be safe to return to the streets of Tehran, the homeland they loved.

An only child, Asadi grew up with the mindset of a refugee longing to return home. As months of exile turned to years, he coped with the harsh reality of his family's unlikely return to Iran, by turning inward. He was uninterested in the typical games, toys, and social interactions occupying other children his age. Instead, the young Asadi pursued activities that would develop him physically and mentally so someday he would be able to make a grand and triumphant return to his homeland.

His parents tried to reach a balance between Western and Islamic cultures, but their son felt disconnected. He attended public school during the week and Islamic services at the local mosque on weekends. They spoke Farsi at home and English when in public. By the age of ten, Asadi could read and write both languages but never accepted Britain as his home, deep down he despised having to live there.

The family lived in the neighborhood of Newham, a suburb of London with a large Islamic population. His parents, concerned about the radical influences their son might encounter on the streets, kept him occupied repairing furniture after school. He enjoyed learning the intricacy of how things worked, but grew bored easily with repetitive activities. Asadi received a generous allowance for his work and was allowed to make frequent trips to the local library, athletic center, and hardware store.

As he grew older, the young man's interests gravitated away from manual labor toward academic studies. All was fine at home as long as "A"s appeared on his report cards, and they did. His foreign heritage and introverted personality made it difficult fitting in at school, but it didn't matter. Most of the time he took refuge in a bedroom full of books and a basement cluttered with the remains of self-initiated experiments. As he became a high school student his internally directed behavior, although hidden from his parents, became extreme. Asadi had little interest in the typical social activities of his classmates because he was destined for greatness, and time was a precious resource not to be wasted.

Some who found his behavior peculiar tried to bully him. He easily defeated schoolyard adversaries, but found having to do so unproductive. He viewed conflict as an unnecessary distraction, but sometimes he would intentionally engage classmates to test his human behavior theories.

In ninth grade, the class bully, Luke, performed his daily ritual of tormenting one of the weaker children. Although Asadi had no compassion for those unwilling to defend themselves, he was curious about how the bully would react if confronted by an unlikely opponent. At least twenty pounds lighter and five inches shorter, he stepped in front of the weaker child to confront the much larger boy.

Luke was shocked by Asadi's bold behavior. He raised his fists and shouted, "Are you looking for trouble, mate?"

Without warning, Asadi smashed the bully hard in the solar plexus. As Luke fell to his knees gasping for air, Asadi turned and walked away without saying a word. He was uncertain of the outcome if Luke actually decided to engage him in a fight, but his theory was, a bully's power came from intimidation. If Luke lost a fight to an apparently weaker opponent then the intimidation factor would crumble and others would line up to challenge him. The next day, several kids warned of Luke's wanted revenge, but as predicted, the bully spent the rest of the year avoiding the confrontation. That day, Asadi discovered the hidden strength in understanding people's motivations and fears, something he would learn to master.

At the urging of a Palestinian classmate, he attended a prayer session led by a local Imam. The religious leader, having heard from others about Asadi's academic excellence, went out of his way to befriend him. They held periodic study sessions together, during which the Imam would indoctrinate the young man with radical interpretation of the Qur'an. It didn't take long for Asadi to develop a strong connection with the Imam and his other followers. The religious leader encouraged him to continue his education and challenged him to push the limits of his knowledge. Soon he was surrounded with young Islamic activists of like minds.

The Imam explained that jihad, waging war against non-believers, was his duty. There was no greater blessing than to be called to jihad martyrdom. In private, the Imam re-enforced the boy's feelings of superiority, telling him that he was special because men with great intellect were more valuable to jihad alive. His Islamic duty was to use his mental powers to swing Allah's mighty sword and leave the dying to others.

Asadi's parents were proud of their son's academic success and distracted by the demands of a successful family business. They failed to notice the religious radicalization of their son until it was too late. Asadi studied biochemical engineering at the local university. He excelled at translating book knowledge into battlefield tactics, inventing creative ways to construct powerful explosive devices. Over time, Asadi became a devout member of an al-Qaeda cell located in London. Fully indoctrinated, he hated the sinful Western life his parents had embraced and forced upon him.

He made one last unsuccessful plea for his parents to reject their Western ways and return to Iran. Now an al-Qaeda operative, he decided it was time to follow his calling. Asadi threw the large travel bag over his shoulder and then stopped at the doorway to take one last look. He watched his parents, busy refurbishing a Tiffany glass table lamp. The look of contempt in his eyes went unnoticed. As he drove down the street of his Newham home, an explosion erupted in the background. When the London Fire Brigade arrived, the building was engulfed in flames, with heat so intense no living organism could have survived.

At Bin Laden's request, the young radical relocated to Iraq. His job was to train insurgents in how to build and use explosive devices to fight American imperialists. His enthusiasm for jihad began to sour as al-Qaeda forces took heavy causalities. He was known as an outspoken critic of Bin Laden's small-minded leadership. Asadi fled to the sanctuary of Iran with the aid of rogue operatives of the Iranian Ministry of Intelligence. The operatives believed his exceptional biochemical engineering skills were worth the risk of hiding him. He was given a new identity and helped to integrate deep into Iranian society. While for the next fifteen years the operatives attempted to keep tight control over his actions, Asadi plotted their demise.

In 2021, the newly elected President of Iran enacted an aggressive campaign of purging Islamic radicals from government ranks. Asadi saw the political change as an opportunity to be free of monitoring. He sent an anonymous package to Iran's President, making it appear to be a product of British Intelligence. It contained information detailing the rogue operatives' unsanctioned support for radical terrorist organizations such as al-Qaeda, al-Shaabab, Hamas, and Hezbollah. Soon after receiving the information, the exposed operatives were expelled from government service. They disbanded and went separate ways freeing Asadi to his own creativity, a decision the operatives would come to regret.

After finishing his prayers, Asadi stood and brushed the wrinkles from his creased trousers, walked over to the large contemporary desk in the middle of the room, picked up the *London Times*, and began laughing uncontrollably at the sight of the headline, "*Tehran Selected to Host 2028 Asia Open.*"

Asadi was astonished by the ingenious deception. Although trained to hold back emotion, he wiped delighted tears from his eyes, certain that *Allah had chosen the game of golf—a game surely created by Satan himself—to deliver his enemies to slaughter.*

CHAPTER 2

In many ways the world was more dangerous. Even though trillions of dollars had been spent fighting terrorism since the first September 11th attacks, the number of potential threats had multiplied. The killing of al-Qaeda leaders during the first decade of the 21st century was offset by the proliferation of weapons pillaged from the stockpile of fallen Middle East dictators. Shackled with enormous national debt and on the edge of fiscal collapse, the U.S. government continued on a path of austerity, enacting deep defense and domestic spending cuts.

With smart weapons trading openly on the black market and rising civil unrest, U.S. Intelligence operations had been stretched to the near breaking point. The nation searched for a low-cost way to detect smart weapons, now scattered across the globe. Since the biggest terrorist threat was the use of its own smart weapon technology against itself, one might say, "*The chickens had come home to roost.*"

Jack Wilson entered the west lot at Langley CIA Headquarters before sunrise. He parked in the same space where he had for over forty years and began the ten-minute walk to the north entrance. Eligible to retire within the year, blissful thoughts of Mediterranean life crossed his mind. *Maybe I should retire in Spain where the climate's warm, the food's superb, and the golf's perfecto*, he thought.

As he strolled by the north lot humming his favorite Italian song, *O Sole Mio*, he opened and closed his aching arthritic hands, wondering if he would ever be able to play golf again without pain. He stopped along the way, took a stance as if to hit a golf ball, pretended to take a backswing, and then continued walking toward the building entrance, convinced his body would withstand another golf season.

Wilson, a senior scientist at the CIA, managed a team of engineers tasked to investigate alternative technology solutions for the Smart Weapons Detection program. After weeks of preparation, he was ready to test a new low-cost concept for detecting the electromagnetic signature emitted by a smart weapon's guidance system.

In theory, common inert objects such as coffee cups, when made with a unique ferrite plasma compound he had invented, would act as recorders, providing an inexpensive way to detect the locations of smart weapon detonations. Wilson had chosen to use a golf ball to test his theory, having injected the ferrite plasma into its core. The test assembly was designed to spin the golf ball at a constant rate and detect change. He expected the simulated test signal to produce a reaction, causing the ball's spin rate to change.

A confident scientist, Wilson smiled with delight when the golf ball's rotation accelerated upon activation of the test signal. The experiment looked promising until the ball returned to its original state upon deactivation. In theory, once subjected to the electromagnetic test signal, the altered state should have remained to create a permanent record of the exposure. After many tries producing the same disappointing result, Wilson declared the experiment a flop and raced off to lunch to update his sponsor.

Wilson stepped into his car, fastened the seatbelt, and then gave verbal instructions to the car's driverless navigation system to proceed to the Virginia Country Kitchen. He positioned himself to take control if necessary along the way. Although safe, driverless cars were programmed to act conservatively when merging with others. Wilson found it faster to take control manually when in "stop and go" traffic.

The car passed through the security gate at CIA Headquarters exiting north onto the Washington Parkway. He instructed his Human Adaptable Interface Device—his HuAID—to notify his colleague that he was on his way. Wilson's personalized HuAID had replaced many devices—watch, phone, electronic notebook, body function monitor, portable navigation unit, camera, and golf distance detector—that now sat in a desk drawer at his home.

A technology geek, Wilson had researched the HuAID's inner workings. The core technology involved a flexible, lightweight, high-resolution, display material that could adapt to a person's body and intended use. The device could fold up to fit easily into a person's pocket, fold out to create a 13x13-inch display, and accommodated many other configurations, such as wrapping around a person's arm like a watch. The device performed a cadre of communications, display, camera, and bio-sensing functions. It also connected to a remote cloud via an ultra high-speed wireless network.

Working in collaboration with the Agency, the HuAID manufacturer had incorporate a special security feature to protect classified information and prevent unauthorized remote tracking.

With the car windows partially opened, Wilson enjoyed the fresh air of the unusually warm February day. His mind wondered to his favorite pastime, playing golf. The snow was almost gone, and the afternoon temperatures felt warm.

Wilson strolled into the Virginia Country Kitchen and gave a wave to the man sitting in the back booth. "Gorgeous day out there," Wilson said, as he approached, "We should be holding this meeting on the links where you could take my money."

"Let's do it. My daughter's college fund is running low," Vaughn replied.

Wilson was no match for his friend and colleague on the golf course. Jason Vaughn was one of the best amateur golfers in Northern Virginia. With his 6'4" height and 240 pound brawny structure, he was a good bet to win the longest drive contest at most tournaments he played. Although over fifty years of age, he was in better physical condition than most of the young players he competed against in amateur tournaments in the Washington, D.C. area.

As an athletically gifted African-American growing up in Brooklyn, Vaughn was accustomed to people focusing on his physical abilities and underestimating his intellect. If he had a nickel for every time someone said, "You probably won't understand" or "It's not rocket science," he would be a rich man. The irony of the situation was, as a Cornell University student, he actually studied rocket science and nuclear physics, too. After graduating with a Masters Degree in Electrical Engineering in 1990, he began his CIA career, ready to put his Ivy League education to work.

Vaughn was one of the best at spy craft. He learned to use the underestimation of others to the nation's advantage. His cover identities ranged from janitor, doorman, and food vendor all the way to Wall Street investor, oil baron, and corporate executive. Within the Agency, he was recognized for exceptional creativity and as the mastermind of many successful clandestine operations. When it came to stealing secrets, Vaughn was one of the best.

After decades of overseas assignments, Vaughn accepted a headquarters job as the Director of the Smart Weapons Detection program. His first action was to task his "go to" scientist, Wilson, to investigate low-cost methods for detecting smart weapon detonations.

For years, Wilson was the person back at Langley inventing special devices for Vaughn to use in conducting his overseas operations. Their alliance in the office extended to being comrades on the golf course.

The two men talked office politics for a while before shifting topics to that morning's activity. Wilson described his experiment, hoping Vaughn might have some new ideas to be considered before shutting it down. Vaughn reminded him the technology guys were always creating devices that the operations guys used differently than originally intended.

Unable to resist an opportunity to poke fun at his colleague, Vaughn asked, "Do you remember those pocket zip lines you developed so agents, if necessary, could scale a three story building in a few seconds?"

Wilson simply smiled because he knew where the story was headed.

"I've yet to find a field agent who actually uses one of those things to scale a building, but they all take one on travel. Agents like clean clothes, and the pocket zip line makes an excellent indoor clothesline."

Wilson snickered.

"You can laugh but hanging clothes outside in plain sight is dangerous. It makes us stick out like sore thumbs," he said, straightening the silk tie around his neck, sending the unspoken message that people in the field had to be more aware of their appearance than headquarters lab dwellers dressed in blue jeans.

Vaughn motioned to the waiter, indicating they were ready to order. Scanning his calendar, he said, "I have a break at 3PM; I'll drop by the lab and see what you got. *Who knows, there might be a pony in there somewhere.*"

The pony reference was a play on an old joke about two children, one a pessimist and the other an optimist. Placed in a room filled with the best toys, the pessimistic child sat there doing nothing because eventually the toys would be taken away. Placed in a room filled with horse dung, the optimistic child ran around looking everywhere because with that much horse crap he figured there had to be a pony somewhere.

•

At 3:05PM, Vaughn walked into the laboratory. Wilson gave a brief tutorial regarding the test configuration and then repeated the experiment.

At the conclusion of the test, Vaughn asked, "What would the golf ball do if exposed to the test signal while in flight?"

Thinking for a moment, Wilson responded, "It should change direction similar to what happens when a golfer hits a golf ball. As the ball slows down, the spin takes over, making the ball move right, left, up, or down, depending on the direction and velocity of the spin."

"So the simulated electromagnetic signal could control the golf ball similar to the way a smart weapon's guidance system controls a missile."

"Yes, you could think of it as a 'smart ball' as opposed to a smart weapon."

"Smartball," Vaughn repeated, letting go with a hearty laugh. "I like it."

"I'm glad you like it," Wilson commented sarcastically.

"Do you know what you've invented?" Vaughn asked.

"No, please enlighten me."

"Jack, you really have to start thinking out of the box," Vaughn said. "You just invented a way to take our golf buddies' money. Just think… you could use Smartball to make all my tee shots go long and straight."

"It's my golf game that needs help," Wilson growled. "You operate the equipment and I'll collect the money."

After a good laugh, Vaughn inquired, "Just for fun, I'd like to know how much a golf ball could actually be controlled in flight."

"Why?"

"Just imagine what would happen if professional golfers got a hold of Smartball. Who knows? Some of those Middle Eastern sheiks, with deep pockets, might be willing to spend a few bucks to give their guys an edge."

The CIA scientist jumped at the chance to continue the experiment. Even better, he now had a valid reason to research golf statistics. In addition to being a brilliant scientist, Wilson was a math wiz with statistical data. He loved being the source of knowledge among his golf buddies; it made up for his lack of on-the-course golf skills.

Within an hour, Wilson had all the key stats associated with tee shots, approach shots, chipping, and putting. This data was readily available from the World Golf Tour website. The World Golf Tour—commonly referred to as the "Tour"—was the premier golf tour, created by merging the PGA, European, and Asian tours. The best golfers in the world played on it. The prize money, by far, was greater than other competitions. In addition to having multiple tournaments each week of the year all over the world, the Tour held four Major Championships each year. The Majors were traditional golf's marquee events. Elite players from all over the world participated in them, and the reputations of the greatest players in golf history were largely based on the number and variety of Major Championship victories they accumulated.

To maintain long-standing traditions, the Tour kept the first three Majors of the PGA tour unchanged and modified the fourth to expand the golf market as follows:

The *Masters Championship*, held at Augusta National in Augusta, Georgia during the first full week of April, continued as the first Major Championship of each year.

The *United States Open Championship*, held within the United States during the second full week in June, continued as the second Major Championship of each year.

The *Open Championship*, held within Great Britain during the third week of July, continued as the third Major Championship of each year.

The *Asian Open Championship*, held within Asia during the fall months, was designated the fourth and final Major Championship of the year. It replaced the PGA Championship previously held at locations within the United States during August.

Data about each shot taken during a Tour event was captured and used to create every metric imaginable, such as average driving distance, percentage of fairways hit, percentage of greens hit in regulation, and percentage of putts made from various distances. Wilson precisely measured the impact of the simulated electromagnetic signal on the golf ball, adjusting intensity and phasing. Working well into the night, he determined the flight of a golf ball traveling a distance of 300 yards could be corrected, left or right, as much as 20 yards.

About to call it a night, it occurred to him Smartball could also be used to improve a player's putting. The actual size of a golf hole was 4.25 inches in diameter. He defined the virtual size of a golf hole to how big it appeared from various distances when the putt was artificially corrected as it rolled toward the hole. The longer the putt, the more opportunity there was for the electromagnetic field to impact the roll of the ball. After more calculations, he determined the hole would appear to be 10 inches in diameter from a distance of 30 feet.

By morning, the CIA scientist was waiting at Vaughn's office ready to brief him on the results of his late night work. When Vaughn saw the tired man waiting at the door, he hoped his colleague's all-nighter was productive.

Wilson poured a cup of coffee and then spent time looking at his notes.

"Ok, enough," declared Vaughn. "Give me the bottom line."

"Smartball could improve a golfer's score by about six strokes," Wilson blurted out.

"Wow, six strokes; that's remarkable."

"Using Smartball an accomplished golfer like you could compete on the Tour. It could have professional players breaking course records on a regular basis, shooting ten to twelve strokes under par. Of course, I had to make assumptions, such as having access to a high speed network and being able to covertly package the equipment within close proximity to the player."

"Wow, ten under par; that's superstar material," Vaughn remarked.

As his friend opened the door to leave the office, Vaughn yelled, "*Hey, Jack, I think you just found the pony.*"

CHAPTER 3

CHARLESTON, SC

With coffee cup in hand, Peter Craft circled the table in the center of the room, studying the 3-D holographic projection from all angles. Over and over, he replayed the golf swing of this year's Cyber Golf Champion. Was Kai Peng's victory legitimate or *cyber magic?* By studying the projection, he could see that Peng's swing mechanics were out of sync with the ball's flight, but proving it was the challenge.

The cyber-golf-craze had started in large Asian cities—Tokyo, Hong Kong, Seoul, and Beijing—and then spread to other cities around the world. The game was played in studios designed to imitate natural conditions encountered while playing the game, such as wind, fairway, rough, woods, sand bunkers, water hazards, and sidehill lies. Networked golf simulation enabled two players in physically different locations to compete against each other, playing any one of thousands of golf courses. Foreign investors, in partnership with golf equipment companies, spent billions making precise digital replicas of the best golf courses in the world. Exclusive courses not easily accessible to the public—Pebble Beach, Augusta National, St. Andrews—were now simple menu selections in the cyber world.

The cyber golf experience would never equate to traditional golf, but it had very attractive features. Cyber golf required skills and equipment similar to traditional golf. It was unaffected by weather, because it could be played in indoor studios all year round. It also could be played in a much shorter time period, because players never had to wait for slower groups on the course. Most importantly, cyber golf extended the golf experience to large inner city populations. In addition, simulators enabled players to fine-tune swing mechanics by providing precise measurements—club speed, spin rate, lunch angle, and other important factors. From a Wall Street perspective, if fully exploited, the revenues generated from cyber golf could exceed those of traditional golf.

Cyber golf gained credibility when some of the game's best players crossed over and became strong competitors at traditional golf events.

Unlike professional golf, anyone willing to pay a modest registration cost could compete in the Cyber Golf Championship. This event involved a match-play elimination tournament starting with a field of over sixteen million players worldwide. Over twenty-four weeks, competitors were eliminated through match play until one player remained unbeaten. The winner would receive the prize money of twenty-five million dollars, unless cheating was proven prior to the payout.

If the cyber golf network was compromised, it was Craft's job to prove it; and time was running out. In four hours, the prize money would be transferred to the winner's account. The cyber golf business was built on trust. People needed assurance that outside entities were not manipulating results to gain unfair advantage. To bolster confidence in the game's integrity, the Cyber Golf Association offered to pay two million dollars to anyone who could provide conclusive evidence invalidating tournament results. While even the best at cyber fraud detection passed on the offer, Craft accepted the challenge, believing his intricate knowledge of the game gave him an advantage.

He had spent countless hours developing an adaptive code to secretively probe the cyber golf network looking for unauthorized intrusions. As a teenager, Craft had developed a curiosity in computer game design. His grandfather, an expert in military intelligence, seized the opportunity to teach him software development skills to include advanced methods for covertly penetrating private networks. In college, Craft developed a friendship with the head of Clemson's Cyber Security Center. He kept his cyber security skills sharp, helping his friend perform forensic analyses of compromised networks.

Five years earlier, Craft had graduated from Clemson University with an illustrious athletic career and a Masters in International Finance. His public image was one of star quarterback of the football team and national swim champion. Only a few close associates knew about his cyber security skills, and he wanted it that way. In college, his cunning ability to elude defenses to throw long passes for touchdowns earned him the nickname "Crafty" among Clemson football fans. In the swimming pool his long, powerful body gliding through the water at Olympic speeds won him national championships. With both the Olympics and NFL draft approaching, local fans were greatly disappointed when unexpectedly the young man from Charleston withdrew from both events. Unbeknown to the community, his grandfather had become terminally ill. Holding immense love for the man who had raised him, he was going to be there until the end. While assisting his mother with caring for his grandfather, he found ample time to earn money testing the strength of corporate security systems.

Looking at the code extracted from a cyber golf simulator, Craft asked his friend at the Cyber Security Center, "Do you see it?"

"I do indeed," his friend replied. "Clever people we're dealing with. They've hidden Trojan code in the simulator unit."

"Thought so. Just wanted your validation. Do you think it's conclusive?"

"Absolutely. A confirmation of the Trojan code discovery is on its way."

His suspicions were now confirmed by one of the top cyber security authorities in the world. *The Chinese military had penetrated the cyber golf network.*

Craft wasn't surprised. The Chinese hated to lose at anything, so it wasn't unreasonable to think the military hacked the network to ensure their guy, Kai Peng, won. Now he had the data to prove it.

"If it was up to me," Craft said, "I'd crash the network and leave bread crumbs leading back to the Chinese."

"Exposing the Chinese could be emotionally satisfying, however, a sizable donation to the Cyber Security Center would be more productive," responded his friend.

"No worries. You'll get your donation," Craft replied, thanking his friend and then shutting down the conference connection.

After sending the evidence to the appropriate authorities, Craft checked to see how his mother was holding up. They both knew the end was near. After insisting his mother take a break and get some rest, Craft sat on the edge of the bed next to his grandfather and began talking softly, hoping the sound of his voice would bring comfort to the motionless man lying next to him. His grandfather mustered enough energy to acknowledge his grandson's presence by moving his fingers. Peter held his grandfather's hand, hoping once again to make that loving connection that had bonded them together for life.

Craft talked in confidence to his grandfather as he had so many times before. He said, "Dad, I fear the game of golf is headed downhill. Sure, the Chinese have found a way to cheat but that's to be expected. Golf played in a simulator doesn't mesh well with golf's time-honored traditions. Maybe the strategy and mechanics are the same but the cultural divide is enormous. You taught me to respect golf and play with honor. The notion of abiding by a set of rules, regardless of who watched, is unnatural to cyber golf's "gamer" culture. In the cyber world, the network is always watching. The gamers have a hacker's mentality. Those clever enough to break the rules without getting caught are idolized, rather than despised."

Although his grandfather was too weak to speak, he could imagine his grandfather's words, "In my business, Peter, you have to deal with the facts, and it's effective intelligence that will get you those facts. Don't be afraid to ask critical questions and most of all, face reality head on. It doesn't get any better by ignoring it. Who knows? You might even have a chance to change the outcome once in while."

CHAPTER 4

Jason Vaughn had requested a special meeting of the Executive Oversight Council. The council, composed of mostly men with over twenty years of experience conducting clandestine operations, was responsible for reviewing new projects. In the past, projects would move under the radar from development into operations with funding hidden in obscure budget line items. As a result of budget cuts, Director Walker implemented aggressive controls to get visibility of early expenditures. Establishing the Executive Oversight Council was one of those controls.

The council members filed into the 7th floor Dulles conference room, taking their assigned seats at the horseshoe-shaped mahogany conference table. Most of the members were division chiefs accountable for directing intelligence within their area of responsibility—Eastern Europe, Middle East, Africa, South East Asia, and other areas of the world. Vaughn had enticed the members to attend in person, instead of sending lower-level staffers, by distributing material in advance. The read-ahead material outlined a technology breakthrough that could potentially transform intelligence collection.

The conference room, named after Allen Welsh Dulles, the first Director of Central Intelligence, was furnished with state-of-the-art equipment. New virtual boardroom technology enabled members at remote sites to interact as if physically present in the conference room. A device that looked like a robotic head hung over the high-back conference chair of each remote member, giving the appearance of a person sitting in the seat. The 180-degree ultra-flexible display enabled the remote member to see, and be seen, as if in the room. In fact, it was so realistic that when things got heated, it was easy to forget the remote members were not actually in the room.

The Director of the Clandestine Service, Clifford Beaumont, marched in with two staffers following close behind. Beaumont, a short man of French decent, had a reputation for using aggressive behavior to compensate for his small physical stature. Behind his back, some staff jokingly referred to the DCS as a direct descendent of Napoleon Bonaparte, the domineering man who installed himself as Emperor of France in 1804. Without saying a word, Beaumont made a quick gesture to start the meeting.

Standing at the front of the room, Vaughn's large stature dwarfed others sitting around the conference table. Well aware of Beaumont's reputation for seizing control, Vaughn decided to establish the rules of engagement up front. He slowly walked into the center of the horseshoe conference table, approaching the shrinking man like a giant. While looking down upon the height-challenged individual, Vaughn placed his large hand down on top of the briefing book in front of the Frenchman, sending the unspoken message, "You don't intimidate me, so let's play nice."

Vaughn said, "Sir, if you need to leave early, this book contains the essential information."

Vaughn was one of the few people at the CIA who could get away with confronting the DCS without severe consequences.

The agitated Frenchman responded, "As the chairman of this council, when I leave…the meeting is over."

"Of course it is, sir," Vaughn replied with a large ear-to-ear smile.

After offering a short welcome, Vaughn began. "It's not my intention to bore you with slides or drown you in numbers. Those who want the data can access it using the instructions in your book. Now, I ask each of you to put aside your immediate concerns, open your imagination and think of the possibilities."

He waited a few seconds for the suspense to build. "What if we could create an iconic figure, a superstar with the spycraft skills of a field agent? What if this person was so famous that people around the world opened their doors to embrace him?"

"Enough of the what if questions," The DCS demanded. "Get to the point, Mr. Vaughn."

"The point is… I believe we can create a golf superstar, a player capable of dominating the Tour."

After a moment of silence, tense chatter among members began to erupt.

Beaumont began the inquiry. "Tell me exactly what we're talking about. Quite frankly, I am lost."

Vaughn knew the man was anything but lost. A truly brilliant person, the DCS was in mental overdrive contemplating the broad range of possibilities. Beaumont's high interest was evident to those in the room. The members knew the DCS was being pushed hard by Director Walker to investigate alternative methods for obtaining better Iranian intelligence.

"I have been collaborating with Jack Wilson from Directorate of Science & Technology on the development of an inexpensive smart weapon detection capability," Vaughn continued. "By chance, a golf ball was used as the test object. Although the experiment was a bust, what was discovered is referred to as *Smartball*. My team believes an electromagnetic signal, similar to those produced by smart weapon guidance systems, could be covertly used to correct the flight of a golf ball to optimize its trajectory. Anyone familiar with golf knows it's a game of inches. The difference between having a difficult shot from a greenside bunker and an easy putt from on the green could be a couple of feet variance in the flight of the golf ball. Similarly, the difference between holing a ten-foot putt for birdie and having six-footer to save par is a fraction of an inch variance in the roll of the golf ball. Bottom line, small changes to the trajectory of the golf ball could have a dramatic impact on a person's score. Based on Wilson's analysis and vetted by my staff, the score of a professional golfer could be improved by several strokes, enough to set records and dominate the Tour."

The room erupted with side conversations among the members, already forming coalitions to protect their turfs.

"Assuming it could be done," the Chief of African Operations asked, "why would we want to do it? And what's the risk?"

"Excellent questions," Vaughn responded, "I'll address the why first and then risk. It's no secret we've invested heavily in conventional methods to get on-the-ground intelligence in the Middle East with limited success. I believe we can create a golf superstar with such an exceptional global image that nations around the world will line up to have this person come to their country to promote golf. Social pressures will require Islamic leaders to open their doors to welcome the best Tour player in the world and it will be our guys going through those doors. The Smartball's technology offers a viable alternative to other conventional intelligence collection methods."

Vaughn shifted the discussion to risks. "Although most sports have an element of dishonesty, such as getting the other team's playbook or bribing an official, golf is viewed by most as a game of ultimate integrity where players are expected to call infractions upon themselves. A public discovery of golf results being manipulated for any reason, no matter how deserving, could be met with global outrage that our enemies and citizen alike could use to bring the country to its knees."

The DCS thanked Vaughn for sharing his discovery and its potential, and then ended the meeting before others could start throwing their daggers. The room was buzzing as Vaughn and Beaumont walked out together like old friends. Within two hours, the CIA Director had been briefed. By early afternoon, Vaughn was told to work with security to place the project under special control, a major step in getting a program approved.

Vaughn dropped by Wilson's office to give him the news. "You know that pony we've been talking about? *Well, it's a racehorse, and it's going to be running on a fast track.*"

CHAPTER 5

CHARLESTON, SC

Callie, the greens-keeper at Charleston Manner Golf Club, was extracting soil samples from the green at the 9th hole when she saw the silhouette of a tall, athletic man moving at a fast pace through the morning shadows come into view. She scanned the clubhouse parking area, and when she saw his car, her body filled with excitement. After months of solitude, he had returned to the golf course to once again perform his daily morning workouts.

Emotionally drained from his grandfather's passing and the formalities of the previous day's funeral, Peter Craft forced his legs to go faster and faster with each stride. When he reached the outer perimeter of the golf course, he knelt down on the soft pine needles and began a series of push-ups, one after the other, until his arms could no longer lift his body. He rolled onto his back, soaked in perspiration, and raised his arms to the sky and in a symbolic gesture, asking for strength to continue life without the man who had been his guiding light.

Callie continued her green-keeper duties. *Why had he shut her out when she was needed most?* Lost in her own thoughts, she sprinkled water on the new flowerbed behind the 16th tee area.

Approaching quietly from behind, Peter kinked the hose so the water would stop flowing. When she turned to investigate the problem, there he stood.

"Hi Cal, how are you doing?"

"I've been better," she replied, offering a cold response.

He turned to leave.

"So you're just going to walk away?" she said throwing the hose on the ground.

He turned back around. She could see the sadness in his eyes. "Do you like the flowers?" she asked. "The crew planted them in memory of your grandfather. Everyone around here misses him."

Finding it hard to speak, he said, "The flowers are beautiful. Please thank the guys for me."

"We could go by the maintenance building right now, and you could thank them yourself."

When he didn't respond, she gave him a hug, as she had so many times before. "I am angry with you," she whispered, "Why shut me out? Your grandfather was amazing. You know how much he meant to me."

"I know," he answered. "I wasn't thinking. Helping Mom cope and spending as much time with him as possible took all my energy. I wasn't much fun to be with…"

"I wasn't looking for fun," she said while pounding her head lightly on his chest. "I wanted to be there for you and Miss Amanda. I wanted to help. Your family has always been there for me. It was my opportunity to return the love."

"Do you have time to talk?" he asked. "I have to make an important decision soon and would like your advice."

She took in his ocean blue eyes, shoulder-length black hair, boyish smile, and physically awesome body and thought the view might just be powerful enough to make a gay girl go straight… but unfortunately, not this gay girl. With some concern she noticed how vulnerable he looked. "I haven't had a day off in weeks. Let's go to the beach," she said. "My friend has a beach house on the island. We could go there."

"Let's go. I'll drive."

"Only if you put the top down," she demanded.

•

The house rested on big wood beams, high above the ground with a wide and long staircase connected the porch to the sandy beach below. Wearing sweatshirts to keep warm from the brisk coastal wind, they sat at the top of the stairs looking out at the eight-foot surf crashing down, the result of a storm a few miles off the coast.

Putting her head on his shoulder, she said, "No fairy tales please. How are you really doing?"

"I can't believe he's gone. Nothing seems right. My mother walks around the house looking at pictures and knick-knacks, trying to recall every memory of us together."

"Your mother had a lot of heartbreak in her life. She just needs time to grieve."

"My grandfather was a remarkable man," he said, remembering some of the great times they had together.

"Hell, your grandfather was more of a father to me than my own dad," she confided.

"I never thought about what life would be without him. Well, now I know. It sucks!" Craft proclaimed.

She turned to face him so he could see the concern in her face. "I shouldn't say this but I'm going to anyway."

"Okay, let's hear it."

"You have to move on with your life, and it's not here in Charleston," she declared.

"Where is it, then?"

"It's on a football field, in a swimming pool, on a golf course, in a computer laboratory, or some place on the other side of the world. I don't know; but it's not here."

"I get the feeling you're trying to get rid of me."

"When we were in high school, I wrote in my diary, *Peter Craft is driven by the circumstance surrounding his birth, the love that consumed his parents, the tragedy that left him longing for a father he would never know, and the grandfather who stepped in to pick up the pieces and inspired him to pursue a path of excellence. While I tend to flowers in the garden, my best friend will be changing the world.*"

"Oh, come on," he said, embarrassed.

"All I am saying is, if you're going to change the world, then you better get going. Time's a wasting."

He removed a letter from his pocket and handed it to her. The letter was a conditional employment offer from the United States Institute of Peace in Washington, D.C.

After reading the letter, she asked, "Why you?"

"Why me? Maybe my education in international finance, interest in Middle East affairs, and ability to speak a few foreign languages caught someone's interest," he answered.

"Peter, I know you're well educated and they would be fortunate to have you as an employee," she responded. "It was the 'Peace' thing that threw me a curve. I see you as a 'kick their ass guy' not an 'olive branch guy', that's all. Anyway, are you going to accept?"

"Do you think I should?"

"Are you ready to give up a career in professional sports for a desk job in D.C.?"

"The government offers a lot of opportunity."

"So, you're going to accept."

"Do you think I should?"

"Absolutely. Then I can come visit you. When would you leave?"

"The government needs to complete my security background investigations. From what I here, it could take weeks."

"So what will you do in the mean time?" she asked.

"Workout, comfort my mother, and bother you."

"I'm looking forward to it already."

"Seriously, my leaving will break my mother's heart," he admitted.

"Miss Amanda is tough; she'll do fine. Maybe if she doesn't have you to look after, she might get on with her own life."

CHAPTER 6

NORTHERN VIRGINIA

Vaughn read the memorandum, signed by Director Walker, establishing the program, code name *Red Crescent*. He then got in touch with the security officer to get a Sensitive Compartmented Information Facility—SCIF—assigned. A human inhabitable vault, the SCIF provided the team a place to work and store classified mission-specific information. After discussing options with the security officer, Vaughn selected a location at a covert site twenty miles west of CIA headquarters on Interstate 66 in close proximity to many golf courses where Smartball could be tested.

Led by Vaughn, the handpicked team began planning the Smartball Operational Demonstration. After reviewing and making some changes, he sent the plan forward. The DCS responded almost immediately with direction to increase funding and reduce the schedule from six to three months. The team figured the compressed timeline had something to do with the Asian Open in Tehran. By the end of the day, the revised plan was approved.

Wilson briefed the Smartball design to Vaughn. The design was composed of three major components:

- The *Launch Detection Unit* would detect the initial speed, direction, and spin of the ball when struck by the golf club.
- The *Real-time Computing and Communications Network* would process launch data and other information about the golf hole to calculate the correction signal.
- The *Flight Correction Transmitter* would send the correction signal to optimize the trajectory of the golf ball.

Vaughn approved the design. Two weeks later, the team technician assembled the Smartball prototype in a secure aircraft hangar in Northern Virginia. At one end of the building hung a massive 100 foot-wide by 200 foot-high wall pad incorporating an electronic grid to detect where the ball hit the wall. The wall pad was perfectly centered to a long white line down the middle of the floor with distance indicators placed every 20 yards.

With Wilson leading the way, Vaughn strolled into the massive building carrying his golf clubs and smoking a big cigar as if he were headed for the 1st tee. When he reached a point 200 yards from the wall pad, he dropped a golf mat on the floor, put on his golf glove, grabbed a four iron out of the bag, and started hitting golf balls at the wall to calibrate the equipment. The team used the measurements from the *Launch Detection Unit* to calculate where each ball was projected to hit the wall, compared to where it actually hit. After reviewing the data, Wilson was satisfied the variance between actual and projected ball flight was small enough to continue testing.

Resuming the demonstration, the technician connected the three major components to the full test assembly.

"Let's start by correcting the ball flight five feet to the left," said Vaughn.

After a few tweaks to the software, the ball was consistently hitting the wall 5 feet to the left. Vaughn hit at least two hundred balls from different distances providing the team plenty of data to analyze.

Getting tired and observing that Wilson was becoming a bit anxious, Vaughn asked, "Jack, would you mind hitting a few balls so I can observe the equipment?"

Wilson quickly put on his golf glove, grabbed a 5 iron and took aim. The first ball went flying off the toe of the club missing the wall pad altogether. Embarrassed, he tried again and soon began hitting the wall with ease. Wilson thought, *this beats office work any day.*

The team worked into the evening refining the software, tweaking the equipment, and collecting plenty of data for analysis back at the SCIF. It required three more trips to the airplane hangar to convince Wilson that the ball flight could be corrected in accordance with his initial calculations.

•

Although the success of the prototype was good news, much work still remained. Next, the team assessed packaging alternatives. They brainstormed for days, before converging on the idea of incorporating Smartball functionality into the golf bag. It would take some innovative engineering, but the golf bag was large enough to hold the equipment and putting it in the bag enabled it to be operated by the caddy in close proximity to the player.

Even though the Agency was the world's best at miniaturizing and hiding electronics in covert environments, the high visibility of the Tour presented a serious challenge, not to be taken lightly. For the Operational Demonstration, the incorporation of Smartball into the golf bag did not have to be perfect; it just needed to demonstrate reasonable feasibility. Six days later, the golf bag was ready; however, the bag was too heavy to be easily carried and had a size and shape that would attract unwanted attention.

Vaughn decided it was time to try Smartball in a real golf environment. The team scheduled morning and afternoon golf rounds at golf courses within an hour drive of the SCIF. In the morning Vaughn played a normal golf round, followed by an afternoon round using Smartball. To not draw unwanted attention, the team practiced operating the special equipment while appearing to others as a normal foursome playing a round of golf.

Vaughn, an exceptional amateur golfer with a 2.3 handicap, normally shot scores in the low 70s on a regular basis and scores in the high 60s occasionally. The morning score was used as a reference for assessing the level of improvement with Smartball.

•

The first day, Vaughn showed little, if any, improvement scoring 74 in the morning and 73 in the afternoon. The team huddled back at the SCIF for hours trying to think through the process. After watching a slow motion video, it became apparent Vaughn was subconsciously making changes to his swing based on visual feedback. Under normal conditions, doing so made sense, but the unintended consequence with Smartball was false visual feedback, because the ball was being manipulated by technology during its flight. Vaughn would have to learn to trust his swing and only use the feel he knew to be true and ignore the flight of the ball.

The second day, after a few software tweaks and learning to ignore the ball's flight, Vaughn showed improvements, shooting 73 in the morning and 69 in the afternoon. The last day of testing, he shot a 71 in the morning and his lowest round ever of 64 in the afternoon with nine one-putts.

The technology worked but whether it could be used undetected during Tour events was still an unknown.

The CIA Director sat at her desk, holding the Red Crescent folder. A career civil servant, Catherine Walker had worked her way up through the Agency starting as an intelligence analyst. Faced with crippling budget cuts, she made a name for herself leading efforts to streamline Agency processes without jeopardizing critical mission operations. Walker was one of the best at using risk management techniques to prioritize needs and allocate resources. The staff both loved and feared her hands-on approach to leading the Agency. Her insistence on challenging the status quo stressed out those resisting change. When confronted by the Director, many of the staff had found themselves on the defensive when asked the simple question, "*why?*" Walker truly believed that the U.S. National Security mission was too important and resources too precious to be wasted on low value activities. If it was worth doing, then you should have a thought out answer for why, and if you didn't have one, then a one-on-one with the Director was sure to follow.

Walker began to read the Red Crescent concept and demonstration results. The idea of creating an agent with an ultra-high profile, a superstar golfer, was fascinating because it reversed the status quo. The traditional approach to clandestine operations involved the use of low profile assets with the ability to hide in plain sight. The James Bond type was for the movies. The status quo was the janitor who copied all the secret papers or the secretary who listened in on the phone calls. The Red Crescent concept did the exact opposite by creating a person with idol status.

While the idea of using high profile assets had been around for quite some time, the ability to execute was the game changer. In the past, the Agency attempted, with limited success, to use persons with superstar status in sports and entertainment to perform very specific intelligence functions. For the most part, these people neither had the skills nor motivation to act as agents for the nation, not to mention having to deal with the inherent danger of being caught.

The Director could see the technology's uniqueness. It enabled the Agency to create a superstar with the needed skills and motivations, but she knew that was easier said than done. These ideas tended to look good on paper, but fell short in execution. On the other hand, Vaughn had a record of success. Because of that, if for no other reason, Walker felt Smartball should be given a fair chance.

She reviewed the concept looking for an answer to the "why" questions. Why golf? Why Smartball? The five key points summarized in the report were:

I. ***Strong Alignment With the Potential Terrorist Target:*** Golf provided the ability to integrate US intelligence activities into day-to-day Tour operations in advance of the Asian Open.

II. ***High Interest by the Host Nation:*** Iran had demonstrated a high interest in golf by aggressively competing to be selected as host for a Major tournament.

III. ***Achievable Within Required Timeframe:*** The time period for creating a golf superstar was remarkably short. Defined by historical precedence, achieving superstar status could be accomplished within a few months by winning Major Championships. Achieving superstar status in other sports—basketball, baseball, soccer, and hockey—required consistent exceptional performance over years.

IV. ***Required Skills Were Obtainable:*** Although difficult, finding an agent with the needed golf skills, motivations, and commitment to the U.S. national requirements was achievable within the timeframe.

V. ***Undetected Execution:*** Other sports having global appeal required players to interact with a common object—basket ball, soccer ball, hockey puck, and tennis ball. Given the nature of player-to-player interaction, undetected continuous manipulation was implausible. Golf was different. Each person played with his own golf ball and when hit, the ball moved at high speed influenced by many factors. A simple gust of wind could change the trajectory of a golf ball several feet.

After studying the Red Crescent concept, Walker called for a meeting.

She thanked everyone for attending on short notice. "The purpose of this meeting is to discuss the Iranian situation as it relates to the Tour event being held in Tehran in October of next year with the focus being on the merits of the Red Crescent concept. Any question before we begin?"

After responding to general questions and concerns, she continued. "We have talked about the suspicions that Iran has been sheltering al-Qaeda operatives for years, but we still have no proof. The current security assessment, based on years of fusing data collected from many sources, looks like a big mosaic with many missing pieces. Some of you think Iran's intensions are now pure, citing valuable intelligence shared by Iranian authorities. Others in this room believe the U.S. is letting down its guard enabling the viper to strike, citing religious extremists and missing al-Qaeda operatives as justification. For those of you who are sports fans, the clock is running out, and yet we repeat the same things, hoping for a different result."

She listened to the Chief of Middle East Operations give his assessment of the security situation in Iran, basically repeating the Director's points but at the same time trying to make the case that more resources were required.

Director Walker was determined not to get off track. "In sixteen months, thousands of Westerners will be going to Iran to attend the Asian Open. These people may, or may not, be walking into the Viper's nest. I don't know, and neither do you. Congress is pressing for a definitive security assessment, and we can't give them one. What makes matters worse is I don't see us getting any closer to having one. Please correct me if I off base here."

Again, the Middle East Chief made an appeal for increased resources.

"I'll be frank," Director Walker responded, "If I thought doing more of the same would get us there, we wouldn't be having this meeting. So, unless you have something new to say then I suggest you keep an open mind and listen."

After waiting a moment, she continued. "Our intelligence networks are drowning in data, but what it all means remains a mystery. I recently discussed the security situation with Tour executives, hoping they might reconsider holding the Asian Open in Tehran. They're blinded by the big money opportunities of the Iranian market place. Nothing short of the President issuing an Executive Order is going to stop American participation at the event. And given the current administration's pro-business attitude, that's not going to happen, without actionable intelligence."

The Director paused to take a drink of water. "Now I don't want to seem paranoid but if the vipers are waiting to strike, as some of you in this room think, then the Asian Open makes the perfect target. The non-Islamic attendees could be viewed as infidels transgressing on holy land and the Islamic people who attend can be viewed as unholy people bending to Satan's temptations. To say I am concerned is an understatement, and I am not the only one. The White House has added the Iran security update to the President's daily briefing. We are discussing this now because putting in place a clandestine operation the magnitude of Red Crescent takes time. Please put aside for the moment any moral concerns you might have and focus our discussion on mission considerations."

Wanting to kill the idea but at the same time to appear to be open minded, the Middle East Chief started the discussion. "Madam Director, quite frankly, the Red Crescent concept seems far-fetched, but I must admit initial results are impressive. Although Tehran has moved toward an open society, the leaders have cut deals to give more power to the local governments. There are areas within Iran still locked down tight and, if the vipers are hiding in wait, then these areas are the places to be looking. With that said, it's not evident how the Red Crescent program gets us intelligence in these areas."

Jason Vaughn spoke up. "The idea is to create a golf superstar who becomes the de facto ambassador for youth golf. Revenues from tournaments would be donated to promote golf among the youth of emerging nations. The golf superstar would volunteer to participate in the advancement of golf, targeting areas where we wish to open doors, to include raising funds through donations. For those of you non-golfers, winning major tournaments is a big deal. Winning all four in a single year, 'The Grand Slam of Golf', is an accomplishment that many sports analysts say is no longer achievable by mere mortals. The timeline is important. The hype cycle starts the first week of April with a win at the Masters. It then grows exponentially the third week of June, with a second Major win at the U.S. Open. Maximum hype is hit late in July with a third Major win at the Open in Scotland. At this point, the golf superstar is a true contender needing only a fourth Major win at the Asian Open to complete the grand slam. My team thinks the hype would be so fervent after winning the Open in Scotland that Iranian secular leaders would force the intelligence ministry to open the doors to any area the golf superstar wanted to visit in preparation for the last Major and to promote youth golf."

"I hate to be the pessimist here," the Middle East Chief interjected, "but do you really think we can pull off manipulating the outcome of three Major golf tournaments without being detected?"

"The process is no different from any other operation we execute," Vaughn responded, "If the probability of success is not high enough, then it's a no go. As always, the Agency's involvement will be guarded through layers of protection, leaving no loose ends."

The meeting continued until everyone had been heard and a consensus was reached. Although the Middle East Chief did not like the idea, he could not come up with a viable reason why it would fail. Everyone agreed the Red Crescent concept had merit and should be pursued as one viable alternative for dealing with the Iranian security situation.

Shifting the discussion, the Director said, "Like most of you, I study history, hoping to avoid repeating past mistakes, yet repeating them seems inevitable. We failed to take out Hitler, Yamamoto, Castro, and Bin Laden during their rises to power, and the world has paid dearly. I believe there's a lesson to be learned. Our waiting for situations to develop to the point of moral certainty can have devastating consequences."

The Director stopped to take another drink of water while assessing the mood of the meeting. "Given the intensity of the hallway talk, it's a good time to put things in perspective. As I understand it, Red Crescent is not about the moral uncertainty of taking lives. It's about cheating at a game to obtain valuable intelligence in areas where we've been unable to collect it through traditional means. On a scale of one to ten of dubious things the Agency does for the good of the nation… it might at best be a three. Let me remind you, *we are in the business of stealing secrets*! From where I sit, cheating at golf doesn't seem to be over the top. If you think I am off base here, please speak up."

After a few half-hearted attempts to make moral cases against Red Crescent, the Director had heard enough. She ended the meeting by informing the staff that going forward with the program was approved.

"Are we going to get the White House involved?" the Director of Science and Technology asked.

"Yes, but when the time is right," Walker said, "I'll deal with the White House."

CHAPTER 7

Jason Vaughn initiated a search for the CIA agent with the right skills. He used a set of weighted criteria to evaluate candidates and, of course, the ability to shoot golf scores at a professional level was the most important criteria. Vaughn rummaged through his desk looking for eye drops to soothe his aching eyes after hours of reading candidate profiles. The Agency had an abundance of people with the needed spycraft skills but professional golf skills were hard to come by. A few people, if given intense golf training, might make the grade but going down that path would be a last resort.

He opened a message from the Director. The message contained the resume of a new hire in process. The Candidate was a U.S. swimming champion and quarterback for the Clemson University football team. In addition, the Candidate had won the South Carolina Amateur Golf Championship when he was seventeen years old.

Vaughn wondered, *what motivated a man who could be earning millions playing professional football to pursue a professional career with the government?*

The Candidate had been given a conditional offer of employment from an Agency cover organization. The employment offer was contingent upon the successful completion of a background investigation and poly-scan test. A few years earlier, the poly-scan had replaced the polygraph as the preferred method within the Intelligence community for lie detection. The poly-scan monitored a person's brainwaves while responding to a series of question covering topics such as drug use, finances, contact with foreign entities, and other important security topics. The poly-scan had proven to be more reliable and people being tested found it more comfortable than the polygraph that required a person's body to be connected to a rat's nest of wires and sensors. The poly-scan simply required the person to sit in high-back chair with a built-in scanner.

Given the candidate's background investigation had been in process for weeks, Vaughn used a four-letter word to express his dissatisfaction with recent budget cuts. He picked up the phone and called the Security Director to get a status update.

"Hello, Conrad speaking," the man answered.

"Good morning John. How's your golf game coming along?" Vaughn inquired.

Recognizing Vaughn's voice, Conrad replied, "If you're looking to shake a few bucks out of me, then you better look someplace else; not playing much golf these days. We're so low on staff, pretty soon I'll be doing the background investigations myself."

"Speaking of background investigations, will you check the status of a new-hire for me?"

Vaughn provided the candidate's name: Peter Craft. Conrad accessed the security system and pulled up the security file. "You're in luck. His background investigation is complete and waiting for final adjudication."

Knowing his inquiry must be important, he offered to do what he could to move it along.

"Since you're in an accommodating mood, I have another favor to ask. Will you give me access to the candidate's background investigation?" asked Vaughn.

"Yes, provided Director Walker approves it, and then you'll have to come to my area to see the file; it's encrypted on a stand-alone system."

•

By mid afternoon, Conrad sent a message, "Received the Director's OK, come on down to my area."

Within minutes, Vaughn was buzzing the door to the security office. He shook hands with Conrad and thanked him for the quick response. While walking to the back of the office, the Security Director announced the candidate's security clearance had been approved and his background investigation could be accessed on an old stand-alone computer setup in the back of the room. Vaughn studied the report trying to connect the dots. Vaughn left the room believing he knew the answer to why an exceptional athlete would pursue a civil service career.

Peter Craft arrived at the Naval Weapons Station Charleston to take his poly-scan test, the last step required to receive his U.S. Top Secret clearance. He wore a dark gray suit, white shirt, red-white striped tie, and polished black shoes. A slender middle-aged African-American woman with short black hair was waiting when he walked through the front door. The poly-scan technician introduced herself and then eagerly mentioned that her nephew, Zachary, had played with him on the Charleston Academy football team the year they won the state championship. Zachary was a fast, tough running back. The technician's face glowed with pride, as Craft described Zachary's spectacular end-zone catch in the last seconds of the championship game. He avoided mentioning her nephew's career-ending knee injury at the University of South Carolina. They engaged in local sports talk while walking to the testing area.

He sat in high-back leather chair with embedded brainwave measuring technology. The technician explained the test procedure and then began asking a series of "yes" or "no" questions, one after the other, for an hour. She sat at a nearby desk looking at the graphical display of his brainwaves as he responded to each question. Then without explanation, she escorted him to a small windowless conference room, asked him to wait, and suggested he have a cup of coffee. On the counter next to the coffee container were two silver-plated cups engraved with Central Intelligence Agency emblems. His mind filled with exhilarating thoughts. *Who was his real employer?*

From a nearby office, a man observed the new recruit through the hidden camera. He thought the young man had a distinctive persona, handsome looks, towering height, and an athletic build that could easily fit the image of a golf superstar. His dark, wavy hair and Mediterranean complexion should appeal to the Islamic community, although toning down the bright blue eyes with contact lenses might be necessary.

The conference room door abruptly opened. "Good morning," a man extending his hand, "I am Jason Vaughn."

I must have missed the business casual memo, Craft thought, as he gazed at the hefty middle-aged African-American man in casual attire.

"Hope you're enjoying the coffee," commented Vaughn.

Holding up the coffee cup and pointing to the CIA emblem, Craft inquired, "Are these hard to get?"

"Not if you're an employee," responded Vaughn, placing papers on the table with CIA letterhead. "I am here to offer you employment with the Central Intelligence Agency."

Caught off guard by the offer, Craft asked, "How soon would you like me to start?"

"Right now!" declared Vaughn.

Within minutes, Craft had taken an oath of loyalty to the nation and signed papers acknowledging his Top Secret clearance had been granted.

"Congratulations, you're now an employee of the United States Government," Vaughn announced, raising his coffee cup in a toast.

"I am honored, Mr. Vaughn, but why the personal attention?"

"At the moment you have skills in high demand."

"I'm flattered, but my skills are quite common."

"If that was true, Mr. Craft, I wouldn't be here."

"No disrespect, I am just trying to understand."

"I'd appreciate your patience while I ask you some questions."

"Yes sir," Craft answered, trying to slow his racing mind.

"Why would the starting quarterback for Clemson University accept a low paying government job?" asked Vaughn.

Rubbing the shoulder he injured playing football, Craft answered, "Out running large men for a living is hazardous to one's long-term health."

Pulling down his shirt collar to show a large scar below his neckline from a knife wound, Vaughn countered, "Agency work can also be hazardous to one's health."

"Risking injury for a worthy purpose is different. It's taking unnecessary risk that bothers me," Craft responded.

"Don't you think the big money of professional football is worth the risk?"

"There're other ways to make big money."

"You mean like pocketing a couple million dollars from the Cyber Golf Association," commented Vaughn. "By the way, the cyber security geeks think the code you developed is quite innovative. If you pass on my offer then they want you."

"You've done your homework."

"Fortunately for you," declared Vaughn.

"Why's that?"

"The Chinese were close to discovering your real identity."

"So what?" Craft responded, as if it was no big deal.

Leaning forward across the table to make direct eye contact with the new recruit, Vaughn said, "Well, we wouldn't be having this conversation because you'd be dead."

Having never considered the potential consequences of his actions, Craft nervously asked, "Is anyone else in danger?"

"Not anymore. We've sent the Chinese on a wild goose chase that will have them wasting resources for years if they continue to pursue it."

"I have much to learn," Craft confessed.

"Let's begin right now," Vaughn said in an absolute serious tone. "Always… I mean always… no exceptions…*work as a team.*"

After giving the new employee a moment to grasp the importance of his words, Vaughn summed it up by saying, "*Agents who work alone, die alone.*"

Is he just making a point or is he telling me I am going to be an agent? Craft wondered. After an uncomfortably long delay, he replied, "I will."

"You will what?" Vaughn barked.

"Work as a team," answered Craft.

"I believe you will," Vaughn responded, "because you're a born leader and a leader needs a team to lead."

They both sat in silence with folded arms looking at each other contemplating the conversation that had just taken place.

"You intrigue me. So I am going to continue with more questions."

"I have no secrets," Craft replied.

"After receiving a big payday, you give most of the money to the university. Do you have an aversion to wealth?"

"Absolutely not. But having a big bank account can make you a target."

Vaughn laughed, "As a government employee that's a problem I've never faced."

"Oh, come on," Craft said jokingly, "You must have bank accounts hidden all over the world."

"You watch too many movies." Vaughn stood up to pour more coffee. "So let's talk golf."

"I prefer playing," Craft responded.

"I am sure you do. So, why not play professional golf for a living?" Vaughn asked.

"You may need a shrink for this one," Craft responded.

"I am not a psychologist but let's hear it anyway."

"Well, I grew up playing golf with my grandfather. We played to enjoy the outdoors and escape life's pressures. On the golf course you just don't think about life's problems. If golf were my job, then its therapeutic value would be lost."

"I know what you mean," remarked Vaughn. "If I didn't have golf to escape life's pressures I'd be in the nuthouse for sure. But still, giving up a chance to play on the Tour for a government job..."

"Looking back, would you really have given up the important work that you do for the nation to play a game?"

"Now who's being the psychologist?" asked Vaughn. "But if you're really looking for a candid answer, then you are correct, I wouldn't have been satisfied playing a game." Intrigued, Vaughn continued. "You qualified in swimming for the Olympic swim team but then withdrew. Why?"

"That was a hard decision," Craft said in a somber tone. "When I found out my grandfather was ill, my life unraveled. Simply put... I lost it. My participation would have hurt the team. Looking back, my emotional maturity wasn't where it needed to be."

Vaughn admired the young man's honesty but wondered if Craft could be counted on in tough situations. That would have to be evaluated going forward. "Would you be interested in an assignment applying your athletic abilities?"

"Mr. Vaughn, I believe you have something important on your mind."

"Let's cut with the formalities. Please call me Jason."

"Okay, Jason, what's up?"

"How good is your golf game?"

What does golf have to do with anything? Craft wondered. "I have a plus four handicap."

"Impressive! When was the last time you played?" asked Vaughn.

"Yesterday. Playing golf has been my way of feeling close to my grandfather since his passing six weeks ago."

"Do you have your clubs with you?"

"Yes, in my car."

Vaughn stepped out of the room, and returned a few minute later with a golf shirt, handed it to Craft and suggested he lose the jacket and tie; they had a 1PM tee time.

After a couple of warm-up shots on the range, they were ready to play.

"What's the bet?" Craft asked.

"If you win, you'll get the respect of an old company man. If I win, you'll have to teach me how to throw a football with a tight spiral."

Craft hit the golf ball like a machine, outdriving Vaughn by many yards on a regular basis. After nine holes, Vaughn knew the young man had world-class golfing skills, but did he have the temperament? On the back nine, Vaughn tried to annoy him, talking excessively, hitting out of turn, and making sudden movements while Craft was putting. Walking off 18th hole, Vaughn glanced at the scorecard to see Craft's impressive score of 68 next to his dismal score of 82.

•

When they returned to the secure building, Vaughn raided the refrigerator for sandwiches and drinks.

"Well, you have earned my respect on the golf course. Now let's talk business." Vaughn briefed the new recruit on the Red Crescent program.

Craft listened with swirling emotions. Cheating at golf was unimaginable. "Let's see if I understand," Craft said. "You want me to win three Major golf tournaments in a row with the assistance of Smartball, so the Agency can do spy work in Iran in preparation for the Asia Open in October 2028."

"Exactly," Vaughn replied, "Are you the right guy for the job?"

The excitement burning inside went cold. He had never considered the possibility of such an assignment. "I am not sure. A man needs to sleep at night and cheating at the greatest game ever played would give me nightmares."

Vaughn thought this guy was unquestionably right for the job. "I have done things for the good of the nation that would make most people sick to their stomachs, and I have no problem sleeping because my motives were pure. But I can tell you this... the things keeping me up at night are those times when I could have done something that would have made a difference and I let my personal reservations get in the way."

Deciding to push the point harder, Vaughn admitted, *"I could have taken out Bin Laden in 1998, three years before the 9/11 attacks but didn't.*

Now that's something I'll always regret."

After waiting a few moments for the young man to think, Vaughn continued. "I believe Bobby Jones had it right when he said, '*playing golf for money would ruin the game.*' Let's face it, golf is no longer a game; it's big business with a massive global market. There's nothing innocent about big business. In fact, the Tour executives are willing to risk lives to grow market share in Iran. I truly believe if you decide to be part of this operation, you will not lose sleep over deceptive golf; you will find inner peace knowing the world is a better place because you had the balls to stand up and make a difference."

"You know," Vaughn paused for a second, "working for the CIA really is like 'Mission Impossible' when it comes to an assignment. You can choose to accept (or not accept) this assignment without retribution. As I mentioned the cyber security guys would love to get you on their team."

Vaughn closed the conversation by asking him to think about it over night and be ready to talk in the morning. Just as Craft was about to walk out the door, Vaughn added, "By the way, you're not in this alone. I plan to be with you every step of the way; you're going to need a good caddy."

Craft was awake most of the night, trying to reconcile his mixed emotions. He understood the concern regarding a potential terrorist attack at the Asia Open. At the same time, cheating at golf tore into the core of his personal integrity. He'd almost lost the amateur championship because he called a penalty stroke on himself when his ball moved in the rough after grounding his club. Craft had always played by the rules, and using technology to alter the flight of the golf ball was certainly against the rules. Could he really justify such deception as being for the good of the nation?

The next morning, Vaughn repeated the question, "Are you the right guy for this job?"

Without hesitation, he answered, "Yes."

Then Vaughn briefed him on the covert aspects of the Red Crescent program, emphasizing his quick rise from hometown amateur to superstar had to be believable, withstand extreme scrutiny and most of all, have no connection to the Agency. Vaughn explained that his cover would be different from other members of the team. Other members could use pseudo identities and when necessary, use disguises to protect their actual persona. Craft would be using his real identity as opposed to a pseudo identity. This meant his association with the CIA would have to be untraceable by the public and closely controlled within the intelligence community.

"The team has examined your life with a fine-tooth comb and there are a couple of loose ends we need to address. Please tell me about your father?" Vaughn inquired.

"Can't tell you much because he died before I was born. He was a New York City firefighter killed in the 9/11 terrorist attacks."

"Who else knows this?" asked Vaughn.

"To my knowledge, only my mother, deceased grandfather, and Callie," answered Craft.

"Who's Callie?"

"A childhood friend."

"Are you romantically involved?"

"No, just friends."

"Why no contact with your father's family?"

Craft told the story of his mother never having met his father's family, moving back to Charleston after his father's death, and then discovering she was pregnant. Not being married, his mother decided it would be best to keep the pregnancy a secret rather than run the risk of tarnishing his deceased father's reputation. Craft admitted he always wanted to have a relationship with his father's family but not at the expense of hurting his mother.

Vaughn explained that public discovery of his father being a 9/11 victim could bring unnecessary attention because a key factor that potential adversaries used to connect people with the Agency was *motive*. Right now all they had was Craft's grandfather worked for Naval Intelligence. Vaughn didn't think that was enough to draw much attention. On the other hand, connecting his past with the 9/11 attacks would be a much stronger motive. In fact, Vaughn knew that the Iranian Intelligence tracked family members of 9/11 victims, suspecting that some would join forces with the CIA looking for vengeance. He asked Craft to continue keeping the family secret.

CHAPTER 8

Craft showed up for his first day of work at the Williamsburg Golf Course. After a short meet-and-greet with the staff, the financial manager escorted him to the money room, a secure area of the clubhouse where the money from business operations was collected, counted, and then loaded into an armored truck each day for transport to a local bank. Once inside, the financial manager handed him a classified package containing instructions. Craft went to the secure unify communications and collaboration unit—the UCC unit—in the back of the room, inserted the provided personal identity card, entered the pin code, and Jason Vaughn appeared on the display. The team leader stressed the importance of being perceived by the staff and members as an assistant golf professional employed by the Williamsburg Golf Course.

For the first two weeks, Craft worked at the golf course introducing himself to everyone, hitting balls on the range, and playing a few holes now and then. He even gave instruction to a few new golfers. It wasn't long before he was a regular among the staff, drinking a couple of beers after work and being invited to social events. One morning, Craft entered the money room, proceeded through a back door to a garage, then jumped into the back of the armored truck that had come to pick up the money from the previous day's operations. At the next stop a few miles down the road, he transitioned to a parked car. When he entered a special code into the navigation unit, the driverless car started to move. Fifteen minutes later he arrived at a gated entrance to a heavily wooded area outside of Williamsburg. The gate automatically opened and then closed as the car passed through. Soon the vehicle stopped in an enclosed parking lot.

As he stepped out of the car, he could see Jason Vaughn walking in his direction. "Hello, Peter," he said, shaking the new agent's hand. "It's time you meet the team face-to-face."

As they entered the building, exercise machines lined the perimeter of the room. They walked to the back of the room where the team had gathered in the kitchen area. As Vaughn began the introductions, Craft did his own assessment. No surprise, the man with a short military haircut and muscles bulging from every part of his body was responsible for physical conditioning. Dr. Page, responsible for psychological training, appeared a bit mysterious. She seem to be a sweet middle-aged lady who should be home baking cookies, but something in her demeanor told him otherwise. Ms. Kim, responsible for technical preparedness, reminded him of a young Asian girl he knew in college who was both a computer geek and cheerleader. Mr. Gul, responsible for Iranian operations, could have been one of the students who took over the U.S. Embassy in Tehran in the 1970s.

Just as the introductions were wrapping up, the door opened and in walked a man of Japanese heritage. With a confident swagger, the man came strutting through the room wearing a leather jacket, sunglasses, and holding a motorcycle helmet under one of his arms. Vaughn explained that the operation required motorcycle skills and Mr. Tagami was responsible for the training. Within the hour, Craft was racing a motorcycle around a track with a wild man yelling instructions he could hardly hear through the speakers in his helmet.

After hours of riding, it was time for him to sit down with the shrink. Dr. Page sat on the desk so she could make direct eye contact with him. She asked, "Mr. Craft, do you think you're ready to be a superstar?"

"I never really thought about it," he answered.

"It's time you do," Page responded. "This mission is much more than playing golf; it's about branding an image. Everything you do in public will be visible to the world."

The doctor's mild-mannered appearance was deceptive, he thought. *She was a tiger ready to attack.*

Dr. Page showed a series of video clips featuring Tiger Woods, a person many thought was the best ever to have played the game of golf. The first clip covered the early 2000s when Woods won four Major tournaments in a row. The crowds were so wild that the media coined the phrase "Tigermania" to refer to crowd craziness going on around him as he tried to compete on the golf course.

The next clip showed a full range of media coverage and how viewership increased by manipulating situations to create conflict. In his early years, the media put Woods on a pedestal and used interviews with other players to create conflict. Woods learned to think before responding to media questions and then choose his words carefully. When he showed frustration on the golf course after hitting a bad shot, it made headlines. If he responded to a negative comment made by another player, it made headlines. The last clips showed how the media could be brutal, invading all aspects of his personal life.

"Mr. Craft, this assignment requires you to function in a world most never experience," she told him, "You are about to become a star acting on the world stage with a live audience. Some of your actions will be scripted, but most will be adlibbed. If the role of being a golf superstar is not hard enough, you must also function as a secret agent for the U.S. government. This means you are expected to perform under extreme pressure, both on and off the course. Basically, this operation requires a full 24/7 commitment. You will be stressed both physically and mentally. We don't have time for on-the-job training, so you'll have to get it right the first time."

•

Over the next few months, Craft underwent intense physical, psychological, weapons, and spycraft training. His time at the golf course became the relaxing part of the day. Vaughn was delighted that the agent-in-training was effective at keeping his cover while progressing on schedule.

Operational security, a major consideration for all successful clandestine operations, required special arrangements. The Agency assumed at some point adversaries would be monitoring the training site. It was important that unauthorized observers not be able to link the training site with golf-related activities. As a result, great care was taken to ensure golf activities were performed inside access-controlled areas and spycraft techniques and procedures were used to conceal any outside activities.

Ms. Kim, the technical engineer, was ready to train Craft on the intricacies of the Smartball technology and the required changes to use it effectively. She was delighted by his interest in the design details. Based on the questions he asked, she thought he must have an engineering degree; she had missed the part of his bio describing his advanced software development skills.

Kim determined a few things in his golf game would have to change to get the best results. She displayed a diagram of Craft's ball flight of a right to left draw, typical of many good right-handed players. The case was made that hitting a draw shot with a lot of sidespin was inefficient when compared to a straight shot with minimum sidespin. A golf shot pushed to the right could be given a sidespin to make it appear to be a slight draw, curving it back to the left. Alternatively, a shot pulled to the left could be given a sidespin to make it appear to be a slight fade, curving it back to the right. The straight shot had the best chance of getting the ball in the optimal position and least chance of detection as being manipulated, because many professionals hit balls with fades and draws depending on the situation. It was called *working the ball.*

Kim led him to a building with an indoor cyber golf simulator. He hit thousands of golf balls while she monitored the equipment. It didn't take long before he consistently hit straight shots with low spin, high ball-speed and optimum launch angle.

After reading Kim's progress report, Dr. Page determined it was time to see how well Craft could perform under stress conditions. For two days, he was subjected to extreme physical and mental exercises and periodically required to hit balls in the golf simulator. To Page's surprise, his performance level was exceptionally good. It took three days before Craft's performance degraded to an unacceptable level. On the third day, his ball-speed had slowed dramatically and he had difficulty striking the ball in the center of the clubface.

With the emergence of winter, work demands at the golf course were minimal. Only a few diehard golfers showed up each day to play. After months of intense training, he looked forward to a free weekend. He left the clubhouse early Friday afternoon, ready for some down time. As he walked toward his blue Mustang in the back of the parking lot, a large F150 Ford truck with dark tinted windows pulled up alongside him. When the driver side window went down, it was Kim driving. She motioned for him to get in.

NORTHERN VIRGINIA

Four hours later, they pulled into the same airplane hangar in Northern Virginia used for the initial Smartball testing. Vaughn had arranged for them to have access to the site over the weekend to work out technical details.

Kim explained the importance of the golf bag location and positioning of the launch detection unit. She tried to make it as easy as possible, so he could keep his mind focused on tournament competition. It was the caddy's job to position and operate the Smartball equipment. The only thing Craft would have to do was wait for the caddy to signal the equipment was ready. She walked through the process, pretending to be the caddy. She demonstrated how the caddy would hold the bag until Craft selected the club to be used. Then the caddy would back away, positioning the bag to about twenty feet in a good position to activate Smartball. When the equipment was ready, she showed how the caddy would signal by taking the towel off the bag as if getting ready to clean the player's club before putting it back in the bag. Alternative bag positions were worked out to accommodate different ball locations and unmovable objects such as a tree. They worked together to refine the player and caddy interactions to make them appear natural.

He hit many shots from different distances as Kim worked the Smartball equipment. Kim was delighted that he had mastered hitting straight shots with low spin, and the data showed it. Although the technology could deliver up to 14 yards of correction to hit the optimal position, on average, Craft only needed 8 yards of correction. By the end of the weekend, she was comfortable he was proficient using Smartball from off the green, but performing on the green was still an unknown.

TEHRAN, IRAN

The day's first light glowed dimly from the peeks of the snowy mountains to the north. The cold air rushed through the open windows as he shook his head back and forth rubbing the back of his neck with one hand while steering the pickup truck with the other. Still an hour outside of Tehran, the CEO tried self-stimulation methods to shake off the hypnotic affects of driving hours on a dark country road. Having shaken free of the cobwebs that clouded his thoughts, he continued mentally preparing for the morning meeting that would put Allah's plan in motion.

Twenty-five years earlier when given a new Iranian identity, Asadi began his movement up the corporate ladder. His biochemical engineering education, calculating mind, and willingness to work outside the system, set him apart from his peers. Unbeknown to the company's owner, Asadi led a black-market drug smuggling operation. He used drug profits to boost his financial performance within the company. While other staff struggled to keep their jobs, his influence within the company grew.

While his demeanor with customers and staff was professional, his contempt for them was immense. To him, they were empty vessels, traveling through life without purpose. Like pieces on a chessboard, he manipulated them to achieve his objectives. In moments of compassion, Asadi would pray for Allah to judge them mercifully in Jannah—the eternal place for Muslims. Having carefully studied each person's mental makeup, he knew which buttons to push to get things done.

As his position within the company strengthened, Asadi's ability to assert control increased. Customers, and staff alike, looked to him for leadership and advice. After years of being patient, the opportunity for Asadi to take control of the company developed. The owner, now in his sixties, wanted to retire but continued working for financial reasons. After a series of family misfortunes, secretly orchestrated by Asadi, the owner accepted a buyout offer requiring Asadi, the new CEO, to make quarterly payments for five years. The buyout deal included the owner's son being in charge of corporate finances. Although unstated, the owner wanted a trusted party watching corporate funds. To avoid suspicion, Asadi gave the owner's son full access to the company books. He believed the complex transaction used to launder black-market profits would go unnoticed as long as the corporate balance sheet remained strong. He was right. The son spent most of his time playing computer games. To keep him busy, the new CEO requested a cadre of financial reports.

With no one looking over his shoulder, Asadi built a network of loyal customers by offering quality chemical products at low prices. He kept his real intension well hidden except for a small group of collaborators he had systematically placed in the company's security organization. They held planning sessions and coordinated smuggling activities late at night after the regular employees had gone home for the evening.

With the Asian Open now driving the timeline, the urgency of today's meeting with Ali, the owner of a rug manufacturing business, had intensified. Over time, Asadi had gained the young man's trust by offering favorable prices for chemical products and helping him obtain a larger building under favorable terms. Their relationship was more than business. Craving a father figure to show interest in his business success, Ali had turned to the chemical company executive for an elder's advice.

Asadi's relationship with the young man was of strategic importance. Ali was the son of the cleric, Gilani, a direct descendent of Mohammad.

Prior to the moderate government's takeover in 2021, Gilani had been next in line to become the supreme leader of Iran. To Gilani's disappointment, his son Ali was more interested in growing a rug business to provide economic stability for his young family than continuing the family line of fundamentalist Islamic clerics. Deep down, Ali had longed for his father's admiration, something he never had. Over time, the young man became reliant on Asadi's fatherly advice to help him cope with his father's never ending demands.

When Asadi entered the building, Ali greeted him saying, "Salaam."

"Salaam," the elder responded.

As they walked through the large manufacturing area to Ali's office in the back, Asadi commented, "I see Allah has blessed you with prosperity."

"Allah has blessed me with a good friend," Ali replied, acknowledging the CEO's help obtaining the new facility.

Asadi explained his assistance was self-serving because producing more rugs required the purchase of more chemical products. After discussing business for an hour, Ali's wife brought tea for them to enjoy a mid-morning break.

While having tea, Asadi mentioned the topic of the Asian Open being held in Tehran. Ali took the bait, expressing his frustration with his father's constant calling for Jihad to stop the invasion of foreign infidels. Ali joked about enticing invaders to purchase his rugs and bring them back to their homelands.

Seething inside at Ali's callous comment, Asadi asked what had stopped his father from taking action. Of course he already knew the answer. Although Gilani had built a cell of fundamentalist followers intent on ousting Iran's moderate government, his ability to fund his efforts was dismal. People were still suffering from the economic sanctions that had had a stranglehold on the nation for many years.

Asadi suggested that sometimes leaders had to form alliances with others sharing common interests, even if their objectives were different. When Ali asked for an example, he pretended to think hard for a moment and then brought up the topic of funding.

He said, "Amir Turani's intension to bring foreign wealth back to Iran is well known."

"Are you suggesting my father join force with Turani? He despises the man," replied Ali, wondering why the elder would propose such a crazy idea.

"You misunderstand," he responded. "The money fueling Turani's dream would have to come from somewhere else. So, who loses if Turani wins?"

Ali sat back in his chair, thinking. "I've heard the Saudi tycoon, Baahir, has much at stake."

"Yes, I believe Baahir manages much of the wealth held by Islamic people outside of Iran," he said, delighted with the direction of the conversation.

"Unfortunately, Baahir is a mercenary uninterested in my father's call for Jihad."

"Baahir may not be interested in Jihad, but he still might fund an operation that hurts his business competition," replied Asadi.

Observing that Ali had grasped the idea, the CEO looked at his watch and then apologized for having to leave to meet with another customer.

CHAPTER 9

After returning to a normal routine of physical and mental conditioning, Craft was summoned to another building at the training site. Inside the building was a large manufactured two-tiered green. Kim discussed the limitations of the Smartball technology explaining that its software was designed to use a highly precise geographical contour map of each green. The equipment would not emit a correction signal that might appear to defy the laws of physics. In other words, it wouldn't create a spin to make the ball break uphill.

The player had to hit the putt with a bias to the uphill side to get the best results. The technology added (or reduced) spin as the ball broke downhill to the hole. Craft understood the technology, but for him putting was the "feel" part of his game. Kim had study video clips of his playing golf. His tendency was to lag long putts. Lagging putts was a strategy to minimize the possibility of a three putt. The player took a higher line, anticipating the putt would break more as it slowed when approaching the hole. Kim highlighted that his lag putts had about a 50/50 change of going past the hole. This was a problem because Smartball could slow down a putt that was going past the hole but was unable to speed up a putt hit short of the hole. He would have to make an adjustment to ensure his putts had enough speed to get to the hole.

To complicate matters even more, Kim informed him his game was so good that Smartball would only be required some of the time. This meant he would have to be able to shift seamlessly between normal and technology-assisted golf.

Craft was excited about the possibility of playing as much as possible without the use of Smartball, but changing his putting style after years of practice was going to be a challenge. Putting came naturally to him, and he felt that having to think about the mechanics would be a difficult transition.

Smartball detected the ball and hole locations and provide an indicator to the caddy of the direction and magnitude of the break. The caddy

52   Tour of Deception

would point to a spot on the green indicating the aiming point. Kim spent two weeks working with him to smooth out the putting process. Just when it appeared they had the process down, he would revert back to his natural putting stroke. When Kim mentioned she had to cut training short to meet with Dr. Page, he dreaded what was coming next.

After 48 hours of intense physical and mental stress, Craft's putting skills rapidly declined. Dr. Page was concerned that his mental focus was lacking, so she put him through a series of drills designed to help him perform under high stress conditions. Tired of the abuse, he figured the mental and physical punishment would continue until he could withstand three days of hell. Not enjoying this part of the training, he worked hard to stay alert after two days with no sleep. It worked. His putting performance on the third day of stress testing was good enough to win a Tour event.

CIA HEADQUARTERS
MCLEAN, VA

The CIA Director received correspondence from the White House Chief of Staff requesting a special update on the Iranian situation. She knew that after the holidays the President would shift into full campaign mode for his second-term reelection. The Asia Open in Tehran was considered a high political risk. The campaign faced a dilemma. If the President issued an Executive Order stopping U.S. participation in the Asia Open without hard evidence of a terrorist threat, then it would be viewed as anti-business and anger the pro-business voting base. Alternatively, if the tournament was held as scheduled three weeks before the November election, it left no time for damage control if Americans were harmed.

As was customary, the President would be spending the holidays in his home state of Florida. After complaining about freezing in Virginia while the President enjoyed Florida's warm weather, the CIA Director volunteered to go there and give an update on the Iran security situation. The White House was surprised when Walker requested a one-on-one golf match with the President prior to the meeting.

The President, an avid golfer with a respectable handicap of thirteen, frequently shot scores in the mid-80s. Catherine Walker, a novice golfer with a twenty-two handicap, kept in excellent physical shape. Her disciplined conditioning stemmed from her childhood years, when she was a gymnast, participating in competitions throughout the southeast. The President preferred playing old style golf, walking the course with a caddy carrying the clubs as opposed to riding in a cart.

With the intent of hyping the match, Walker encouraged friendly wagering between the CIA and White House staff. The White House Chief of Staff wanted to know how many strokes the President would have to give to make the match fair. Based on the handicap differential, Walker should receive nine strokes but she only requested five. The CIA staff lost their enthusiasm when they heard the boss was giving the President a four-stroke advantage.

WEST PALM BEACH, FL

The morning of the match, the President was gracious, offering to give the Director additional strokes, but Walker politely declined, indicating she felt especially lucky this day. The CIA Director was taking a shellacking with the President going six up after nine holes. The President, feeling guilty she had not taken all nine strokes, wondered if she was this bad at Agency negotiations. The tide turned when Walker won seven straight holes on the back nine, shooting five pars and two birdies to go one up after the 16th hole. The President was impressed by her competitive nature, but losing to a twenty-two handicapper, not to mention a woman, would have been embarrassing. The President made a comeback on the last two holes to win the match one up. They shook hands and then in Spanish, the President muttered to his caddy, "Sandbagger—twenty-two handicap my ass."

•

Walker started the afternoon meeting, "Thank you, Mr. President, for giving me the opportunity to update you on the Iranian security situation. It's not by chance that we played golf this morning because the subject of this meeting is a golf tournament in Iran. As you have been briefed on multiple occasions, the Asian Open would make a perfect target for terrorists. I know you want a more definitive assessment regarding the terrorist threat but we haven't one, and time is running out. We believe at this time there are two reasonable courses of action. One of which you are well aware of—issue an Executive Order stopping U.S. involvement and pay the political consequences. What I am here to talk about is a new second alternative. Before going any further, I request everyone except principals, leave the room and all recording of this conversation be shut down."

She waited until the CIA staff assistant gave her the okay and then left the room. Walker went through the Red Crescent program and the Smartball technology. The President, intrigued by the idea, assessed the political implications. His political adversaries would love to catch him cheating at many things but golf was nowhere on the radar. On the other hand, he thought cheating at golf to defeat terrorists was brilliant.

"How do you know Smartball would work in real operation?" asked the President.

"Mr. President, its operational readiness was validated this morning during our match. I played the first nine holes without Smartball assistance and then used it for the next seven holes. In all seriousness, sir, neither you nor the Secret Service was able to detect anything, yet it worked very effectively to improve my game."

Laughing out loud, the President indicated he had been fooled. The National Security Advisor and Director of National Intelligence were conflicted. They were unhappy the CIA Director had briefed the President without going to them first, but at the same time thought the Red Crescent program had real potential.

"While the secrecy of all of our clandestine operations is important," Walker continued, "the highly visible nature of this one requires the absolute smallest number of people to be granted special access. If we go forward, I strongly recommend the knowledge of this operation outside a small group within the CIA stays with the people in this room."

Walker gave the President an Operational Order to sign authorizing execution of the Red Crescent program and use of the Smartball technology.

Before signing, The President asked, "Do any of you have a good reason why I shouldn't sign this document?"

With no objections being voiced, the President signed the document, stood up and said in a serious tone, "The nation needs you to succeed. If there's anything I can do to assist, do not hesitate to ask."

CHAPTER 10

After months of training and being pushed to the brink of breakdown on a regular basis, Craft started to believe Red Crescent was more than just a practice drill. Up until now, the operation seemed improbable. In the back of his mind was the thought of preparing for a game that would never be played. In the last two weeks, the tempo and intensity of training had increased to a level that made him think the operation would begin soon.

With shaving cream on his face and water pouring into the sink below, he looked at his reflection in the mirror, as if in a trance, overwhelmed with uncertainty. *Who am I? What have I become? Is this really necessary? How did I get here...?*

He missed his grandfather more than ever, the man who had always been by his side to listen, mentor, challenge, motivate, comfort, and when necessary, provide a deserving kick in the butt. Feeling sorry for himself, he recalled Vaughn telling him he would not be going through this alone. And he felt alone, having to face the crazy motorcycle instructor, demented drillmaster, possessed shrink, and cunning spies putting him through daily hell. Then a moment of relief set in as he thought about how much he enjoyed his time with Kim, the techno geek. After a few minutes of doubt and self-pity, it was time to go to work.

As usual, the armored truck stopped at the drop-off point when an oversized, white, SUV pulled up. With the driver side window down, the man inside said, "Hello Peter."

After getting into the car, Vaughn handed him a cup of coffee and a letter, and then with a big ear-to-ear smile pronounced, "Well, the practice is over, it's game time."

Where in the hell have you been while I been getting the crap beat out of me on a daily basis? He wanted to ask but decided to act professional.

Scanning the letter, it was an invitation from the Florida Citrus Association to play in the Orlando Open. The tournament winner would receive an invitation to the Masters. The Agency had shortcut the normal process for being invited to play in a Tour event by securing a Sponsor

Exemption. Most players on the Tour held "official status" obtained by achieving top rankings on one of the less lucrative tours. To boost ticket sales, tournament sponsors received a limited number of exemptions they could give to people without official status. Unknown to Craft, his Sponsor Exemption was a result of the President pulling strings in his home state of Florida.

Vaughn pulled out a new HuAID unit with the built-in security, handed it to Craft, and told him how to invoke the built-in encryption for secure communication. Traveling west on Interstate 64 and seeing his luggage and golf clubs in the back, Craft breathed a sigh of relief at the realization his grueling days of training were behind him.

SAUDI ARABIA

He waited at a desert villa near the city of Al Majmaah located two hundred miles from Riyadh. In secrecy, he had made the pilgrimage to Saudi Arabia to meet with the wealthy Saudi businessman, Azzam Baahir. The harsh trip through the Persian mountains, the marshlands of southern Iraq, and the Saudi Arabian desert had taken its toll on the cleric's sixty-year-old body. With throbbing back pain muddling his thoughts, Gilani tried to think through his takedown of the current Iranian leadership. He had already received word Baahir needed assurance his operation would not involve mass killing. He knew if he took the money and failed to comply, the Saudi businessman could be ruthless. At the same time, some of his followers would only support his Jihad movement if it involved the annihilation of those attending the Asia Open.

A skilled politician, Gilani planned to create a security threat big enough so the current Iranian government couldn't ignore it. His Jihadist followers would take action, believing those attending the Asian Open would go to their graves. In actuality, they would never have the full means to execute the threat. His real objective was a last minute cancelation of the tournament. As usual, he expected the United States and its allies to respond by reinstating sanctions. The global embarrassment and return of sanctions would be sufficient for citizens to question the Supreme Leader's competency. Then Gilani's network of fundamentalist clerics would use the power of the mosque—the ability of religious leaders to engage the congregation at daily prayers—to ignite a grass roots revolution. Of course, as a direct descendent of Mohammad, he would step forward to offer spiritual guidance as the new Supreme Leader of Iran.

After bathing and trimming his beard, he unpacked a neatly folded tie, long-sleeve shirt, and business suit. Even though his alliance with Baahir was an action of last resort, he was prepared to show respect by dressing in appropriate business attire. He hoped Allah would not judge him harshly for dealing with a man who worshiped money. Still trying to rationalize his actions, he found comfort knowing his deal with the mercenary might provide the impetus to return Iran to Sharia law. In his mind he could hear his son, Ali's words, *"Great men focus on the righteousness of their objectives while remaining flexible with the methods used to achieve them."*

Gilani waited for hours at the villa for the Saudi businessman to arrive. As the sun moved over the horizon, he remembered how much he loved the vibrant colors of desert sunsets. When the cleric began his evening prayers, a stranger appearing out of the darkness knelt down next to him. After praying together, the man apologized for Mr. Baahir who would not be coming in person because of an urgent family matter. In actuality, the Saudi businessman had never intended to meet with the Shiite cleric. The Saudi had requested Gilani come to Riyadh as a test of conviction, knowing a man of his stature would only make the trip if he had a serious plan. Baahir had no interest in details, he just want to know the cleric agreed to his terms.

The stranger handed Gilani a hand written letter from Baahir. The letter stated that forty million in gold would be given to assist the cleric's political ambitions with the special stipulation of no mass killings. The remainder of the letter contained specifics regarding the demise of Amir Turani. After the cleric had read the letter, the man asked, "Do you agree to the terms?"

"Yes, I agree," answered the cleric.

The man retrieved the letter and handed him instructions of where to find the gold in Tehran. Then the man left the home, vanishing into the dark. Gilani stood on the terrace feeling the desert breeze on his face. After pondering the agreement, the cleric got an uneasy feeling that the wrath directed at Turani was more rooted in personal vengeance than business interests.

Just after midnight, they pulled into the driveway of the Johns Island residence, located in a rural area a few miles south of downtown Charleston. The modest three-level house sat back from the road on a large open lot away from neighbors with a fence around the perimeter. Surrounded by marshlands, the house was only accessible by visitors from the front. The ground level contained a two-car garage with a large staircase in the middle connecting the ground level to the house entrance on the second level.

The ocean breeze and smell of fresh salt air stirred warm feelings of being back in Charleston, the place Craft loved and would always call home. When the garage door opened, there stood two high-performance Japanese motorcycles.

"Get comfortable," said Vaughn. "This is going to be your home for a few weeks."

After a good night sleep, Craft prepared for a long run in an early morning February mist. In addition to a lightweight rain jacket, he wore gloves, socks, and headband to keep his hands, feet, and ears warm. While he was out pounding the pavement, Vaughn sat at the kitchen table drinking coffee and scanning news headlines from around the world.

Mid morning, they drove to a nearby discount golf store in North Charleston. After a short conversation, the store manager led them though a doorway into an employee only area. They descended down a flight of stairs and through a second door. The stairwell was equipped with sensors and optics to detect and view anyone in the area.

Once inside with the door closed, Vaughn said, "This is a secure facility code named '*The Shack*' and as long as you have your HuAID, the upstairs and downstairs doors will detect your biometrics and open. We'll use this space to work out operational details. As your fame grows, additional precautions will be necessary to maintain operational security. Only Agency people are working here so they'll keep an eye on things and alert us if there's any unusual activity in the area."

Director Walker appeared on the secure 3-D holographic display. Although in her office at CIA Headquarters, the quality of the virtual meeting made it seem as if she was in the room. "Hello, Mr. Vaughn and Mr. Craft. On behalf of the nation, I thank you for accepting this important mission. I pray for your safety. Jason, my comrade and friend, once again you've stepped forward to answer the call of duty. And Mr. Craft, the word 'extraordinary' comes to mind when I think of your willingness to accept this assignment. If you have any questions or concerns, please feel free to voice them."

After waiting a few moments, Walker continued, "As stated in the signed Operational Order, you are now authorized to execute the operational phase of Red Crescent program. Again, I thank you. The nation owes you a debt of gratitude."

Within seconds, the Director's image disappeared. Craft thought something about her seemed familiar but he wasn't sure what. She reminded him of someone he met as a child, but he wasn't sure where.

They sat in silence for a moment, reflecting on the importance of the mission and personal interest shown by the Director. The Operational Order stated the specific intelligence collection objectives and the allowable means that could be used to achieve those objectives. Next came the caveats. The Agency would disavow any knowledge of the operation and the people involved.

An attachment to the order described the team, the roles and the operational security. In addition to leading the team, Jason Vaughn would perform the role of caddy and assume the identity of a man named Jefferson, a wounded warrior from the Iraq War. Vaughn put his personal identification into a safe and reached for a package containing a full set of new identity credentials—driver's license, passport, and other identity documents. Also, the package contained Jefferson's detailed bio.

After reading Jefferson's bio, Craft asked, "What if someone wants verification of your war injuries?"

Vaughn lifted his shirt to show a gruesome scar, a wound received twenty years earlier during a clandestine operation in Iraq. Before walking out of the room, he handed over the car keys. "From now on, we have a player-caddy relationship outside of this room. I will meet you at 1PM at Charleston Manor. Also, by now, your invitation to the Orlando Open is public knowledge."

CHAPTER 11

CHARLESTON, SC

When Craft arrived at the Charleston Manor Golf Course, the staff with Callie leading the parade made a celebratory orange juice toast in honor of his having received an invitation to play in the Orlando Open. After socializing for a while, he thanked the staff for being so gracious and planting the elegant flowerbed in memory of his grandfather by the 16th tee, and then left the clubhouse to go practice.

At the practice range, he barely recognized Jefferson, the caddy, because the disguise was so transformational. Vaughn looked ten years younger, but weather beaten like a cowboy who spent years baking in the sun. Before hitting balls, he tightened the clasp on his bright orange Clemson golf hat so it wouldn't blow away in the stiff ocean wind. After hitting balls for two hours in the cool winter air, he moved to the putting green with Jefferson lugging the clubs close behind.

While working on his putting stroke, he caught a glimpse of a familiar looking woman walked down the cart path toward the putting green. She wore a pink sweater, much too tight for playing golf, but perfect to draw attentions to her female curves. The high heel shoes were a dead giveaway the woman was not there to play golf.

Waving frantically as she approached, the woman said, "Hi Peter, you probably don't remember me."

He blushed at sight of the once spicy college intern who had been the object of his affection in 8th grade, the provocative older woman he often dreamed of when he was a young teenager.

"Of course I remember you, Ms. Bates. Are you still working for the *Charleston News?*"

"Yes. You probably remember me when I was an intern, following your mother around like a young pup."

Craft motioned for his caddy to come over. "This is Mr. Jefferson, the man who'll be lugging my clubs around for the next few weeks."

Jefferson acknowledged the news reporter with a smile and a tipping of his hat, "Good afternoon ma'am, pleased to meet you."

"Welcomed to Charleston, Mr. Jefferson," she responded with a sweet southern drawl and then offered a gentle handshake.

"We were about to take a break. Would you care to join us?" asked Craft.

"I'd be delighted," said Bates, batting her eyes flirtatiously.

Still remembering him as a young boy, she marveled at the stunning man he'd become. She wondered which of Charleston's fine ladies would be lucky enough to win his heart, wishing she were single and ten years younger. "I was surprised to hear you received an invitation to play in the Orlando Open."

"To be honest, Ms. Bates, I was also surprised. During my grandfather's illness, playing golf didn't matter much to me. Now golf is my future."

Reaching out to hold his hand, she said, "Your grandfather's death was a great loss for Charleston."

He gave her a somber look. "I needed to get away for a while, so I went to work at the Williamsburg Golf Club in Virginia where I discovered a renewed passion for the game of golf. While Williamsburg gave me the time away I needed, Charleston will always be my home."

Pleased by Craft's media presence, Jefferson excused himself and went outside to tend to the golf clubs.

Bates continued the inquiry. "Why did you get the invitation rather than some of the other professional golfers in the area?"

"That's an excellent question for the Florida Citrus Association, but I can tell you my thoughts."

"Please do."

"I believe it was a simple business decision. A tournament sponsor can offer exemptions to anyone they think will increase ticket sales. Who knows? Maybe some Clemson fans might go to Orlando to watch one of their own play on the Tour."

Bates asked, "Do you think your mother, the Mayor of Charleston, pulled strings to get you the invitation?"

"I am sure my mother being mayor was a factor; however, it's my understanding sponsors can give exemptions to anyone they think will benefit their cause, and I am thankful they chose me. I hope to not disappoint them."

The news reporter began shaping the news article in her head. She would write the story in a way so readers could speculate about how much influence the mayor exerted to get her son the invitation. "Given you'll be competing against the best players in the world, do you think you can win?" she asked.

With a confident smile, Craft answered, "Sure I can win. But even the best players fail to win most the time. So, my odds of winning are a long shot. Then again, the Charleston Academy Tigers were also a long shot to win the state football championship, but we did."

"How did you meet your caddy, Mr. Jefferson?"

"We met in Williamsburg. He's an excellent caddy and a great American who risked all to defend this nation. He was wounded years ago during the Iraq War. I think it's important to reach out to those who've given so much for our freedom."

Excited to get back to the office and write the story, the *Charleston News* reporter concluded the interview.

Craft continued practicing until the secure message indicator on his HuAID began blinking. After activating the decryption, a message appeared, *The Shack 17:15*. Glancing at the clock by the 1st tee, he had just enough time to bathe and change clothes before going to the Ops meeting.

Once in the secure area, Vaughn complimented Craft on his first media encounter and shared ideas about what to do next. As quarterback for a top-ten college football team, Craft had been interviewed many times by both friendly and hostile reporters.

They agreed to meet the next morning at 7am at the golf course. As the young man stood up to leave, Vaughn said there was one more topic to discuss. "An agent's life of secrecy is especially difficult when around friends and family. Every new agent needs a mentor, an experienced agent with similar interests but not directly involved in the operation. Your mentor will have the needed clearances, so you can talk about anything," said Vaughn.

Thinking the last thing he needed was an old guy sharing war stories, Craft asked, "So when will I get to meet my mentor?"

Handing the young man a piece of gum, Vaughn ended the conversation by saying, "Read it, remember it, and then eat it."

Printed on the gum was the following text. You will know your mentor by the following verbal exchange:

When asked—*Have you ever played Saint Andrews?*

You will respond—*No, but I would love to.*

The reply must be—*Maybe someday we can play the old course together.*

Thinking this was old school spycraft stuff he ate the gum and walked out the door.

He stopped by the Johns Island residence for a short rest and then gave his mother a call. She insisted on meeting for dinner at their favorite restaurant, Magnolias.

After a warm embrace and some casual conversation, he asked, "Whatever possessed you to run for mayor?"

Craft's mother thought for a moment and then replied, "Your grandfather's passing. You know he treasured Charleston's great heritage and his protective nature consumed him during the last few years. He watched as unprepared cities were vandalized when anti-government protests escalated out of control. The thoughts of Charleston burning haunted him. After doing some research, it became evident the city leaders did not take the threat seriously. So becoming mayor was my way to get their attention. Contingency plans to protect the city are almost done so I don't plan to be mayor much longer. Truthfully, other members of the council are better than I am at the city's general administration."

Changing the subject, Craft's mother asked, "I heard you're going to play at the Orlando Open? Charlotte Bates has already given me her version of today's interview, and if I do say so myself, her version is quite provocative. You are the knight in shining armor who has returned to Charleston to win the heart of a beautiful southern princess."

"I don't remember any provocative discussion."

"Charlotte is famous for turning every interview into a romance. You're lucky she isn't a few years younger; you would have a stalker on your hands."

After sharing a good laugh, he said, "If you don't already know, Ms. Bates has the notion that you pulled strings to get your son the invitation."

"No worries; she'll be fair. And so what if people think I pulled strings for my son? Around here, pulling strings to help your family is admirable. What's even better is the city council believing I have this much influence."

After a toast, some antipasto, and sharing a few family memories, Amanda asked, "So give me the truth. How did you really come by the invitation?"

He knew to be careful about what he was going to say because his mother could read him like a book. He hated having to lie to his mother although he knew she would understand. He told her the head professional at the Williamsburg Golf Club used his Florida connections to get the invitation.

Craft's mother reached for his hand, looked him in the eyes as she had done many times before, and asked, "Is playing golf what you really want to do with your life?"

"Yes it is, and I am good at it."

"If you're happy then I am delighted. Golf is a lot safer than playing quarterback," she said, pointing to the shoulder he hurt playing football.

While sitting at the table having a second glass of wine, Amanda Craft said, "I have a work opportunity that's popped up and I need your thoughts."

"What's up?" he asked.

"I've been offered the lead scriptwriter position on a movie to be made in Australia. It's a great offer but the work has to be done on site. If I accept, it means I will be out of the country for several months starting next week."

"Mom, it's your dream job. You have to take it," he insisted.

"But I won't be there to watch you play your first professional tournament," she said with a sad face.

"You've been there for me my whole life. It's time you do something for yourself," he said, and then asked, "What are you going to do about being mayor?"

"The city council can designate one of the other members to be acting mayor. If they do a good job while I am gone, then I'll step down permanently."

They talked for another hour before saying good night. He stopped by the local convenience store, picked up some snacks and a six-pack of beer. After drinking a beer and skimming a couple golf magazines, he went to bed. Thoughts of the day's events ran through his head. The CIA Director's pep talk, the signed operations order, interview with Bates, dinner with Mom, his secret life, ... *He woke in a cold sweat consumed by thoughts of the shame to be placed upon family, friends, and community if his golf deception was ever exposed.*

•

Craft met Jefferson at 7AM. After playing a few holes, it became apparent to Jefferson the agent had lost focus. To no avail, Jefferson did as much as a good caddy could to assist his player through troubled waters. After calling it a day, Craft received an encrypted message, *"The Shack 17:30."*

Once inside the secure area, Vaughn started the questioning, "Peter, what's going on? Do we have a Doctor Jekyll and Mr. Hyde thing going on here? Yesterday, you were the cool-collected guy handling the press like a pro and today you're having a meltdown."

Vaughn knew exactly what was going on. No training could totally prepare an agent for his first clandestine operation, especially when it took place close to home. Going into your home environment was a big adjustment. Based on experience, he knew facing the demons upfront was much better than down the road.

"You need a few days off. Spend some time reestablishing yourself in the community, getting reacquainted with friends and most of all, get your head on straight," Vaughn firmly stated. "The next time we meet, you need to be ready to work. This operation needs you; there's no backup plan."

Furious with the conversation, Craft exited the secure room without saying a word. He stopped at the house to pick up his swimsuit, then on to the local community center for a long swim. He dove into the pool and began moving with long strokes back and forth across the 50-meter pool for forty-five minutes without stopping. Then, physically exhausted, he was ready for self-analysis. He went for a long walk on the beach and reflected on the situation.

Walking into a strong wind with waves crashing hard on the sandy beach, he could visualize Dr. Page saying, *"Golf will never define you. You are a U.S. government agent, working on the side of good to defeat evil. You live a life of secrecy so others can have freedom…"*

Craft left the beach feeling more at peace but still unsure about the future. Returning home, he accessed the *Charleston News* media center to see the headline, *Mayor's Son Invited to Orlando Open.* He read the article and concluded his mom was right. Ms. Bates gave a fair report with a definite flare for romance. Tired from the day and having found some comfort in the words of Dr. Page, he fell into a deep sleep.

CHAPTER 12

CHARLESTON, SC

At morning's first light, he fired up one of the motorcycles and drove up the coast along route 17 to Georgetown. Feeling rested when he returned to his residence, he thought it might be fun to play golf at a public golf course on Johns Island. Given it was a weekday afternoon, most the people at the golf course were staff and retired folks. By now, the locals knew the mayor's son would be playing at the Orlando Open. When Craft walked into the pro shop, people went out of their way to offer congratulations and well wishes. As always, he took time for personal conversation, asking how each was doing and inquiring about their family members. Peter's interest in other people was genuine and his positive attitude contagious. He treated people with respect, using Mister and Ma'am, when appropriate. Growing up in the south, talking to people in a direct, caring, and personal way was natural. Since his youth, the people of Charleston had taken a personal interest in him. He was known for winning the right way, through mental preparation, hard work, dedication, and leadership. He had a special gift for balancing confidence and humility. It was never about him; it was always about the objective.

Not having a scheduled tee-time, the starter asked Craft if he would mind joining another golfer who waited on the 1st tee. He was pleased to see the other player waiting by the 1st hole professional tee—the tee area on each hole the farthest away from the green.

Walking on to the tee, he extended his hand, "Hello, I am Peter Craft. Do you mind if I join you?"

"It would be a pleasure," responded the man, offering a hearty handshake and a big nice-to-meet you smile. "My name is Kekoa Kalani."

At the starter's request, Craft moved his clubs into the cart with Kalani and then began to size up his playing partner. The man looked Hawaiian, but also could be Hispanic, near retirement age, short, stocky, ex military, and personable.

Craft hit first, launching an excellent tee shot into the middle of the fairway. Then Kalani stepped forward and blasted a drive 15 yards past him. They both missed mid-length birdie putts to score par on the 1st hole. When Kalani suggested a friendly wager where the loser would buy the winner a drink at the 19th hole, Craft upped the bet to include a sandwich. The 19th hole was a term used to refer to the place where bets were settled up after a round of golf, typically over a drink.

It was a sunny February day in the mid 60's and windy. The informal match was even after five holes, and Craft started to pay attention to the precision with which his playing partner hit the ball. Kalani had a simple but powerful swing, finely tuned for a shorter body with wide shoulders. His swing started with a slow and deliberate take away making a big body turn. By the time his club was about half way to the top, everything was in place for the down swing. His transition toward the ball was both controlled and powerful, going from a dead stop to 120 miles an hour in a split second. The golf ball exploded off the clubface. His short game was finely tuned to control distance with a shoulder turn accelerating through to the ball. Although older in age, his physical conditioning was exceptional. Craft couldn't see a mechanical flaw in the man's game. In fact, Kalani had a highly repeatable swing, something he had never mastered.

Both were at two under par heading for the 10th hole, a 565-yard par five with a sharp dogleg to the left. Kalani hit a beautiful draw with the ball coming to rest in prime position, leaving 210 yards to the green. Craft resisted the temptation to hit a power draw around the corner, leaving a comfortable second shot to the green. As trained, he hit a straight shot which left his ball 240 yards from the green.

Craft went for the green in two, pushing the ball to the right, catching the front right bunker. Then Kalani hit a laser like second shot landing the ball 8 feet right of the pin in good position for an eagle putt. Although Craft made a routine sand shot landing the ball a few inches from the hole for an easy tap-in birdie, Kalani dropped the eagle putt to take the lead by one stroke.

At this point, you would have thought the two competitors were playing for a million dollar purse. Both were digging deep, hoping to get into the zone—a mental state when the body and mind come together with intense focus to play flawless golf. On the 17th hole, a long 225-yard par 3, Kalani hit a shot online to the pin, but a wind gust pushed the ball several feet to the right. One stroke down with two holes remaining, Craft was ready to take a calculated risk. He hit one more club than normal and took a high line out to the left and let the wind bring the ball back to the right. As the ball started to slow down, the wind pushed it sharply to the right landing two feet from the hole, leaving an easy birdie putt.

The match was all square going into 18th hole, a long 465-yard par four. The flagstick was positioned in the difficult back left corner of the two-tiered green. Both hit 300-yard plus drives, landing within a few feet of each other in the middle of the fairway. Then, both hit approach shots, landing in the middle of the green, eighteen feet from the hole. The two balls were less than a foot apart. The players looked at each other to see who should putt first. Not sure which ball was the farthest from the hole, Craft offered to go first, knowing Kalani would get the benefit of seeing the line his putt traveled. Having played the course many times, he knew what line the ball should take. He aimed six feet to the left of the hole and stroked the putt. The ball broke hard to the right as it slowed down, dropping softly into the bottom of the cup.

Without a word, Kalani looked at the putt from every angle, and then after a couple of practice strokes, hit the putt. The ball followed the same line as Craft's and was headed right into the center of the cup but the ball stopped. Both looked at the ball in total amazement. The odds of a ball rolling down hill stopping on the edge of the cup were probably one in a million. The suspense was building.

In accordance with the rules of golf, when the ball overhangs the lip of the hole, the player is allowed enough time to reach the hole without unreasonable delay and an additional ten seconds to determine if the ball is at rest. If by that time the ball has not fallen into the hole, the player must add a stroke to his score.

Kalani walked to the hole, stopped, looked down and after 3 seconds, with both players watching intensely, the ball fell to the bottom of the cup. They gave each other a high-five, acknowledging the splendid competition and suspenseful ending. In traditional form, the men removed their hats and shook hands, each acknowledging the other's good company. Craft couldn't remember the last time he had such an invigorating golf match.

As they walked off the 18th green, Kalani asked, *"Have you ever played Saint Andrews?"*

Caught off guard, Craft hesitated for a couple of seconds and then answered, *"No, but I would love to."*

Kalani gave him a pat on the back and replied, *"Maybe someday we can play the old course together."*

In absolute astonishment, he now knew the man who had inspired him to play his best was also his mentor.

"I hear you're into motorcycle racing. I'll come by your place around eight tomorrow morning," Kalani said.

Before Craft could respond, his mentor was walking toward the parking lot.

He returned to the house refreshed from playing golf and excited about meeting his mentor. Now it was time to connect with friends. He got in touch with Chris Davis, a friend from his football days. Even though they hadn't seen each other since college, both had kept in touch exchanging messages, mostly regarding sports news. After talking for a while, Chris suggested they meet for a drink at Jacksons, a new tavern a few miles south of downtown Charleston.

•

When Craft arrived, the tavern had only a few patrons. He ordered Harbor Ale, a new blend from a local brewery, and then strolled around the room looking at sports pictures hanging on the wall. When the big man with snowy white spiked hair entered the tavern, everyone took notice. At 6' 5" and over 300 pounds nothing was ordinary about Chris Davis. After a "hello" chest bump nearly knocked Craft to the floor, they moved to a table where they could talk quietly.

They caught each other up on friends and the local goings-on, then the conversion turned to football. Chris reminisced about winning the high school state championship and how they could have been college national champions if injuries had not sabotaged them, such as Craft suffering a separated shoulder from a blindside hit in the 1st quarter of championship game against Alabama. In the spirit of moving forward, Craft didn't mention it had been Chris' assignment, as left tackle, to protect the quarterback's blindside.

On his way back from the restroom, Craft's friend stopped to talk to an attractive but unfamiliar girl standing by the bar. While they talked, he gauged the situation from across the room. Dressed in old jeans, a plain blue top, and wearing no visible makeup, the stranger didn't fit the image of someone looking to hookup. Since Chris had a steady girlfriend, his interest in the lady was probably of a casual nature. If Chris was aiming to fix him up with a date as he had many times before, then his judgment had improved immensely.

Craft couldn't take his eyes off the young lady as he walked across the room to join the conversation. She was of Irish or Scottish heritage, Craft thought, as he walked closer. She may have dressed down to hide her natural beauty but no drab clothing could conceal her tall, slender, fine-tuned physique. She turned and smiled as he approach. Her reddish-brown hair flowed, with a slight curl, down the side of her face and over her shoulders, partially covering the curves of her breasts.

"Jennifer, this is my friend, Peter Craft."

Extending her hand with a friendly smile, Jennifer Wilkins introduced herself.

Giving a gentle handshake, and leaning in close so he could be heard over the music playing in the background, Craft introduced himself and then asked, "What bring you to Charleston?"

"Work," she answered.

"Jennifer is a friend of Doreen's," responded Chris, referring to his girlfriend.

"Doreen took pity on the new girl in town and invited me to join them for lunch at the downtown market last Saturday," Wilkins said.

"What kind of work do you do?" asked Craft.

"I am a consultant. My job is to assess the city's vulnerability to anti-government movements."

"How did you meet Doreen?"

"We met at a city council meeting where she presented her hospital's contingency plans for people who might be injured during a violent protest. You wouldn't by chance be related to the mayor?"

"You know my mother?" he responded.

"We've never met, but I know your mother is the person driving the city's contingency planning."

In a shameless attempt to impress the young lady, Chris proudly announced, "We're here tonight to celebrate Peter receiving an invitation to play at the Orlando Open."

Rolling her bright emerald-green eyes, she said, "Congratulations, Peter," then asked, "What's the Orlando Open? Are you a tennis player or something?"

A bit embarrassed by his friend's hard sell, Craft turned on the charm and redirected the conversation toward life in Charleston.

Chris said his goodbyes before rushing out of the tavern just in time to pick up his girlfriend, whose shift was about to end at the hospital.

They sat at a quiet table near the back of the tavern talking for another hour, having drinks and sharing chicken wings. When it was time to go, she handed him a business card and invited him to call sometime.

Not wanting to ruin the pleasant evening by being too forward, he gave her a friendly goodbye hug and suggested they meet again soon to continue the conversation.

With the mystery woman gone, he sat alone tapping his fingers to the music as if playing the piano. Jennifer Wilkins was the complete package, he thought. Her intellect, beauty, and charm were intoxicating. He stared at the card with her name and phone number fighting the urge to call, knowing another drink might have him making a damn fool of himself. He settled on sending text, "When can we meet again?"

She responded almost immediately, "Call me tomorrow."

He departed Jacksons thinking *today was a good day,* but he told himself to proceed with caution and, of course, *expect the unexpected.*

TEHRAN, IRAN

Asadi attended morning prayers at the Imam Khomeyni Mosque, a religious center known for conservative, traditional Islamic beliefs. At the conclusion of the prayer service, he entered into a conversation with two brothers known as followers of the cleric Gilani. One brother, spoke passionately regarding the cleric's new commitment to Jihad. When Asadi inquired to its purpose, the irritated man began to rant, *"The infidels must be punished... Sharia must be returned to Iran... Satan's pawns must be banished from the government..."*

"Forgive my brother," the other man interrupted. "Sometimes he gets emotional about recent changes to our country."

"I understand. These are emotional times," replied Asadi. "Do you feel the same?"

Suspicious the stranger might be a government informant, instead of answering the question, the man asked, "Who are you?"

After introducing himself, the chemical company CEO cleverly mentioned the names of some of his clients in Tehran, hoping to put the brothers at ease. They asked him many questions about business, religion, family, and politics. As always, Asadi answered with ease giving no indication of his actual intentions. He shared innocuous information while steering the conversation toward events of interest. By the time he was ready to depart the mosque, he was confident that Gilani had obtained the financial resources to fund his activities. One brother mentioned Gilani's recent trip to Mecca where he received the vision for Jihad. Asadi suspected the cleric's trip to Mecca was a cover for going to Saudi Arabia to meet with Baahir. A picture of Gilani's activities was beginning to take shape; however, important pieces were still missing.

After bidding the brothers good day, he left the mosque headed for a teahouse near the Tehran Bazaar to meet with the cleric's son, Ali. Deep in thought, he tried to envision how the conversation might unfold. He would use his position of trust with Ali to coerce him into revealing details regarding his father's activities, if not now, then soon. He would convince the young man it was in his best interest to stay connected with his father.

•

When Ali arrived, he apologized for being late, explaining that one of the machines had jammed and apparently he was the only one who knew how to fix it, holding out both hands to show the red bruises on his fingers. They talked business while drinking tea and eating fresh fruit. Then they entered into a lengthy discussion regarding the importance of living a healthy life style to include regular exercise. They compared weekly exercise routines.

Observing that Ali was in a talkative mood, he said, "Your father was the center of conversations at the mosque this morning."

"My father is busy organizing his revolution," Ali answered, rolling his eyes to show his dislike for his father's politics.

"You once mentioned your father's difficulties funding his activities."

"This conversation has to stay between us," Ali whispered.

"I assure you it will."

"My father received funding from Baahir."

"Where did he get the idea of joining forces with the Saudi?"

"From me."

"I hope you didn't mention my name in your discussions?"

"No. If my father knew of your brilliance, he would recruit you. Then you would raise my chemical prices in retaliation."

Laughing, the CEO responded, "You are correct about that."

After long pause, he asked, "Are you concerned for your family's safety?"

"Should I be?"

"From what I know, Baahir can be heartless in his business dealings."

"Baahir is the one who should be concerned. My father is a serious man."

"Let's think about this. If I am hearing about your father's Jihad plans at a local mosque, who else knows? As the Asian Open approaches, I suspect the government will be watching anyone opposed to current government policies, and I suspect your father is near the top of the list."

"You're right. Maybe I should be concerned," responded Ali. "Maybe I should keep my distance?"

"A better option might be staying informed without getting involved. Then you'll be in position to take action, if necessary."

"I appreciate your concern. Now, enough about my family, tell me about yours?" Ali asked.

The CEO talked in generalities about his fictitious family providing details he knew could not be easily validated. He told a story of how his son had joined an extremist group. He admitted feeling guilty having put business first and failing to rescue his son before it was too late. His fictitious son died in the Syrian conflict in 2014. Having never forgiven him for putting business before family, his wife moved back to her family in Britain.

As the older man talked, Ali promised himself never to put business before family. He asked to meet more often to share information and to get advice on how to navigate his father's Jihad plans as they developed. Asadi graciously agreed to weekly meetings.

CHAPTER 13

CHARLESTON, SC

The next morning, Kalani pulled up in front of the Johns Island residence riding a Harley motorcycle. A garage door opened and out drove Craft on a Kawasaki. Off they went with his mentor leading the way. Just like the golf match the previous day, it turned into a competition. They raced along back roads for most of the morning before stopping at Melvin's, a country diner. Sitting at a table away from other people, Kalani pulled a small box out of his pocket, placing it on the table along with his wallet, money clip, and HuAID. A few years earlier, Jack Wilson had designed a small matchbox sized voice scrambler so anyone trying to listen in on conversations would hear only noise.

After some small talk and play-by-play of the previous day's golf match, Kalani started the serious conversation. "Peter, it's not by chance I am your mentor."

Jokingly, Craft responded, "Vaughn must have searched high and low to find someone as good as you at golf."

"You don't understand," he said in a serious tone. "In 1992, I led an Army Special Forces team during the first Iraq War. Pete Sullivan was one of the soldiers on my team."

Feeling the blood rushing to his head, Craft asked, "Are you saying you knew my father?"

Kalani replied, "Yes, the men you go to war with are family. Believe me when I say, I loved your father like a brother."

His mentor told stories about the team and tried to answer all of Peter's questions about his father. He made the point that he could see many similarities between them, but there were differences too. Peter wanted specifics about the differences.

"For example, the way your father would introduce himself. He would give a big smile, shake your hand and say, 'Hello, I am Pete Sullivan.' Your father was direct, friendly and informal, putting you at ease in the first few seconds. Remember, I only have a few data points on you, but you're more formal and mysterious. Anyway, your father was a brave and physically gifted man, and I see that in you. But you have an added dimension. You think strategically. Your father had many admirable qualities, but strategic thinking was not one of them."

Craft had dreamed of some day meeting a person, other than his mother, who knew his father, and now he had. "How did you get so good at golf?"

"My father was a chemical engineer who worked building sugarcane processing plants. We lived in many places, starting in Hawaii where he met my mother. Most of the places were Spanish-speaking countries in warm climates. The family loved golf and I played with my father and brothers as much as possible. Two of my brothers played on the Tour in the 1980s and 1990s. High-level competition was the norm around the homestead, with some of the best players stopping by to play and wagering a few bucks."

Changing the subject, Kalani asked, "Is there anything about the mission you want to talk about?"

Craft responded, "This is a dangerous business and my weapons training has been limited."

"I hear you're an excellent marksman, especially from long distance."

"My grandfather and I were frequent visitors to the shooting range."

"No worries, you'll get more weapons training; every agent does. The short timeline for the current mission required the Agency to take a team approach and you have an exceptional team. Vaughn is one of the best."

"I met a new girl in town last night and she didn't seem to fit the picture," Craft commented. "You might say she was too good to be true."

With a big grin on his face, Kalani responded, "She's probably one of us."

"I thought so but couldn't be sure."

"I recommend you have some fun," Kalani said. "Think of it as professional jousting. She knows all about you and is testing to see if you're going to give up secrets. You're not supposed to know anything about her, other than what she chooses to reveal. Your challenge is to discover things you shouldn't know and reveal them at the right moment. An agent is trained to have a mental picture of how the other person perceives them. When that self-portrait gets distorted, the agent will retreat. Truthfully, this is one of the things I love about the job; it keeps you sharp."

"Did you know my father's family?"

"Well, your father had a younger brother, John, who was in the Army. I don't believe John ever met your mother because he was on a two-year deployment in Korea when your father passed. I had a chance to talk with your uncle at your father's funeral. Of course, he was devastated by his brother's death. After finishing a four-year tour in the Army, your uncle John joined the NY Fire Department to continue in your father's footsteps. I don't know if your mother ever told you why she had never met your father's parents."

"Not really. I think she said something about being too busy with school work."

"Your dad once told me that whenever he brought a girlfriend home to meet the family, they would befriend the girl. The next thing he knew the girl would be getting invited to family events. Then his parents would be devastated when they went their separate ways. Before meeting your mother, he made a promise that the next girl he brought home would be the one he planned to spend the rest of his life with. The weekend after 9/11, they had planned to visit your grandparents and announce their engagement."

"I know they have passed away but did you ever meet my grandparents?" Craft asked.

"Yes. I met them once and in the grand Irish tradition, they treated me like family because I was a friend of their son. Similar to many of the New York Irish immigrants, they smoked and enjoyed a stiff drink now and then. They lived good lives, although they died much too young. When I met your grandfather, he was about to retire from the Fire Department. He was just waiting for your dad to complete his hitch in the Army, so the Department would not be left without a Sullivan in its ranks."

Kalani gave him a card with contact information and told him to use it if he needed to talk. He would be coming around from time to time to check on him.

•

Back at the house, Craft called the phone number on Wilkins' business card.

"Hello, Jennifer speaking," she answered.

"Hi, it's Peter Craft. We met last night."

"Yes, I remember," she replied. "I am with a client, could I call you back?"

He sent a message, "Will you join me for dinner tonight at Magnolias at 8PM?"

Soon he received a response, "Yes, I'll meet you there."

Craft dropped by the secure facility (*The Shack*) and accessed the high-side computer system. He found a profiling application used to find Agency personnel. After entering identity features of what he could remember about Jennifer Wilkins, he began scanning through pictures. He kept refining the search until he discovered what he was looking for. Her real name was Victoria Beach. He entered her name into the skills search application designed to help find Agency people with specific skills. The profile for Victoria Beach showed up on the display. She grew up a farm girl in Nebraska and graduated from University of Nebraska in 2024, majoring in Business Management. He had all the information he needed.

•

He arrived at the restaurant, wearing the same suit, shirt, and tie he wore his first day of work. Wilkins strolled into the restaurant dressed in an elegant white silk dress with a modest cut to show her sleek long legs as she walked. He was convinced she would have looked good in anything, but tonight she looked spectacular. Just a smile from her made his heart race. *Thank God we're on the same team,* he thought.

Craft ordered an excellent Pinot Noir and turned on the charm to throw her off her game. Every time she asked a question targeting his recent activities, he changed the subject to life growing up in Charleston. After enjoying an exquisite dinner, he started to go on the offensive. He reached for her hand and through body language, sent a clear message that he found her very attractive; it was easy because he did. She returned the gesture, telling him he looked especially handsome in a suit. Finding it hard to focus, he could see how professional jousting, as his mentor referred to it, helped you sharpen your spycraft skills.

Wilkins opened the door with an innocent question, "Why did you decide to play football at Clemson University?"

Seizing the opportunity, Craft answered, "I guess it was the desire to follow in my mother's footsteps and stay close to home. After winning the state football championship in high school, recruiters tried to entice me to attend various universities. Our team won with a running-option offense similar to those used by midwest colleges. I thought being the quarterback for a great football school such as Nebraska would be exciting. Then the reality of living far away from home set in. After talking through it with my grandfather, I decided to go to college in state."

Seeing the mention of Nebraska hit a nerve, Craft asked the charming woman across the table to go for a walk. It was a cool February night and they snuggled together as they walked down the street. As they walked by the corner florist shop, they stopped to look at the flower arrangements in the window.

Gently pulling her close, he held her so they could feel the warmth of each other's body. Without saying a word, they communicated to each other the intense desire consuming them. While trying to stay in the moment, thoughts raced through her mind. *Was his mentioning Nebraska coincidental? Did he really want her? Was he playing her?...*

Within seconds, they were kissing and the surreptitious behavior made it all the more stimulating. Walking back to the restaurant to say good night, he decided a change in strategy was necessary. He didn't want her to retreat at all. He quite enjoyed her clever inquiries, trying to get him to reveal secrets she already knew.

•

By morning, Wilkins had discovered that the University of Nebraska had indeed offered Craft a football scholarship. Still uncertain regarding the emotional encounter the previous evening, she knew Peter Craft was the perfect choice for the Red Crescent program. She notified Vaughn that she would accept the assignment. Now she could relax, the Orlando Open was still weeks away.

Running along the beach during the early morning hours, Craft received a secure message, *The Shack 10:15*. Was he ready to go back to work? He felt ready but his emotional state was still questionable. By attending the meeting, he would be implicitly accepting his role in the big deception. If he didn't attend the meeting then the program would be shutdown.

•

The team waited anxiously so they could begin the operations briefing. Vaughn stalled, covering some administrative details—timecards, expense reports, and upcoming events. At 10:29, Craft walked into the secure facility, apologized to the team for being late, and then sat down at the conference table. Vaughn took one look at the young agent and could see he was back on track.

Thank you Kalani, I owe you one, Vaughn thought. After welcoming everyone back, Vaughn turned the meeting over to the Iran Ops Director.

Gul displayed a series of pictures of an older Iranian businessman, "This is Amir Turani, the owner of Century Capital, a financial investment firm based in Tehran. He is known for bringing golf to Iran. His company built the first golf course community as a way to entice Western clients to Iran."

Gul showed pictures of a young Iranian man, "This is Amir's son, Kamran. You might recognize him. He's the only Iranian player on the Tour. In addition to playing professional golf, Kamran is infatuated with high-speed motorcycle racing. Don't underestimate him; he is well educated, an excellent athlete, and exceptional at long distance running. He is known on the Tour as one who entices players into big money bets."

Next Gul showed pictures of an older man dressed in military uniform, "This is Kamran's uncle, Farzad Shirazi, a general in the Quds Force, the elite division of Iran's Islamic Revolutionary Guard. The uncle is a direct report to Iran's Supreme Leader. Shirazi has led the elimination of the extremists component of the previous administration. Kamran is a frequent guest at his uncle's home in a remote area near the city of Qom, where he races motorcycles. His uncle lives at the entrance to a paved stretch of road leading to a secure military facility affectionately referred to as VIPER I. This road is closed to the public and the uncle controls the schedule of vehicles traveling on it. We suspect the facility stores nuclear fuel from Iran's suspended nuclear program."

A male team member hooted when a picture of a gorgeous Iranian woman, taken from the cover of a women's magazine, flashed on the display. After cautioning the disrupter to act professionally, Gul said, "This is Kamran's sister, Daria Turani, the owner and editor of *Persian Woman*, a popular glamour magazine. The magazine is designed to attract the interests of Middle East women living in Western nations."

The Iran Ops Director finished the presentation showing pictures of the VIPER I facility and the surrounding area.

Vaughn spoke up, "Craft will get us access to the VIPER I facility by building a relationship with Kamran Turani, starting at the Masters. We'll work out the operational details over the next few weeks."

●

Craft settled into a daily routine of morning golf, afternoon physical conditioning, early evening operations planning, and then finishing the day sharpening his cover skills bantering with his fellow-agent, Jennifer Wilkins. They shared long walks, late night dinners, romantic moments, and hours of personal stories.

Each morning at the crack of dawn, Craft stood on the 1st tee, looking for Jefferson to give the OK signal to hit the ball. Without the use of Smartball, Craft posted scores in the high 60s, good enough to do well in most Tour events. With the assistance of Smartball, the scores improved by as much as eight strokes. The system worked so well that they started picking target scores and then using Smartball intermittently to hit the target. They found the best approach to hit an exact score was to get a couple of insurance strokes ahead of the target score and then give them back with a missed shot here and there on the last couple of holes. The system wasn't perfect; there was no room for big mistakes, such as hitting the ball out of bounds on the 18th hole or dropping a couple in the pond.

The evening before Craft left for Orlando, Wilkins waited at the house while he purchased a few dinner items at the local market. She danced to music while sipping a glass of Merlot and reading an electronic book on the kitchen display. Reacting to the sudden loud noise from behind, she whirled around sending the wine flying in all directions.

Craft peered through the kitchen window at Wilkins frantically trying to wipe the big red stain of her white top. He had no idea his tapping on the window to get her attention would cause such chaos, but at the same time it was quite hilarious. After a good laugh, a sincere apology, and helping clean up the mess, he left the kitchen and returned with a bright orange football jersey. It was the jersey—Number 11—he wore playing quarterback for Clemson University. She affectionately accepted the peace offering and went into the bedroom to change.

Craft prepared dinner while waiting patiently for Wilkins to change clothes. After what seemed to be an eternity, she strutted out of the bedroom with her hair pinned up on top with ringlets falling down the sides of her face, a small football under her arm and wearing only the jersey. She pranced around the room as if the leading lady in the feature film, "Miss America Turns All American."

He chased her around the house pretending to be a defensive player in hot pursuit. She bobbed and weaved climbing over furniture to escape his clutches. Exhausted from behaving like rambunctious children left alone at home, they fell onto the soft rug in each other arms. She gave all the signals of wanting him but he failed to act. Soon the moment of intimacy had passed. As much as he wanted to experience all of her, *now was not the time.*

As they sat at the table eating dinner, reality set in, and the mood turned dark. With his mind in overload, he reflected on the situation. Soon Jennifer Wilkins (aka Victoria Beach) would be gone, on to the next assignment, a new identity, probably never to be seen by him again. As much as he enjoyed their time together, this was not a game. His feelings were real but she was not. He looked across the table at her wearing his jersey, something precious to him, with conflicted sentiments. Her feelings seemed sincere. But how could they be? Everything about her was an illusion. She didn't grow up Jennifer Wilkins, a child of military parents living in locations around the world. That was a cover story, make believe, a persona the Agency created to appeal to his international interests. She was Victoria Beach, a farm girl from Nebraska. If she could be so convincing at sharing an international fantasy, then pretending to have feeling for him was child's play.

Not wanting to add to his obvious emotional turmoil, Wilkins kissed him good night, wished him good luck, and assured him she would be there to celebrate his victorious returned from Orlando. He walked her to the car, and began an overly dramatic goodbye.

After letting him ramble for a short time, she touched his lips signaling him to stop talking, waited a moment until he was ready to listen, and then said, "Peter, I know you think this is the end of the road for us. *Please trust me... it's not!*"

CHAPTER 14

ORLANDO, FL

Upon arrival in Orlando, Craft attended the mandatory meeting for first-time Tour participants to review rules and special considerations. The course had several areas where temporary facilities had been constructed to accommodate spectators, such as portable bleachers along the fairways. The head official demonstrated procedures for taking line-of-sight relief and appropriate behavior interacting with spectators. The players were reminded every second of the tournament was recorded. The official reviewed cases where players had been disqualified based on recorded visual evidence of infractions.

The team gathered at a secure facility in Orlando to discuss final preparations. Dr. Page began the meeting by saying, "Tomorrow, our mission moves out of the shadows into public view. Please remember when it comes to public image... *perception can become reality*. With today's 24/7 global media access, a public image can spin out of control at warp speed. We must be ready to adapt to developing situations as the operation progresses. Potential image issues must be exposed and, if necessary, adjustments made before they become big problems. To help in this area, Ms. Jennifer Wilkins will be joining the team."

Wilkins walked into the room. After a moment of awkwardness, Craft moved to make room for the new team member at the conference table.

Dr. Page continued, "Congratulations, Mr. Craft, for your detective work using the Agency's profiling applications to discover Ms. Wilkins' true identity. Some day you'll have to learn how to avoid leaving a trail, but I digress. In public, Ms. Wilkins will be the business-media consultant accompanying Mr. Craft to golf tournaments. She will have special status reserved for player's guests, enabling her to maintain situational awareness within the wives and players circles. Also, her job will be to build relationships with the media, so we get the inside scoop on emerging stories."

Wilkins continued the meeting, revealing her plan and expectations for image management. She talked about how simple mannerisms on the golf course between the player and caddy could drive public image in the wrong direction, requiring significant efforts to repair. A public disagreement of what shot to hit could have the appearance of a young southern white male taking a superior position over the older black caddy, potentially giving rise to a fabricated racist image. Alternatively, the caddy appearing to have too much control of decisions could undermine the player's leadership image.

Although Wilkins' role on the team was defined, the nature of their relationship remained uncertain. A few hours ago he was haunted by thoughts of her leaving forever. Now he was faced the prospect of her managing every aspect of his life. *Who was she really?*

Noticing the uneasiness between the two agents, Vaughn spoke up, "Whatever is going on between you two, you better fix it fast. For God's sake, establish some ground rules. You might want to start with the mission comes first."

After agreeing to start their relationship over under new terms as business associates, they talked through what to expect when the tournament started in the morning. They both knew there would be a time in the future when they would have to sort out their true feelings but now was not the time.

•

The first two days of the tournament went smoothly. Craft, a virtual unknown on the Tour, scored well enough to make the Friday cut, but not well enough to draw unwanted attention. Without needing to use Smartball, he was nicely positioned at six under par, just five strokes off the lead. Few in the media went out of their way to talk with him and those who did were more interested in talking about the possibilities of his playing professional football than his performance on the golf course. With Wilkins close by, he stayed on message politely and eloquently answering reporters' questions. A reporter made the comment that sports betting had set the odds of his winning the tournament at one in ten thousand.

Jokingly, Craft commented, "If I win there are going to be some elated Clemson fans because they would be the only people crazy enough to bet on me winning."

After Friday's round, Jack Wilson, back at Langley, crunched the numbers based on Craft's position in the tournament relative to the rest of the field. Taking into consideration the projected weather conditions for the weekend—sunny, a high of seventy-five, and the risk of occasional thunderstorms in the afternoon—the target for Saturday's round was to finish within five strokes of the lead. This would ensure a greater than 99 percent probability of winning the tournament on Sunday using Smartball. Based on the Saturday pairings, the last group would be on the 12th hole when Craft completed Saturday's round. This left seven holes of uncertainty. After further analysis, the target was set for the CIA agent to finish the 18th hole within three strokes of the lead, leaving two insurance strokes to accommodate the uncertainty of what the leaders might do on the finishing holes. Wanting to minimize the chance of detection, the team hoped Craft could hit Saturday's target score without technology assistance.

•

All was going according to plan on Saturday when Craft approached the 18th tee. He only needed a routine score of par to finish within three strokes of the lead. He proceeded to hit his drive on the 18th hole—a 425-yard par four with water all along the left side of the fairway. In the middle of his swing the foghorns blasted causing him to flinch, pulling the tee shot hard to the left. The ball crossed into the water hazard only 40 feet in front of the teeing area. Tournament officials had sounded the foghorns to signal that tournament play was suspended because of lightening in the area. Although the sky was blue, a fast moving thunderstorm was about to pass over the course.

After a 35-minute delay, the foghorns sounded again to restart play. Having assessed the situation, Craft decided to re-tee under the rules of golf taking a one-stroke penalty.

At 4:23PM, play resumed. Before hitting a second tee shot on the 18th, the caddy Jefferson signaled that Smartball would be used in hopes of minimizing the damage. Craft pushed his tee shot out to the right and with the assistance of Smartball, the ball drew back into the center of the fairway, leaving a 125-yard short to the flagstick. After walking down the fairway to his golf ball, he waited patiently for the group in front to clear the green. Craft checked his watch to see it was now 4:43PM. The group ahead had taken an unusually long time on the green. He hit the approach shot to the 18th green and with Smartball's assistance, it landed two feet right of the pin for a tap-in bogey five. He was relieved to have limited the damage to one stroke, having finished the 18th hole within four strokes off the lead. One of the Friday leaders in the last group scored an unexpected four under par on the last seven holes. After all the players had finished Saturday's round, Craft was seven strokes off the lead with only a 73 percent chance of winning on Sunday. Needless to say, the Red Crescent team was concerned.

CIA HEADQUARTERS
MCLEAN, VA

Maj. Frank Young was killing time scanning recent changes to the officer's training manual while manning the watch station for the Smart Weapons Detection Network at CIA Headquarters. At 16:24, the watch station visual and audio alarms activated with the arrival of an Emergence Action Message from the National Security Agency, indicating a smart weapon detonation was detected in the Orlando, Florida area. At first, Maj. Young was skeptical of the message because the intelligence community had recently begun the rollout of the smart weapons detection capability to domestic locations, with Orlando being one of the first locations to implement it. The Major called air traffic control at the Orlando International Airport to inform them of the situation and requested the status of all aircraft in the area. At 16:44, the watch station received a second Emergency Action Message indicating another smart weapon detonation in the same area. In accordance with emergency action procedures, Maj. Young ordered an immediate grounding of all air traffic in the Orlando area.

Catherine Walker sat in the director's office at CIA Headquarters, catching up on paperwork. A high priority message ordering air traffic shutdown in Orlando flashed across the display unit. Realizing Smartball emissions had set off the smart weapons detection sensors, the Director immediately rescinded the order.

The CIA Director stopped by to visit Maj. Young to explain that a military operation was conducting smart weapons testing in Orlando and had failed to coordinate their activities. Relieved no aircraft were in danger, Maj. Young updated the database by mapping out of the problem area and continued his study of the officer's training manual.

Walker said a prayer of thanks, knowing she just averted a major disruption to the global air traffic. A few more minutes of delay in cancelling the shutdown order would have had a similar impact to a major weather event. The movement of aircraft around the world was so tightly synchronized any disruption would have had a ripple affect impacting all major airports. The collective fuel costs and traveler impacts would have been massive. Most of all, the CIA Director was thankful she would not be spending the next few weeks on the Hill, explaining the unfortunate event to Congress.

•

On Sunday, the CIA Director relaxed at home, watching Craft come from seven strokes behind to shoot ten under par to win the Orlando Open by one stroke. Relieved that the CIA agent would now receive an invitation to the Masters, Walker sat at her desk handwriting a thoughtful letter to the young agent's mother to be delivered by a personal courier.

CHAPTER 15

NORTHERN VIRGINIA

The aircraft began its midnight decent into Dulles International, an airport Vaughn had come home to many times. With the soothing effects of Captain Jack's Rum flowing through his body, his mind flowed with tender thoughts of home and family. He scrutinized pictures of his two grandchildren, twin three-year-old girls, feeding goats at the local petting zoo. The twins seemed to have endless energy, something he discovered when he volunteered to babysit the little darlings over a long weekend, enabling his oldest daughter and son-in-law to attend an out-of-town wedding.

He exhaled with a loud sigh while looking at two year-old pictures of his youngest daughter's first day of the Georgetown Medical Residency Program. What troubled him was the reality of time slipping away—high school, college, and then medical school—with no way to slow the clock. Immensely proud of having the first doctor in the Vaughn family lineage, he said a prayer of thanks to his father-in-law, a highly regarded pediatrician in Washington, D.C., who helped his daughter get accepted into the medical program.

Weary of life on the road, he stopped promising years ago the next trip would be his last. Now he cherished the warm reception of coming home to the person he loved, and who loved him, especially a partner with the wisdom not to seek answers to questions that should never be asked. He recalled how his wife was stressed over buying their first home, one they really couldn't afford but was perfect for their young family. They agreed to cut spending and watch every penny. To Vaughn the idea that a boy from the Brooklyn projects could raise a family on a half-acre mansion was daunting. To many a four-bedroom colonial in Herndon, Virginia, five miles from the airport, would hardly qualify as a mansion but it was all about a person's perspective. No stranger to poverty, Vaughn spent much of his career overseas in the poorest countries in the world. To this day, he believed his Herndon home was a palace to be treasured.

He arrived at CIA headquarters early the next morning with the intent of spending time in his office before meeting with the executive team. While in Orlando, the DCS, Beaumont, alerted him the Middle East Chief was lobbying the Director to pull the program's funds for another operation.

He scanned messages on the internal high-side network. Good news, he thought. The operational security assessment indicated his disguise at the Tour event had worked. The probability of anyone outside the program connecting him with the caddy, Jefferson, was highly unlikely. Of course those who were cleared into the program were going to pull his chain for getting paid to carry golf clubs but that's what the Ops guys did for fun.

Vaughn waited with the others in the Director's conference room for Walker to return from the daily White House intelligence briefing. After sizing up the meeting attendees, Vaughn figured the Middle East Chief felt threatened and was probably going to use the air traffic screw up to justify killing the program. Attempting to show his more personal side, Beaumont came to the meeting ready to poke fun at the infamous Jason Vaughn. He projected on the wall a collage of pictures captured over the weekend of Jefferson lugging golf clubs, raking sand traps and soaked in sweat trying to keep up with the fast walking Tour players. He joked about his daughter being a golf fan with a big crush on the younger attractive Jefferson.

"What could be so humorous this early in the morning?" Director Walker asked, hearing the hoots coming from conference room.

With pictures of Jefferson still on the wall, she began giving her own critique, commenting that he needed to get to the gym more often. She complimented Vaughn on the success in Orlando and cautioned everyone to pay more attention to the details. She mentioned the Smartball fiasco had nearly given her a heart attack, and then turned the meeting over to the Middle East Chief.

"We have intelligence the cleric Gilani is on the move," he said while handing each member of the team a folder with intelligence details. "We know General Shirazi of the Quds Force is tracking Gilani's activities. We believe the operation is being conducted out of VIPER I near his estate in Qom. We need access to the facility as soon as possible."

"There're many reasons for wanting access to VIPER I, but why is Gilani driving the timeline?" Vaughn asked.

"We think his recent activities are somehow connected to the Asian Open," responded the Middle East Chief. "So when will you deliver access to VIPER I?"

"June at the earliest," answered Vaughn.

"That's too late," declared the Middle East Chief.

"Goddammit! You've had years to get into VIPER I," responded Vaughn sternly. "June will have to do. The timeline's fixed."

Director Walker spoke up, "Jason, the chief wants to move money to fund a specific effort to track Gilani. My thoughts are...if Shirazi is already doing it then we just need to find out what he knows. Let's assume whatever Gilani is up to, it has something to do with the Asian Open, then getting access to VIPER I in June still gives us three months to adjust. So bottom line, how confident are you the Red Crescent team will deliver?"

"We'll deliver," said Vaughn. "If you need to hedge, then go ahead and fund tracking Gilani. Just don't pull the funds from Red Crescent. It would be a big mistake."

Beaumont chimed in, "I agree with Vaughn, the Red Crescent program should continue as planned."

Vaughn excused himself from the meeting indicating he had a lunch date with a beautiful woman. They all knew he was referring to his wife, who worked at CIA headquarters in the Recruitment Center two floors below.

CHARLESTON, SC

He raced through the park. The sound of the skates hitting the pavement told him his pace was slowing. His leg muscles strained to maintain speed but his body had reached its limit. Bent over with hands on his thighs, and gasping for air, Craft coasted toward the parking area. Unhappy with his performance, he thought, tomorrow I'll swim, let the legs recover, and then try again.

Since winning in Orlando two days earlier, his attention had shifted to training for the VIPER I operation. In the shower with the warm water spraying against his aching body, he reflected on how to improve performance. In-line skating was a new experience, so his technique was crude.

Poor mechanics translated to slower speeds and increased risk of injury. He needed videos of expert skaters to analyze.

After bathing and chugging down a protein shake, he lounged in a large sofa chair while giving voice commands to the integrated entertainment system. The music played as he scanned messages of congratulations, mostly from friends and Clemson fans. With Vaughn at headquarters, Wilkins busy with the media, and his body recovering from a hard physical workout, Craft pondered what to do next. What he really wanted to do was play the piano, but the house didn't have one. Soon he was in the car headed to his mother's home in Mount Pleasant, a suburb north of Charleston.

He entered the home through the back door, rummaged through the refrigerator, finding beer in the back behind the bottled water. With a cold brew in hand, he walked into the living room, sat at the piano, and commenced with a warm up routine he learned as a child. Soon he launched into his rendition of the Blues—*Crying in the Rain, Starting Over, Do I Really Know You, So Lonely*—letting his emotions flow.

•

Callie stopped by her mother's house to drop off groceries. While backing out of the driveway, she noticed Craft's white SUV. Still psyched about watching his unbelievable victory in Orlando, she got out of the car and walked up the street to visit, hoping to surprise him.

As she approached the Craft family home, the sound of downbeat music caught her attention. After listening for a while, she began to laugh. Only a woman could have him playing with such fervor, she speculated. She discovered a long time ago the music he played was a true measure of his emotional state. She wished her female partner's emotions could be deciphered so easily, instead of hours of probing just to get an inkling of what was going on inside.

Glad to see his friend come through the door, he played the melody to her favorite song with one hand while motioning for her to sit next to him at the piano with the other hand. With some prompting she began to sing, *Stay Another Day*, a tribute to her father, a Navy technician, who frequently deployed to sea for months at a time.

Ready to rekindle old memories, he went into the kitchen and returned with two beers. They touched bottles in a toast. He instructed the integrated sound system to play the sound track, *Drink a Beer*. They raised bottles high in the air and began to sing like old times. With fond memories of life by the sea, they enthusiastically bellowed the chorus, "*I am going to sit right here on the end of this peer and watch the sunset disappear... and drink a beer.*"

With childhood bonds revived and wanting to understand his mysterious behavior, Callie asked, "What's up with you?"

"I thought we were having a good time," he responded.

"I am having a good time. It's just strange you've won you're first professional golf tournament, more money than most people will make in a lifetime, and you don't want to talk about it. I drop by to find you playing the Blues."

"Nothing's wrong. I just need to unwind. Golf has sucked all my energy."

"Are you getting soft?" she asked while playfully punching at his hard body.

Ignoring her comment, he said, "My winning will help fund Charleston's youth golf program."

Her emotions softened as she thought of his awesome generosity. She knew with him it was never about the money. It was always about achievement. She recalled as kids, he talked about someday building a golf course dedicated to youth golf. She had promised to be the greens-keeper if he was fortunate enough to raise the funds. Wow, she thought, he just might do it some day.

"If we're going to talk about strange behavior then let's talk about your current relationship," he said.

She was surprised by his directness. "What do you know about my current relationship?"

"Nothing," he answered, making the point she had been holding back.

"Chris Davis mentioned you been seeing a new girl in town."

"Jennifer Wilkins is her name. She's my business manager," said Craft.

"Your business manager. Who wouldn't want to be your business manager?" asked Callie.

"She's quite attractive. You're not jealous, are you?" Craft joked.

"She's chili, but not my type," she answered with a provocative smile. The word "chili" was local slang for an attractive, sexy girl.

"How do you know?" he asked, realizing she knew more than he expected.

"We've met," she answered. "She dropped by the golf club looking for you."

He doubted the meeting was coincidence. Wilkins was doing her job, trying to manage all aspect of his life.

"Were you successful at scaring her off?"

"No. She's actually quite charming. I don't know why but she really likes you."

"How would you know that?"

"A girl can tell these things. Her interest in you is more than business."

"So what do you think?" he asked.

"As always, I am going to be honest," she confided. "I haven't liked the girls you've been interested in in the past, but Jennifer's different. I see the connection. Just be careful."

"Be careful... what are you trying to say?"

"Well, she's not some crazed cheerleader chasing a jock. I am probably a little paranoid, but who is she really?" she asked. "I'm certain her feelings for you are sincere, but then it seemed too easy. As you've reminded me many times, it takes me time to warm up to people. In just a few minutes with her, we were talking like sisters... and I don't even have a sister. It was so easy and comfortable but that was the strange part..."

"You've managed to get into the middle of my personal business while keeping your own private," he said as they walked to the door.

"I have to go. Let's continue this conversation tonight at Jacksons? Meet me at 9 o'clock."

•

While on his way to meet with Callie at Jacksons, he received a voice message from Wilkins, "Be a gracious winner." He wanted to scream, *I didn't win anything* but instead he pulled the car to the side of the road. He was now an actor on a world stage and the audience expected him to act as if he had just won his first Tour event. At the same time, the hollowness he felt inside made him physically ill. Sitting there shaking, he contemplated turning the car around and going back home. Then the words of Dr. Page entered his mind, *"It's not about you. Your feelings are irrelevant. Your motives are pure. Keep your pride in check and do your job. People's lives depend on it."*

When Craft walked into Jacksons, the tavern was filled with friends who had come to celebrate his first Tour win. Several of his football and swimming teammates had travelled from long distances to be there. Many of the guests had won thousands of dollars from sport gaming by betting a few dollars on him, a long shot, to win.

With Wilkins and Callie off in the corner talking, Craft put on a happy face and began working the room. With drink in hand and jokes flowing freely, he took a walk down memory lane, caught up with friends, and proceeded to be a gracious winner. As much as he hated the deception, seeing his friends was good medicine for putting the blues behind. The night came to a close at 2AM with Chris Davis leading Clemson fans in singing the school's fight song, *Tiger Rag*.

•

The next morning, following the operations meeting, he asked Wilkins if they could talk in private regarding Callie. He tried to explain their long friendship revealing nothing she didn't already know.

After listening patiently, she finally said, "Enough with the background, I get the picture. What's on your mind?"

Craft said, "Callie's acting strange. She's keeping secrets."

"So how can I help?" she asked.

"You two seemed to be getting along well last night, maybe you could... oh, never mind," he said.

"I'll find out what's going on," responded Wilkins.

Wilkins already knew why his childhood friend had clammed up about her love life. Callie had a secret "on-again, off-again" relationship with Chris Davis' girlfriend. Revealing this information would put Craft in the burdensome position of having to choose between friends. Rather than put him in the middle, she was prepared to create a situation where Callie's secret affair would become public, but only if necessary.

CHAPTER 16

AUGUSTA, GA

The smell of fresh azaleas welcomed spectators to Augusta National for the final round of *The Masters Tournament*. The hum of lawnmowers mashed in chaotic harmony as the maintenance crew put the final touches on the pristine landscape of the most magnificent golf course in the world. Difficult conditions—cool temperatures, high winds, lightning fast greens, and hard pin positions—set the expectations for another electrifying Sunday finish.

Craft stood alone on the terrace of the Augusta National Clubhouse contemplating the future, knowing today his life would change forever. During the first three days of the tournament, the young man went unnoticed while Tour regulars dominated media coverage. Today would be different. Soon he would take center stage at the most watched golf event of the year. With months of grueling training complete, he was both mentally and physically prepared to execute the mission. He had to win; *American lives depended on it!*

A confident competitor, Craft walked to the end of the practice area to join Jefferson, his caddy. These days, a team of two at the practice range was an unusual sight. Golf was big business, each player a mini corporation. With millions of dollars at stake, players practiced with a full entourage—golf coach, fitness trainer, health consultant, data analyst, business manager, sports psychologist, and of course, the caddy.

After brief stops at the chipping area and putting green, he checked in at the 1st tee starter station. Several strokes behind the Saturday leaders, he would tee off hours before the last group. Today he would be playing with Kamran Turani, the only Iranian player on the Tour. After shaking hands and wishing each other good luck, Craft, instinctively began comparing first-hand observations of his playing partner to what he already knew from the Ops briefings. He could see the man's striking similarities to Persian royalty. His distinctive bronze complexion with dark wavy hair combed back to show his long slender face. Bushy black eyebrows outlined his deep, piercing brown eyes. His lean, six-foot body appeared strong, agile, but under developed for maximum power.

The starter stepped forward to announce, "First on the tee for the 11:40 pairing from the Islamic Republic of Iran . . . Kamran Turani."

A few spectators politely applauded as the Iranian teed the ball, made a practice swing, and launched a 300-yard drive into the middle of the fairway.

The starter continued, "Second on the tee for the 11:40 pairing from Charleston, South Carolina . . . Peter Craft."

A spattering of southern gentlemen at the 1st tee erupted with loud cheers hoping to rally the young man from Charleston. Craft teed the ball, executed his routine, looked at Jefferson for a moment, then with great precision, hit a drive that started down the right side of the fairway and then drew back into the middle, landing 310 yards from the tee. The two players walked in unison down the fairway, taking long strides, with the two caddies trying to keep pace. The crowd of spectators grew larger with each birdie, as the rookie from Charleston moving up the leader board, scoring birdies on four of the first ten holes.

Craft arrived at Amen Corner—a name given decades earlier to holes 11, 12 and 13—one stroke off the lead. He left Amen Corner headed for the 14th tee with a two-stroke lead, having scored birdies on all three holes. Stunned by the rapid rise of the name Craft to the top of the leader board, the previous day leaders now on the 2nd hole began "flag hunting" in hopes of scoring birdies. Given the taxing course conditions, many of the high-risk shots turned into bogeys, resulting in the previous day leaders falling farther behind.

The typically reserved Masters onlookers, rushed to get in position as the tournament leader arrival at the 18th hole. Feeling the energy in the air, one British announcer told the viewers a Yank winning the Masters would be huge for the United States. The enthusiasm for the young man from Charleston was amplified by the memory of when U.S. players once dominated the Tour and the harsh reality of America's failure to win the Masters in recent years.

The 18th hole was one of the most famous finishing holes in professional golf. The uphill 465-yard dogleg right had two bunkers protecting the left elbow of the fairway and another two bunkers guarding the green. Craft stepped onto the 18th tee needing one last birdie to break the single round course record of nine under par set by Nick Price in 1986 and later matched by Greg Norman in 1996. Breaking the course record was inconsequential, winning and then cultivating a relationship with the Iranian were the day's objectives.

He drove the ball left expecting it to fade back into the middle of the fairway with the help of Smartball, but the ball unexpectedly continued on a straight line coming to rest in the middle of the second fairway bunker. While walking down the fairway, a text message containing the number "−10" flashed across Jefferson's HuAID indicating a score of ten under par for Sunday's round was needed to assure a win. Back at CIA Headquarters, Wilson had calculated the target score using a complex formula, taking into consideration the current status of each player and the number of holes remaining to be played.

"Do we have a problem?" Craft calmly asked.

"Not at all," Jefferson responded, "because you're going hit the next shot close to the pin and make the putt."

For Craft, who by nature was fearless in competition, choking under pressure was never an issue, but every shot had risks. The best a player could do was remain focused and then be prepared to deal with the unexpected. Above all, never think about the consequence of failure. He stepped into the large white sand bunker, and with folded arms looked down at the lie of the ball, surveying the situation. The ball settled about a half inch below the sand, so picking it clean was not an option. *It would take a near perfect strike of the ball to clear the front of the bunker with enough elevation and speed to reach the green,* he thought. For most golfers, hitting a 165-yard soft sand bunker shot was nearly impossible. With the leverage of his tall body frame, strong arms and fine-tuned golf swing, the shot was difficult but not impossible. He had to keep the clubface moving down the target line as it plowed through the sand. He visualized the shot as if in a trance, blocking out all negative thoughts. Under normal conditions, he would have hit a 100-yard sand wedge and then tried to get up and down to save par. Today a birdie was needed so going for the green was the only option.

He pulled a seven iron slowly from the bag, one club more than he would use if the ball had landed in the fairway. Jefferson offered a gesture of confidence by laying the golf bag on the ground, rushing to pick up a rake a few feet away, and motioning he was ready to rake the sand as soon as the shot was played. Craft gripped the club much tighter than normal to keep the clubface from turning at impact. He took aim and made a smooth powerful shoulder-arm swing, keeping his lower body still. The ball cleared the front of the bunker with only a few inches to spare, traveling on a line left of the pin coming to rest ten feet from the flagstick.

As Craft walked out of the bunker, Jefferson whispered, "Impressive!"

"Know your limits," replied Craft.

He was referring to the agent-training program that emphasized knowing one's limits could be a matter of life and death.

The massive collection of spectators cheered loudly as the young man from Charleston walked down the middle of the 18th fairway with the presence of someone out for a brisk walk in the park. He was in the zone, unmindful of the craziness surrounding him. He was performing on a world stage with the presence of a Broadway star. Tournament marshals tried in vain to quiet spectators feeling compelled to yell cheers urging him on.

Overcome by the moment, the Iranian quickly executed a 30-foot putt and then a 2-foot tap-in to finish the tournament four under par. Craft fixed his ball mark and then began to survey the 10-foot putt needed to post a total score of 274, fourteen under par, giving him a 99 percent chance of winning the tournament. As the suspense built, he relied on his extreme psychological training to keep his mind focused on the mission. He concentrated on one swing thought, to keep the ball above the hole and let the magic happen. He looked intensely at Jefferson for guidance. One of the network cameras zoomed in on Jefferson pointing to a spot on the green indicating the ball would break slightly to the left.

The network announcer stationed near the 18th green appeared puzzled by the caddy's read of the green because he had watched other putts from similar locations and none broke left. By now the world was watching, and millions were glued to their full-view televisions—FVTV—waiting in anticipation for the record-breaking putt. The new television technology fused inputs from many cameras, effectively digitizing the full viewing area. This capability enabled viewers to control the viewpoints they chose to watch. Virtually everything going on around the 18th green could be seen from every angle.

With a smooth delicate stroke, Craft started the ball rolling toward the hole. It rolled on a line just outside the right edge and then gradually broke left enough to catch the hole and fall to the bottom of the cup.

The Saturday leaders, getting ready to putt on the 7th green, were visible shaken by the thunderous roar from the clubhouse area.

Craft removed his hat, shook hands with the Iranian and his caddy, and then turned to respectfully acknowledge the crowd by offering a big smile and a polite gesture of gratitude. He continued on to the scorers' station to sign and submit his scorecard just as he had the last three days. The difference being, today the world was watching.

Word quickly traveled to the remaining players on the course that Craft had broken the course record to take a three-stroke lead. The buzz was so great well-seasoned players regressed, recording bogeys and double-bogeys on critical finishing holes. Craft watched in seclusion, as the other players one-by-one completed the 18th hole with scores too high to win. With two groups remaining on the course, it was now mathematically impossible for anyone else to win the 2028 Masters Championship.

"I am truly astonished today, in watching Craft," said the broadcast announcer, a retired hall of fame golfer. "He has a confidence and composure similar to some of the great players of the past. It's as if he expects to win and to do otherwise would be unacceptable. And the remarkable way he overcame the difficult lie in the bunker on the 18th was the mark of a true champion. I have a feeling we'll be seeing a lot of this young man in the future."

Another network announcer chimed in, "Craft has competed in two Tour events, winning both by coming from far behind on Sunday. We might compare him with racehorse greats, the ones that remain in the back of the pack until the clubhouse turn and then sprint to the finish-line to win."

The tournament director led the Masters Champion to the famous Butler Cabin. As Craft put on the trademark green jacket, he could only think of the mission ahead.

•

Totally exhausted from the tournament, Vaughn held a short meeting with the team and then boarded a private aircraft to Virginia. Even though the team had succeed at winning the Masters, much still needed to be accomplished before nights end.

Craft, the new Masters Champion, accompanied by Wilkins, was the guest of honor at the formal closing ceremony. Wilkins had arranged for the Iranian and his guests to be seated with them at the head table reserved for the tournament winner. When Kamran arrived at the ceremony, accompanied by his sister Daria, they were escorted to the head table. In three years of playing on Tour, Kamran had never experienced anything close to today's excitement. When Daria had received word her brother would be playing on the weekend, she rearranged her busy schedule and caught a flight from New York City to Atlanta, and then drove to Augusta in time to watch him tee off on Sunday morning.

Unbeknown to Kamran, his sister had spent much of the day with Jennifer Wilkins following the two players around the golf course. They were part of a group following the Craft-Turani pairing. Both wore badges reserved for special guests. After a couple of holes, they started talking; by the end of the round, they were protecting each other from the thousands of spectators that gathered to watch the record breaking round.

Soon after sitting down at the table, the ladies were deep in conversation. Craft could not believe how beautiful they looked after a day in the sun walking around Augusta National. Both girls looked magnificent, but Daria's Persian splendor was mesmerizing. While the girls talked, Craft scanned the room filled with women draped in fine jewelry. The Masters was an invitation-only tournament, so most of the participants were wealthy. The female guests were no strangers to traveling and looking first class.

The President of Augusta National thanked the members and volunteers for their hard work in continuing the Masters grand tradition of being the best golf tournament in the world. Then Craft gave a short and humbling speech, talking about the good fortune bestowed upon him this day and the great honor of having his name listed along with all of the other Masters winners.

After the formal ceremony, Craft engaged in casual conversation with the Iranian. They talked about the market competition between traditional and cyber golf, and the emergence of golf in Iran. Craft shared his experience of both learning golf in Charleston at an early age and his desire to promote youth golf, especially in emerging nations. After a few minutes of exchanging general interests, the two converged on the subject of motorcycle racing. The Iranian talked with great enthusiasm regarding his passion for motorcycle racing and was delighted to know that Craft shared a similar interest.

After comparing schedules, the next time both players would be competing in the same tournament was the Players Championship at Sawgrass in early May. They agreed to meet at Ponte Vedra Beach, Florida the weekend before the Players for some beach time and informal motorcycle racing. Craft volunteered to arrange for the accommodations and motorcycles. *The agents completed the evening having accomplished the day's mission critical objectives.*

CHAPTER 17

A security guard frisked the man before allowing him to enter the CEO's office. Asadi got up from behind his desk, motioned for the security guard to leave, walked to the door and extended his hand to greet the man.

"Welcome to Hamedan Chemie," Asadi said.

The man walked past Asadi, took the sword off the wall, turned around, walking back toward Asadi.

"Tell me why I shouldn't kill you right now?" said the man.

"Because you hate what's happening to Iran as much as I do and…"

"And what?" asked the man.

Asadi walked over to his desk, picked up an envelope, pulled pictures out of the envelope and placed them on the desk.

"You love your family!"

On the desk was a collage of pictures of everyone in Moein Tehrani's family. Moein was the lead operative who had provided Asadi with a new identity twenty-five years earlier.

After placing the sword back on the wall, Moein asked, "What do you want?"

"I want you to be part of Allah's plan to *enact vengeance upon the earth.*"

"What about the others?" referring to the other operatives that had played a role in hiding Asadi.

"They declined the offer and now stand before Allah in judgment."

PONTE VEDRA, FL

Craft was authorized to spend tournament winnings to maintain his rising-star tour image and support the mission. He leased a beach house in Ponte Vedra a few miles from TPC Sawgrass, the course where the Players Championship would be played. For image purposes his winning the Players Championship was not necessary, a top-ten finish would do. This phase of the mission was about getting an invitation from the Iranian to race motorcycles near the VIPER I site in Qom, Iran.

Two days earlier, Kamran had flown from Tehran to Washington, D.C. where he had stopped to visit old school friends. Craft checked to see the flight from Washington, D.C. was on time before leaving the beach house. As the CIA agent drove along the beach, he marveled at the spectacular sea green colors reflecting off the crashing surf and relaxed to the soothing music of a modern classical British pianist. Thirty minutes later, he pulled into short-term parking at the Jacksonville airport.

He strolled into the terminal wearing casual golf attire, a stylish pair of sunglasses, and wireless headphones. As he walked through the terminal, he placed the sunglasses on top of his hat above the visor. The sunglasses incorporated a camera and secure radio transmitter. When activated, equipment would send live video to the Agency's identity detection database. The terminal arrival display indicated the Iranian's flight had landed, and passengers would soon be passing through the security checkpoint.

When his guest came into view, Craft motioned to get his attention. He welcomed Kamran to sunny Florida. After talking for a while, they exited the airport. The Iranian toted a travel bag with enough clothes for the weekend. To make travel easy, his luggage had been shipped to the Sawgrass Marriott where he would be staying during the tournament.

They engaged in casual conversation about the good weather, tournament preparation, and their weekend plans. At first, the conversation was awkward with Kamran giving short responses to broad probing questions. Once the conversation turned to the topic of their weekend plans, the Iranian talked with exuberance about their common interest in motorcycle racing.

"After getting settled at the beach house, I thought taking an afternoon motorcycle ride to Daytona Beach would be fun," Craft said.

"Sounds good to me," replied Kamran.

"Tomorrow afternoon we have two hours on Jacksonville Motor Raceway. Of course, we'll have to sign our lives away before they'll let us on the track."

"What's my share of the cost?"

"I have it covered. You just be ready to ride."

"No problem. I'll be ready."

After showing Kamran around the beach house, he told him to help himself to food and refreshments during his stay.

Kamran retrieved two beers from the refrigerator, handed one to Craft and then said, "Let's get this weekend off to a good start."

They had an early lunch by the swimming pool overlooking the beach. Craft excused himself and went into the poolside bathroom to read an alert on his HuAID. After activating the decryption, he could see a close-up picture of a man exiting the Jacksonville airport with a short message, *Ahmad Reza, Member of Quds Force, reports directly to the Iranian's uncle.*

When he returned to the pool area, they began an easy conversation, getting to know each other. Kamran spoke openly about the importance of golf to his father's business plans and his education at an Iranian-owned boarding school in Northern Virginia. Rumor had it his father made a generous contribution to the school in return for the school incorporating a quality golf program into the curriculum. He didn't really mind because he liked attending school in the states. Even though Kamran appreciated his life on Tour, he made it clear motorcycle racing was his true passion.

Craft shared his experiences at Charleston Academy, a small private high school that won the state football championship his senior year. He spoke of the challenges playing quarterback for a top-ten college football team while at the same time trying to get a quality education. He told a story of when the coach threatened to cancel his scholarship if he didn't attend a spring practice scheduled at the same time as a final exam. The coach freaked out when he discovered that his starting quarterback was the only player on the football team attending the university on an academic scholarship.

Kamran was interested in why an exceptional athlete would choose to play the game of golf instead of professional football. Craft admitted he missed the excitement of game day, and then proceeded to talk about how football had become too specialized and too violent. As a quarterback, the risk of serious injury was high including long-term brain injury from repeated hits to the head.

Jokingly, Craft said, "If I am going get hurt then I'd rather it be racing bikes than by a monster-sized linemen slamming my body to the ground."

"When it comes to blood on the raceway, I've lost a few pints over the years. My sister can attest to that," Kamran replied.

The Iranian revealed his motorcycle racing was so notorious on the streets of Tehran, his father had to cut a deal with his uncle to keep him out of prison. His uncle lived in a remote mountain area of Iran on a private paved road perfect for motorcycle racing. To keep the peace, Kamran had agreed to move his motorcycle adventures out of the city to his uncle's estate.

Craft tried not to appear too interested in Kamran's arrangement with his uncle; there would be time in the future to continue the conversation.

After finishing their lunch, they went to the garage and fired up the two road-ready Kawasaki 650cc motorcycles and headed down the coast to Daytona Beach. Different from other Florida beaches, Daytona allowed small motor vehicles to drive on the hard-packed beach sand. Looking up at the bright blue sky, Craft thought for once the weatherman had it right, mid 80's and no rain in sight. The two bikers rode side by side at normal highway speeds, stopping only once at a roadside convenience store to use the restroom and have a cold drink.

Although the beach was crowded with people trying to get an early start on their summer tans, there was still plenty of room to park their bikes and enjoy the warm breeze, light surf, and scantily clad young ladies. The two sightseers stopped at one of the many biker bars in Daytona for beer and barbecue. Craft noticed Ahmad Reza, the man who worked for the Iranian's uncle, in the bar, having made no effort to conceal his identity. On the way back from the restroom, Kamran stopped to talk to Reza. He could hear the Iranian telling Reza in Farsi to be more discreet. Reza looked out of place in the biker bar wearing a white sports jacket.

"Is everything all right?" Craft asked.

"Not everybody in Iran is cool with my playing golf on the Tour. My uncle insists on providing protection, so he sent one of his security goons to look after me. I wouldn't mind, but he doesn't know how to blend in. Tell me, does he look like he belongs in here?" Kamran asked.

"Not at all, but he looks tough enough to take on everyone in the bar," Craft answered.

Rather than probe for specifics about who might want to hurt him, Craft decided that relating to his situation might be the best tact. He told Kamran he was considering security protection given his win at the Masters. After a couple of beers and some fabulous barbecue, they returned to the beach house.

While relaxing by the pool, Kamran began comparing the laid-back environment of golf to the wild-exciting environment of motorcycle racing.

"The thrill of making a long putt just doesn't compare with the excitement of racing through "S" turns at light-speed with another racer ready to put you into the wall if you lose your concentration, even for a second," the Iranian exclaimed.

"Let's face it, golf can be boring, but you don't have to worry about anyone picking up your body parts off the fairway after a mistake," Craft responded.

"I have to admit, playing with you on Sunday at the Masters was sensational. The excitement in the crowd on the back nine was like a rumbling volcano getting ready to erupt. You were so focused on golf I don't think you even noticed. I was so pumped you would have thought I was the one breaking the course record."

"I was plenty nervous," said Craft. "But being able to take the crowd out of the game is something I've worked hard at since my high school years playing sports for a small school that played big schools with big crowds. Whether the crowds were cheering for or against us, it didn't matter, to me it was just noise."

Kamran shared some stories of the antics that go on behind the scene on the Tour. "The players have so much money they'll bet on just about anything. I know two players that bet ten thousand dollars on their five-year-old children's soccer match. One player who used to be a Navy underwater diver made big bucks getting players to bet on how long he could hold his breath under water. We've had several Grand Prix races with golf carts on dirt tracks. Some of the guys like motor-cross racing with dirt bikes and quite a few are into car racing. A few players actually sponsor race teams and have a big showdown at the Daytona 500 each February. You're the only one, other than me, interested in high speed motorcycle racing."

"You have to admit motorcycle racing is comparable to riding a rocket. Probably on the dangerous side for players who can make millions hitting a small white ball," Craft responded.

After a couple of beers, Kamran started to reveal his serious side. "My being Iranian is not easy on the Tour. Some of the guys think one day I am going to stroll into the locker room with a bomb strapped on and blow the place to kingdom come so I can have 72 virgins in paradise. Some of my playing partners get bent out of shape when they see spectators following me wearing traditional Islamic clothing."

"I just finished reading a book about the life of Jackie Robinson, the first black man to play professional baseball. Can you imagine the strength of character he must have had, to deal with all the hatred hurled in his direction? It's always hard for the ones who lead the way."

"To be honest, I really haven't performed well enough to earn much respect. I suspect some of the guys know my heart isn't in the game, and it bothers them because most of the other players live to play golf. A few have made snide remarks about my playing to help Daddy's business prospects."

"The players I know say you're a good guy who loves to make crazy bets. There's always going to be some jerks stuck in the old ways, but that's their problem. If we push each other, we all become better players and better people too."

"Speaking about pushing each other, I am hoping we can play more together, so some of your intense focus on the course will rub off on me. To tell you the truth, after a few holes, I start daydreaming. Your ability to keep focus at the Masters was astonishing."

"Let's plan on playing a couple of practice rounds early in the week before the tournament starts," Craft proposed.

"Are you interested in a friendly wager?" Kamran asked.

"Your reputation precedes you. I think I'll just keep my money in my pocket," Craft answered.

The moonlight shining off the water provided just enough light to see the surf crashing on the shore from the beach house. After sitting on the deck for a while enjoying the tranquility, they decided to call it a night.

Before going to bed, Craft said, "I plan to work out in the morning; you're welcome to join me or just relax and save your energy for the racetrack."

"I'll join you," Kamran replied.

Craft woke up early and made breakfast, preparing a large bowl of fruit, mixing melon, strawberries, bananas, and blueberries. After breakfast, the two athletes began a four-mile jog on the beach.

In excellent condition, the Iranian was a strong long distance runner notorious for having won thousands of dollars from other players who had dared to challenge him. He thought it wouldn't be good form to entice his host into an unfair bet, so a casual jog would have to do. The runners started jogging north on the beach at an easy pace. After reversing directions at the two-mile point, Kamran accelerated the pace, sprinting into the lead.

Anticipating the morning run might turn into a competition, Craft caught up to the Iranian and then throttled it back to where he easily kept pace. Craft could have taken the lead at any time but kept his ego in check. Kamran pushed harder, trying to go ahead but Craft stayed by his side step for step. The Iranian knew this was not the typical Tour player who thought he was in much better condition than he actually was.

He had read about Craft's athletic accomplishments in his biography, but wanted to see for himself. He now knew Craft was a real athlete with exceptional endurance. The two competitors passed in front of the beach house running nose and nose, each trying to cross the imaginary finish line first. They gave each other a pat on the back agreeing to call the race a draw.

After a short recovery time, they rode street bicycles to the local swimming pool. Without hesitation, Craft dove into the pool and started swimming laps. The Iranian, sprawled out on a lounge chair, watched in awe as his new friend, a past member of the national swim team, glided through the water. Sure that the American was the best all-around athlete he had ever encountered on Tour, but did he have the skills on a motorcycle to match his athletic abilities?

They stopped by the clubhouse at Sawgrass for lunch and then onto the raceway. The manager met them at the entrance and gave a short tour of the racetrack. He drove them around the track in a customized electric cart, occasionally pointing out areas where they should be especially careful. The outside track was a big oval designed for high-speed race cars. The inside track was designed for high-speed motorcycle racing with the north side of the track having a long straight away and the south side of the track having "S" turns.

After taking the tour and signing the waiver forms that released the racetrack owner from liability in the event of injury, the manager escorted them to a garage area housing two identically customized 900cc MotoGP class motorcycles. The room had a selection of race gear including helmets, jackets, gloves, and leather pants. The two racers cruised several laps around the track to get a feel for the best racing lines to take in and out of the turns. Craft hoped all the hours of practicing with Tagami at the training facility had prepared him for what was to follow.

The Iranian proposed a twenty-lap speed trial to see who would post the best time. Kamran went first. He was simply amazing on a motorcycle. Craft knew he didn't have the skill to compete in the turns. His objective was not to beat the Iranian, just to have a competitive time. While the Iranian raced around the track, Craft poured a gas supplement concocted by Wilson into the fuel tank. The chemicals would boost the horsepower on the straightaway to make up for the time he would lose in the turns.

During the final lap, the Iranian was pushing the envelope and nearly crashed the bike into the wall. For a second, Craft thought the Iranian's lack of fear might compromise the mission. Soon after Kamran finished the time trial, the racetrack manager announced the twenty-lap time was the best ever recorded at the raceway.

Craft hit the track hard, needing to make up time early, because the Iranian's final laps were outstanding. After nearly dropping the bike in the second turn, Craft narrowed his concentration. One mistake could end everything, including his life. He crossed the finish line twenty seconds slower than the Iranian but fast enough to gain respectability.

The Iranian could see his friend was visibly shaken from the near crash but had recovered to record an excellent twenty-lap time.

Craft was humbled by the experience. "Maybe some day I'll be good enough to give you some real competition."

"You're sound, just some technique issues. Nothing good coaching can't fix," replied Kamran.

"You know a good coach?"

"Let's make a deal. You help me improve my performance on the golf course, and I'll help you improve your technique on the racetrack."

"You have a deal," Craft said, offering a hearty handshake to confirm the agreement.

The two motorcycle enthusiasts spent the rest of the afternoon at the raceway, working on technique in the turns. At the end of the day, they drove away from the Jacksonville Raceway in Craft's Mustang convertible with the top down. Craft felt a huge sense of relief that no one was injured, allowing the mission to continue on track. After nearly hitting the cement wall at high speed, he had a new appreciation for living on the edge.

They each received a message containing Players Championship pairings. The tournament would start with a field of one hundred and fifty players, paired in groups of three. By chance, the two were paired together for the first two rounds of the tournament along with a third player, Taylor King, from Atlanta, Georgia.

The Players Championship at Sawgrass had a special status above other

Tour events. It was sometimes referred to as the Fifth Major, although it did not have official status. Owned and managed by the Tour players, the tournament was held to collectively benefit the players themselves. As a result, the Players Championship consistently had the largest prize money and attracted the top players in the world.

For over forty-five years, the Players Championship had been played at the TPC Sawgrass in Ponte Vedra, Florida. Sawgrass was the first golf course designed with spectators in mind. The designers implemented stadium seating around tees and greens to give observers unobstructed views of the action on the course. The short par three island green 17th hole at TPC Sawgrass was one of the most famous in golf. Traditionally, on Sunday, the final day of the tournament, the flagstick would surely be placed in the low right portion of the green, a few feet from the water. While the rewards for aggressive play might yield birdies, the consequences could be devastating.

CHAPTER 18

PONTE VEDRA, FL

Early Monday morning, the two Tour professionals arrived at the TPC Sawgrass Golf Club to practice and prepare for the tournament. The private practice area for Tour professionals was occupied with early arrivals hoping to get an edge on the rest of the field. As this year's Masters Champion walked toward the practice range, reporters jockeyed for position to ask him a few questions. Also, several established players stopped by to offer congratulations. By now, golf analysts had watched and scrutinized Craft's play at both the Orlando Open and Masters, looking for his weaknesses. They now agreed that Craft was going to be a force to contend with on the Tour for many years.

Some of the Tour caddies welcomed Jefferson, a wounded warrior, with open arms, going out of their way to show him the tricks of the trade. Jefferson (aka Jason Vaughn) now had a reputation as a skilled card player and a fun guy to spend after-hours with, drinking beer and telling stories. Craft was amazed that many of the players, while not being very warm toward him, greeted Jefferson like an old friend.

In the afternoon, Craft and Kamran played a practice round. They both shot respectable scores of three under par. While having a drink in the clubhouse, the Iranian asked, "How do you keep from getting distracted on the golf course?"

Craft thought for a moment before saying, "I am taking a risk here."

"Why's that?" Kamran asked.

"Because you're probably the only one who could take my advice and actually use it to beat me," said Craft.

"I don't think you have much to worry about," responded the Iranian.

"I am serious, you can do it. The concept is easy to understand, but you need the right experience to execute it and most don't have it," replied Craft.

"Okay, you've have my attention, please enlighten me."

"In essence, you must transfer the mental concentration you have during out-there-on-the-edge competitions, like motorcycle racing, to the golf course. As you know, to compete on the racetrack, you have to suppress fear without being reckless. When control is lost for a split second coming out of a turn, you don't think about how you almost crashed, there's no time. You have to look forward and do better in the next turn. You have to mentally block out the spectators because the race demands your full attention when danger waits around the next corner. Of course, it's hard to keep focus on the golf course because you have too much time to think between shots. The mental conditioning part is to look forward and approach the next shot with the same intensity that you approach the next turn on the racetrack. Bottom line... *no looking back, only forward while on the course.*"

Kamran understood the comparison and asked several questions about practical ways to execute. Craft volunteered to show him some practice techniques in the morning. Next, the two competitors took their rivalry to the putting green. Kamran proposed a friendly wager with the loser buying dinner. The two had battled to a stalemate as darkness approached, so Kamran intentionally missed a couple of putts so he could buy dinner for his gracious host.

The next day they played a practice round, during which they practiced concentration techniques. As Tuesday evening approached, the two said their goodbyes and went their separate ways to prepare for the tournament. Later that evening, the Red Crescent team met at a secure facility near Jacksonville to discuss tournament strategy. Craft gave an update and provided helpful insight regarding the Iranian's motivations. After much discussion, the team agreed on a course of action. They would promote healthy competition between the two players during the tournament. As long as Craft was on track to finish in the top ten, then Smartball would remain inactive.

Wilkins informed the team of a media issue that was heating up. She referred to a social media site where golf reporters share information. Craft's "odd behavior" at the Masters was a topic of discussion.

Ready to offer her professional opinion, Dr. Page said, "I think Craft's behavior at the Masters appeared mechanical and emotionally disconnected from the moment. It's okay to be confident but I suggest he needs to show more emotion as if winning and losing actually matters. I recall years ago, ABC's Wide World of Sports used the tagline *'the thrill of victory and the agony of defeat'* to sum up the emotions of those playing competitive sports. They would broadcast a series of pictures showing joyous celebration by winners and utter devastation by losers. Mr. Craft gave a polite wave after winning his first Major tournament, hardly the display of immense joy."

Craft knew she was right but, then again, he was only human. Showing immense joy while deceiving the world might be an act beyond his theatrical abilities.

Early the next morning, Craft walked to the TPC Sawgrass practice range with Jefferson following closely, to prepare for the pro-am tournament. This year's Masters Champion would be paired with three amateur golfers having paid thousands of dollars to play with him in the 18-hole tournament with the proceeds going to charity. Having read bios on his three partners, Craft knew these were well-connected people whose perception of him would have to be carefully managed.

By midmorning, the practice range was filled with the Who's Who of golf. Previous Masters Champions would drop by to congratulate Craft for being this year's winner. He found playing in the pro-am relaxing and the three businessmen he played with were easy-going, looking to trade a day in the office for one out in the fresh air with the guys on a beautiful golf course. The businessmen knew each other well, and spent most of the time between shots telling jokes and trading jabs. As the round progressed, Craft joined in making jokes along with the rest of them.

The Players Championship would start with morning and afternoon sessions held during the first two days of the tournament with players starting on both the 1st and 10th holes. If you played in the morning the first day, then you played in the afternoon the next day. The Thursday morning players, not having to tee off again until Friday afternoon, were notorious for engaging in after-hours activities. Craft's group was scheduled to tee off starting on the 1st hole at 8:40AM on Thursday and then starting again on the 1st hole at 1:10PM on Friday.

•

Thursday's conditions were right for aggressive scoring—70 degrees, a slight morning breeze, and favorable pin positions. With the heat of the afternoon, the ocean breezes would become strong gusts, making the course more difficult for the afternoon session. Unlike the first two tournaments he played, a large crowd of spectators waited for him, this year's Masters Champion, to arrive at the 1st tee.

Giving Craft a handshake, the Iranian said, "Play well, my friend."

"I have a good feeling," Craft replied.

They both hit outstanding tee shots on the 1st hole, a 423-yard par four. King, on the other hand, letting his nerves get the best of him, pushed his drive wide to the right, staying in play by only a few feet. King took his medicine, punching the ball out of trouble into the middle of the fairway.

With intense focus, the Iranian hit a gap wedge 125-yards, coming to rest six-foot right of the pin. Craft hit a safe shot to 20 feet short of the pin. Gathering his composure, King hit his third shot close to the pin for a tap-in par.

They walked off the 1st hole with Kamran leading the group at one under par. All three players reached the 2nd hole, a par five, in two shots. Craft made a 16-foot eagle putt and the other two had tap-in birdies. All three players continued to play solid golf. By the 6th hole, both players, Craft and Turani, showed up at the top of the leader board at three under par.

Kamran took to heart his friend's advice of bringing racetrack focus to the golf course. He moved from shot to shot, as if he was the only one on the golf course. In actuality, the players had to contend with hundreds of spectators following the groups as well as all kinds of distractions. Staunch discipline was required not to let the actions of others into their consciousness.

The three players stood on the tee area for the famous 17th hole, a two-tiered green surrounded by water. A steep slope separated the back-upper and front-lower potions of the green. The flagstick was positioned in the lower left corner, about 128 yards from the tee and twenty feet from the water. Thousands of spectators sat on the bank surrounding the hole. Since it was the first day, the demeanor of the crowd was calm, with soft cheers for good shots and quiet sounds of disappointment for balls landing the water. With the wind behind them, all three players hit gap wedges past the flagstick into the up slope, drawing the ball backwards off the slope to within a few feet of the pin. They walked by the crowd to the sounds of cheers and onto the island green.

Craft and Turani were now tied for the lead, at six under par and King remained three strokes behind. The green was fast and a missed putt could slide past the hole by several feet, so gauging speed was important. The calm crowd erupted with a loud cheer when Craft' rolled a 10-footer into the center of the cup.

The Iranian, beaming with confidence, sunk his 8-foot putt. Again spectators exploded with an ear piercing cheer, and some of the Islamic spectators made yells of celebration customary in the Middle East. Distracted by the crowd, King pushed his 5-foot birdie putt and then missed the 4-foot par putt coming back for a bogey four.

After completing the 18th hole, Kamran and Craft walked together to the scorer's station, both seven under par and tied for the lead. It was the best first round either of the players had ever shot in competition. When they left the scorer's station, the press waited to interview them. Reporters wanted to know about their new friendship and how it had helped them post excellent first round scores. They answered media questions mostly talking about their motorcycle racing adventure.

Ready to burn off some energy, the Iranian suggested a rematch run at the beach. They agreed to meet at 4PM.

•

At 3:55PM, cars started pulling up in front of the beach house. Apparently, Kamran had invited a few of the guys to join them for the four o'clock run.

After saying hello to everyone, Craft asked, "What's the wager?"

The Iranian explained, "It's a team relay bet. It's us against them. The losing team cleans the winning team's shoes."

"I am not sure I understand your math. If we lose, we clean six pairs of shoes and if they lose, they clean two pairs of shoes."

"Not exactly. If they lose, they clean our two pairs of shoes the next three days," Kamran said. "Trust me, I have it under control. All you have to do is what you do best... run fast. I will run the first two miles, and you run the last two miles," Kamran strategized. "The other team can place their six runners at whatever intervals they choose to cover the four miles."

Hesitant at first, Craft thought the race was a good opportunity to build a positive off-the-course relationship with some of the players. They agreed to start the race at exactly 4:30PM, leaving time for the runners to get into position. The other team decided to have their six runners equally distributed across the four miles. Craft noticed the players on the other team appeared to be in good shape and each had to run only 2/3 of a mile. He did the math in his head. If Kamran could finish no more than twenty seconds behind the other team then he might have enough in the tank to catch the last of the six runners close to the finish line.

At 4:30PM, Kamran and his competitor started sprinting north on the beach. After a quick start, Kamran settled back into a steady pace. Craft stood at the two-mile mark, waiting for his teammate. He could see the other team's runner with a significant lead, but Kamran was closing the gap fast. The other team started running south towards the beach house with an eighteen second lead.

As Kamran crossed the two-mile mark, Craft sprinted down the beach, catching up just as the other team transitioned to a fresh runner. Craft fell behind as the fresh runner moved ahead and then began to slow. Craft caught up again right at the last transition. Craft knew it was going to be a close finish, given that the other team's anchorman was their strongest runner. Kamran and the early runners, having gotten a ride back to the beach house in a car, waited at the finish line. Craft sprinted across the finish line to win by two seconds.

With Craft bent over trying to catch his breath, the Iranian gave him a pat on the back and said, "You're a great athlete; we're going to make some money, my friend." The players lounged around the pool for a couple of hours, having drinks, snacks, and enjoying the late afternoon sun.

Craft realized the Iranian was more calculating than he'd originally thought. He suspected Kamran knew he had held back during their first run on the beach. So the Iranian intentionally created a situation to see how fast Craft could run. To overcome an eighteen second lead against three fresh runners, Craft would have to move at near Olympic speed, running two miles in close to eight minutes. In the future, he would have to be more vigilant before engaging in unexpected events.

•

The next day, they teed off at 1:10PM on the 1st hole. The weather forecast projected wind gusts of 15 to 25 miles per hour with the threat of rain all afternoon. By the time they started, there were four players, including themselves, leading at seven under par. The other players tied for the lead, having played in the morning session, had already completed their second rounds. The day proved to be difficult with two rain delays and the wind blowing the ball off target, but Kamran and Craft persevered. Both players had the lead at ten under par as they walked to the 16th tee area.

After both players hit good drives, the Iranian pushed his second shot on the 16th hole, going for the par-5 green in two, finding the water down the right side. Discouraged by scoring a bogey on a birdie hole, the Iranian's focus was slipping away. As he walked off the 16th green, Craft whispered, "Look forward to the next turn, my friend."

Kamran smiled. Hitting first, Craft landed the ball safely on the back tier of the green several feet from the flagstick. The Iranian stepped up to the tee, and with confidence, selected a nine iron with the intention of going for the back pin position. The wind had gone still, but a gust could come at any moment. He hit the shot high and on a line straight at the pin. The ball hit the flagstick and dropped six inches from the hole for a tap-in birdie. Both players finished the second round at ten under par, having a two-stroke lead on the field. As the tournament leaders, they would be playing together in the final pairing on Saturday. After the round, Kamran thanked his friend for the helpful words.

The story of the two men beating a team of six in a relay race had reached the media. In an effort to hype the tournament, the media framed their relationship as "partners in crime." Concerned this image might draw unwanted attention Wilkins worked behind the scenes to shift the developing image to one of fierce competitors.

By the time they teed off on Saturday afternoon, the media referred to them as "prizefighters ready to do battle." The weather conditions were excellent; it was going to take six under par for the day to keep pace. The crowds squeezed around the 1st tee, waiting for Friday's leaders to tee off. Kamran now believed he could win the tournament, but his opponent would have to go down. The battle began with both players getting birdies on the 1st hole. After the first five holes, they were back in the lead at thirteen under par. It was an intense battle between them, and the networks were cutting short commercials, afraid they might miss the action on the golf course. The announcers spent much of the broadcast commenting on the interaction between the two players and projecting how each player interpreted the actions of the other.

Vaughn, disguised as the caddy Jefferson, had never enjoyed an Agency assignment as much as this one, but the hard work was still ahead. Not having to deal with Smartball made his job easier but the pace was so quick the two caddies had to work as a team just to keep up. Having spent three days in a row together, the caddies had the routine down pat.

A major network broadcast announcer said, "Maybe Craft and Turani are friends but on the golf course they are fierce competitors. They are out to match each other shot for shot as if no one else is playing in the tournament. I've yet to see either player look at the leader board. Don't they know the best players in the world are playing in front of them?"

The duo finished Saturday's round, with Turani shooting eight under par, two strokes ahead of Craft and four strokes ahead of the rest of the field. The press waited for hours to have a chance to interview them. For the Iranian, it was no longer about beating the other golfers, it was about beating Craft; he was the competition.

Craft was grateful for the physiological preparation with Dr. Page. It was as crazy as she had indicated. The press tried everything possible to create tension between the two players. Craft found ways to compliment Kamran, without appearing weak. Before ending his last interview, Craft mentioned he would be making a major announcement before teeing off the next day. Media speculation, fed by the image manager, was all over the place, from announcing a new clothing line to his leaving golf to play football.

The golf battle at TPC Sawgrass dominated sports media all over the world. The news of the Iranian being in position to defeat an American at the Players Championship was broadcast on all media outlets in the Middle East. Some Western news networks had political analysts projecting the potential impact of Sunday's outcome on international relations if the American came from behind to win.

•

Saturday night, Kamran stopped by the beach house. He wanted to assure his new friend that win or lose, he greatly appreciated his friendship off the golf course and assistance on the golf course.

As the Iranian started to leave, Craft said, "Get a good night's sleep. I want you playing at your best tomorrow, because that's what it's going to take to win."

"Good fortune, my friend. It's too bad one of us has to lose for the other to win," the Iranian said as he walked out the door.

•

The reporters jockeyed for positions, as Craft arrived at the golf course for Sunday's round. Calm and rested from a good night's sleep and a long run on the beach, he was ready to engage the media. With Wilkins standing close by, Craft said, "It's my intention to sponsor a youth golf program around the world. This endeavor will require financial resources, so I've have made a commitment to donate a large portion of my tournament winnings to fund youth golf activities. This morning, I signed papers donating two million dollars to setup the First Light program in memory of my grandfather, Mr. William Craft. This is not a hands-off operation. I plan to be directly involved in helping the program succeed. Thank you."

Craft went into the clubhouse, leaving Wilkins to answer questions. By the afternoon, the morning rain showers had passed, and the weather forecast was for a beautiful, sunny blue sky, seventy-five degrees, and light winds. While the pins would be placed in the typically difficult Sunday positions, the greens would be softer than normal, enabling the players to go at the flagstick.

Broadcast announcers were hyping the match, wondering who would flinch first? Being two strokes behind, the pressure would be on Craft to be more aggressive, but a two-stroke lead was not much to sit on waiting for others to make mistakes. Some of the premier players a few strokes back were visibly upset the networks were not giving them the usual high level of attention.

They teed off in front of a massive crowd. While the cheers were loud, a few spectators made off-color remarks trying to rattle the Iranian. Although the match was not about Craft winning, he could feel his competitive juices going into high action. Two players on the back nine had climbed within one stroke of the lead, but not for long. Kamran and Craft went three under par on the first five holes, extending the lead to four strokes. With Craft one stroke behind Kamran, they both drove the par five 16th hole in two and walked off the green with two-putt birdies.

The 17th hole had the traditional Sunday pin location about ten feet from the water on the lower right portion of the green. The tee markers were at the back of the teeing area, leaving 134-yards to the hole. Craft watched as the Iranian reached for his pitching wedge; he was playing safe, intending to hit the ball to the middle of the green leaving a 20-foot, or longer, putt for birdie.

Ready to make a statement, Craft pulled a nine iron out of the bag but Jefferson did not take the bag away. The player and caddy locked eyes with each other for an unusually long time. Slowly Jefferson moved the bag to the side of the tee and then turned to face Craft.

Loud enough for those around the tee area to hear, Jefferson said, "Knock it stiff."

The Iranian, who had kept his concentration on high all afternoon, could feel his heart pounding while waiting for Craft to tee the ball. Was his friend really going at the pin? Was he being fearless or reckless? The Iranian thought his opponent must have seen replays of the many aggressive Sunday shots having found the water. Although thousands of people crowded around the 17th hole, it was quiet enough to hear a pin drop. Craft took aim, and with a beautiful smooth swing, hit the ball directly at the flagstick.

Spectators cheered as the ball hit the ground three feet in front of the hole, then a huge gasp, as the ball hit against the flagstick and began rolling to the right toward the water. The green was fast, having dried in the heat of the afternoon sun. The ball rolled slowly toward the water. For a moment, it appeared the 18 inches of fringe grass on the side of the green would stop the ball. The world watched in suspense as the ball trickled off the side of the island green to fall softly into the pond. Craft stood watching in disbelief, with his hands above his head holding the club dangling behind him and then slammed the nine iron into the ground as the golf ball found its resting place in a sea of despair.

A broadcast announcer, attempting to rationalize the implausible, blurted out, "Sometimes this game just isn't fair. Craft hit a near perfect shot. His ball had more chance of going in the hole than in the water, but in the water it is. Hitting the flagstick must have taken the backspin off the ball, and it just wouldn't stop rolling. The young man from Charleston is visibly shaken. But who wouldn't be?"

The Iranian wanted to give his friend a gesture of condolence, but the stakes were too high and he still needed to get across the finish line. Choosing not to go to the drop area closer to the hole, Craft teed the ball again, and hit a second tee shot with a nine iron, and the ball landed two feet from the pin. The Iranian walked off the 17th green with a two-stroke lead.

On the 18th tee, Kamran hit a safe shot out to the right and then a long second shot to the front of the green. After a long two putt, the Iranian raised his hands in victory, having just won this year's Players Championship. Kamran's sister and father were there to share in his celebration as he walked off the 18th green.

As Craft walked to the scorer's station, he tried hard not to smile. There couldn't have been a better ending to the tournament if he had scripted it himself. Although he found it hard to display the thrill of victory at the Masters, today it was easy to express the agony of defeat. He wondered if Dr. Page had enjoyed watching his colorful display of emotions. It was the first time in his adult life he had pounded a club into the ground during a golf match, and it was quite refreshing. Craft left the clubhouse, avoiding the press, not wanting to take the spotlight away from the winner.

•

That evening, Wilkins and Craft attended the closing ceremony. Kamran insisted his friends sit with him at the head table. He agreed, but cautioned that their sitting together might not be good for the image of two warriors ready to do battle. After being introduced, Kamran's father, Amir, thanked Craft for bringing good fortune to his son.

After thanking everyone, the tournament director turned the podium over to this year's Players Champion. Visibly nervous, Kamran paid tribute to the long-standing tradition of the Players Championship and thanked the sponsors. The Iranian acknowledged his playing partner who had pushed him to play his best, and had even offered words of encouragement along the way.

He said, "I have come to discover that my friend, Mr. Peter Craft, is a much bigger person than can be demonstrated on the golf course. In the spirit of giving back, I commit half of today's winnings to the new First Light program, in hopes of helping the youth of Iran."

Following Kamran's gracious act, the tournament director asked this year's Masters Champion to say a few words. Standing at the podium, Craft said, "If anyone was to benefit from my disappointment today, I am sincerely delighted it's the man sitting at the head table. His generous donation is greatly appreciated. Let this be an example of how two people from diverse nations can come together to help others. With Mr. Turani's approval and help, I plan to kick off the First Light program in his home city of Tehran."

After the formal ceremony, Craft spoke of his intention to play overseas in Dubai tournament the first week of June, two weeks before the U.S. Open. Seizing the opportunity, Kamran invited him to come to Tehran the weekend before the Dubai tournament to kick off the First Light program and to enjoy motorcycle riding at his uncle's estate in the mountains.

As the evening concluded, the team had accomplished the critical mission objective of obtaining an invitation to the VIPER I site.

CHAPTER 19

TEHRAN, IRAN

He arrived in Tehran on a direct overseas flight from Atlanta. Tired from the many hour flight, Craft was not looking forward to the hassle of waiting in the long line to clear customs. An immigration officer approached and motioned for him to step aside.

Speaking English, the officer said, "Sir, please follow me."

Faced with the possibility of an intense interrogation, he prepared himself for the worst. Speaking in Farsi, the officer pulled his handheld radio off his belt and announced to whomever was listening on the radio that he was escorting the American golfer to the customs area reserved for dignitaries. Craft could feel his pulse returning to normal. Once in the VIP room, the officer welcomed the Masters Champion and expressed empathy for the bad luck encounter on the 17th hole at Sawgrass. By now, Tehran's local community had watched video of the Players Championship, to see the fearless Iranian triumph over the American competitor. Craft found it ironic that his losing at the Players had done more to build a favorable image in the Middle East than his winning at the Masters. It really wasn't losing that made him famous; it was how he lost. From an image building perspective, Craft's Sawgrass defeat was spectacular. People all over the world could relate to the disappointment of having made an excellent effort, only to be sabotaged by fate.

The immigration officer quickly opened and scanned the American's luggage, and a few minutes later he was headed out of the airport. While Kamran waited for his American friend, a crowd gathered. After saying hello to each other, the Tour players posed for pictures and responded to a few questions. Although Craft understood the questions being asked, the Iranian acted as a translator. People wanted to know when the two warriors would do battle again. Craft redirected his answers toward the First Light program and the importance of building bridges between the two nations.

While walking to the waiting car, Kamran said his win at the Players had elevated him to superstar status around the city. From a security perspective, his newfound fame had to be taken seriously. The progressive people of Iran welcomed his high profile accomplishments on the golf course, as well as his commitment to the youth of the community. Others hated him as the son of Satan for his Western ways and for befriending the infidels.

Without a word, the driver loaded his luggage into the trunk of the black Mercedes sedan and began the slow drive through north Tehran to the family home in the Darrous neighborhood. Concerned that Reza, the man sent to protect Kamran in Florida, drove the vehicle; he hoped team members back at Langley were tracking his movements.

They ate lunch in the home's botanical gardens with Kamran's father. After a short rest in the palatial guest suite, the Tour players boarded a helicopter for a flight to south Tehran to officially begin the First Light program with a youth golf workshop. Thousands of children wanted to participate, but attendance was limited to two hundred children selected by a lottery.

As the helicopter approached the landing area, the glare of sunlight reflecting off the ground concealed the hundreds of children waiting, many more than those who had received lottery passes. They landed far enough away to avoid covering the children in dust from the downdraft of the spinning blades. With the temperature near ninety degrees, they hoped there would be plenty of refreshments for all the children to eat and drink. The workshop was held in a field designated by the local community to become a future public golf course.

Both boys and girls were allowed to attend but great care was taken to comply with Islamic protocol, keeping the boys and girls sufficiently separated. While all the children were allowed to watch and enjoy the refreshments only children with lottery passes received a golf glove, hat, shirt, and golf balls. Craft and Kamran, accompanied by recruits from the Iranian's home golf club, worked for hours with the children, telling stories, giving lessons, and performing golf tricks. The smiles and excitement of the children was truly gratifying to both players. Their hands were aching from autographing two hundred hats and countless other items.

The local media recorded video for the evening news. At the conclusion of the event a local politician thanked the Tour players and gave them each a large leather travel bag with their initials embroidered on the outside and filled with small Persian trinkets and handmade linens with elegant designs. As the helicopter lifted off the ground, both young men, fixated on the hundreds of children waving goodbye, began to grasp the awesome realization they could truly make a difference.

Craft went to the guest suite to rest. In two hours, guests would begin arriving for the western barbecue Kamran was hosting in his honor. He emptied the leather travel bag, opening the secret compartment in the bottom containing spy equipment. He extracted one of the three power outlets designed by Wilson. The devices enabled the National Security Agency to record conversations throughout the complex and then forward them to the CIA for analysis. The CIA scientist had discovered a way to use the common ground wiring and a unique voice frequency matching technique to listen to local conversations occurring within the building complex.

He replaced one of the power outlets in his room, taking care not to disrupt the building's electrical system. Using his HuAID with wireless earphones, he listened and recorded conversations via the power outlet. Resting on the bed almost asleep, he heard Kamran speaking with someone. Initially, Craft wasn't sure whom the Iranian was talking with, but soon it became apparent the other person was his uncle, Farzad Shirazi, the Quds Force General. He played back the conversation.

Speaking Farsi, General Shirazi said, "My apologies, but urgent business keeps me in Tehran for the next few days. I must leave here immediately. Please enjoy tomorrow's visit to my home, but it's important we talk today in person."

"No need to apologize. I know you have your hands full trying to keep us safe and I have not been making it easy for you." Kamran said.

"No you're not," responded Shirazi. "Dangerous people are looking for someone to make an example of, and you and your sister are becoming targets. Your friendship with the American is comparable to poking a stick into the serpent's nest."

"Is there something I need to know about the American?"

"No, but some of my associates still view America as the enemy, making you and your sister collaborators. Some go as far as to label you, American spies."

"An American spy," repeated Kamran. "That's ridiculous."

"Maybe so, but these are serious people."

"I am fortunate to have such a powerful man for my uncle. I am sure my security rests in good hands."

"Don't confuse powerful with invincible; everyone has their limits."

"Uncle, as you have told me many times, I must follow my dream."

"Your dream or your father's dream?"

"I share my father's dream for a prosperous and progressive Iran."

"You know I love you and your sister like my own children. You are a man now; consider the consequences of your actions. Treacherous people are plotting; I know this for a fact. Iran hosting the Asian Open has forced a dangerous confrontation. Please take some time off; go to a safe place, enjoy life, and let the storm pass. Soon it will be impossible for me to ensure your safety."

"Dear Uncle, I would not want to be in the shoes of those who harmed your family."

"Listen to me. Do not underestimate the forces at work!"

Given the urgency of the uncle's appeal, Craft believed General Shirazi had intelligence indicating something big was in the works. He was now confident the Red Crescent program was headed down the right path.

Kamran eagerly introduced his American friend to the guests as they arrived. Many attending the barbecue were of American Iranian heritage, well versed in Western traditions and fluent in the English language. Although some guests wanted to talk about sensitive topics such as the adequacy of security at the Asian Open, Craft was masterful at giving friendly, innocuous responses and then redirecting conversations toward youth golf. Many offered cash donations on the spot. He responded by giving them a card with information of how to make First Light donations.

Early the next morning, Reza pulled the Mercedes sedan in front of the family home, ready to begin the two-hour drive to General Shirazi's estate. They would be driven instead of flying because the military base was off limits to non-military aircraft. After a quick breakfast and a short workout in the fitness room, they put their travel bags into the trunk and stepped into the car. Kamran sat in the front passenger seat next to Reza. Craft sat alone in the back seat, taking a position where he could keep an eye on the driver.

Reza navigated through the streets of Tehran with ease and merged onto the Persian Gulf highway, Highway 7, traveling southwest to Qom. Soon a second black Mercedes sedan was following close behind.

Craft wanted to send a message to the team to check out the trailing vehicle, but was operating under strict OPSEC restrictions. He could receive encrypted messages from the team, but could not transmit over the airwaves. Iranian security could potentially detect the unique signal, and pinpoint it to his physical location. He trusted that the team was monitoring his every move, and would send an alert if the trailing car posed any danger.

"We have company," said Kamran in Farsi, referring to the car following close behind.

"Your uncle ordered additional security to assist us outside the city," Reza calmly replied.

Given his uncle's face-to-face warning of danger the previous evening, Kamran did not protest. It wouldn't have mattered anyway. The security force was trained to follow orders to the death, if necessary. Kamran informed his guest the trailing car was additional security. Craft continued scanning a golf magazine pretending he hadn't noticed.

The landscape soon turned to semi-desert, with the outside temperature rising to the low nineties. They passed the time talking about the previous day's experiences with the children, and shared ideas for improving the youth golf program. At one point, Reza spoke up in English, suggesting they could build public support by accelerating construction of the public golf course in south Tehran. Although Reza's ideas made sense, his sincerity was questionable.

QOM, IRAN

As they approached the city of Qom, Reza exited Highway 7 onto a back road leading to the General Shirazi's estate, located on a remote military base. Kamran changed the conversation to motorcycles, giving a short tutorial on what to expect when racing on a mountain road. Reza glanced into the rear view mirror to study Craft's reaction, as Kamran discussed the dangers ahead. Craft was well aware of the potential dangers, having studied high-resolution satellite pictures of every inch of the 26-mile road, from the uncle's estate to the VIPER I facility. The Iranian emphasized the importance of staying on the main road, implying off-road areas were hazardous. What the Iranian actually meant but did not say was the off-road areas were covered with minefields.

Kamran delighted in the adventure of having an inexperienced American on his home turf. On the other hand, he was genuinely concerned his friend might not be taking serious enough the potential dangers of racing on a winding mountain road with loose rock on its uphill side and unprotected steep ledges on its downhill side. Kamran emphasized they would need to be on the lookout for fallen rocks, small animals, and sandy patches in the road. He concluded the lecture with a final warning of letting go of the bike quickly if it slid out from under you. Otherwise, the bike's momentum would pull you over the ledge.

To lighten the mood, Craft asked, "How fast can the medical personnel respond to a motorcycle accident?"

"Don't know, never had one," replied Kamran.

"Well, I don't plan to be the first."

Reza slowed the vehicle at the entrance to the military base, giving the guard time to open the gate. Soon the car pulled up in front of two golden gates guarding the entrance to the General's estate. As the car approached, the gates opened and they proceeded up the winding road. Tall palm trees and the vibrant green foliage created a picture perfect landscape. Craft thought it had to take an army of gardeners just to maintain the manicured grounds.

The General's property was positioned at the entrance to a mountain range and the road to the VIPER I facility. As the car pulled in front of the residence, a young low-ranking soldier waited. Upon exiting the vehicle, the young man offered, in barely understandable English, to take their luggage. Craft politely declined but the soldier insisted, picking up the luggage with both hands. Apparently, he was not really asking, just trying to be polite.

Kamran commented, "Even though I have been here many times, the staff still treat me like a first time visitor. I find it's better to just let them do their jobs."

The dining room table contained an assortment of fruits, pastries, and drinks for lunch. Craft enjoyed a small lunch and then began exploring the estate. His every move was under surveillance by the uncle's security force. Sipping a glass of lemonade, Craft stood on the back terrace, acting surprised to see a grand golf green below with an elaborate chipping area.

Joining his American friend on the terrace, Kamran said, "You may have noticed my uncle has taken an interest in the game of golf. Our Supreme Leader, educated in Great Britain, is a golf enthusiast. I am told he holds retreats here to fine tune his short game."

After relaxing for a while, the two competitors went to the large garage, which contained an assortment of motorcycles and equipment. For the sake of safety, Kamran recommended they ride the less powerful 600cc motorbikes.

Craft mounted one of the bikes, and began test riding around the driveway area. He hit a pile of dirt by the edge of the driveway, throwing it all over himself and the vehicle.

Kamran laughed at the American and motorcycle covered in dirt.

Craft went into the garage, wiped the dirt off his clothes and then picked up a towel and secretly sprinkled Wilson's special lotion on it. He returned outside and began wiping the dirt off the motorcycle. He carefully wiped the tires with the towel containing the special lotion, making sure to get the dirt out of the tire treads. The lotion was designed to leave a glowing florescent trail on the road that could only be seen at night, using specially designed night vision goggles.

They wore helmets, equipped with headsets and microphones, enabling them to talk with each other as they raced along the mountain road and, if necessary, with the people in the security control center who could warn them of pending issues, such as an approaching dust storm or a rockslide.

The two competitors exited the estate, and began racing up the road to VIPER I. Kamran pointed out obstacles to watch for as they moved through the turns. The scenic views were breathtaking. As their speed gradually increased, Craft found it necessary to devote his full attention to navigating the road.

When they reached the entrance to the VIPER I facility, Craft casually stopped, turned off his motorcycle, took off his helmet, and signaled Kamran indicating he wanted to talk. The Iranian pulled up next to him, shut down and also took off his helmet. Craft asked questions, using the opportunity to view the VIPER I facility in daylight. Not wanting to look too interested, Craft tried to commit to memory details needed for his late night spy mission. He could see the best place to traverse the 30-foot wall protecting the secret site. Although Craft had detailed satellite pictures of the facility, his mission would be executed in the dark of the night, so viewing the facility up close in daylight was vital.

With the engines shut off, they could hear the sound of another motorcycle approaching. Kamran did not act surprised. Soon a man riding a motorcycle pulled up alongside of them. It was the young soldier who had carried their luggage. He talked in Farsi to Kamran proposing a bet, but the terms were not clear.

"You're probably wondering what's up," Kamran said when the conversation ended. "Javid is the fastest motorcycle racer in my uncle's force and it would be disrespectful to not accept his challenge. My uncle considers betting on motorcycle racing part of his morale program. The soldiers are allowed to bet but not with money; only barter arrangements are acceptable. Apparently the odds are five-to-one in my favor, but Javid received a vision last night of a glorious victory. Would you be kind enough to start the race?"

Craft wondered how his team had missed briefing him on what appeared to be a common practice at the uncle's estate. On the other hand, this distraction allowed him to have extra time to survey the secret facility. He took off one of his gloves, held it out and asked Kamran to tell Javid the race would start when the glove fell to the ground. After waiting until both racers indicated they were ready, he opened his hand to let the glove drop.

The racers quickly accelerated their motorcycles to dangerous speeds. Craft was in a position where he could see them racing down the road for a few miles. The lead had changed four times before the racers went around the mountain out of sight.

Craft took his time putting on his helmet and starting the motorcycle, trying to fight off the demons of seeing danger everywhere. He raced down the road, hugging the uphill side of the mountain, hoping not to come across a deadly accident. In his headset was the voice of someone at the security center announcing the race to the troops. When Craft reached the uncle's estate, Kamran was consoling the soldier, wishing him better fortune next time.

After a short rest and cold drinks, they began racing back to VIPER I. Craft could appreciate why the road was perfect for MotoGP training. The repeated pattern of "S turns" connected by straight lengths of road resembled a racetrack laid out in a straightaway, instead of in a circle. After listening intensely to Kamran's instructions on the way up to VIPER I, he was ready to see if he could keep pace on the way back. The two competitors raced down the mountain road but he was no competition for the Iranian. Kamran's road knowledge and ability to keep speed through the turns without losing control was masterful. At the same time, Craft, knowing his limits, was not about to push the edge and put the mission at risk.

Back at the estate, they sat in the shade of a big tree, drinking cold drinks, reminiscing about the excitement of Sunday at the Players. The Iranian revealed he was considering taking time off from the Tour. Having heard the conversation between Kamran and his uncle, Craft had thought about how to respond if the topic surfaced. The danger facing him and his family were real but losing the option to leverage their relationship could be a major mission setback. He walked through the pro and cons of Kamran continuing on the Tour, mentioning his importance to the First Light program and the goodwill they were building between the two nations. It didn't take much persuasion for Kamran to agree to finish the year. Craft felt an overwhelming sense of responsibility, but that would be something to deal with later.

They both turned their heads in the direction of the garage to the sound of a motorcycle engine starting just in time to see someone coming at them at a high rate of speed. The person slammed the cycle to a skidding stop, jumped off and began walking slowly towards them. The mystery person had the body curves of a young woman. Off came the helmet. Gently shaking her head while brushing back her long flowing black hair, Kamran's sister was ready to ride.

Would the surprises ever stop? Craft wondered. Daria was supposed to be in New York, directing a photo shoot for a special edition of the *Persian Woman* magazine. He wondered what other surprises were in store, although he had an idea where this one was headed, given she had flown halfway around the world to join them.

"My brother is not the only one in the family who enjoys motorcycles," Daria commented and then asked, "Will you join me so I do not have to ride alone?"

Craft graciously accepted the offer. They rode toward the secret facility with Daria leading the way. Halfway to VIPER I, she pulled over to the side of the road at a lookout area with a panoramic view of the lowlands below. The mountain range partly blocked the sunlight, creating a magnificent palette of shadows and colors in the lowlands. Aware they were being watched, both leaned against their motorcycles, keeping an appropriate distance—close enough to talk, but far enough apart to meet the protocol for the distance between a man and woman. This was the first time Daria had a chance to talk with him in private. They talked about the beautiful scenic view, and then she got to the point.

"What's your relationship with Jennifer?" she asked.

Thinking for a few seconds about the professional jousting at the core of their relationship, Craft responded, "She's my business manager."

"I thought there might be more to it, given she talked so affectionately about you."

"Is there a reason for your interest in my personal life?" he asked.

"The romantic interests of young golf stars sell magazines."

"So, you're only interested in my personal life is selling magazines?"

"I didn't say it was my only interest," Daria replied in a soft seductive voice.

"What other interest might you have?" Craft asked, pretending to be puzzled.

"I think it's time to head back before it get dark." Reluctantly, Craft decided he would have to dampen her enthusiasm for the sake of the mission. At this critical point, he couldn't take the risk of unnecessary complications. The last thing he needed was Daria slipping into his room in the middle of night, only to find the bedroom empty.

"The next few months are a critical time for my golf career," he explained, "and that requires my full attention."

With a look of disappointment she responded, "My career is also important. Finding balance makes life more pleasurable."

"I agree. I intend to take some time off after the Asian Open in October. I hear fall in New York City is delightful."

She climbed back on the motorcycle. "Yes, fall in New York City is beautiful."

They raced their motorcycles back to the uncle's estate, having fun taking turns moving into the lead. He was impressed by her ability to handle the bike, and could see she was a person who enjoyed adventure. She was a beautiful woman who could capture the heart of any man she chose, so his resisting her mild advances would probably be taken as a challenge. He tried not to think of her as a potential love interest but the way she blended Western and Persian cultures intrigued him.

CHAPTER 20

After cleaning up, the three met in the dining area for a traditional Iranian dinner. They sat on big beautiful Persian carpet around a white dining cloth. The military kitchen personnel placed bowls of food on the white cloth, containing rice, roasted meats, fruit, and other items. Although knowledgeable about Iranian dining traditions, Craft asked for guidance from his hosts. He ate food, only using the fingers on his right hand; doing otherwise would be disrespectful. They talked for hours, comparing the traditions of both countries. Although not religious, Kamran and Daria were sincerely knowledgeable and proud of the ancient traditions of their Persian culture.

Craft could not take his eyes of Daria; she looked absolutely stunning in the soft evening candlelight. As midnight approached, he excused himself to retire for the evening. Once in the bedroom, he activated the HuAID application designed to detect cameras, motion detectors, and listening devices in the room. The application indicated the room did not have cameras but did have motion and body heat sensors as well as listening devices to detect if he left the room. He opened the secret compartment in his carry bag and went to work, counteracting the sensors so it would appear he was in the room while he was executing the late night mission.

Craft rested and used a nightlight to study the operations plan and satellite pictures until 1:30AM, then slipped into his athletic jacket and pants specially designed to disperse body heat, to avoid infrared detection. He put on a black hood to cover his head, leaving just a small area for breathing and to see through the specially designed goggles. He slipped out the window into the darkness of night. As they expected, the outside lights were turned off so the estate did not present an easy target for air attack. He worked his way to the garage area, and then connected inline skating wheels onto his specially designed shoes. With the goggles on, he could see the florescent trail on the road left by the lotion on the motorcycle wheels.

He began skating at a steady pace of eighteen miles an hour, reaching the 30-foot wall of the VIPER I facility at 3:02AM. Timing was extremely important. At 3:07, the two guards protecting the facility would be at the farthest point away when he entered the facility. At 3:05, Craft pulled out the pocket zip-line. He fired the zip-line, hitting the wall about six inches from the top. At 3:06, Craft used the zip-line to scale the wall and was on the ground on the other side at exactly 3:07. Moving quickly along the wall, he threw a furry object onto the ground in a hard-to-get-to area.

Craft had three minutes to get to the building entrance where food supplies were dropped off. The refrigeration equipment in the supply area would draw electricity from the building power system. His mission was to find a power outlet, and replace it with one of Wilson's devices. Craft found the loading area and an exposed outlet. Everything was going as planned, until he replaced the outlet and it failed the test validating its correct operation. He quickly reinstalled the device, but again the test failed. The guard would be coming by the food supply area in four minutes. He concealed himself until after the guard passed. He waited another five minutes for the guard to get far enough away to resume operations.

Craft activated the secure satellite call through the NSA network to the CIA personnel on standby. Talking as low as possible into the microphone, Craft calmly explained the situation. They asked him to uninstall the device and send them a picture. Within a few seconds, the analyst could see the problem. But Craft had to shut down again, because the guard was about to return. Time was now becoming an issue because the darkness of the night would begin to lift soon, starting at 4:55AM. By 5:10AM, he would be visible to security. Once the guard passed, he worked fast to execute the analyst's instructions. The power outlet passed the test.

Checking the time, he knew if he waited for the guard to complete another cycle before leaving VIPER I, it would be impossible to get back before daylight. The guard was about two minutes away when he activated a diversion. The object discarded upon his entry into the secure facility was a fake rodent. When activated, it made a loud screeching noise, imitating an animal being mauled. Craft hoped the noise would distract the guard long enough for him to get over the wall. The exploding rodent made a putrid smell, discouraging anyone from getting too close. Craft ran to the exit point, activated the zip-line, and quickly scrambled over the wall. At 4:07AM, the agent re-attached the inline skating wheels and began sprinting back to the uncle's estate. He pushed his body to the maximum, placing one leg in front of the other, leaning forward to reduce the wind drag. To avoid detection, he needed to travel twenty-six miles in fifty-five minutes, beating his best time in training by ten minutes.

The tracker built into his HuAID indicated he was on pace to reach the estate in seven minutes, when he hit something that let out a wild scream. A small animal had run in front of the skater, undetected in the dark. He crashed to the ground, sliding down the road face first. The fall on his chest left him gasping for air. Instinctively, Craft rolled over onto his back, then twisted to get his feet in front of him and with all his strength, dug the metal back of the skates into the ground, hoping to come to a stop before going over the ledge, which meant falling several feet to rocks below.

Just by chance, he came to an abrupt stop, smashing against a rock on the side of the road. His HuAID smashed into pieces. In immense pain, he struggled to regain his balance and then began skating again. He could feel his injured ribs and a sharp pain in his abdomen. He was now in the danger zone of being detected with the sun starting to rise over the horizon. He travelled as fast as possible, given his injuries, and hoped it was good enough.

TOP SECRET LOCATION
NORTHERN VIRGINIA

At 4:53AM Qom time, the Red Crescent team huddled around a display unit monitoring Craft's progress returning to the uncle's estate. The adrenalin rush from overcoming the installation problem at VIPER I was beginning to subside. Astonished by the speed at which he traveled, Vaughn was now optimistic the CIA agent would reach the estate before sunrise, when without warning, the tracking signal transmitted by Craft's HuAID disappeared. He tried repeatedly to use emergency procedures to re-establish secure communications with Craft's HuAID. The device was not responding.

At 4:59AM, Vaughn sent a high priority message to the CIA Director requesting approval to redirect satellite assets to capture high-resolution real-time video of the road between VIPER I and the uncle's estate. By 5:17AM, he had the live video feed and began a close-up visual inspection of the area where the signal disappeared. The team's imagery analyst observed skid marks in the road consistent with a person's body sliding on the surface of the road. The analyst pointed to wheel tracks continuing down the road toward the uncle's estate. After a few seconds, the analyst announced that given the speed and the length of the skid mark, the agent probably took a hard fall but was able to recover and continue the mission.

While assessing the situation, they received an NSA alert indicating the listening device at the uncle's estate was activated. The team let out a sigh of relief, knowing Craft must have made it back. Vaughn was about to send a message to Walker giving her an update when he observed several military personnel assembling near the uncle's estate. He feared the mission was compromised and Craft was in grave danger. Vaughn was about to invoke an emergency action of exploding a nearby fuel supply, intended to divert the attention of the assembling military force and buy time for the agent to potentially escape.

After taking a closer look at the assembling force, he observed the soldiers were only armed with small holster weapons and did not appear to be preparing for a potentially hostile engagement. He watched carefully as the soldiers walked casually up the road to the uncle's estate, entered into the backyard, and stood at attention around the golf green. He listened to the NSA audio feed for any indication of Craft being active within in the estate.

At 7:45AM, he heard a loud knock on Craft's bedroom door. It was Daria Turani inquiring whether their guest would be coming to breakfast. Barely conscious, Craft indicated he had overslept, and needed a few more minutes before joining them. *Vaughn could tell the agent was injured; the question was how badly?*

QOM, IRAN

Craft staggered into the bathroom, holding onto the wall to keep from falling down. Looking into the mirror, he could see a gruesome bruise on his chest and suspected he might have cracked some ribs. The swelling and pain in his abdomen was severe, and his upper body was stiff with major inflammation. Although he knew his team would be listening, he couldn't talk to explain the situation because the Iranian military would also be listening. He took a hot shower, trying to loosen his muscles and regain motion. He swallowed a pill that Dr. Page had given him for such situations. Soon the pain was greatly reduced, but the stiffness remained. After dressing, he was relieved to see in the mirror that his injuries were not visible. The athletic suit had protected his body from skin abrasions. He dressed and finally mustered enough strength to walk downstairs, to join the others for breakfast.

He reverted to an operational contingency plan. He asked Daria if he could use her HuAID to make a call, explaining his had lost its power charge. He called Wilkins, his business manager. She picked up the phone knowing it was Craft because he was the only one authorized to call the emergency number.

Craft began the conversation, saying, "Hello, Jennifer, How was your trip to Dubai?"

Wilkins understood if the conversation started by him asking about her trip, that it was code for needing to return to the U.S. as soon as possible.

Knowing the conversation was not secure and being monitored by the uncle's security, Wilkins replied, "I'm glad you called. The company we talked about last week wants to offer you the endorsement contract, but the deal has to be completed by Friday. The company president wants to meet with you in Atlanta as soon as possible, to hear firsthand about your plans for the First Light program. He said your favorability ratings are off the charts and thinks you are the right person to promote his company. I recommend you cancel playing in the Dubai tournament and meet me in Atlanta first thing in the morning. This deal is simply too good to pass up, and you'll have more time to prepare for the U.S. Open."

Craft replied, "I will be on the next flight to Atlanta."

Wilkins continued, "I will inform the Dubai tournament director of your decision. He's not going to be happy, but I've already checked and he has a long list of alternative players just waiting to fill in, if given the opportunity."

Wilkins could tell he was in pain by the crackle in his voice, but thanked God he was still alive and thinking clearly.

Craft explained to Daria and Kamran his need to return to Atlanta, and apologized for having to delay their next battle on the course until the U.S. Open in two weeks. Craft booked a 4:30PM flight back to Atlanta. With a couple of hours remaining before returning to Tehran, he hoped the pain pills would allow him to function with his injury remaining undetected.

While attempting to eat some fruit at breakfast, Craft noticed several soldiers standing at attention around the green in the backyard.

Smiling at his Iranian friend, he asked, "Another surprise?"

Kamran replied, "No big deal. A few of my uncle's men would like us to put on a short game exhibition."

Craft knew even a short swing with a golf club would be difficult, and draw unnecessary attention to his injury. After hearing all the hype about the two players battling it out at the Players Championship, some of the soldiers were curious about golf and wanted to get a close look.

Seeing an opportunity to deflect attention, Craft said, "Let's give each of the soldiers a chance to try chipping and putting. You demonstrate a few chip shots and I will demonstrate putting. Then we'll let them have a go at it."

Craft was in extreme pain, but tried not to show it. Noticing their guest appeared to be in discomfort, both Kamran and Daria wanted to know if everything was all right. He pacified their interest, by calmly mentioning the bed was a bit soft and his back had stiffened from an old football injury. In reality, the pain was so intense he was having difficulty keeping his head clear and not wincing at every move. While Daria appeared sympathetic, Kamran reacted more like a shark smelling blood in the water.

The soldiers behaved like big kids, waiting for their chance to give golf a try. The two pros gave instruction until all the soldiers had turns, first chipping and then putting. Craft tried to hide the pain he felt as each soldier offered a strong handshake of thanks after receiving his putting lesson.

Ahmad Reza pulled the Mercedes sedan in front of the house entrance and waited until the Tour players were ready to return to Tehran. Craft was relieved to find Javid waiting by his door to carry his luggage to the car. Daria met her American friend in the hallway outside the bedroom to say goodbye. She would be staying behind to have dinner with her uncle, who would be returning home in a few hours.

Looking into his deep blue eyes, Daria said, "I am thinking of going to Washington, DC for the U.S. Open. Would you be interested in joining me for dinner one evening?"

"Only if you let me make the arrangements," Craft responded, straining not to let his physical pain be mistaken for lack of interest.

By noon, they were traveling on the Persian Highway back to Tehran. Craft pretended to read a book, fighting to keep awake, fearing if he didn't, they would not be able to wake him when they arrived at the airport.

At the airport, Craft thanked his host for their weekend adventure and then stood and waved as the car pulled away. In severe pain and barely able to function, he made his way through Customs and waited to board the flight to Atlanta.

Getting weak, he struggling to carry his travel bag onto the aircraft. Approaching from behind, a man with a familiar soft voice said, "Peter, please take a seat and get comfortable. I'll take it from here."

Too weak to resist, he turned his head to see his mentor, Kalani. He managed to get into his seat and then lost consciousness, knowing he was in good hands. During the flight, Kalani diverted the flight attendants' attention away from the injured agent. He monitored Craft's vital signs, fearing internal bleeding was occurring and sent frequent messages to the team, providing an update and requesting special arrangements to get the injured agent off the aircraft as quickly as possible.

Just prior to landing in Atlanta, Kalani informed a flight attendant of the medical emergency, explaining his friend was having a severe reaction to sleeping medicine. The flight attendant informed ground operations of the situation and confirmed that an emergency team was waiting on the ground.

CHAPTER 21

As soon as the aircraft reached the gate, a waiting medical team retrieved Craft from the aircraft and loaded him into a waiting emergency vehicle, and then sped off towards a secure medical center in the Atlanta area. The medical team took quick action to stabilize his condition, now in a state of shock and rapidly approaching the point of no return. The injured agent suffered from extreme internal bleeding, resulting from blunt trauma to the abdomen area. Using special microscopic equipment designed to minimize muscle damage, the medical team operated to stop the bleeding and cleanse the injured areas. To speed his recovery, the lead doctor administered a sedative putting him in a light coma.

Vaughn kept the leadership informed regarding the injured agent's condition. Meanwhile, the team quickly engaged in an aggressive communications campaign to keep rumors under control. Wilkins stayed by Craft's bedside until it was time to wake him. After hours of drifting in and out of consciousness, he finally managed to stay awake.

Craft awoke to the feel of her soft hand squeezing his and a caring look he would never forget. By evening, he was out of the bed, trying to regain movement. With the U.S. Open only two weeks away, every second counted. It hurt just to breathe, but he resisted pain medications because he knew it would screw with his head.

With the U.S. Open approaching, the team held a contingency planning session. Although the preferred approach would be to minimize the use of Smartball, the reality of the agent's condition dictated a change in strategy. The revised plan involved taking the tournament lead as soon as possible, extend it as far as possible and then grind it out to hold on, as the strain of the four days took its toll on the injured agent.

This year's U.S. Open Championship would be held at Congressional Country Club in Bethesda, Maryland. Wilkins called the tournament director to ask for Craft to be exempt from attending the mandatory pre-tournament festivities, because of his medical situation. She continued the cover story of an allergic reaction to an over-the-counter sleeping medicine. The director was accommodating to her request but insisted Craft would have to attend the Wednesday evening mandatory rules session and then submit his golf equipment to the engineering team, to be tested for compliance with Tour specifications.

Although the director didn't say it, a player had made an official complaint claiming Craft's equipment didn't conform to Tour specifications. She thought about the concern, and determined testing would not be a problem because the golf balls with ferrite cores were designed to pass Tour specifications. She feared the suspicions of other players would now bring unwanted attention by placing Craft's tournament play under intense scrutiny.

Pictures of his emergency departure from the aircraft had now surfaced. With the first round of the U.S. Open a few days away, members of the media searched Atlanta hospitals looking for this year's Masters champion, hoping to get a firsthand medical update.

Wilkins issued a press release, providing details regarding his allergic reaction to sleeping medicine. Some players maintained his illness was nothing more than a publicity stunt. She announced Craft was resting at an undisclosed location, and assured everyone he would be ready to play in the second Major of the year.

During the evening, Craft covertly moved to a remote ranch in the Georgia countryside. The team met the next morning to assess the situation. Even with strong pain medicine, he was unable to swing a golf club. He spent the day doing light exercise, soaking in a hot tub and receiving deep heat massage. By Saturday afternoon, the speed healing drugs had begun to take effect. His condition had greatly improved by Sunday night. The next morning, Craft attempted to play golf at a local golf course. With a score of three over par after six holes, he struggled just to walk the course. With the first round of the U.S. Open only two days away, he tried to ignore the pain and focus on golf. The two days of coma had zapped much of his energy. Although he tried hard, the energy just wasn't there. His body instinctively released the club too early from the top of the swing to avoid pulling hard on his abdomen. The slightest flinch during the golf swing sent the ball flying in the wrong direction.

Craft's energy level improved on Tuesday, but the flight of the ball was still quite erratic. The team was thankful when the tournament pairings were announced to see the agent had an afternoon 1:36PM tee time to start the tournament. That afternoon, Craft received another HuAID to replace the one broken during the VIPER I operation. Reviewing the call log, Daria and Kamran had left several messages. He called to assure them he was fine, and to congratulate Kamran on his top ten finish at the Dubai tournament.

Although the medical team was amazed at the pace of Craft's recovery, they cautioned that the aggressive healing drugs could have some side effects. Rapid heart rate while at rest was an example given.

The team held a pre-tournament strategy session. Given Craft's physical condition, his ability to sustain a high performance level through all four rounds of the tournament was unlikely. At the same time, the over use of Smartball could feed into player suspicions. Wilson made the case for getting an early lead to have reasonable chance of winning the tournament. Vaughn made the final decision to use Smartball from the start, and then adapt as the situation progressed.

WASHINGTON, D.C. AREA

He stepped out of the aircraft at the Manassas Regional Airport and into a waiting car. As the vehicle cruised east on Interstate 66 toward the beltway, the driver tried to strike up a conversation but Craft wasn't in a talkative mood. The fast healing drugs prescribed by the medical team elevated his heart rate, an uncomfortable feeling, given his recent low activity level. The car moved at a snail's pace in commuter traffic through Tysons Corner, Virginia toward the American Legion Memorial Bridge into Maryland. Shortly after crossing the bridge, he arrived at a grand, gated home, overlooking the Potomac River, a short distance from Congressional Country Club.

The luxurious riverside home in Montgomery County Maryland—one of the richest counties in the nation—had everything needed to be comfortable and more. After hanging up his clothes, he meandered through the house appreciating the sophisticated Mediterranean decor. His eyes sparkled at the sight of the grand piano in the middle of the sunroom. He tried to play music but his rhythm was too fast and his hands struck the wrong keys. His mind and hands seemed disconnected.

Frustrated with his lack of musical ability, he tried relaxing in the hot tub, hoping to sooth his sore muscles. Unable to unwind, he dressed and waited until it was time to go. When Craft arrived at Congressional, a Tour official pulled up in a golf cart and offered to take his equipment to the engineering team for testing. While attending the evening rules session he received an electronic certificate stating his equipment passed testing. With the sun about to go down over the horizon, he strolled along the paved paths near the clubhouse, getting familiar with the golf course. He could see a few players still on the range hitting balls, probably trying to fix their swings before morning. He attempted to calm himself by slowing his breathing and enjoying the peacefulness of the June evening.

The fast healing medicine, designed to maximize blood flow to his injured body, made it difficult to sleep. He felt like a bionic man with exceptional strength. Instead of sleeping, he imagined lifting weights in the athletic center. Facing the reality of a sleepless night, he got up to embrace the fresh early morning air. At first light, he stood on the back terrace of the Potomac home, drinking a glass of orange juice, and looking through the light mist at the whitewater flowing over the rocky riverbed of the Potomac.

At 6:30AM, Craft walked into the dining room at Congressional Country Club to join his Iranian friends for breakfast. After receiving a warm welcome, he assured them his health was fine. They had a quick breakfast and some easy conversation. Then Kamran bid his sister and friend goodbye to go prepare for his morning tee time.

Standing up to shake hands, Craft said, "Good luck, but remember it's my turn to win."

Clenching his fist, mimicking a prizefighter going into the ring, Kamran replied, "I welcome another battle, but don't count on me going down easily. It's going to take a knockout punch, my friend."

Daria gave her brother a kiss on the check and bid him good luck. "Honestly," she said, "you two are behaving like little boys, flexing muscles, hoping to intimidate each other. What are you going to do next, make scary faces and growl at each other?"

The men laughed and acknowledged she had a good point.

With hours remaining until his afternoon tee time, Craft wanted to relax and give his mind and body a rest. He sat back down at the breakfast table to continue the delightful conversation with Daria. She looked radiant, he thought, with the morning light reflecting off her dark skin and modestly placed jewelry to accentuate her petite features.

Genuinely intrigued by her ability to merge Western and Islamic cultures, he listened attentively as she talked about her life growing up in Tehran as the daughter of Amir Turani, an enormously successful businessman. She expressed thanks for a loving, progressive father who supported her in obtaining an education, and appreciated her role in leading the advancement of women's rights across the Middle East. She believed her father to be a great visionary, forging a path for Iran to become a great 21st century nation.

As Daria talked about the passing of her mother, who had died giving birth to her brother, Kamran, it occurred to Peter that, although separated by ocean and culture, they shared a similar childhood. She spoke affectionately of her grandmother, Mama Shirazi, the unselfish person who raised her to be a woman, and the loss she felt upon her grandmother's passing.

She spoke of the close friendship with her brother, and how much she had missed him when he attended school thousands of miles away in Virginia. She talked about the awful fights they'd had growing up, but how they always managed to patch things up. Although Kamran's reckless motorcycle racing was worrisome, she'd learned to appreciate his ability to push to the edge without going over.

Craft found it interesting that she talked about everyone important in her life, but avoided talking about her own dreams. Daria was the founder of a successful worldwide publication, and notorious among some Islamic communities for advocating ungodly Western behavior. He knew she lived in danger every day from Islamic extremists who scorned her independent ways, but she seemed to pay no attention to it.

She realized the attractive man sitting across the table was not one of those fast-talking Wall Street gents who would say anything in hopes of getting an attractive woman into bed. He seemed to sincerely enjoy learning about her and lacked the self-centered tendencies she had encountered with other men in her life.

Aware three hours had passed, Daria said, "I don't want to distract you from preparing today's round."

"Regrettably, I do have to go now," he said, "Are you free tomorrow night for dinner?"

"Yes, I would love to go to dinner," she responded. "My father recommends a family-owned French restaurant in the city called Marcel's."

"Then Marcel's it is. I'll make reservations for tomorrow night at 7PM."

Daria blushed like a young schoolgirl, as the charming American walked out of the room. She tried to push aside the cultural difficulties that would arise if a serious relationship developed between them. She wasn't even sure her brother would approve. While deep in thought, contemplating the possibilities of a romance, she failed to notice Jennifer Wilkins walking across the room in her direction.

Although they greeted each other warmly, they both tried to keep their true feelings hidden. Wilkins proposed they spend time together, watching Kamran finish his morning round, and then watch Craft later in the afternoon. The two ladies left the clubhouse, planning to catch up with Daria's brother who had just finished the 9th hole.

CHAPTER 22

Craft casually walked through the locker room, stopping to talk with some of the players hanging around inside trying to keep cool. It was obvious by the questions asked his competitors expected the physical stress of the U.S. Open to take him down, given his frail medical condition. Although he portrayed his medical issues as a thing of the past, his rapid heart rate made it more difficult than normal to follow a conversation.

When Craft walked out of the clubhouse, children surrounded him hoping to get his autograph. He joked with the kids but found signing autographs taxing. He figured it would be better to deal with the media now than having them yell questions at him while on the course. After providing basic information, sticking to the cover story of an allergic reaction to sleep medication, he tried to change the focus to the First Light program, but the media persisted in wanting more details about his illness.

Wilkins had just returned from watching Kamran compete his round. She observed that Craft appeared frustrated and his speech a bit convoluted. She interrupted the interview, indicating it was time for him to go to the practice range. She found a quiet spot.

"Are you all right?" she asked.

"The medicine is affecting my concentration. My heart is pounding, and I am overly sensitive to everything going on around me. It's hard to concentrate on one thing."

"The medical team is on standby, and I'll be close by," she said.

"I'll be okay, just give me time to adjust."

Hundreds of spectators surrounded the practice area, waiting for the 1:36PM pairing to begin their pre-round practice routine. Craft would be playing with Tiger Woods and Rory McIlroy the first two days of the tournament. The tournament director had intentionally paired Craft with two iconic Tour players to see if the rookie could handle the pressure.

Although now over fifty years old, Woods was still competitive, and proudly held the title bestowed upon him by thousands of sports writers as the best ever to play the game of golf. Woods had won more Major

146   *Tour of Deception*

championships than any other active player on the Tour. His massive following of devoted fans were known for rattling the nerves of competitors.

In 2011, the rookie Rory McIlroy, after losing a seven-stroke lead on Sunday at the Masters, burst onto the golf scene by winning the U.S. Open Championship at Congressional Country Club. He earned great world respect as someone who could overcome adversity to excel, winning several Major tournaments during his illustrious career to include back-to-back Majors in 2014 with wins at the Open and PGA Championships.

Jefferson chatted with the other caddies while waiting in the shade at the practice area for Craft to arrive. Typical of a Washington, DC June afternoon, the temperature was over ninety degrees with oppressive humidity. The caddies joked about the whiny players complaining about the heat and then expecting them to lug a heavy golf bag and be positioned at the golf ball before they arrived.

Jefferson thought the warm temperature would be an advantage for the injured agent, having grown up playing golf in the summer heat of South Carolina. He knew how to keep hydrated, keep his hands dry, find as much shade as possible, and slow the pace to avoid over exertion.

His playing partners were already in the middle of their warm-up routine, when Craft entered the practice area. The mass of spectators cheered for the Masters winner and sponsor of the First Light program.

Craft went to the end of the practice area, far from the other players. A crowd of spectators also moved to the end of the range to watch. He began his routine of hitting three shots with each club. Vaughn watched, anxious to see if he had the resolve to overcome his injuries. His swing appeared solid, and the warm temperature enabled him to turn freely, with minimal pain.

As Craft walked to the short game practice area, he looked to see four players in the lead at four under par, with Kamran one stroke behind the leaders. After practicing a few chip shots and bunker shots, he continued onto the practice green. A crowd of spectators, having stopped to watch the players practice putting, blocked the walkways. The tournament marshals tried to keep people moving, but crowd control was already out of hand with security staff having to take quick action to keep minor altercations from escalating into more violent behavior.

Amongst all the turmoil, he tried to concentrate, but thoughts of Dr. Page filled his head. He could now relate to the pressures of executing a covert mission in the public spotlight. It was apparent his playing partners had developed an inner strength, enabling them to focus as if it was just another day of work, blocking out all distractions. They learned to turn it into a competitive advantage, expecting the fury of the crowd to fluster less seasoned competitors, and it did.

Although going through the motions of hitting putts, Craft's thoughts were scattered. He wished he had a chance to thank Kalani for saving his life. He wondered if he would have won a gold medal at the Olympics if his grandfather had not taken ill. His mind was comparing what life might be like with Wilkins versus Daria, as he glanced over to see the two young ladies talking with Kamran, who had finished his morning round.

Woods and McIlroy began the proud march from practice green to the 1st tee, followed by their caddies. Giving the signal it was time to go, Jefferson picked up the golf bag and began walking toward the tee area, expecting Craft to be close behind. Halfway to the 1st tee, Jefferson looked back to see the agent standing in the middle of the practice green, gazing up into the sky as if in a trance, seeking spiritual guidance.

Jefferson placed the golf bag on the ground and calmly walked back to the practice green. He put his arm around Craft's shoulder and said, "Peter, it's time to go."

Realizing he had completely tuned out, he looked at the official clock to see he had only one minute to check-in at the starter station before being assessed a two-stroke penalty. If late, he would probably be the only player in professional golf history to be on time to the practice green, and late to the 1st tee. He took off, sprinting toward the starter station.

Craft would tee off first. After being announced by the starter, he teed the ball and stood intensely looking at his caddy for the OK signal. Jefferson gave the signal, lifting the towel ready to wipe the golf club. Craft just stood there while Woods, McIlroy and hundreds of spectators watched. After an uncomfortably long time, the crowd started to make noise, with a few rude people yelling, "Hit the ball." The injured agent began to visibly shake. The iconic players, Woods and McIlroy, both remembered the excitement and nerves at the 1st tee of a Major, but this was over the top. Marshals motioned frantically to quiet the spectators.

Trying to regain control, Craft stepped away from the ball, then bent over and pulled the ball and tee out of the ground. He slowly moved to the other end of the tee box and re-teed the ball. Again, he waited for the

OK signal. Not wanting to draw more attention to Craft's strange behavior, Jefferson gave the OK without waiting for the Smartball equipment to reset.

Craft started his backswing with a low and slow take away, enabling a full body turn and then moved aggressively at the ball with a powerful swing. The ball shot off the club head with a mighty thrust, easily clearing the bunker down the right side of the fairway landing 355 yards from the tee, leaving only 50 yards to the flagstick.

Craft's playing partners looked at each other, wondering if they had just witnessed the world's greatest act or a near physical breakdown. Although they had seen Tour players come unglued over the years, the rookie's behavior was off the charts. It took Woods and McIlroy less than a minute to hit their tee shots.

Walking down the fairway, Woods whispered to his caddy, "Is this guy for real?"

"Real enough to shoot ten under par on Sunday to win the Masters," replied the caddy.

"Let's hope this rocket burns out," Woods commented.

"He's had some health issues, so stamina might be an issue," his caddy replied.

The CIA agent got off to a fast start, hitting a sand wedge to within three feet of the hole for an easy birdie. Jefferson made an on-the-spot decision to only use the Smartball technology, if necessary. With the heavy golf bag hanging from his broad shoulders, he gave Wilkins a big smile as he passed by on the way to the 2nd tee, relieved the young man, who only a week ago was near death, was acting like he was superman, hitting a monster drive. It occurred to him, contrary to Dr. Page's psychoanalysis, some day Craft might actually be the best player in the world.

He birdied four of the first nine holes with seven one putts. His playing partners were giving a solid performance, but their putts failed to find the hole. By the 10th hole, Craft's name was at the top of the leader board at four under par.

Wilkins was in the media room at the clubhouse, monitoring network broadcasts. Clips of Craft's unusual behavior on the 1st tee filled the airwaves with speculation. Was it an act? Was he on drugs? Was he just nervous? She could sense the excitement building in the room as this year's Masters Champion was making a strong showing in the first round of the U.S. Open. When a young sports reporter mentioned the possibility of

Craft making a run at golf's Grand Slam, one of the more experienced reporters quickly responded that the rookie had a better chance of getting struck by lightning on a clear day than winning the Grand Slam of Golf. Tiger Woods fans went on the offense, angrily voicing their opinions that even mentioning the rookie Craft and icon Woods in the same breath was a violation of all common sense.

He stood on the tee of the 523-yard par four 18th hole, needing one more birdie to go seven under par and take a three stroke lead. Several strokes behind, his playing partners both needed a birdie to finish the day one under par.

The 18th hole at Congressional was one of the most beautiful and difficult holes in the world. The long approach shot to the peninsula green, surrounded by water on three sides, required an accurate ball flight to get close to the flagstick. Today, the hole was located in the front right portion of the green, one of the easier pin positions.

Although dripping in sweat, Craft appeared comfortable playing in the hot June afternoon sun. On the other hand, Jefferson was hoping to find the strength to carry the heavy bag one more hole before collapsing in exhaustion. In fact, everyone but the man from Charleston looked drained from hours walking in the sweltering heat.

He hit another long drive over the hill, rolling down the fairway to within 140 yards of the flagstick. After reaching the location of his drive, he waited several minutes for the group in front to clear the green and his playing partners to hit their approach shots.

"Why don't you stick one in there close and we'll call it a day," said Jefferson.

"I feel a right-to-left wind. What do you think?" Craft asked.

"Keep the ball below the tree line, and it should be fine," replied Jefferson.

Craft stood over the ball for quite a while, before backing away. His playing partners saw an intense focus similar to when they played at their best. He put the ball back in his stance and visualized a low right-to-left punch shot with a nine iron, similar to the one he'd hit at the 17th hole on Sunday at the Players. He selected a nine iron, took aim and hit the ball low with a soft right-to-left draw. The ball hit three feet in front of the flagstick, bounced forward, hitting the pin, and disappeared into the hole.

McIlroy raced across the fairway to congratulate him with a high five hand slap, acknowledging the exceptional eagle, two under par on the difficult 18th hole at Congressional. Almost to the green, Woods stopped, turned, took off his hat and bowed.

Craft picked his ball out of the hole and stood off to the side waiting for the others to finish. He shook hands with everyone and then walked confidently off the 18th green relieved he had just shot eight under par in the first round of the U.S. Open. Although gracious, his playing partners were visibly disappointed by their own performance, but there was still much golf to be played.

Craft submitted his scorecards and then asked Woods and McIlroy for a few moments of their time. He apologized for the distraction getting started, and explained how playing in his first U.S. Open with two Hall of Fame superstars was simply overwhelming. Both players accepted his apology, and again congratulated him for his excellent first round score. He then had a private conversation with Wilkins regarding the media situation.

When he arrived at the media area, the multitude of reporters, ecstatic about the excitement of the first day at the U.S. Open, blitzed him with questions. The story of the day was Craft's triumph of overcoming a near breakdown—in front of thousands of spectators and two of the best players on the Tour—to post an eight under par, nearly matching the lowest score of nine under par shot only four times in U.S. Open history.

Craft said, "Let's address the elephant in the room. By now, you've probably seen video of my peculiar 1st tee behavior. Most days, I can keep my emotions in check, but not today. Playing in the U.S. Open has been a lifelong dream. Paired with two of the biggest icons in golf history was simply overwhelming. Hell, I was so nervous, my brain just stopped working. Did you see the look on Jefferson's face? I thought he was going to push me aside and hit the ball himself. Following today's round, I apologized to both of them for my unfortunate behavior. Being true gentlemen, they accepted my apology. I am not the first player to be overcome by their presence, and probably won't be the last."

By the time he finished talking, media members were shaking their heads, acknowledging how a rookie could easily be intimidated by the iconic figures.

Someone asked, "How did you manage to pull yourself together to smash a monster drive?"

"Now, that's a great question," said Craft. "Embarrassed about freezing on the tee, something told me to just swing as hard as possible. I wouldn't be surprised, if the video shows my eyes being closed."

When asked about his medical condition, Craft responded, "I think eight under par speaks for itself."

One of Wilkin's media friends gave him the opportunity to shift the conversation, asking, "How much of the winnings do you plan to donate to the First Light program?"

"There are still 54 holes yet to be played, so talking about winnings is a bit premature. With that said, it's still my plan to donate a large portion of any winnings to the First Light program," Craft stated.

Seeing Wilkins waving to get his attention, he walked over to talk with her briefly, and returned to the media area.

"Ms. Wilkins just informed me the First Light program received this morning sizable donations from my playing partners. Now, I really feel bad for my 1st tee screw-up. In all sincerity, please feel free to thank them for their awesome generosity. I will." He walked through the media area, to a group of children waiting for his autograph. Reporters continued to ask questions, as he signed his name on everything the kids could find to hand him. After an hour with the kids, Wilkins interrupted the gathering to announce it was time for Craft to leave for another commitment.

Wilkins accompanied him to the Cadillac sedan provided by the tournament sponsor for him to use, while attending the tournament. She drove back roads to the Washington Beltway, crossed over the Potomac River, and then pulled into a garage in Vienna, Virginia. She entered a code into the navigation system and the door at the back of the garage opened. It was a secure facility, where Vaughn and a medical team waited to give the injured agent a full check out.

The medical team indicated his recovery was simply remarkable, but caution was still necessary. The fast healing drugs, coupled with the euphoria of competing in the U.S. Open, may have masked the real stress on his body. They recommended nourishment, rest, and some light entertainment to give his mind a rest.

A member of the medical team led them to a room towards the back of the building. As they entered the room, there stood Jack Wilson, the Smartball inventor, wearing a chef's hat. The aroma of freshly cooked pasta and spicy sauces filled the room. Although Wilson was a novice at golf, he was an excellent chef, specializing in classic Italian cuisine.

As they sat down to eat, Vaughn said, "I am starving and the food looks marvelous."

"*Buon appetito*," replied Wilson.

After a delicious and nourishing meal, Wilkins and Craft drove back to the Potomac residence. He tried to begin a serious talk about their professional and personal relationship. Given that a few days earlier his life was on the verge of slipping away, she thought a heart-to-heart conversation could wait until another day. Before Craft went any further, she said, "The doctor recommended rest and relaxation. I thought after today's 1st tee antics, you were going to start hitting chili peppers like in the movie *Tin Cup*."

Craft laughed, having seen the classic golf movie several times. In the movie a Texas driving range pro competing in the U.S. Open Championship is so nervous the first day of the tournament, he keeps hitting shanks, referred to as chili peppers, at the practice range, making fellow competitors duck for cover. Jennifer pressed the button on the controller and the movie began to play.

While watching the movie, she received a request for Craft to submit to a voluntary drug test in the morning. In a pre-emptive move to squelch speculation regarding his behavior, she had sent a message to the Tour Commissioner recommending this year's Masters Champion be given a drug test. Of course, the Agency team would make sure the test results came back normal, only showing drugs consistent with an allergic reaction to sleep medication.

CHAPTER 23

TEHRAN, IRAN

The Course Manager at the Sabz Pardes Country Club tossed the financial report on the desk in frustration. He shouted at Mulligan, the black Labrador, sprawled out on the floor, "Is the old man really surprised maintenance costs are higher than normal? Someone needs to tell him that hosting a Major tournament is not normal." The Course Manager was referring to Amir Turani, the owner of the golf course.

Observing the outburst, Mulligan rushed to his master's side and placed one paw on his lap to offer assistance. After receiving a few soft strokes on the head, the dog, relieved all was okay, returned to the floor to save his energy.

In Iran, dogs led an underground life where ownership was technically a violation of Islamic law. Although some people objected to canines, authorities no longer enforced the restrictions. The Course Manager found Mulligan, a trained water dog, to be a wonderful companion. The spirited Labrador kept the geese in the pond areas so they didn't leave a minefield of droppings that made a putrid mess of grassy areas.

The contract with the Tour required the golf course to meet the quality standards for a Major tournament. The amount of pesticides, fertilizers, and water to keep green areas up to standards was much more than originally planned. There were many reasons for increased costs, but none mattered. The message was clear, find a way to reduce costs without degrading course conditions or start looking for another job.

The Course Manager began rummaging through the stack of chemical proposals on his desk, throwing them one after the other into the wastebasket. Near the bottom of the stack he found one proposal that stood out. The company offered favorable prices and daily chemical deliveries and the golf course would only pay for what was actually used. The amount of chemicals required could vary by as much as twenty-five percent depending on the weather. After working the numbers, he determined the cost savings would be enough to get the financials back on track. He called the company.

The CEO answered the phone. After a polite introductory conversation, the Course Manager verified the terms and then listened to the CEO express his desire to establish a long-term relationship with Sabz Pardes and then offered two weeks of free chemicals so their quality could be demonstrated. Delighted with the offer, the General Manager agreed to proposal.

After ending the call, Asadi sat back in his office chair admiring the replica of Mohammad's sword on the wall, knowing another piece of Allah's plan was in place.

WASHINGTON D.C. AREA

Friday morning, Craft stopped by the medical room, submitted to a drug test, and then on to the practice range to prepare for his 7:50AM tee time. Only a few dedicated spectators showed up to watch the early morning players warm up. His playing partners were already hard at work at the range, determined to put the previous day behind them.

Craft struggled to make a full swing through the golf ball, hitting several shots off target. His injured muscles felt like overly wound rubber bands ready to snap. He shook his head in disbelief, when notified that Wilson had set the aggressive target of having an eight-stroke lead by the end of the second round. Given the way he was hitting the ball, having any lead would be a major accomplishment.

Today's start was uneventful, with all three players hitting solid tee shots into the middle of the fairway. McIlroy made a fast move, going four under par in the first seven holes. Woods birdied the 3rd, 4th, and 5th holes, but stumbled a bit with a bogey on the difficult 6th hole, finding the water on his approach shot. Craft struggled, scoring bogeys on the 2nd and 6th holes.

Jefferson tried to slow the pace, hoping to buy him some time to get back on track. Given the previous day's 1st tee follies, a slow play penalty would surely anger his playing partners. Woods and McIlroy, seasoned professionals, accelerated the pace of play, trying to push Craft out of his comfort zone, and it was working. By the 7th hole, Craft's lead had dwindled to one stroke. Some of his shots were too far off line for Smartball to help.

Craft flinched with pain each time the club struck the ground. To reduce the torque on his body, he releasing the club early from the top of his swing, instead of holding off the arms as the hips turned toward the target.

Jefferson thought, *it's time to roll the dice,* when he started hearing spectators making comments regarding Craft's erratic swing. He handed the struggling player a bottle of water and a small chocolate bar containing a strong painkiller and muscle relaxant. Craft finished the front nine tied for the lead with McIlroy, and several other players close behind.

Craft arrived at the 10th tee to face a long 218-yard par three over water. His playing partners had already hit their tee shots safely into the middle of the green. With the drugs kicking in, Craft felt a jolt of energy as he took two pain-free practice swings. His tight swing had loosened with the warm temperature, now in the mid 80s. He hit the ball solidly straight at the pin, but the ball continued past the flagstick, landing in the bunker behind the green.

Trying not to show his frustration, Craft looked at his golf ball almost completely buried in sand near the back edge of the bunker, and the short-sided flagstick resting in the hole cut a few feet directly in front of the bunker. He looked at the dreadful bunker shot from every side. Hitting a buried golf ball out of a sand trap on a downhill line, with water off the front of the green, was an extremely difficult shot, even for the best of players.

The announcer in the tower overlooking the 10th green commented, "The rookie appears to be going at the flagstick. This shot will take nothing short of a miracle to get up and down. If he hits too deep into the sand, the ball will probably stay in the bunker. If he catches the ball solid, there's a good chance it will fly back over the green into the water. Major tournament archives are filled with stories of rookies who self-destructed on the course, trying to hit high-risk shots instead of playing the odds. The best players have the mental strength for effective course management, but most learned it the hard way."

Jefferson handed the player his sand wedge, assuming he would hack out of the bunker on to the middle of the green. Craft put the club back in the bag and pulled out his 64-degree wedge, the most lofted club in the bag. Jefferson slowly picked up the golf bag and backed away, leaving plenty of time to reconsider. Craft dug his feet in deep and choked up on the club. He raised the club steeply, and then blasted into the sand. A perfectly hit flop shot, the ball few straight up in the air and back down, landing next to the hole for a tap-in score of par. The crowd erupted with ear shattering cheers.

Excited, an announcer commented, "My hat goes off to Mr. Craft, who just made an impossible shot look easy."

Craft walked to the 11th tee, still tied for the lead with McIlroy, with the confidence of having just executed a great recovery shot. The 494-yard hole was rated the most difficult par 4 on the Tour, with trees lining the left side of the fairway and a stream running along the right side, with a water hazard guarding the green, providing a wet landing for overly aggressive approach shots. Most played safe approach shots, aiming at the center left portion of the green. Today, the pin was located on the front right side of the green, a few feet from the water's edge. Years ago, players were more inclined to hit at the front-right flagstick, because a strategically located bunker would stop balls before they went into the water hazard. In preparation for the 2011 U.S. Open, Tiger Woods recommended removing the bunker on the right side of the 11th green to make the course more suitable for a Major tournament.

His playing partners hit their drives to the middle of the fairway leaving a long second shot into the green. Feeling loose and pain free, Craft adjusted his golf swing to get more power into the ball. He hit the ball with a crushing swing but to his surprise, the ball pushed right, flying over the stream deep into the woods. Getting ready to hit a provisional tee shot in case the first was lost, a tournament marshal signaled his ball had been found.

While Craft marched across the stream and into the trees, his playing partners hit safe shots to the left portion of the green. The errant shot had come to rest near a walkway providing spectators access to the 11th hole. Surrounded by trees, even chipping out of the woods, over the stream to the fairway presented a problem. The good news was the ball sat on hard ground so he could get a clean strike at the back of the ball with a full swing.

Not liking the odds of chipping to the fairway, Craft asked, "What do you think? Should we head back to the tee?"

Pointing to an opening in the trees on a direct line to the green, Jefferson responded, "I think you could hit a high five iron on line to the green."

Looking at the opening in the trees, Craft said, "It's a tight shot."

"Piece of cake," whispered Jefferson, handing him a five iron.

Watching Craft prepare to take another risky shot, McIlroy commented, "This kid is fearless. He reminds me of my younger days."

"I'd break your clubs before letting you take that shot," replied McIlroy's caddy.

With a mighty swing, Craft struck the ball, sending it flying through the gap in the trees. After a long period of silence, loud cheers radiated from the 11th green. The ball had landed on the green, coming to rest near the flagstick for an easy birdie putt. His playing partners shook their heads in disbelief.

Craft walked to the next tee with a one-stroke lead. He then birdied five of the next seven holes, recovering from errant tee shots on almost every hole. He walked off the 18th green having shot four under par for the day and twelve under par for the two day total. As they walked to the scorer's station to submit their scorecards, Craft again thanked his playing partners for their generous donations to the First Light program.

Jokingly, McIlroy said, "I have seen all the shots you hit today at one time or another in my career, but never within in the span of nine holes. You could have a second career as a magician. I look forward to playing with you again."

•

Craft retrieved a sandwich and drink out of the refrigerator, and sat by the swimming pool under an umbrella. Seeing dark clouds beginning to form out to the west, he thought the guys playing this afternoon were going to get wet. After eating his sandwich, the agent slipped on a swimming suit and dove into the pool. The warm water felt good and he could feel his strength coming back. He replayed in his head every shot of this morning's round of golf. He couldn't remember a time when he had hit more bad shots in a single round than today. At the same time, he couldn't remember a round when he succeeded at hitting more successful recovery shots. Things were definitely getting out of control.

He looked up to see Wilkins standing on the pool deck in a stylish summer dress. She stood there looking at him with a towel in one hand and the other hand on her hip. "You obviously didn't get the message."

"I've been a little busy today, if you didn't notice."

"Is that what you want me to tell our nation's President?"

"Okay, what's up?"

"The President wants to meet this year's Masters Champion at 3:45PM today at the White House. If you hurry, we have just enough time to get there, if traffic cooperates. It's not a good career move to blow off the President; he's rather important in our business."

Lightly splashing water at her, Craft said, "Meeting the President in wet clothes is not a good move either."

He walked up the steps of the pool and stood in front of her with water dripping off his body. She tossed him the towel and watched as he wiped the water off his back and legs. Although badly bruised, she marveled at his athletic physique. She wanted to take her clothes off and fall into his arms, but they had a mission to perform and time was running out.

He activated the application on his HuAID, to check for bugs in the car, as they drove out of the Potomac home headed for the White House. The car was clean.

"Why do you think the President really wants to meet?" he inquired.

"Although it's an annual tradition for the President to invite the Masters champion to the White House, I suspect he wants to discuss the mission. Recent Intel indicates the Iranian situation is heating up and it's now a re-election issue. He has a no-win situation on his hands. If he issues an Executive Order stopping U.S. participation in the tournament then he will lose 'big business' support. On the other hand, if terrorists strike, he will lose public support three weeks before the election. So, the President has a lot riding on our program and probably wants to meet you in person to assess the odds of success."

"Has the President been briefed on Red Crescent?"

Wilkins told the story about how Director Walker challenged the President to a golf match where she secretly used Smartball, before getting him to approve the program.

"Why didn't I know about this?" he asked.

"You didn't have a need to know until now," she responded.

"I guess you're right. It's hard enough knowing Director Walker is directly involved," he replied.

"How are you doing after today's difficulties?" she asked.

"My body and mind are not connecting the way they should. My tee shots on the back nine were awful. What makes matters worse is my swing felt okay, so I'm not sure what changes to make. If tomorrow is like today then I'm afraid the odds are going to catch up with us, and the outcome won't be good."

Placing her hand on his to console him, she replied, "You'll figure it out."

"So, what's going on in the media world?"

"Well, the sports networks are running nonstop coverage of your miracle shots on the back nine today. They are using flattering terms such as 'Houdini' and 'Tigerlike' to refer to your ability to hit spectacular shots to escape trouble. Also, other players are becoming really annoyed by all the media attention you're getting. You need to be mentally tough. I suspect some nasty stuff is headed in your direction. By the way, Daria called, upset Kamran got into a shoving match with another player who had unkind things to say about you. She said it got pretty ugly."

"Kamran can handle himself," he commented.

Just as they drove into a parking garage at New York Avenue and 15th street, the skies opened up with a downpour from an afternoon thundershower. She pulled two umbrellas out of the back seat, handed one to him, and said, "We have five minutes to go a half mile, check-in at the guard's desk, and be ready to meet the President."

They both started jogging through the rain, trying not to splash water on each other.

On the way she asked, "Do you have identification?"

"I have three different ones. Which one do you want me to use?" he said jokingly.

"Don't be a smart ass," she responded. "The Secret Service lacks a sense of humor."

The guard at the entrance validated they were on the guest list, handed them badges to put on and motioned them to go through the security gate. They put their fingers on the biometric reader and the security gate opened. A staff assistant was waiting to escort them.

As they entered the Oval Office, the President was sitting at a big oak desk, talking on the telephone. He motioned for them to come in, hung up the phone and walked across the room to greet them. After a few moments of casual introductions, the President asked the staff assistant to leave the room, and shut the door. A few seconds later, another door open and a Secret Service agent appeared.

The President led them out of the room to a nearby elevator and then hit an unmarked elevator button, while looking into a mirror. Behind the mirror hid a retina biometric scanner. The elevator started moving downward, no telling how many floors. When the elevator stopped and the door opened, the President led them into a secure room.

The President sat at the end of the table, with Walker, Wilson, and Vaughn sitting on one side of the table and Craft and Wilkins on the other.

"Thank you for coming," said the President. "I wanted to have this talk because you're the people doing the heavy lifting for the Red Crescent program. Thanks to your excellent work, we now have hard evidence Islamic extremists are targeting the Asian Open. Today, we're at a crossroads and a decision must be made soon. Given the evidence, I could issue an Executive Order stopping U.S. participation in the tournament. While politically viable, this option troubles me because the bad guys get a moral victory. Alternatively, if we go forward with the program, then the focus must shift from intelligence collection to threat elimination."

To lighten the mood while everyone thought about the implications of his words, the President commented, "You know my Chief of Staff thinks I've taken my eyes off the ball, watching too much golf, instead of attending to the national security business. I would love to tell him that my watching golf is national security business, but Director Walker has sworn me to absolute secrecy. Did the Director tell you how she bamboozled me into a golf match, to get the go ahead for the program?"

Vaughn spoke up, "Mr. President, would you consider pursuing the elimination of the terrorist threat on an accelerated schedule, leaving open the option to issue an Executive Order as the backup?"

"Yes, but if the word gets out nuclear material is missing, then issuing an Executive Order will be the only viable option," answered the President.

Director Walker spoke up. "We now have hard intelligence a large amount of nuclear waste from the Bushehr Nuclear Power Plant was hijacked the day Mr. Craft arrived in Tehran. Iran's Supreme Leader has assigned General Shirazi to track down the materials and bring those responsible to justice. The Iranian leadership has kept the incident under wraps, hoping to resolve it without disruption to the tournament."

"That explains why Shirazi had urgent business in Tehran, and was unable to be at his estate during my visit," Craft commented.

Talking directly to Craft, the President said, "As you know from firsthand experience, the spy business is dangerous. Given your recent injuries, I am concerned the nation is asking too much of you."

By the look on Vaughn's face, Craft knew his answer would influence the President's decision. "Sir, it a great honor to meet you. It gives me comfort to know you've taken a personal interest in this important program. Some people say golf is not a team sport. In the traditional sense, they're correct. But golf as it relates to this mission is all about a team effort, and I am proud to be a member of this extraordinary team. Mr. Vaughn has led the revival of a program that two weeks ago was on life support, and is now back on track in the fight against terrorism. Everyone on the team has personal motivations driving him or her to excel. I would like to share mine."

Taking a moment to gather his thoughts, Craft continued, "My father was a New York City firefighter who lost his life in the first 9/11 terrorist attacks. Every night, I pray for the strength and opportunity to play a fulfilling role in protecting this great nation. When it comes to fighting the evils of terrorism, the nation cannot ask too much of me."

Moved, the President said, "Over the years, I have come across a few remarkable individuals who always seem to find a way to adapt and overcome whatever obstacles are placed in their way. Watching you the last couple of days coping with injury, the media, and the challenges of a Major tournament, the word that comes to mind is 'amazing.' Watching some of the golf shots you pulled off today on the back nine, a better word would be 'miraculous.' I am confident you will find a way to defeat these evil bastards."

The President asked Wilkins and Craft to accompany him back to his office. Since the cover for their visit was a routine meeting with the Masters Champion, they would have to leave the White House through normal channels. The others would leave through an underground exit reserved for off-the-record visits with clandestine personnel.

After exiting the White House, Craft informed Wilkins of his plans to spend the evening in the city. She didn't push for details because earlier in the day she had overhead Daria tell her brother she would be dinning in the city with Craft.

With two hours to spare before meeting Daria for dinner, he walked over to the National Mall to tour the Smithsonian American Art Museum. He thought about his White House meeting while touring the museum. He figured it was the President's way of creating a sense of urgency. The President's words, "*the focus must shift from intelligence collection to threat elimination*" were fixed in his mind. Did he really expect the team to change into a special operations team overnight? Although eager to engage, and if needed, kill terrorists, Craft knew his limitations.

While strolling down Pennsylvania Avenue toward Marcel's restaurant, he checked his HuAID. With all second rounds finished, he had a four-stroke lead going into the weekend. His lead was half the target score set by Wilson to ensure a high probability of winning. To make matter worse, the forecast for the weekend was sweltering afternoon heat. Although he felt good at the moment, he knew with his weakened condition holding the lead would be a grind.

Craft enjoyed a cold drink while he watched the sports broadcast on the display over the bar at Marcel's restaurant. A local sports station was showing video clips of his morning round. The sports announcer made a bold prediction that the rookie from Charleston would fall apart under the weekend pressure.

A patron also watching the broadcast noticed the U.S. Open leader sitting at the bar. He turned to Craft and said, "He needs to do his homework."

"Why's that?" Craft asked.

"I watched you play at Clemson," the patron said. "You're the least likely person to fold under pressure."

"Thanks you for the vote of confidence," Craft said and then began to talk enthusiastically with the patron about Clemson football, expecting his dinner companion to arrive any moment.

Daria walked into the restaurant, wearing a modest semi-formal black dinner dress. Craft excused himself, and walked over to greet his dinner companion. She captured the eyes of every person within viewing distance. He started to give her a kiss on the cheek, and then pulled back, holding out his hand. *A picture of them kissing broadcast over the Islamic networks would be an unnecessary complication*, he thought. With a look of disappointment, she shook his hand.

The headwaiter showed them to their table. The restaurant, tastefully decorated with classic Belgian-French furniture and paintings, was perfect for a quiet, elegant evening.

Daria said, "I appreciate the dinner invitation. I was dreading another lonely dinner at the hotel."

"I find it hard to believe you have difficulty finding dinner companions."

"Normally I don't, but my brother is totally consumed with the tournament. He's locked in his room watching video of today's round. I probably shouldn't tell you this," she said.

"Why not? I'm good at keeping a secret."

"Kamran had a vision of once again playing against you in the final group on Sunday," Daria confided.

Sensing she was conflicted, Craft asked, "How do you feel about your brother's vision?"

"Of course I want my brother to win."

"Then you must want me to lose," he responded, making a sad face.

"What I want... is a glass of wine," she replied.

They both ordered a glass of French Cabernet Sauvignon and continued talking. Craft asked questions about her work as the founder and editor of *Persian Woman* Magazine. He wanted to know how she found a balance between glamour and modesty that would sell to both Western and Islamic nations.

Daria referred to a market survey that indicated Westerners were tired of provocative girls dressed in clothes leaving nothing to the imagination. They wanted to see beautiful women dressed in colorful, well-designed clothing that captured the imagination. Although the styles contained in her magazine were far from traditional Islamic attire, the most important attribute was an image of modesty and intrigue.

"So you've built a global publication around your own attributes."

Daria smiled, because he'd said what she was too humble to say. The magazine was designed to reflect her life, bridging both Western and Islamic cultures with a Persian touch.

The waiter stood patiently at the table waiting for the two to pause their conversation. Daria ordered lamb tenderloin and he ordered a classic *boudin blanc*.

After eating their dinner, Daria said, "Enough about me. Tonight, it's your turn to educate me about your life growing up in Charleston."

Craft talked passionately about his childhood and how mother and grandfather, made sure he had every opportunity to participate in activities that interested him, and there were many. Daria asked questions, indicating she knew more about him than he had revealed. When questioned, she admitted receiving a copy of his bio from her uncle prior to Kamran's visit to Ponte Vedra Beach.

"You've talked fondly about your mother and grandfather. Tell me about your father," she asked.

Craft was ready to give the cover story that had been worked out by the team, and supported by manufactured evidence, if someone chose to investigate.

"I never knew my father. Unfortunately, he died before my birth. For all practical purposes, my grandfather was the male figure in my life," answered Craft.

Sensing he was uncomfortable about the subject, Daria said, "It's fine with me if you would rather not talk about him."

"No that's okay. It's a wonderful love story that ended much too tragically. My mother is a gifted writer. Right now she's onsite in Australia, writing a movie script. After graduating Clemson University, my mother attended graduate school at New York University with dreams of being a Broadway scriptwriter. During her time in New York, she fell deeply in love with another graduate student from Nashville, Tennessee. During the summer, my father proposed marriage to my mother and gave her a magnificent engagement ring. In August of that year, my father traveled back to Nashville for a friend's wedding. Occupied with final exams, my mother was unable to accompany him on the trip."

Stopping for a few seconds to let his emotions calm, Craft continued, "My father and his parents were killed in a tragic car accident in a severe thunder storm. Brokenhearted by the news, my mother returned to Charleston, only to discover she was pregnant. My mother's father was there from day one to raise me. Of course I missed not having a father, but my grandfather was a wonderful man who had plenty of time to spend with me, having retired from work soon after my birth. My grandfather took ill during my last year of college. After graduating, I returned to Charleston to help my mother care for him until he died two years ago."

"Seeing the way you turned out I would say your parents did a terrific job raising you. I would love to meet your mother some day," said Daria.

When it was time to leave, Craft ask the maître d to arrange for a taxi. By the time they walked out of the restaurant, a taxicab was waiting. Craft opened the door, and Daria slid across the back seat, leaving room for him to sit by her side.

The driver asked, "Where are you going?"

"The Ritz Carlton, at Tysons Corner," she answered.

Seeing the name on the licenses attached to the dashboard, Craft engaged Amid, the taxi driver, in casual conversation. Within seconds, Craft had discovered Amid's interests and put him at ease, inquiring about his city experiences in the nation's capitol. Amazed by the interpersonal skills of her American friend, she listened as they talked.

By the time they reached the hotel, she knew Amid was passionate Washington Nationals baseball fan, visited his parents in India once each year, had two brothers living in the states, one in Boston and the other in Atlanta, was not married but was engaged to a woman from his homeland, knew nothing about golf, and had no idea he was talking with the current leader of the U.S. Open Championship. Arriving at the hotel, Amid jumped out of the car to open the door, and with a big smile, volunteered to wait while Craft escorted the young lady into the hotel.

In the hotel lobby, she stopped, turned, looked into his eyes, and in a sincere tone said, "I had a wonderful evening."

Craft leaned forward to give her a friendly kiss good night. She responded by moving closer so he could feel her body and see the desire in her eyes. They kissed, almost uncontrollably for a few seconds. After saying good night, Daria turned and began slowly walking across the lobby toward the elevator, knowing he was watching her every move. His heart was beating fast and it wasn't the medicine; it was the feeling of having kissed the beautiful Persian woman who left him wanting so much more.

Returning to the taxi, he thanked the driver for waiting, and asked to be taken to the Potomac residence. Soon the car turned into the driveway, Craft entered a code into his HuAID and the front gate opened. He bid the driver good night, wished him well with his upcoming wedding, paid his fare, and gave him a substantial tip. He then walked up the grand stairs leading to the front door. When he opened the front door, he could see Wilkins sitting in the living room reading a magazine. He suspected she had dropped by the house to share some timely intelligence regarding Daria Turani, to splash cold water on his delightful evening.

Visibly irritated by her unannounced visit, Craft inquired, "Jennifer, what brings you here so late at night?"

She pushed aside her jealous feelings for the moment and sarcastically replied, "While you were enjoying the city night life, I spent the evening with Jack Wilson."

"Really," he declared, "Wilson is a nice guy but you could do better."

"Seriously, I have important information to share."

"Did you sweep for bugs?"

"Of course. Now do you want to hear what I have to say, or are more important things on your mind?"

"Okay, what's up?" he asked.

"Wilson replayed the video of today's round. As far as he could see, you were striking the ball solid off the tee but the ball was going off-line just about the time Smartball was supposed to correct the ball flight. Wilson did some calculations and determined the probability of your hitting thirteen tee shots off-line in a single round of golf was one in a million. He discussed his findings with Vaughn, who then asked the technology guys to get involved. They pulled the launch data from the Smartball equipment, and ran a simulation of where your tee shot should have landed, based on the launch data. The data validated Wilson's hunch. Eleven of the thirteen tee shots should have landed in reasonable positions, but they didn't. So the question was, why didn't they?"

Having his complete attention, she couldn't stop herself saying, "Oh, I forgot to ask; how was your evening?"

Not giving him time to respond, she continued, "The technology guys determined the equipment was working correctly, so we started to search Intel databases looking for answers. You won't believe what we discovered."

Enjoying the opportunity to drag the story out, she excused herself to get a drink of water. Craft followed her into the kitchen, insisting she get to the point.

"A Marine Corps group located at Quantico was testing a new intercept capability to take enemy Smart Weapon projectiles off target. The intercept scrambles the electromagnetic pulse controlling the weapon. Did I ever tell you I took computer science in college and love this technology stuff? Anyway, they verified the Smartball signals were being scrambled by the intercept. It didn't affect putts because the ball was on the ground."

Mentally exhausted by her dramatics and barbs, he asked, "So what does it all mean? Will I have to play out of the woods the next two days?"

"No," she said, "the issued been solved. The President asked the Secretary of Defense to issue an immediate directive requiring a strategic pause to the Smart Weapon Intercept program."

"Are you telling me, the President had to get involved?"

"Yes, and Director Walker, too," she answered. "It has been a crazy night, but don't worry. I covered for you, and made sure no one interrupted your evening plans. Oh, you better watch your back. Some pretty pissed-off Marine generals will be attending the golf tournament tomorrow. Don't worry though; the storm will blow over in a couple of days when the strategic pause is lifted."

Unable to resist, she declared, "I've been doing all the talking. Please tell me about your evening."

"Why couldn't you wait to tell me this tomorrow?"

"I thought after your erratic performance today, you might be contemplating some early morning swing changes."

Even though she was taking great pleasure at irritating him, he could see the bloodshot eyes of someone who had worked nonstop for hours. He sincerely thanked her for the information, and suggested she stay the night in the guest room, rather than drive back to her hotel. She picked up the travel bag containing her clothes that was hidden behind a piece of furniture, and then preceded to the guest room. Craft caught a glimpse of the magazine she left on the coffee table. It was the June issue of *Persian Woman* with a glamour shot of Daria Turani dressed like a Persian princess on the cover. He picked up the magazine with both hands, and scrutinized the photo. He thought the close-up of Daria's face perfectly captured her dark complexion, strong jaw, long flowing black hair, and deep enchanting eyes. Having studied Persian culture, he marveled at the similarities between her face and those he studied of ancient royalty.

CHAPTER 24

When Wilkins woke the next morning, she strolled into the kitchen, wearing the Clemson Tigers football jersey, Number 11, covering her body down to her knees. The kitchen table had place settings for two, with coffee, orange juice, toast, and a bowl of fruit ready to be served. She scanned messages from the team, and then activated the application used to track team members. The tracker indicated Craft was somewhere downstairs on the first level. With a glass of orange juice in one hand and a piece of toast in the other, she went in search of him. She roamed from room to room, until she heard sounds similar to wind from a big fan cycling between high and low speeds. She peeked around the corner to look into the room where the noise originated.

Craft was engaged in intense exercising, working out on a rowing machine positioned so he could look out at the Potomac River below. He was dressed in shorts with his shirt off. She could see the power in his back and legs as he moved back and forth on the machine. After taking a moment enjoying the view, sipping the juice, and eating the toast, she flicked the wall light switch to get his attention.

"Good morning," he said. "I see you're wearing my jersey."

"Do you want it back? I could take it off right now."

"No. It looks better on you than it ever did on me."

"Then, I suggest we have some breakfast and then get to work."

"Good idea."

While eating breakfast, they discussed plans for First Light and prepared for the media attention that would intensify over the next two days. Looking at the clock to see his 2:44PM tee time was still hours away, he stood, walked around the table, reached out to take her hands, and then gently pulled her out of the chair. She looked into his deep blue eyes and then rested her head on his chest, with his strong arms wrapped around her.

Craft said, "It's time we talk about us."

Tentatively, she agreed, although she would rather just stand there all day in the comfort of his embrace. They sat next to each on the sofa in the family room.

Craft began the difficult conversation. "Our time together in Charleston when we first met was special, but…"

"But what?" she interrupted.

"It wasn't real. You were testing the new agent and I was having fun seeing how far you would go. Simply put, our relationship was a fantasy."

"In our business, what's wrong with pretending?" she said, putting her head against his shoulder.

"Life isn't a game," he responded, showing the frustration lingering inside him.

"Did you think I was pretending when I sat by your bedside, praying for you to find the strength to make it through the night?"

"That's my point!" he proclaimed, "Were you praying for me to make it through the night because the mission depended on me living, or because my death would deeply hurt you?"

She pulled away, annoyed. "If you really want to know, the answer is both."

He put his arm around her shoulders and pulled her close again. In a soft tender voice, he said, "I suppose, for some people it could be both, just not for me. I want a relationship built on honesty. To do that, we have to know each other as real people, not manufactured images created by the Agency."

"You're making it too complicated. Let's enjoy our time together, and see where the journey takes us."

"What journey? Our relationship can't go anywhere," he proclaimed. "It's a dead end."

"If you have already made up your mind, then why are we talking?"

"I am trying to explain," he said in frustration.

"So what's really bothering you?" she asked.

"My life as Peter Craft from Charleston, South Carolina is real. Your life as Jennifer Wilkins is an Agency creation. I will never get to know the real you, Victoria Beach from Lincoln, Nebraska, because that's a connection that must never be revealed. So, when you go back to being Victoria, our relationship must end."

She knew on one level he was right. When the mission ended, the life of Jennifer Wilkins would end. A plane crash, a car accident, a house fire, street violence—the how didn't matter, but it would end, like the final act of a theater production.

She thought through what he was saying. "We both want the same thing; we just have different ways of getting it. I also want an honest relationship. That's why I have chosen not to live my life as Victoria Beach. Sure, within the databases I am the girl from Lincoln, Nebraska, but that's not me. Since my parent's death years ago, the life of Victoria Beach is just a memory, a wonderful memory, but still a memory. My personal life and professional life are one and the same. I am Jennifer Wilkins and anyone else that I have to be in the future."

"That might work for you but I will always be Peter Craft from Charleston."

"Do you really think you can have an honest relationship with someone and hide your secret life as an agent? If you can, then go for it. I know I couldn't."

He was at a loss for words. His mind told him there was truth to what she was saying, but she was a professional at manipulating people. While the concern in her eyes appeared real, what was going on in her mind was a mystery and probably always would be.

"You might not want to admit it, she continued, "but, like it or not, we're connected."

"We have a professional relationship, that's all," he insisted.

"Think about it from my perspective. It's my job to be thinking about you twenty-four hours a day, seven days a week. When we lost track of you during the VIPER I operation, I felt as if the fate of my best friend was uncertain. I held the phone in my hand, wanting it to ring with your voice at the other end. Our relationship may be artificial to you, but it's more than real to me."

Craft thought about what she was saying. One thing he knew to be true. Jennifer Wilkins was a person he could trust with his life and someone he would go to the ends of the earth to help, if he thought she was in danger. They talked for hours, before it was time to put the conversation aside and turn their attention to the mission at hand. They agreed to put the mission first, and again put their personal relationship aside for now.

A strong-willed person, Wilkins ended the conversation by having the last word. "With regard to our relationship having to end with the mission, all I can say is... *motivated people find a way.*"

CHAPTER 25

POTOMAC, MD

The hype around a rookie player being in contention to win a second Major was heating up. Security waited in the reserved parking area to escort them to the clubhouse. The security force pushed aside the aggressive reporters, blocking the way as they walked to the clubhouse.

Craft glanced at the leader board in the locker room to see the name of Turani had moved nearer to the top. The Iranian, along with four other players, was within four strokes of the lead.

His mind was clouded with an endless list of thoughts: *his meeting with President, dinner with Daria, yesterday's debacle on the back nine, his conversation with Wilkins, the First Light program, the media, his mother, the weather…*

His psychological training automatically took over. He began an exercise of deep breathing and mind control meditation. Before long, he was ready to play, with a total focus on golf and the mission, his mind cleansed of other thoughts, at least for now.

By the time he teed off on the 1st hole, Kamran Turani had just posted a remarkable score of nine under par, to take a three-stroke lead. The Red Crescent team did not see this coming. Wilson had put the chances of the Iranian being in the last group on Sunday a long shot, based on past performance. Wilson determined Craft would have to shoot seven under par to retain a four-stroke lead going into Sunday.

With the help of Smartball, he performed exceptionally well hitting fairways and greens, and making putts. Toward the end of the round, his physical condition was beginning to deteriorate, hitting shots astray. Hours in near hundred-degree temperatures had taken its toll on both player and caddy. Craft and Jefferson walked slowly down the 18th hole far behind the others. Craft took three shots to reach the 18th green, he then three putted the green to finish with a score of double-bogey. Even with a score of six on the 18th, he had managed to post a six under par to retain a three-stroke lead going into Sunday.

The scorer's station was at the top of a long hill next to the clubhouse.

Craft could feel the energy draining out of his body, and making it up the hill was going to be a struggle. He pretended to be discussing the score with Jefferson.

Seeing the player's eyes beginning to dilate, Jefferson signaled Wilkins, who was standing close by, that Craft was in trouble. Wilkins pulled off the scarf around her neck, reached into a cooler of nearby marshals and soaked the scarf in ice water. She flashed her VIP pass, and stepped under the rope to join the player and caddy. She put her arms around Craft, pretending to be his girlfriend giving him a big hug, but holding the cold scarf to the back of his neck. She kissed him for all to see, taking the attention away from his weakened condition.

As he struggled to walk, she whispered into his ear, "We are going up the hill together."

He put his arm around her shoulders, and they walked up the hill with her supporting most of his weight. It took all her strength to walk up the hill with the weight of his 220-pound frame leaning on her. Trying to take his mind off the situation and not show his weakened physical condition, she softly whispered a phrase she learned as a child, about a small train struggling to go up a big hill, "I think I can, I think I can, ..."

When they reached the scorer's station, Jefferson assisted him with reviewing and signing the scorecard, while she asked an official inside the scorers' station for two bottles of cold water. She helped him drink one bottle, while holding the other bottle on his neck. Craft's signature on the scorecard was unrecognizable. The scoring official asked him multiple times if he was officially submitting his score. The officials could see he was having difficulty responding and suggested calling the medical team. With Wilkins holding the cold water on his neck, his physical condition started to improve.

Finally, Craft asked the official scorer if he could take another look at his scorecard before submitting it. He reviewed the score of each hole with Jefferson and Wilkins. The math didn't matter, what was important was having the score right for each hole played. After correcting an incorrect score on the 16th hole, Jefferson agreed the scorecard was correct. Craft signed with a legible signature, and the official scorer checked it against the computer and gave the okay.

Still recovering, he sat in a chair in the players' locker room, pretending to watch the news. Having played in the last group, it wasn't long before all the other players had departed the clubhouse. He managed to get himself into the shower, letting the cold water bring his body temperature back to normal. Feeling better, he left the clubhouse through the back entrance to the reserved parking lot, and began driving back to the Potomac residence. While driving, the thought crossed his mind that Kamran's vision was coming true. They would be playing together in the final group of the U.S. Open Championship. This was a situation of unintended consequences. The possibility that the Iranian might shoot nine under par to be positioned in the last group of the tournament was a remote possibility he never considered.

When he turned down the street to the Potomac residence, Craft saw a crowd of people blocking the gated entrance. Reporters were irked he had not given a public interview so they decided to pay him a visit. Driving through a crowd of screaming people was not an image he wanted broadcast around the world. With only seconds to think as the crowd approached, he asked himself what would Wilkins do. He threw his HuAID into the glove compartment, pulled to the side of the road, stepped out of the car, and began walking confidently toward the crowd.

With a big smile, he said, "By the looks of things, you would think someone important lived around here."

The press started pushing and shoving. Craft said, "Please, let's be civil. I will stay as long as necessary to answer your questions."

"Why did you leave without giving a press interview?" A reporter asked.

"First, I want to apologize for leaving. I know you're just trying to do your job. Family obligation drove my behavior. My mother was waiting for my call immediately after the round. I always call to give her an update, but this time my HuAID was missing, and her number is programmed into the device. I knew she would be concerned if I didn't call. For those of you who do not know, my mother is temporarily on assignment in Australia. As you might expect, she worries and might feel the necessity to fly back to the states to make sure everything is okay. Now, I could stand here and answer your questions, or go into the house and make an important call. Which do you prefer?"

One reporter spoke up, "I am from Charleston, and worked with Amanda Craft at the *Charleston News*. I suggest it's in all our best interests to let the young man go call his mother."

Craft thanked everyone for understanding his dilemma, and promised to be at the clubhouse early the next day to be interviewed and answer questions. He drove the car slowly down the street, through the gates, and into the garage. He reached into the glove compartment, and pulled out his HuAID device. He called Wilkins, and asked her to drop by to discuss the media debacle.

Craft used his application on the HuAID to sweep the house for bugs. With all the media attention, he needed to pay particular attention to security. When Wilkins arrived, he explained the situation and told her about the story he contrived. She suggested he call his mother immediately to explain what happened, before she heard it from someone else.

"You can bet the electrons were already flying around the world," said Wilkins.

Reporters were already speculating about what occurred after today's round; mostly about the subject of the day, "Wilkins' relationship with Craft."

"Sorry for the public love scene. Given the situation, it was all I could think of at the time," she explained.

"You did what you had to do," replied Craft. "I don't believe how weak I got out there today."

"I talked with the medical team," responded Wilkins. "They are amazed at how well you have held up with your injuries, the medication, and the heat. As good as you are, everyone has limits, and today we were out there hanging on the edge. Tonight, you need rest, a healthy home cooked meal, and plenty of fluids."

Craft called his mother while she cooked dinner and pretended not to be listening to the conversation. Having studied Amanda Craft's bio, she could project the nature of her inquiries. It was evident his mother wanted to know how he was holding up given his medical issues. She listened as he gave his mother details about the tournament, his Iranian friends, and other personal things. She knew at one point Amanda must have asked about their relationship, because he quickly changed the subject.

He hung up the phone. "She still treats me like a child. I am surprised she didn't ask if I brushed my teeth this morning."

"I think that's a common quality of good mothers," Wilkins responded. "I suspect your mother is a fascinating person and I hope to meet her some day. Do you think she'll make it to Scotland for the Open?"

He had a feeling she already knew the answer. "I suspect the Agency has something to do with my mother's exile. It's too much of a coincidence she gets an offer to be a scriptwriter for a new movie in Australia the day I return to Charleston to begin the mission. I have to admit it's a win-win situation. She has an opportunity of a lifetime, and I don't have to deal with my mother's involvement, on top of everything else."

"I didn't know about that, but I suspect you're right. What I do know is your mother would have found time to be at every tournament, if she was anywhere in the States. I suspect it bothers her greatly not being there to see you win the Masters, and tomorrow when you win the U.S. Open, her guilt will be even greater. Honestly, I wouldn't be surprised if she tells the movie director, like it or not, she is going take a few days off, to see her son play at the Open. I hope she does, so I can meet her."

Wilkins had prepared swordfish and a salad. After dinner, Craft decided to take a swim in the pool, to relax and think through the unexpected situation of being paired in the last group with the Iranian. It was the first time the thought of losing passed through his mind. He knew that Kamran was determined, and would be a fierce competitor. He was floating on his back relaxing when he felt a splash. He stood up to see Wilkins gliding through the water with the strokes of someone who had been well trained in competitive swimming.

She stopped for a moment. "You don't think you're the only one who knows how to swim, do you?"

He stepped out of the pool, dried off, and sat in the chair watching her long, lean body swim up and down the pool. Seeing her swim with such grace and power reminded him again that she had a great advantage in their relationship. She knew everything about him, and he still had much to discover about her. For a brief moment, *he delighted in the possibilities of the unknown.*

CHAPTER 26

As promised, Craft arrived early at Congressional on Sunday, and went straight to the media area. With a standing room only crowd of reporters, he answered questions for more than an hour.

When Craft was about to leave the room, Christopher Reed from the *London Review* asked, "What is your relationship with Ms. Wilkins?" He held up a picture of them kissing after completing the previous day's round.

Craft jokingly responded, "What can I say? The picture speaks for itself."

Reed persisted. "Do you think Kamran Turani approves of you dating his sister?"

"Kamran is well aware of my friendship with his sister," answered Craft.

Reed asked, "Then does this picture speak for itself?" He held up a picture of Craft passionately kissing Daria Turani in the lobby of the Ritz Carlton hotel.

Wilkins calmly interrupted the interview, indicating it was time for the tournament leader to prepare for today's final round. Visibly angry at being caught off guard by the media trap, Craft marched out of the room without saying a word.

In a private area of the clubhouse, she pulled him aside and placed her hand on his wrists so she could feel his pulse. His heart was beating fast. His body was reacting to the embarrassing situation.

In quiet but sincere voice, Wilkins said, "Please listen to me for a moment."

She waited to make sure she had his full attention. "We each have a job to do. Your job is out there on the golf course, and mine is in the media room."

"That son of a bitch, Reed, is lucky I didn't kick his ass all the way back to London."

"Listen to me, they're trying to mess with your mind," Wilkins insisted. "Don't let them waste your energy. Beating the Iranian today is going to take all you got. Remember, we're a team. You said so yourself to the President."

"Okay, I get it, we're a team," he responded, still steaming at Reed waving around the picture of him kissing Daria for all to see.

"Let me take care of Reed. You take care of business on the golf course."

While listening to her words, he recalled Dr. Page's grueling psychological exercises to groom him for the vicious media coverage. Page showed him how the media would use any means possible to build him up and tear him down—whatever it took to make news. Page would wait for the most vulnerable moments during training, and then move in like an attack dog, shouting, "Don't fall into the trap of thinking it's all about you. Don't let your pride get the best of you. You're going to make mistakes. You have a team and you're going to need them to succeed. At the end of the day, *the only thing that matters is the mission.*"

Wilkins felt his pulse return to a calmer rhythm. "I want you to consider doing your warm-up in the player's locker room and then go directly to the 1st tee. Don't play into the big hype of the American against the Iranian. Let Kamran be wondering where you are and if you're going to be ready. Walk to the 1st tee with the same confidence you did on Sunday at the Masters."

"Okay, tell Jefferson to meet me at the 1st tee."

Wilkins gently let go of his wrists and squeezed his hand for good luck. She sent Vaughn a message, explaining what happened and telling him to be at the 1st tee at 2:25PM. She spent a few minutes coordinating with the other Red Crescent team members, and then she was ready to go on the offense.

Wilkins sent a broadcast message to her long list of media contacts to join her in the media room at 1:50PM. When she walked into the room, the crowd chatter was loud. She went to the podium located next to a large display unit on the wall, checked to make sure the video on her HuAID could be projected on the wall unit, and then spoke into the podium microphone to get the attention of the people packed into the room.

"Mr. Craft has authorized me to represent him while he prepares to win this year's U.S. Open Championship. First, I would like to clarify a potential misunderstanding." Wilkins displayed the picture of her kissing Craft the previous day at the 18th hole on the wall unit.

"When Mr. Craft responded that the picture could speak for itself in the previous interview, the video tells the more complete story." She displayed in slow motion a video of her taking the scarf from her neck, soaking it in ice water and running over to give him a hug and a kiss, and then walking up the hill to the clubhouse.

"As the video shows, while I was kissing Mr. Craft, I was actually holding a scarf soaked in ice water on his neck, trying to relieve the effects of heat exhaustion. Look at how Mr. Craft is leaning on me as we go up the hill. Given he was on the verge of physical breakdown, I didn't want to give the competition any insight into his weakened condition, so I acted to conceal the situation. If you look at his face when I kissed him, it was more the look of surprise than affection. I am telling you this now because it doesn't matter, the players are already on the golf course with more important things on their minds. So the picture does speak for itself with some narration. For those who care, I assure you my current relationship with Mr. Craft is strictly professional, but who knows the future. For those of you who want the juicy stuff, I have to say kissing him was delightful."

She stopped to take a drink, and the chatter erupted. It was obvious to everyone her actions the previous day were that of a devoted business manager protecting her client.

She continued, "With regard to the second picture presented by Mr. Reed from the *London Review*, Mr. Craft did not respond because he did not recognize the picture."

"Please be patient and I will explain," Wilkins requested. "Three weeks ago, Mr. Reed published a picture of Mr. Preston Jackson. For those of you who might not know, Mr. Jackson is a British movie star who recently married." She displayed the picture of Jackson walking down the street, holding hands with a woman dressed in a skimpy nightclub dress. The caption read, *"Trouble in paradise for Jackson marriage."*

She then showed the original picture of Jackson walking down the street, and with a young lady walking behind. With some Photoshop magic, she manipulated the picture to bring the young lady forward, and then connected their hands to make it appear they were holding hands. "My intent is to reveal the lack of integrity behind Mr. Reed's reporting. His purpose is not to report the news; it's to create a fantasy to feed his pathetic subscribers. To further illustrate my point."

She pointed to a picture on the display unit of Mr. Reed with his wife at the pool of a local hotel. In the picture, Reed stood at the bar, ordering a drink with his wife lounging by the poolside, watching. A young girl, probably underage, also stood at the bar. Wilkins pushed a button, and the picture slowly changed to show Mr. Reed's arm around the young girl, with a horrified look on his wife's face.

"Mr. Reed is not the only person who knows how to create fantasy," Wilkins joked, "Would anyone like to suggest a caption for this picture?"

Red-faced with embarrassment, Christopher Reed departed the room to the sounds of laughter.

"I guess Mr. Reed has more important business than to stand here discussing this bogus picture. When Mr. Craft wins the tournament, I would appreciate keeping your questions related to golf."

•

Kamran, his caddy, and Jefferson were standing at the 1st tee, when Craft casually walked up one minute early. He walked over, shook the Iranian's hand and congratulated him on the previous day's record breaking round.

After playing three rounds of golf surrounded by spectators, Craft didn't notice the crowd, but he could see in Kamran's eyes, and by his body language, he was ready to compete. Craft felt strong, but knew the day would be a grind. He would have to start fast, and then fight to hold on. While waiting for the group ahead to reach the 1st green, he looked at the leader board. Kamran, along with four other players were now three strokes behind his lead.

The Iranian and Craft had aggressive starts, going three under par on the first eight holes. Even with the use of Smartball, Craft was unable to extend his lead. As they approached the 9th tee, he scanned the leader board, and determined only the Iranian could catch him, as long as he shot par or better on the next ten holes.

The 9th hole at Congressional was a long 620-yard par five, with a big ravine crossing in front of the green. From the start, Kamran planned to take three shots to reach the par five, so the Iranian stroked a smooth drive, landing 295 yards from the tee.

Feeling his endurance beginning to wane, Craft decided it was time to make a move, to put some pressure on his competition. It would take two monster hits to reach the green in two. He stood up taller and reached more with his arms to the ball. Craft increased his club head speed to 123 miles per hour, about eleven miles faster than his normal 112 miles per hour swing. The ball launched high, and the trailing wind carried the ball 343 yards into the middle of the fairway.

In hope that Craft would start a charge similar to Sunday at the Masters, the crowd began shouting patriotic American chants. Several yards behind Craft's drive, Kamran hit a safe shot short of the ravine, leaving 120 yards to the flagstick. Some of the American spectators started yelling insults, heckling the Iranian. Intensely focused on the next shot, Kamran was oblivious to the crowd. Scuffles started to breakout in the crowd, as Islamic spectators cheered for the Iranian.

Craft had a perfect lie and a trailing wind. He selected his three-wood, believing he had a chance to extend his lead by one or two strokes. He hit a long straight shot going right at the flag. It appeared to have enough to reach the green, when the flag on the flagstick switched directions, reacting to a change in wind direction. The ball hit on the front of the green and then started rolling backwards downhill toward the ravine. It came to rest on a steep slope, in thick grass, but still playable. A marshal standing by the green walked down the steep slope and placed an orange stake in the ground, marking the location, making it easy for Craft to locate the ball.

Kamran hit his approach shot twelve feet below the hole, leaving a reasonable length birdie putt. The bank was too steep for Jefferson to carry the bag down to the ball, so he handed Craft his sand wedge. Craft walked carefully down the steep slope, trying not to slip on the slick grass. With both hands, he gently pushed back the grass to verify the ball was his without causing it to move. He could see the golf ball had his unique markings.

The hill was so steep, Craft found it difficult to get his shoulders level with the slope of the terrain. His right foot was two feet below his left foot, making it difficult to maintain balance during the swing. The shot required a steep, hard descending swing in order to get the ball elevated quickly enough to carry over the ridge at the front of the green. Unable to see the flagstick, Craft walked part way up the hill. Jefferson walked over and stood at the front of the green, to give a visual line between Craft's golf ball and the flagstick. Craft used Jefferson as the reference point, as he descended back down the slope to his ball. Once Craft was ready to hit the ball, Jefferson moved out of the way. Craft made a strong swing into the grass. The club stopped quickly, as if hitting a tree trunk with an ax. The ball came flying out of the grass high into the air. By the cheers of the crowd, he knew the ball must have landed close to the hole. Craft felt a strain on his body when the club came to an abrupt stop, but thought nothing of it.

By the time he made it up the hill and marked his ball located three feet below the hole, he began to bleed in the abdomen area. The impact of the swing had ripped open the area where the surgical equipment had cut through the stomach muscle to operate on the abdomen. The bleeding wasn't serious, but if noticed, could call attention to his injury.

Kamran missed the birdie putt, tapping in for a par five. When Craft squatted down to line up the three-foot putt, Jefferson noticed a blood spot beginning to form on his light green shirt. Craft made easy work of the short putt, scoring birdie to take a four-stroke lead. As they walked by the clubhouse toward the 10th tee, Jefferson stopped to talk with Wilkins telling her about the blood. She went to the clubhouse, and escorted by security retrieved a change of clothes from Craft's locker.

Jefferson positioned the golf bag in a standing position at the back of the 10th tee area, enabling him to look through the bag for bandages he had put in the bag as a precaution. He approached Craft, who was drinking a bottle of water and eating an apple, placed the package of bandages into his hand and suggesting he visit the restroom. Noticing the bloodstain on his shirt, he began walking toward the restroom reserved for players, when Wilkins caught his attention. She handed him a clean shirt, identical to the one he was wearing.

The afternoon temperature was nearly a hundred degrees. Jefferson reached into a cooler to stock up on cold water and juices, to ensure Craft stayed hydrated, hoping to avoid a repeat of the previous day.

It had been a tradition for decades that a young amateur walked along with each golf group, holding a sign on top of a pole showing the name of each player in the group and their score. The young man who carried the sign lowered it to the ground to change Craft's score, when the pole struck the golf bag containing the Smartball equipment. The golf bag fell over the bank, crashing to the ground several feet below with golf clubs flying out of the bag. Jefferson scrambled down the bank, quickly gathered the golf clubs, checking for damage, picked up the bag, and lugged the golf bag and clubs back up the hill.

Craft returned to the 10th tee, wearing a clean shirt with a bandage underneath, to see a frightened young man sincerely apologizing to

Jefferson for knocking over the golf clubs and Jefferson trying to calm the young man. Craft pulled a couple of cold drinks out of the cooler, walked over and lightly touched one of the ice-cold bottles to the back of the young man's neck. He turned quickly to see Craft standing there.

"Do you really think a little fall is going to hurt those clubs after the beating I have given them the last few days?" Craft asked jokingly.

The young man smiled.

Craft handed him one of the cold drinks and said, "No worries…"

The golf clubs were fine, but the Smartball power unit had disconnected, and there was no opportunity to repair it. As Craft prepared to address the ball on the 10th tee, Jefferson signaled, by placing the towel around his neck, that the Smartball capability was shutdown. One thing Craft had learned by now was to expect the unexpected. In most situations, having a four-stroke lead with nine holes remaining, would almost guarantee a win. But not today, with the mission on the line, he was playing in a weakened state against a man who had gotten a taste of victory at the Players Championship. Wilkins was right; the Iranian was going to push him to the limit.

Craft managed to make a ten-footer for par on the 10th while Kamran made a five-footer for birdie cutting the lead to three-stroke. On the long par four 11th hole, Craft's drive was short, leaving 230 yards to the flagstick. He pushed the ball right, landing in the water hazard on the right side of the green. Kamran hit a safe shot to the left portion of the green. Scoring a bogey five, Craft's lead dropped to two strokes.

On the next four holes, Craft fought to score par, while Kamran missed short birdie putts, burning edges on all four. The Iranian turned up the heat on the 579-yard par five 16th hole, driving to the front of the green in two, then scored an easy birdie to cut the lead to one. On the 17th hole, Craft dodged another bullet, holing a long putt to make par, while Kamran missed an eight-foot birdie putt. Frustrated by missed putts, the Iranian marched to 18th tee, one stroke off the lead, with the energy of a physically fit man who was used to running long distances in the heat of the day. Kamran knew his American friend was in trouble, and the long 524-yard 18th hole could be the break he needed, to tie, or take, the lead.

Under ordinary circumstances, Craft would welcome the competition. With the mission on the line, he needed to push his pride aside and do whatever was necessary to keep things on track. Desperate to slow the pace, Craft noticed the President seated in a guarded area, behind the 17th green. Instead of walking directly to the 18th tee, he asked Jefferson to retrieve extra gloves and balls out of the golf bag. He walked over to the President's grandchildren and handed them each a golf glove and ball. The President motioned for him to wait while he stepped out of the bullet-proof seating area. They shook hands, and the President handed him a ball marker with the Presidential seal. Tired of waiting, Kamran hit a long drive down the right side of the fairway over the hill. The ball rolled down the slope leaving 185 yards to the flagstick, which was positioned in the back left portion of the green, a few feet from the water's edge.

Not feeling his usual strength, Craft tried to turn his upper body more, to get extra power. Feeling his arms lagging behind his body core, he threw his arms at the ball, trying to catch up in the swing. The ball flew long left over the bank, and down a several foot incline, into deep rough. The American spectators who were so vocal on previous holes were stunned by the turn of events. The Iranian's ball rested in excellent position, to attack the hole, while the American's ball was nearly out of play.

Although Jefferson tried not to show concern, he analyzed the situation to determine the best move going forward. The U.S. Open had special rules. If tied, the two players would have to play a full round of eighteen holes the next day, to determine the winner. On the positive side, they could have the advantage of Smartball. On the negative side, Craft's fatigue was showing, and the urgency of neutralizing the threat of the missing nuclear material was now driving the agenda. As they approached the ball, Jefferson had concluded they needed to find a way to win it right now.

Kamran waited in the middle of the fairway, trying not to show his frustration with the slow play. They had already been given a slow play warning. If Craft didn't hit the ball soon they could be given a two-stroke penalty.

After looking at the lie of the ball, Jefferson handed him a nine iron, expecting the agent to pitch out on to the fairway, and then try to get the next shot close for a score of par. Craft continued to assess the position of the ball in the high grass. It was an unusual occurrence where tall thick grass rested behind the ball, and short grass in front of the ball.

Jefferson (aka Jason Vaughn) was an accomplished amateur golfer. So Craft asked, "What do you think the ball would do if I hit it hard with a four iron with a light grip?"

"The heel of the club would dig in the grass, causing the club face to close fast, creating a sharp hook driving the ball into the ground a few feet ahead."

Then Jefferson realized that's what would happen when the ball had thick grass on both sides of the ball. With short grass in front of the ball, the ball would elevate a few feet off the ground with a sharp hook. Jefferson handed him a four iron, knowing exactly what Craft was going to do.

The tournament official approached, signaling for him to hit the ball or a penalty for slow play would soon follow. He took the club back with a deliberate swing, maintaining a light grip. The ball flew up the bank, just clearing the ridge by about three feet, and sharply hooked left, rolling down the fairway. The ball rolled downhill on the ground for 100 yards, into the middle of the green, leaving a 25-foot putt for birdie. Thousands of spectators erupted into earsplitting cheers.

After watching the incredible shot, Kamran recalled the advice his American friend had given him during a practice round at the Players. When faced with pressure situation where going long could find trouble areas, choose a club that would have to be hit perfectly just to reach the pin. From 185 yards, the Iranian selected a nine iron instead of an eight. Sure enough, he hit the nine iron perfectly, flying two feet past the flag-stick, and spinning back, leaving the ball six feet from the hole in excellent position for a birdie. The crowd erupted again, this time with great respect for a brilliant shot in the most difficult of competitive situations. The two competitors walked down the fairway to thunderous cheers.

After reaching the green, Craft and Jefferson looked at the 25-foot putt from all angles. Jefferson calmly walked over to a light spot on the green, and pointed, indicating the aiming point for the putt. Craft hit the ball at the light spot. The ball broke slightly right and then sharply left, heading directly for the hole. The ball caught the edge of the cup and spiraled around the cup in a motion similar to water going around a drain, before falling to the bottom of the hole.

Kamran stood for a moment, on the side of the green in disbelief. While the disappointment was enormous, the intense competition was electrifying. Craft tried to quiet the crowd, now singing *God Bless America* for all to hear. The Iranian made the short putt for a birdie, finishing the tournament in second place one stroke behind the lead, but earning world's respect as a competitor who knew how to finish strong.

After the reality of losing set in, Kamran congratulated his American friend, saying "I had you on the ropes."

"Yes you did."

They walked off the 18th green, with their arms around each other for the world to see. Knowing the danger facing his Iranian friend, he sincerely hoped they would be able to compete again under more favorable conditions. As the tournament chairman presented Craft with the U.S. Open Championship Trophy, *he wondered what his role would become as the mission changed to threat elimination.*

CHAPTER 27

CHARLESTON, SC

By the time the team reached Charleston the news of Craft's second consecutive Major win dominated media outlets across the globe. The operations center, set up to handle his business affairs, received a deluge of messages offering congratulations, endorsements, major talk show invitations, and other tributes. Fans around the world clamored for information about the mysterious man who, in a short time, had emerged from obscurity to dominate world golf.

The media management team, led by Wilkins, worked overtime to ensure the information flowing across the network supported a positive image of the golf superstar. The team engaged in all forms of social media, to continue the process of image building. Complex search capabilities roamed cyber networks, looking for hotspots where information was being shared regarding the emerging golf icon. The team covertly engaged in collaboration with virtual groups around the world in many languages, to shape common consciousness and, when necessary, to squash the perception of improper behavior. Sites persistently promoting negative images were mysteriously overcome by technical challenges, diverting their attention.

The perception across the Islamic populous regarding the competition and friendship that had taken center stage between Craft and the Iranian was generally positive, with some pockets of extreme anger. The team used advanced big data analysis techniques to identify and characterize real threats from those simply wanting to vent their frustrations.

For security reasons, Craft relocated to a gated residence on Kiawah Island, twenty-five miles south of Charleston. It had been weeks since he had been visible in the local community, and the team was concerned some Charleston natives might get the notion he had forgotten his roots. They decided it was time for Craft to visit downtown. He stopped to say hello to people at his favorite establishments. His presence during lunch hour turned into an impromptu block party, with people crowding around to congratulate him and asking questions about his golf adventures.

A young police officer pulled up in front of the group of people surrounding the Tour player and blasted the siren for a few seconds to get their attention. It was Joe Miller, an old teammate who had played center when Craft was the quarterback in high school.

Vigorously shaking Craft's hand, the officer said, "I have to tell you, you're a living legend around here. But honestly, playing golf instead of football... I just don't understand it."

"How are you doing, Joe? It's good to see you're on the right side of the law these days. It must be the free donuts," joked Craft.

After talking briefly about their families and the goings-on around town, the officer said, "Would you mind going for a short ride? The Mayor wants to talk with you. Don't worry. He's just sucking up to your mother, hoping if he treats you well, your mom will stay in Australia and let him run the city."

"No problem, let's go see the Mayor," responded Craft.

He said goodbye, and stepped into the police car with his schoolmate. Unbeknownst to him, Wilkins had given the local media, the mayor's office, and police chief advance notice of his being in the downtown area around lunchtime. Hearing the news that Amanda's son was in town, the Mayor coordinated with the police chief to arrange a Town Hall celebration for the hometown hero, who had brought such pride to the city. When the police car at the corner turned onto Broad Street, Craft could see a large assembly of people standing in front of City Hall.

"Don't get nervous," Officer Miller said, "but these people have come on a moment's notice to celebrate your outstanding golf accomplishments. I've been told business in the city is at a standstill. Don't take this personal... Oh hell, we're friends; you can take it personal... I wish we were celebrating your winning the Super Bowl instead of a wimpy golf tournament."

"Are you still pissed about my kicking your ass in the junior golf league when we were ten years old?" asked Craft.

The Mayor stood on a red carpet at the street's edge, ready to welcome the golf icon. As the car transporting Craft approached, the citizens of Charleston cheered and held signs of admiration. When he stepped out of the police car, the crowd noise became so loud he couldn't hear a word the Mayor said. They walked along the red carpet, up the stairs onto a high veranda at the entrance to City Hall.

The Mayor approached the podium, and began talking into the microphone, for all to hear, "It's with great pleasure that I have the privilege to welcome to the podium a man who has brought enormous pride to the people of Charleston, the winner of this year's Masters and United States Open Championships, Mr. Peter Craft."

As Craft stood at the podium waving, the massive crowd applauded for several minutes. In the front were hundreds of children, wearing First Light tee shirts and waving U.S. Open flags and Masters golf towels. Each time Craft started to talk, the crowd erupted with applause. He humbly and graciously thanked everyone for their support and gave special thanks to those who helped shape his character. He talked about the pride he felt representing the citizens of Charleston, and how much their support meant to him, especially during the tough times.

Wilkins approached the podium and handed him the U.S. Open Trophy to hold up for all to see. Craft told the people assembled, that with the Mayor's approval, the trophy would be displayed at City Hall for the next year as a thank you to all who worked so hard to create a community that made it possible for a child to turn a big dream into reality.

Holding up the trophy, Craft ended the speech by saying, "You do not win one of these without hometown support, and I have the best support system in the world—you, the great citizens of Charleston South Carolina."

The Mayor concluded the celebration by presenting Craft with a ceremonial key to the city. Overcome by the outpouring of public support, he was beginning to lose track of where he was, when in his head, he could hear Dr. Page's words, "*Golf will never define you. You are a U.S. government agent, working on the side of good to defeat evil; you live a life of secrecy so others can have freedom...*"

Following the ceremony, Craft made the rounds to his favorite local golf courses to chat with the staff, and helped promote their marketing by offering photo opportunities with the hottest player on the Tour. He was about to head back to his Kiawah Island home, when he received an encrypted message "*Shack 17:30 – EM required.*" The EM in the text indicated his travel to the secure facility would require evasive maneuvers, to avoid detection. With his newfound fame, people watched his every move. Using his HuAID, Craft accessed the secure navigation system, to hear voice instructions guiding him to a route that would avoid detection. The navigation system directed him into a private parking garage with multiple exits. Craft changed cars, and then drove into a garage behind the building where the secure facility was located. He entered the golf store through a back entrance, where he could proceed undetected to the secure facility. The evasive maneuvers took longer than expected. He walked into the secure facility a few minutes late.

The team was waiting when Craft arrived. First, Vaughn acknowledged everyone's hard work, and then the team did a mission walk-through, starting with the VIPER I operation and ending with the City Hall celebration. Vaughn made the point that now with the second Major tournament win, maintaining operational security would be much more difficult.

When the mission walk-through reached the last day at the Masters, Craft pointed out that, like Wilson, he also was good with golf stats. He figured the probability of Kamran Turani missing six putts from inside twelve feet were one out of a thousand.

Wilson responded his calculations were correct, unless the Tour player used a modified putter with a molecular structure having a random coefficient that increased with the heat of the day. Then, the probability of missing the putts was closer to 80 percent.

Ready to give her assessment, Dr. Page said, "This difficult mission has been a success to date, because of your commitment and ability to adapt to changing conditions, and despite some major screw-ups."

The immediate response in the room, to Dr. Page's comment, was one of contempt, but they knew she had a purpose. As a college athlete, Craft had experienced many teambuilding exercises led by psychologists. She was attempting to build team unity by creating a common villain. He could see she enjoyed playing the bad guy.

Dr. Page continued, "Yes, you heard me right, 'major screw-ups' I repeat. Our golf star crossed the line by becoming too personally involved with the Iranian family, adding unnecessary complexity and nearly compromising the mission. Our media manager publicly embarrassed a powerful member of the media, making Reed an enemy for life. Our mission leader failed to protect critical equipment. It's hard enough when we have to deal with unexpected events such as the Smart Weapon Intercept program and Craft's medical issues. We don't need to make things harder."

There was no sense in getting defensive or trying to explain. The team knew she was right. The mission was going to get harder, and they would have to do better. Craft never imagined how difficult it would be to keep his emotions in check. A few hours before, he was receiving a key to the city, and now he was being reprimanded as a screw-up. For a moment, "*I quit*" crossed his mind, but he knew the terrorists were not quitters.

Vaughn thanked Dr. Page for her frank operational assessment and after the doctor logged out of the virtual meeting, he addressed the team. "Now that we have heard Dr. Page's assessment, I want to give you mine. I think Mr. Craft said it best last Friday, when he told the President of the United States, that he was proud to be a member of this extraordinary team. When Director Walker asked for my operational assessment this morning, I simply responded, *we're getting the job done.*"

Re-invigorated by Vaughn's vote of confidence, the team was ready to move forward with mission planning. As expected, Craft's rise to fame had created some operational security concerns. This would be the last face-to-face meeting with him. To maintain close coordination, Wilkins would become the interface between Craft and the team. To increase the time for coordination, their public relationship would become romantic, to explain Wilkins spending her evenings with Craft.

Vaughn didn't tell them all the reasons for the change. He wanted to stifle the Iranian girl's romantic ambitions and give Christopher Reed an opportunity to save face before he started digging in the wrong places. It better positioned Wilkins to manage the emerging Amanda Craft situation, and reduce the motivation of the countless young girls who would be competing to gain his affections. The most important reason for the change, Vaughn thought, was making it easier for the two agents to watch each other's back as the mission became more dangerous.

The team leader talked about what it meant for the mission to change from intelligence collection to threat elimination. He explained that in most situations involving threat elimination, they would integrate with a Special Ops team. This scenario would be different because success depended on keeping minimal exposure. Vaughn displayed a picture of Craft's mentor, and informed the team that Kalani, an agent with extensive Special Forces skills, would be taking an active role on the team. In this case, Kalani would build the team by hand picking individuals from a cadre of special operations forces. He ended the meeting, advising that Gul would soon be ready to outline the next phase of the mission.

Craft left the secure facility, using evasive maneuvers to return back to the private parking garage, where his car waited. When he arrived at the

Kiawah Island residence, Wilkins had the kitchen table set for dinner, and was ready to serve the Chinese food she had picked up on the way. They ate dinner without saying a word to each other. After dinner, she motioned for him to follow her. She led him downstairs to the Communications and Entertainment Center—CEC—and then closed the door, pushed a button to activate the security system and waited until the blinking red light on the control panel turned green. The CEC was a large room with one wall having an integrated communications unit that either projected onto a single large display or divided into multiple video displays. A sofa and comfortable chairs sat in front of the display wall. In the back of the room was a kitchen area, with a table and chairs. Also in the back of the room was an entertainment area with a variety of electronic and classic arcade games.

Wilkins said, "This is a secure facility now; it is the only place in the house we can talk about the mission, so we'll be watching a lot of movies."

She sat down on the sofa. "Before we go out in public together, I think we need to be on the same page."

"I watched the video clip of your press conference yesterday. Your handling of Reed was incredible."

"Well, Dr. Page didn't think so."

"Page is just doing her job. To tell the truth, when things get crazy, it's Page's physiological rants that bring me back into focus. Just today, I was caught up in all the hoopla at City Hall, when a vision of Page telling me it's not about me; it's about the mission, popped into my head."

They both agreed Page was a pain in the butt, but a real asset to the team's success.

"So, what do you think about the new arrangement going forward?" she asked.

"If I am willing to deceive the world at golf to protect the nation, I suppose pretending to have a thing going on with my adorable business manager is not too much to ask."

"Don't underestimate the perceptiveness of the public. If the feelings aren't there, the public will see through it. Our time together in public will be under a microscope. Experts will be reading our body language. Trust me, it's not hard to detect a fake relationship; I am really good at it. We need to find a way to stay connected on an emotional level."

"I understand what you're saying, but controlling feelings is beyond my capacity. I can tell you, we have a major obstacle to overcome."

"What is it, so we can deal with it?"

"You already know."

"Well, tell me again."

"My life is an open book and your life is locked in secrecy."

"Okay, I will make this commitment. To you, my life will also be an open book. I have never told anyone and by the end of the night, you'll know why."

Craft went to the bar area in the back of the room, filled the bucket on the counter with ice, and opened a vintage bottle of Chardonnay. He returned to the sofa, handed her a glass of wine and then raised his glass to make a toast. "I cannot think of anything I would rather do right now than to discover the real you."

He had no idea of what she was about to tell him. As far as he knew, she grew up a Nebraska farm girl, went to the University of Nebraska, and was recruited by the agency out of college.

"Like you, my grandfather had a profound influence in my life. I am the only granddaughter of the late James Crawford, one of the wealthiest men in the world, who made a fortune in the early 1990s developing a high-speed computer network with proprietary software algorithms, that made computerized stock trades on Wall Street. In the mid 1990s, he sold the rights to one of the big investment firms for billions of dollars."

She could see the intrigue in Craft's eyes. She used her HuAID to access childhood pictures of her with the grandfather.

"My grandfather had one son, John Crawford, my father. After my grandmother Crawford passed away in Hampton, New York, my father grew tired of the big city life and the pressures of being a wealthy man's son and the sole heir to the Crawford fortune. In 1998, my father moved to Nebraska, looking for a simpler life and became captivated by farming. My father had a Christmas time affair with Doreen Beach, my mother, a young girl from a small farm town near Lincoln. I was born at my father's ranch on August 2, 2001. Although he proclaimed his love for my mother, they never married. I suspect my grandfather had something to do with stopping their marriage plans, but I don't really know. My mother named me Victoria after her deceased mother. I remember little about my mother, because she passed away from lymphoma before I turned three years old. My father and grandfather were the only family members I ever knew growing up."

She showed pictures of herself as a young child with her parents, and the farm animals. Craft said, "Not many kids have a horse at three years old."

She replied, "In Nebraska, most farm kids learned to ride a horse and shoot a gun at a young age. I am really good at both."

Reminiscing about the past filled her with all sorts of emotions, good and bad. After pouring another glass of wine, she continued the story, "After the first 9/11 attacks, my grandfather, a very patriotic man, committed his life and much of his wealth to fighting terrorism around the world. He setup businesses to provide cover for U.S. covert operations. Up until the age of thirteen, I had a normal life as a Nebraskan farm girl. I really didn't know much about the 9/11 attacks and didn't really care."

Wilkins showed pictures of her winning horse riding contests and 4-H ribbons. She truly loved country life, and spending long hours helping her father doing chores around the farm. While many of her school friends complained about having to do farm work after school, she couldn't wait to get home to tackle another job with her dad.

"In 2014, my grandfather believed his connection to the Agency had been compromised and as a result, the family was in danger. I don't know the details but my grandfather convinced my father that going undercover was necessary. My father didn't really care about his safety, so he decided to continue living on the farm. They cut a deal to send me off to live at private boarding schools around the world under aliases. In 2016, my father died as the result of a mysterious farm accident. My grandfather discovered my father's death was no accident; he had died at the hands of foreign government agents. I have been told my grandfather personally administered vengeance. So, from the time I was thirteen until the age of twenty-two, I lived at boarding schools around the world. I never stayed long enough at any one place for my real identity to be discovered. You might say I have basically lived my whole life under different identities. I was who ever I needed to be to survive."

He was astonished by the story. "You grew up without a home and family."

"I don't want to make it sound worse than it really was. My grandfather lived a private life, traveling around the world. I never knew when he might show up, but when he did, which was quite often, we had a wonderful time together. He was truly a brilliant man; I wish you could have met him, but unfortunately he died in a boating accident a few years ago. It really was an accident, although he was going much too fast."

"Being the only heir to the Crawford fortune, why are you doing this?"

"Why are you doing what you do?" she asked. "You could be rich playing sports or hacking computers."

"Good point," he said.

"Money never meant much to me. I have a generous trust fund if I ever need it, but most of my grandfather's money was donated to a covert fund to help us fight the bad guys. I do just fine living on my government paycheck. Although he would never have admitted it, my grandfather had been training me for this life since my first days at boarding school. Although unconventional, I've had the best teachers and experienced things that other children only dreamed of. It would take days for me to tell you all things I have done. I speak most European languages and have an extensive education in various technologies."

They talked through most of the night. She talked about her long list of interests, including equestrian, gymnastics, swimming, sailing, and snow skiing. She also mentioned her training in self-defense, a broad range of weapons and piloting a full range of commercial and military aircraft.

"Is there anything you haven't done?" he asked.

"Well, I've never gone ice skating," she said.

"Me neither. We don't do too much ice skating in Charleston, but I bet it's fun," he said.

Craft thought he had lived an interesting life, but his was elementary in comparison. She had to be telling the truth, he thought, because the details were verifiable. Now things made sense. The stories she shared when they first met were actually true. It also explained why the cover story behind Jennifer Wilkins had her living in boarding schools around the world, because that's exactly what she did, so creating a paper trail consistent with her actual life experiences was clever.

About to fall asleep, she said, "There is still one more thing I need to tell you."

"I cannot imagine anything could top what you've already shared," he replied.

"It's about how we met."

"How we met doesn't seem all that important now. I am just glad we did meet and we're on the same team."

"I still think you need to know the truth. When Vaughn explained the mission to me, I didn't believe he had found a person capable of pulling off being both an agent and golf superstar. Let's be honest, we're in uncharted territory with a lot at stake. Truth be told, I needed to see firsthand if you could resist the lure of fame and fortune. Don't let this go to your head, but I knew you were special the night we met. I had already signed on to the mission when you invited me to dinner. For what it's worth... I spent time with you in Charleston before the Orlando Open because I wanted to, not because it was my job."

•

Up early, Wilkins drove to the secure facility to attend the operations meeting. The Iran Ops Director, Gul, began the briefing. "This is Azzam Baahir, the owner of a privately investment firm headquartered in Riyadh. He's built a powerful empire managing the financial assets of the upper class of Islamic society. We have a strong suspicion he is somehow connected to the hijacking of the nuclear waste. He stands to lose billions, if Amir Turani is successful at bringing wealth back into Iran. Make no mistake... This man is ruthless. The globe is littered with the bodies of adversaries who attempted to get in the way of his business ambitions. We could leverage Baahir's business interests in Middle Eastern golf and the First Light program."

Wilkins spoke up, "Since Craft's U.S. Open victory, we've been flooded with endorsement offers. I propose that he does free public service announcements promoting healthy living in the Middle East. Soon his image would be commonplace in Islamic households. Then, we'll be in position to entice Baahir into a deal, trading Craft's endorsement of the Saudi businessman's financial services, in return for his support of the First Light program in Riyadh."

Based on Wilkins recommendation, the team outlined the Riyadh operation. The primary objective would be to gain access to the Baahir's office and then the company's computer network. Wilkins would push for face-to-face negotiations at the Saudi businessman's compound in Riyadh. Playing the role of production manager, Vaughn would accompany Wilkins to Riyadh, to assess the filming options, while in reality they would be assessing the compound's security. The evening before the First Light kickoff in Riyadh, the agents would attend a reception at Baahir's compound. While Craft held the spotlight, Wilkins would systematically release a network of decomposable biosensor devices.

Vaughn played a video prepared by Jack Wilson, demonstrating how the biosensors worked. Propelled by nanotechnology, the sensors acted like small bugs that, when released, would seek remote areas of the room—walls, ceiling, plants—then change colors to blend into the environment. After forty-eight hours, the devices would decompose into dust-like material.

A contact within the Saudi government would divert security forces from the businessman's compound, by making an official request for Baahir to provide security personnel at the First Light event. The commercial production team, Vaughn and Kalani, would show up at the compound during the First Light event to begin equipment setup. The biosensor network would give them intelligence regarding the location of people in the compound. They would search Baahir's office, and copy data from the internal computer network.

Talking with Vaughn in private, Wilkins said, "I am concerned about Amanda Craft's behavior. It doesn't make sense that someone who had been actively involved in her son's life for years, is now willing to sit on the sidelines while he achieves #1 ranking on the Tour, winning two Major championships. I understand the requirement for her to be on-site in Australia, but there is no evidence of her being active on the network. Amanda Craft is a media professional. I think she may have figured out a way to cover her tracks."

"Your concern is timely," Vaughn responded. "The Director just sent a message this morning, recommending you two take a trip to Australia to visit with Ms. Craft, before she reads about your romance in the news. While at the movie site, you can film Craft's public service announcements."

Both excited and anxious about meeting his mother, Wilkins returned to the Kiawah Island residence, just as Craft finished his morning run. She talked with him about the general plans for the day and the kind of things romantically involved people would talk during the course of a day. When the conversation concluded, Craft left the room to go bathe and change into casual dress.

As he walked away, she decided it was time to see where things stood in their relationship. She waited at the door until she heard the sound of the shower and then took off her clothes and went into the bathroom. She stood where he could see her naked. "Is there enough room for two?"

"Sure, there are two showers, so you can have your own."

"I was thinking more like, I could wash your back and you could wash mine."

Craft knew if they were going to carry out a romantic relationship, then being naked in front of each other was going to be a normal occurrence, so he better get used to it. He reached out, grabbed her hand, pulled her into the shower, and began rubbing soap all over her body. Within seconds, she was so aroused she thought her body was going to erupt just standing there. With her hair and body washed, she took the soap and began lathering his body. She could tell he was trying not to get aroused, but it was not working. As she brushed near his genitals, his body came to full attention. After washing the soap off his body, she stepped out of the shower and handed him a towel. They dressed where each could see the other, and then proceeded to the CEC room where they could talk.

Wilkins said, "Maybe it's time we visited your mother, before our romance goes public."

"You must've read my mind. This is something she needs to hear face-to-face," he replied.

Holding two tickets in her hand, she said, "We have tickets for a 4PM ultrasonic flight from Miami to Brisbane, Australia. We'll arrive around 11am local time."

CHAPTER 28

BRISBANE, AUSTRALIA

News spread quickly through the airport that the golf star, Peter Craft, was about to arrive in Brisbane. The American agents cleared customs soon after arriving at the airport. Amanda Craft, most of the movie crew, and many locals were waiting to greet them when they walked into the public terminal area. Amanda gave her son a motherly hug and kisses to the cheers of the welcoming public.

Before he could say a word, Wilkins spoke up, "It's a pleasure, Ms. Craft. I've been looking forward to our meeting for quite some time."

Amanda, without hesitation, embraced the young lady with a warm southern greeting usually reserved for family and the closest of friends. "No need for formalities. Please call me Amanda. Would you mind if I called you Jen, or would you prefer Jennifer?"

"Jen is fine; that's what my friends call me."

Amazed by his mother's beauty, Wilkins only hoped to look as good in twenty-five years. After further inspection, she could see her attractiveness was the result of wholesome living, and not Hollywood magic. After spending a short time socializing with the movie crew, they traveled a short distance to a beach complex.

Craft's mother escorted them to a grand penthouse suite on the top floor of an eight-story building, reserved for one of the movie stars who would be arriving in a week to begin on-site filming. The suite had beautiful ocean views with a large wraparound terrace.

Intent on giving them time alone, Wilkins put on a light jacket, and headed out the door to enjoy the cool breezy walk on the beach. Soon after Wilkins' departed, Amanda insisted her son take off his shirt so she could see firsthand his injuries.

Tears dripped down her checks at the sight of his badly bruised body. "You really need to be more careful."

"How did you know?"

"Oh Peter, I have watched you swing a golf club since you were ten years old. Did you really think I wouldn't notice? The only reason I didn't get on the first plane to Atlanta was Jen's assuring me you were in the best of hands, and her promise to stay by your bedside until you were out of trouble. She cared enough to give me regular updates on your condition. Let's say we talked a lot."

He assured his mother he was all right and then explained his having taken a bad fall while in Iran, but avoided giving any specifics. To his surprise, she didn't push for more details.

Relieved he was going to fully recover, she retrieved a couple of cold drinks from the refrigerator, handed one to her son, and then asked, "Tell me about your friend."

He told the story of how Chris Davis had introduced them. In preparing for the Orlando Open, he realized he was not ready to deal with the business and media aspects of professional golf. Jennifer agreed to be his business manager after much pleading on his part, accepting a payment arrangement on a commission basis, before he had ever made a dollar winning on the Tour.

"If you want my opinion, Ms. Wilkins is a highly skilled professional. Don't be surprised if other players try to steal her away. Based on our heartfelt conversations during your illness, she has a personal interest in you that is more than just monetary. If you ask me, I think she's in love with you and not because you're winning golf tournaments."

"Jennifer is a special person in my professional and personal life," he replied.

"Do you love her?"

"We've only known each other for a few months; there is no need to rush things."

"I fell in love with your father the day we met. It's not about the time, it's about feeling the connection."

"Given your unusual interest in romance, have you met any charming Aussie bachelors?" he asked.

"Yes I have, and you're going to meet him tonight," she answered.

"Don't mess around with me. I've never met anyone you've dated, if you've dated anyone, in my whole life."

"You're a man now, with a life of your own. Your father would be so proud of you. It's time for me to put his death behind and move on. Don't get me wrong. I will never love anyone the way I loved your father, but with your grandfather gone and you on your own, it's time."

With mixed emotions, he commented, "I can't wait to meet him."

Craft thought just to be on the safe side, he would have Wilkins do a background investigation. He didn't expect to find anything out of the ordinary, because his mother was an excellent judge of character and not one to be taken in by a sweet talking man.

Amanda wanted her son to share all the details of his rise to golf stardom while she had been in Australia. Exhausted from the long flight, he tried to give details that would satisfy his mother's interests and be consistent with his cover story. Then the conversation turned to his trip to Iran. She wanted to know about his friendship with Kamran Turani and the rumors about him being in a romantic relationship with his friend's sister. Most of all, she wanted to know what lapse in common sense drove him to pursue high-speed motorcycle racing. She made a sarcastic comment that he was lucky to have returned from Iran with only bumps and bruises, instead of in a pine box.

The conversation became easier after Wilkins returned, and the topic shifted to the Charleston Town Hall celebration. It took an hour for him to mention all the people he had talked with during the course of the day. His mother requested updates on everyone's family. She asked questions, expecting him to remember all the details about everyone, showing disappointment when he failed to remember what college someone's daughter was going to attend in the fall or the name of a new grandchild.

Amanda treasured the time spent catching up with her son but it was now time to go get ready for the evening celebrations. As soon as his mother walked out the door, he began sharing his conversation with Wilkins.

"It's great seeing my mother, but it's tiresome answering all her questions, especially the probing questions about our relationship."

"She knows you're at a critical point in your life, and she wants to be part of it," responded Wilkins.

"Do your friends really call you Jen?"

"Yes, my close friends."

"Like who?"

"Your mother."

"I guess you two became quite chummy during my down time."

"I was just doing my job. Your mother wanted to stay informed, and I could only imagine what it would be like being halfway around the world while my son is fighting for his life."

Pulling her into his arms, he said, "My mother is very perceptive, and she thinks you were doing much more than your job, taking care of me."

"What do you think?"

He avoided a direct answer to the question. "I think you need to be careful tonight. My mother has a way of getting people to reveal details they would rather not. She's going to ask questions about your life, and analyze everything you say, looking for consistent and reasonable answers. It's just her nature as a news reporter."

"Your mother is darling, but I plan to never underestimate her mental sharpness."

Wilkins placed clothes for him on the bed, and then went into the second bedroom to get ready for the evening celebration. She made sure he would be dressed appropriately for the occasion, and the conservative superstar golfer image. He would be wearing dark blue cuffed pants with sharp creases, an open collar light blue cotton shirt, business-like casual black leather shoes and a navy blue sport jacket with gold buttons.

After bathing and getting dressed, he waited in the living room, reading the scripts for the next day's studio recordings.

He could hardly believe his eyes when Wilkins walked out of the bedroom,. She was wearing the same elegant white dress she wore the night they went on their first dinner date. While helping her put on a wrap to keep her shoulder warm, he said, "You look incredible."

Giving him a quick thank-you-for-noticing kiss, she commented, "This dress brings back fond memories of a wonderful evening with a charming man. A day in my life that some day I would like to relive."

A limo arranged by the studio drove them to a local restaurant, where his mother had arranged for a dinner celebration, with seventy guests. They walked into the restaurant holding hands conveying an image of their relationship being one of a romantic nature. They stayed together as a couple, greeting guests and thanking them for making the night special. He marveled at the ease with which she connected with everyone, skilled at directing conversation in a way to make each guest feel welcomed.

As the crowd around them began to thin, Craft caught a glimpse of his mother standing next to a man, while talking with guests. He assumed the man was his mother's friend. He immediately assessed the situation. The man was well dressed, handsome, tall, appeared to be middle-aged with an exceptionally dark tan. *Had she fallen for a Hollywood type, all glitter and no substance?* He wondered.

Feeling the tenseness in his arms, Wilkins said, "Lighten up; it's a party."

His mother and friend made the first move, walking over to greet them. Reaching out to shake Craft's hand, the man introduced himself, "Jeremy West, pleased to meet you."

After a few minutes of pleasantries, Craft offered to get everyone a drink. Wilkins volunteered to go with him.

"Okay, I need some information. Who is this guy?" he asked.

"Relax. He is an Englishman who moved to Australia a few years ago to start a charter boat business. Mr. West owns a small fleet of boats offering tourists customized packages for fishing, sailing, snorkeling, and other water adventures. He is an outstanding citizen in the local community, and every eligible woman his age has tried to capture his affections."

Craft smiled, "I would have bet a million he was one of those Hollywood types. But when we shook hands, I could tell he was an outdoorsman. A sailor; now that's a pleasant thought. My mother loves boating and the ocean."

"Give him a chance. Rumor has it he has fallen head over heels for your mother. I wouldn't be surprised if he hasn't already popped the question."

"I've never thought about my mother getting married," he confided.

"To be honest, it's sweet seeing you fret over your mother's love life."

After a rocky start, West and Craft talked passionately about life by the sea. In many ways, Brisbane was similar to Charleston—friendly, family-oriented people living by the sea. The two couples had a highly animated conversation with everyone there, telling entertaining stories. His mother told funny stories about her son's childhood, like the time he played a piano concert with one hand, because he had banged his other with a hammer helping his grandfather build a bird house.

Peter told about the time the cat ate a holiday turkey after his mother left it on the kitchen counter to cool.

Wilkins divulged a story about her horse deciding to come to a dead stop in the middle of a riding contest, sending her face first into a pile of dung.

West had many boating yarns, about people he married at sea on the ship deck and the outfits they chose to wear, if any.

Wilkins was surprised his mother had not asked about her background. She suggested they have lunch the next day, while Peter was at the studio filming the public announcements. Craft mildly protested his media expert would be gallivanting around with his mother, leaving him to deal with the studio crew alone. She assured him the studio had the script, and she would be there to review the filming later in the afternoon.

After dinner, the lack of sleep caught up with them. Amanda suggested the exhausted travelers go back to the suite, and she would thank the guests and bid them good night.

Once back at the penthouse suite, thoughts of romance quickly turned to total fatigue. Together, the two agents slipped out of their clothes, and climbed into bed. With their bodies comfortably intertwined, both fell fast asleep almost immediately. When Peter woke up the next morning, he was in the bed alone. He vaguely remembered getting into bed, and then nothing after that. He figured the evening must have concluded with them falling asleep, because his first sexual encounter with her would not be something he would forget.

Throwing on a shirt and shorts, he wandered into the kitchen area. Wilkins sat at the kitchen table, wearing a robe and drinking a cup of coffee. She had been up for hours, coordinating with the team. Her romantic desire from the previous evening had been overtaken by mission urgency.

"Is everything okay?" he asked.

She gave him a warm embrace. "I woke up early, probably from jet lag. Lying there next to your naked body was delightful, but unproductive. I decided to catch up on work before going to lunch with your mom."

She wasn't going to tell him his mother had become a high security risk. Ms. Craft's behavior was totally inconsistent with that of a mother who had taken a very active role in her son's life. Now that her son was the top player on the Tour, her involvement in his life just didn't seem right. Being a computer savvy writer and reporter, Wilkins expected to see Amanda's fingerprints all over the network, piecing together a world perspective of her son's image. As far as the team could tell, either Amanda was inactive on the network or clever enough to cover her tracks.

Wilkins needed answers, and she needed them now, or it would be time to raise the red flag to Director Walker. This wasn't just any person; she was Craft's mother, a person she had come to admire. On the other hand, Wilkins couldn't manage what she didn't know about. In collaboration with Vaughn, she decided to take an unconventional approach of engaging Ms. Craft directly.

The team arranged for a bungalow on the beach, where they could have lunch and talk freely at a top-secret level. The agency people would be monitoring any surveillance activities in the area, and the people preparing and serving lunch would be insiders. They met in the front of the complex, and were transported by an agent, posing as a taxi driver. Wilkins indicated she had a surprise. The driver took them to a remote beach with a bungalow set up for a catered lunch.

After enjoying the cool ocean breezes and some casual conversation, Wilkins directed the conversation to the task at hand. "Ms. Craft, there is a lot I would like to talk to you about regarding your son, but before I can do so, you will have to read and sign a national security nondisclosure agreement."

Amanda put her finger on the HuAID device being offered, entered the private pin code, and then hit the "Accept" button, to digitally sign the document.

Before Wilkins could say another word, Amanda said, "Jen, you can relax now. I am aware of who you are and why we're meeting."

Stunned by Amanda's declaration, Wilkins asked, "Who am I?"

"Let's make a deal, I will answer your questions provided you tell me about your relationship with my son."

"Okay, we have a deal."

"You're Victoria Beach, the daughter of John Crawford, and granddaughter of James Crawford. Before I forget, thank you for funding the movie. It is going to be a blockbuster."

Wilkins was shocked. She had never considered the possibility that Craft's mother worked for the CIA, under an unofficial cover.

"Why are we meeting?"

"You're spooked by my behavior. It's inconsistent with the profile you have built on me. From your perspective, I would never sit idly by, while my son ascended to the top of the golf world."

"Are you aware of the mission?"

"Jen, you can verify with Catherine Walker that I have been cleared into the Red Crescent program on a special need-to-know basis. Let me save you some research time, by telling you about the connection. Kate Walker and I met at gymnastics summer camp as teenagers. We became close friends during our college years and when she began a career in national intelligence, my father, a naval intelligence officer, volunteered to be Kate's mentor. As a freelance reporter, I frequently contracted with the Agency to support covert operations around the world. When Kate realized my son was the best fit for the mission, she granted me special need-to-know access, so we could discuss the mission and its potential danger. To make it easier for my son, we concocted a plan to get me out of the U.S. for a few months. My son is unaware of my Agency involvement, so please keep this between us."

"Yes, ma'am," responded Wilkins, still trying to comprehend the situation.

"The reason I have not been active on the network is, because Director Walker assured me you were the best and my son's image was in good hands. From what I have observed, she was correct. If you don't mind me saying, you have a gift. You not only kept me informed of his medical condition, you also gave me great comfort by relating to my situation. I will never forget your care and compassion."

Humbled by the turn of events, Wilkins asked for her professional opinion regarding the program. Amanda indicated that any information she had assembled was strictly for the care of her son, not to meddle in the mission.

Amanda changed the topic. "So, let's have some girl talk. How are things between you and Peter?"

"We came here so you could know of our personal relationship, before it's revealed to the public."

"So what's really going on between you two? Don't give me the Agency party line... I am interested in the real stuff."

"Well, our relationship got off to a rocky start." She told Amanda about how they met; the complexity of their relationship, intermingled with the mission, and then there was the Iranian girl.

Amanda listened patiently to the young lady. "Do you love him?"

"I am still trying to sort out my feelings."

"I think he is trying to do the same," Amanda confided.

She shared Peter's concern of their relationship having to end when the mission ended, leaving both of them brokenhearted.

"I have watched a lot of girls try to gain the affection of my son, and he never let one of them get close, except Callie."

"I've met Callie."

"Then you know they will never be more than friends."

"Yes, I know about her sexual preference."

"I can tell you this, the way he looks at you is special. It's like the way his father looked at me. I think his emotions are jumbled. My son has always lived life where he's been a step ahead of everyone else, and now with you, he's just fighting to keep up. I think he finds his relationship with you both exciting and frightening at the same time."

"I appreciate your interest, but why are you telling me this?"

"Jen, my interest is the personal safety and happiness of my son."

"I am not following you," she responded.

"Since learning about his father's tragic death, my son has dreamed of being a superhero, defending the world against evil. Metaphorically speaking, all the superhero types I know of are dead. I want my son to have a reason not to take unnecessary risks. Also, two agents who care for each other will be there to watch each other's back. Let's just say, I think the Wilkins-Craft team is a winning combination."

"Knowing more about his father might bring us closer."

Amanda told the story about her time in New York, and the love she shared with Pete Sullivan. She described in detail their first sightseeing date in New York City, and the events leading up to their engagement weekend. Wilkins listened intently to every word, like a young girl hearing about the Cinderella fairy tale for the first time.

As the story progressed to the dreadful terrorist attack on September 11, 2001, Wilkins interrupted, seeing Amanda overcome with emotion. Although over twenty-five years in the past, the feelings for the man she loved came forth as if yesterday.

Wilkins responded by sharing personal aspects of her life as the granddaughter of James Crawford, living in boarding schools throughout the world. Needless to say, the ladies spent an afternoon bonding.

When it was time to bring this warm encounter to an end, Wilkins said, "I am so glad we had this conversation. Maybe we could spend some more time together in Scotland at the Open, if you decide to attend."

"Thanks for the offer but my staying out of the way is best. With regard to your relationship with my son having to end with the mission, all I can say is... *motivated people find a way.*"

CHAPTER 29

After reviewing the staffing plan, the Course Manager at Sabz Pardes Country Club knew he had a problem. Finding workers in Iran with golf course maintenance skills was difficult under normal conditions, but with the Asian Open on the horizon it was nearly impossible. The social tensions among Islamic fundamentalists and progressives created a stressful work environment for golf course employees, a problem that even increased pay had been unable to fix. During the past week, two maintenance workers had quit and others were now complaining of being over worked. He heard a knock on his office door. *It must be the new applicant*, he thought. A middle-aged man dressed in work clothes stood at the door. He invited the man into his office, offering a chair and cup of tea. The man thankfully accepted the tea.

"What's your name?" asked the Course Manager.

"Vahid Salehi," the applicant answered.

"Where are you from?"

"Tehran but I've been working outside the country."

"Where?"

"Most recently in Bahrain."

"I am looking for men with golf course experience, do you have any?"

"Yes, I can operate equipment, cut grass, and apply chemicals."

Surprised by the applicant's confident response, he asked, "Where did you get your experience?"

"Britain," the applicant responded.

"Do you speak English?"

"Yes."

English-speaking employees were highly desirable, given the large number of Westerners that would be attending the Asian Open. Observing that the middle-aged applicant looked in good physical condition, the Course Manager requested his references. The applicant placed his resume on the desk.

After scanning the impressive list of references, he asked, "Are you willing to begin work right now?"

"It depends. How much will I get paid?"

"Let me see how you do today and then we'll talk pay. If you are as good as your resume, you will be paid very well," responded the Course Manager before taking him to meet the staff at Sabz Pardes.

When the first day of free chemicals arrived at Sabz Pardes, it was Vahid Salehi standing on the loading dock ready to receive them.

CHARLESTON, SC

By the time they had returned from Australia, Craft's healthy living promotions were playing on media outlets throughout the Middle East. Vaughn gave the team the go ahead to move forward with the Riyadh operation. Wilkins called the Vice President of marketing at Baahir's investment firm and went over the proposal. Her client, Craft, would promote his firm's financial services, in return for Baahir's support of the First Light program within the Riyadh area. When the VP showed lack of interest in the offer, Wilkins turned up the pressure, mentioning that Amir Turani's planned to leverage his son's recent growth in popularity on the Tour to market his company's financial services.

Soon after ending the initial conversation, Baahir personally called Wilkins requesting details about Turani's marketing plans. She divulged just enough information to convince the Saudi businessman she had the inside track. It didn't take much convincing for him to agree to the proposal. She steered the conversation in a way that led to his offering to shoot the commercials at his compound in Riyadh. Intent on beating Turani to the punch, Baahir pushed to accelerate the schedule, requiring the event to take place within two weeks. After a mild protest, Wilkins agreed as long as she would be able to meet with his people this week at the Riyadh compound, to survey the site and work out the details.

She talked with the Saudi Minister of the Interior to coordinate the kickoff of the First Light program in Riyadh. She discussed security with the Minister and suggested it might be in the government's best interest to request Baahir provide the security force for the event. The Saudi official graciously accepted the offer of VIP tickets to the Open in Scotland.

Disguised as the image specialist responsible for directing the commercial, Vaughn would be traveling with Wilkins to Riyadh. Craft would stay in Charleston, rest and keep a low profile while the hype of his possibly winning a third consecutive Major built. Given the advanced capabilities of Baahir's security forces, installing sensors inside the compound would be too risky. The two agents would have to work as a team to create a mental picture of the compound's security layout, without the assistance of electronics.

With Wilkins in flight to Riyadh, Craft sat alone at the piano playing intensely emotional songs—turmoil, love, commitment, betrayal, agony, perseverance, triumph—letting his feelings out. His hands moved like a virtuoso, across the keyboard of a perfectly tuned grand piano. The music drained the emotion from his body, allowing his mind to think clearly.

He got up from the piano and called the number Daria had given him for the New York office.

"*Persian Woman*, Anna speaking?"

"Hi Anna, could I talk with Daria?"

"Who may I say is calling?"

"Peter Craft."

Looking at Craft's face on the display, she said, "Ms. Turani is on location doing a photo shoot. Would you like me to have her get in touch with you?"

"No, that's not necessary. I was hoping to surprise her. I'd appreciate it if you would tell me the location of the photo shoot?"

"Sorry Mr. Craft but I am not at liberty to do so," she said while holding up to the camera a mockup cover of next month's addition of the *Persian Woman* magazine with the word "Kitty Hawk" written on the cover.

"I understand," he responded.

He threw some clothes in a travel bag and disconnected the power from his HuAID so the signal couldn't be tracked. Dressed in jeans, an old tee shirt, and wearing a helmet with a dark lens, he drove a motorcycle out of the back exit used by delivery personnel to begin the trip up the Atlantic coast to the Outer Banks of North Carolina.

Soon after passing the "Welcome to Kitty Hawk" sign, he stopped to use the restroom at a local convenience store. He noticed an elderly lady making sandwiches in the deli section of the store. The lady had bleached blond hair and weather beaten skin, probably from years of sunbathing on the beautiful North Carolina beaches. Glancing at the name on her badge, he said "Good afternoon, Ms. Morgan."

"Would you like one of our fine sandwiches?" asked the lady.

"Do you have one that you recommend?"

"All the sandwiches are good. My favorite is the turkey on rye."

"Then I'll have a turkey on rye, with extra mayo."

"So what brings you to Kitty Hawk?"

"My friend works for a film crew, doing some filming in the area," he responded.

"One of the locals told me a fancy city magazine is taking pictures of girls on the beach, about six miles down the road. You want to hear something funny?"

"Sure."

"Yesterday, big Mike comes into the store with a long frown on his face. When he heard they were filming beautiful women on the beach, he went rushing down to the site to watch. He expected to see young girls wearing skimpy swimsuits. Big Mike said the girls were dressed like peacocks, wearing colorful beach clothes entirely covering their bodies."

After enjoying a good laugh, Craft thanked Ms. Morgan for the sandwich and wished her well. It was late in the afternoon when he arrived. The filming site was roped off, with security patrolling the perimeter. One of the men guarding the entry looked familiar. It was Javid, the young man he met at General Shirazi's estate.

Javid recognized the Tour golfer when he approached. He asked Craft to wait and then walked to the filming area a couple hundred yards away, where he disappeared into a temporary building. The guard returned with a note from Daria, containing the address of the beach house where she was staying and the security code to get in.

When Craft opened the front door to the beach home, a young man lounging by the pool jumped to his feet. Seeing the frightened man, Craft introduced himself and apologized for not knocking first.

Introducing himself as Maurice, the young man said, "So you're the elusive Mr. Craft. Daria has mentioned you once or twice or a few thousand times; who's counting?"

"Pleased to meet you, Maurice. If you don't mind, I'll relax in the living room until Daria returns."

"She is so right. You're dreamy," said the young man.

"Yes, I am a dreamer," replied Craft.

"Well, it's time for me to skedaddle and give you two some alone time."

Before walking out the door, he handed Craft his business card and said, "If you're ever looking to make a fashion statement, please give Maurice a call."

"You're the first one I'll call."

Maurice was a world famous fashion designer, specializing in a unique blend of American and Persian style clothing. He had designed the colorful clothing that big Mike had referred to, as "women dressed like peacocks." Craft smiled as he thought of the reaction he would receive wearing some of Maurice's colorful creations on the golf course.

Covered with sweat from the long motorcycle ride in hot summer Carolina sun, Craft reached into his travel bag for a swimsuit, slipped it on, rinsed off in the shower by the pool and dove into the cool water. When Daria arrived at the beach house, Craft was lounging by the pool, drinking juice, and reading a current copy of *Persian Woman*. He delighted in the opportunity to experience the Iranian princess on his own. She didn't look like an airbrushed model on the cover of a magazine; she had the look of a real woman returning home after a hard day of work, mentally and physically drained.

Daria had mixed emotions. She wanted to give him a passionate welcome, but was disappointed by his thoughtless behavior following the U.S. Open. She suppressed the desire to make a hurtful remark and instead gave him a friendly embrace and said, "I am surprised to see you. Shouldn't you be in Scotland, preparing to win the next big tournament?"

"Yes, but we need to talk."

"You could've called," she remarked.

"Then I would have missed seeing you in person."

"Enjoy yourself, because this is the real me. Directing a photo shoot isn't all that glamorous. If you think Tour players have big egos, walk a day in my shoes."

She showered, changed into comfortable clothes, and then emerged from the bedroom, refreshed with a new attitude and food on her mind. "I am starving; let's talk during dinner."

"Please let me help," he replied.

They worked like a team making dinner. She teased him on his cooking technique, and he intentionally bumped her whenever she moved into his space. He made a mango salad and she made Kobab Torsh, a tenderloin beef marinated in a paste made with crushed walnuts, pomegranate juice, chopped parsley, olive oil, and crushed garlic. Daria set the table in the pool area, turned down the lights, and lit a candle in the middle of the table. Craft activated the entertainment system, accessing over the network the private collection of classical piano melodies that he had recorded.

Daria remembered an article in a popular golf magazine, portraying Craft as an accomplished pianist who played for pleasure and relaxation, but mostly in private. She knew this was his way of sharing something personal that only a few chosen people had experienced. Having taken piano lessons for years as a child, she could appreciate the sound of a truly gifted musician and his ability to play with such passion. She knew the music told a story, a life experience and some day she would ask him to share it.

They sat across from each other at the small dining table, gazing at each other through the flickering candlelight, like two lovers longing to be with each other, but forbidden by social prejudices. He apologized again for showing up unannounced. She admitted that Anna had mentioned the possibility of his visit.

"I enjoyed our evening in D.C.," he said.

"You have an strange way of showing it," she snapped. "We share a delightful evening together, and then nothing, no messages, no calls ..."

"You have to know by now, the picture of us kissing caused public outrage in areas of the Middle East. The image of an Islamic woman and a Western man together is socially unacceptable to much of the world's population, and especially in Iran."

In a huffy voice, Daria added, "Everything I do offends the righteous!"

"This is much bigger than you and me. It's about building bridges between our nations and right now, those bridges are fragile. One well intended but thoughtless action could take those bridges down," replied Craft.

"Try to see it from my perspective. My life has been devoted to bridge building; that's why I started *Persian Woman*. The hardest part of my job is dealing with self-centered girls wanting to move too fast. I am the one reminding everyone to take it slow, stick to the plan, be responsible..."

"So, let's deal with the truth. The truth is I didn't drive several hours to see you in hopes of a one-night stand. I am looking long-term."

"I am glad you got the possibility of having a one night stand out of the way up front."

"Be honest, you didn't fly halfway around the world just to spend a few hours with me at your uncle's estate." Taking the dishes to the kitchen, she disingenuously remarked, "I flew halfway around the world to be with my brother; you just happened to be there."

Daria returned with after dinner drinks made with watermelon juice. As they sipped the juice, she couldn't help wonder what was really going on in the mind of the man across the table. Was life dealing her a deserved twist of fate? By the seriousness in his tone, tonight was payback for all the times she left adoring suitors craving more. She would be the one left unfulfilled tonight.

"How is Kamran? We haven't spoken since the U.S. Open."

"Along with many of the other players on the Tour, he's been spending most his time in Scotland, getting ready for the Open at Saint Andrews. The notion of a first year player dominating the Tour has strengthened the bond among the veteran players. My brother took the loss at the U.S. Open hard, especially missing so many short putts with the tournament on the line. Kamran is leading the charge, trying to get the veteran players to step up their games."

"Your brother's loss at the U.S. Open was just bad luck."

"Kamran doesn't believe in bad luck; he thinks practicing harder is the answer. I now have two men in my life driven by the obsession of golf."

Surprised that she considered him a man in her life, Craft replied, "You're right, golf is consuming me. I am not going to make excuses. I am on track to win the Grand Slam of Golf, something so challenging that only one person has ever done it, Bobby Jones, and that was decades ago. If history is any indication, I will never have this chance again. Tiger Woods came close by winning the four Majors in a row, but not in the same year. He never came close again. So what I am saying is, this is a once in a life-time chance."

"If we are going to be truth telling, then I have something to share. My feelings on Sunday at the U.S. Open were conflicted. Although I love my brother dearly, I prayed for you to win. Although I felt disloyal to my family, there is something about you and it took me awhile to figure it out."

"What did you figure out?"

"You're complex," she said. "You function at a higher level than other Tour players. When we first met, you had just won the Masters, and your mind was already focusing on the next step in your personal journey."

"I am a small town boy from Charleston, South Carolina. Winning the Masters was surreal."

"That's what you want me and others to believe. I have a different theory. You're an extremely complex person, and anyone who listened to you play music would know it. You're not motivated by winning golf tournaments, not even the Grand Slam of Golf."

Concerned she was making connections that might put the mission at risk, he asked, "So, what is it you think my motivations are?"

"Please, don't let this go to your head?" she asked. "I am surrounded by men with oversized egos. For you, golf is just a means to an end. You're destined to make an impact on the world in a truly profound way. You're using your golf skills to open doors to change the world. What saddens me most is... you came here to ask me to sit on the sidelines."

"Sorry to disappoint you, but right now my concern is winning Majors. If wanting to use golf to build a closer relationship between our nations for the greater good is what you are talking about, then I am trying to change the world. The reality is, in October of this year, thousands of people will be traveling to Tehran for the last Major of year. If you have been following the news, then you know the President is under great pressure to cancel American participation. If the tournament is cancelled, I can't win it, and our nations are dealt a setback. Tensions are mounting, so we must proceed with caution. On top of it all, the paparazzi monitor everything I do."

"You made it clear in Qom your focus is golf, so why are you here?"

"It's going to be publicly announced that Jennifer Wilkins and I are romantically involved. Our having a relationship plays well in the eyes of the public, and doing anything to reduce tension between our two nations going into the Open, is a good thing."

Offended by his confession, she asked, "Why are you telling me this?"

"Because I thought telling you in person was the right thing to do, and you would understand the security concerns going forward."

"Right now, my capacity for understanding is weak. It might be better if you leave."

"Before I leave, there is one more thing you need to know."

"And what might that be?" she asked.

"What I am going to say will anger your family. Please tell them I am a friend."

"My family is skeptical of everyone. Our survival depends on it."

"I will be doing a commercial for Mr. Baahir to promote his financial services company, in exchange for his supporting the First Light program."

Stunned by the news, there was nothing left to say. Craft thanked her for dinner, and she graciously walked him out to his motorcycle parked in front of the beach house. She watched the backlights of the motorcycle disappear into the night, trying to comprehend what happened this evening. *Was he asking her to wait? Was his relationship with Wilkins a fraud? Was he saying goodbye?...*

CHAPTER 30

CHARLESTON, SC

In the secure area of the beach house, Wilkins talked at length about the trip to Riyadh and the challenges they would have to overcome in order to search Baahir's office.

Shifting the conversation, she asked, "Did you enjoy your free time?"

Initially, he didn't plan to talk about the trip to Kitty Hawk, but something worried him. "I met with Daria Turani in Kitty Hawk."

At first she acted totally surprised and then asked, "Did you meet Maurice?"

"Are you kidding me? Maurice is one of our guys."

"Let's just say, he keeps an eye on things."

"Her name is Daria," responded Craft.

She leaned forward so he could see her cleavage. "No offense, but even the most disciplined men have a problem thinking clearly around a seductive woman." She pressed her body against his, so he could feel the firmness of her breasts as her hand gently rubbed against his groin. "It's simply fact that women have taken advantage of this evolutionary flaw in men since the beginning of time."

Within seconds, they were kissing and frantically taking off each other's clothing. Partly undressed, Wilkins froze. She gently backed away and began putting her clothes back on, as he stood watching.

"Is something wrong?" he asked. "I thought you wanted to see where things would go."

"I do... but at the same time, I don't. Not like this anyway. It's different now."

"What's different?"

"Our relationship."

"How?"

"I met your mother."

"So what? She really likes you."

"I know, but things are different now. I truly apologize for sending mixed signals."

He gently held her, to show he was ready to listen. "What does your change of heart have to do with my mother?"

"When we had lunch, your mother told the most wonderful story of her falling in love with your father. Their first date in New York was the most romantic story I have ever heard. Although it was years ago, her eyes sparkled like diamonds as she talked about their time together. That's what I am looking for in a relationship."

When the heat of the moment passed, they switched back to business. He shared the essence of his dinner conversation at Kitty Hawk, careful to provide just the needed details, without revealing any of the intimacy. As he talked, Wilkins wondered if he would ever be able to return the feelings she had for him. After listening to him stumble his way through, she assured him the Iranian girl's motives were innocent and she truly believed he was playing golf to make the world a better place.

Exhausted from the trip to Riyadh and their emotional encounter, Wilkins told him she would be meeting with the executive team at CIA Headquarters soon. As she was in midsentence, he hit the button on the wall and the green light disappeared, indicating the area was no longer secure.

"We can talked about business later. Right now you need rest," he insisted.

She agreed and went upstairs to the bedroom where she slept for hours. The next morning, after showering and getting into comfortable beach clothing, she went downstairs to continue discussing business. When she walked into the secure area, he handed her a drink and a turkey sandwich and pushed the button on the wall, and waited for the light to turn green. "What's up? It's obvious you have something big on your mind."

"To create havoc, some of the Tour veterans are promoting a conspiracy theory, that you and Kamran have joined together in a clever way of cheating at golf. His defending you at the U.S. Open didn't help the situation. We've tried to redirect the focus, but our traditional methods haven't worked. Some members of the executive team are concerned this could turn into an international problem and are putting pressure on the Director to shut down the program."

"Let's think it through, starting with the facts."

"Okay, the facts. Your favorability among the Islamic population is solid. Wilson has determined you really don't need Smartball to win.

He believes you would have won the U.S. Open by three strokes if we didn't use technology assistance. Some of the Tour veterans have united to make veiled accusations that you and Kamran have conspired to win tournaments."

"So we need to change our approach. Let's create a wedge that will expose our accusers, and then make them look like fools in public."

"If we go on the offensive, there are going to be casualties, and your reputation will be on the line. To date, you have been portrayed as a 'good old boy' from Charleston who has been fortunate enough to win golf tournaments. It's a very likable image. If we go on the offensive, your image will become more dominant, forcing people to take sides. In other words, people will either love you or hate you, but most will have a strong opinion."

"In the words of Dr. Page... *this isn't about me.*"

She looked at him with concern. "You're also human. It's your all-star reputation that's going to get trashed."

"Well, if that happens then you can rehabilitate it."

"If I get the go ahead, then by the end of the week the media frenzy will be so loud, it's going to be deafening. I mean, crowds of people camped outside the house and following us everywhere we go. Are you really prepared for this?"

"If it's necessary, then I am ready."

"Okay, then, I need to know the real deal on your physical conditioning."

"I'm fully recovered."

Handing him a letter, she said, "You better be because tomorrow morning you are working out with the Miami Dolphins football team. They are going to put you through the combined workout given to rookies in preparation for the football draft. Based on historical performance, you should have the fastest 40-yard dash time of any quarterback this year, score high enough in the strength and agility drills, and easily charm everyone. The unknown is how well you'll do throwing the football, given you haven't actually played football in a while."

"You don't forget how to throw a football."

•

Craft invited a couple of his friends to meet him at a local athletic center for a football workout. After a few warm up drills, he began moving around the football field and throwing like a quarterback again. After the workout, he thanked the guys, buying drinks and hors d'oeuvres at a popular beachfront lounge.

When Craft returned to the beach house, Wilkins commented it was a beautiful day and suggested they go for a walk. They walked along the beach with the warm waves splashing over their feet. With the sun low in the sky, soon to be over the horizon, the heat of a summer day had passed. Wilkins tossed the football back to him, pretending to be the center hiking the ball. He moved as if pretending to dodge an approaching defender, and with the flick of his wrist, send the football sailing through the air, careful to ensure the ball landed on dry sand. On the way back to the beach house, they walked hand in hand, like two lovers out for a stroll. In front of the beach house, they sat on the steps watching the waves as the moon in the night sky reflected on the water.

CIA HEADQUARTERS
MCLEAN, VA

Director Walker began the executive team meeting with an emphatic appeal, "I need you to come up with a real plan to locate the stolen nuclear material."

She didn't say it, but the political pressures of a vicious reelection campaign had the White House breathing down her back. Her frustration with the Agency's inability to use in place intelligence assets to locate the missing nuclear waste was evident. When the Chief of Middle East Operations began his standard response that more financial resources would be required, Walker signaled her attack dog, Beaumont, to take over and then exited the meeting.

Now a strong proponent of the Red Crescent program, Beaumont said, "I think we have an actionable plan. My gut tells me the stolen nuclear material is part of the Saudi's plan for protecting his financial empire. I suspect he's funding Gilani. We just need to prove it. The Saudi is a control freak, getting access to his private network will give us the intel we need. We have a plan. The plan is to go forward with the Riyadh operation."

The Middle East Chief protested, making the case that the fundamentalist Shiite cleric, Gilani, would never join forces with the Sunni business tycoon, Baahir.

The Frenchman verbally ripped into the Middle East Chief. "You were wrong about VIPER I and your wrong now. Vaughn's team has delivered more critical intelligence in a few weeks than you have in years. I am telling you right now, the Riyadh operation will confirm the connection between Baahir and Gilani and lead us to the hijacked nuclear waste."

While sitting there quietly listening to the DCS' tirade, Vaughn appreciated Walker's bulldog chewing on someone else's ass instead of his. Most of all, the DCS was creating a sense of urgency to change the status quo mindset of the Agency culture.

After more discussion and another attempt by the Middle East Chief to raise his concerns, the team agreed to execute the Riyadh operation.

Next, Vaughn brought up the issue of the emerging conspiracy theory linking Craft and the Iranian in a cheating scheme and how it could complicate an already difficult mission. Wilkins provided the status of the current media situation and outlined a revised course of action. After briefing the executive team and answering many "what if" questions, approval was granted. She could see the executive team members were relieved that going forward would no long require the use of Smartball. Only Beaumont expressed concern about the potential negative impact to Craft's public image; the others simply thought of it as an occupational hazard. None of the people at the table ever had a public image to worry about, so being concerned about Craft's was unnatural. Their career success involved obtaining intelligence by hiding in the shadows, and changing colors like chameleons to blend into the shifting global environment.

MIAMI, FL

He relaxed in a teal colored Bentley convertible, reading the sports page of the *Miami Herald* newspaper while soaking up the Florida morning sun. The aircraft sent to pick Craft up in Charleston would soon arrive. The Miami Dolphins' GM, also a Clemson University graduate, prepared to give the #1 ranked Tour player the fanfare he deserved. Eager to meet him, the GM spent the previous evening reviewing Craft's bio and exchanging messages with the many Clemson staff having coached the quarterback in college.

Craft was surprised the GM had come to the airport to escort him to the athletic center and was delighted to learn they shared Clemson roots. During the ride, they engaged in a deep discussion of Clemson's recent football successes and disappointments. Both agreed if not for late session injuries, the Clemson Tigers would have won the 2024 National Championship.

Given that Craft had taken five years off from playing professional football and had a successful golf career going, the GM inquired as to why consider the NFL now? Craft explained that it was a matter of market timing. The length of his football career was, at best, a few years while his golf career could last decades. He also wanted to dispel the media bias that a professional football player couldn't compete on the Tour, and the reverse.

Being off-season for the players, he thought his tryout would be a low-key operation, with the coaching team going through the motions of testing his football skills to please someone in the front office. To his surprise, the entire football team stood outside ready to greet him when he arrived at the training complex. Craft drew attention when during warm-up drills he started throwing 60-yard downfield passes with grace and ease. Before long, the wide receivers were volunteering to run patterns. Seeing Craft's skills, the coaches huddled and then changed the agenda. They started running basic plays full-speed with no pads. Craft's ability to escape trouble and go down field with long passes to wide receivers was impressive. After two hours of intense practice with the starters, the coaching team continued with the skills and speed testing. It was a formality, given the coaching staff had already validated the young man's exceptional athletic abilities. Craft sensed the coaching team was eager to work out a deal, but why he wasn't sure. He was good, but there were lots of good quarterbacks with proven NFL experience and no gap in their careers.

CHAPTER 31

When Wilkins walked into the secure room at the Kiawah Island house, returning from Virginia, Craft was on the floor stretching his legs to relieve the cramping from his extreme workout in Miami. At one point on the flight back to Charleston, the pain had been so strong he had to stretch out in the middle of the aisle to relieve a cramping abductor muscles in his right leg.

After securing the room, Wilkins sat down on the floor next to him. "So they worked you hard today."

"In addition to doing all the testing drills, I spent two hours running full speed with the starting team. It was fun, but my body is paying the price."

"I can visualize you escaping from the grasp of the converging defensive line, ready to pound your face into the ground, to let the ball fly downfield into the hands of a sprinting receiver crossing the goal line." Wilkins jumped up, and started dancing around like a cheerleader for the football team. "Do you think I could make the Miami Dolphins cheerleading squad?" she joked.

"You're not tan enough. The Dolphins' cheerleaders look like bronzed goddesses."

"Give me a couple of days on the beach, and this farm girl becomes a true beach babe."

"Given your light complexion and Irish freckles, you must be mistaking a red burn for a brown tan."

"I like my freckles. They give me character," she said while pointing to the freckles on her arms.

"I like them too," he responded, pointing to the freckles on her red cheeks.

Getting the conversation back on track, Craft said, "By the way, my being at the Dolphins training complex was the worst kept secret in the world."

"Who said it was a secret?"

"My hand and back hurt from all the handshakes and backslaps I received, walking into the facility. Many players brought their children, and probably most of the neighborhood children too. I spent the first hour, giving golf lessons and signing autographs. Instead of bringing footballs the kids brought golf clubs. These kids have better equipment than I do."

Sitting down on the floor next to him, Wilkins said, "Believe me, you're playing football is no joke to the Dolphins' management. They're seeing big dollars. As soon as you left Miami, the receivers went as a group to meet with the GM, endorsing the idea of giving you a contract to be backup quarterback. As soon as the receivers left, the starting quarterback was in the GM's office, demanding a contract modification to ensure he kept his starting position. You seem to cause trouble wherever you go these days."

"There are a lot of good football players; I am really not that special. Not sure what the big fuss is about."

"Tell that to the Dolphins' management. The GM has already sent a one-year contract offering eleven million dollars for you to play back-up quarterback, with an option to start if the team losses three or more of their first six games."

"At this point, nothing surprises me but I'll ask anyway. Why would any football team pay millions for someone who hasn't played in four years? Oh, I get it. Your trust fund owns the team."

"You may have studied International Marketing, but you don't know your own value. You're worth a lot more than eleven million dollars. You're their insurance policy. The Dolphins are facing a difficult early season schedule, and could be out of playoff contention in the first few weeks of the season. If that happens, then replacing the starting quarterback with you could fill the stadium with fans wanting to see if a professional golfer can survive the brutality of professional football. What you demonstrated today was the athletic ability to survive, at least a few games. The difference between having 90,000 people versus 40,000 people at the game equates to $300 million dollars in revenue."

"So what you are saying is… the Dolphins plan to feed me to the lions, to keep the citizens coming to the coliseum?"

"That's an interesting way to look at it."

"Is Vaughn on board with this?" he asked.

"Sure Vaughn is on board. The entire executive team is on board. They think it's quite brilliant."

"What's brilliant? Me getting mauled by lions?"

"Hey, you told the President the nation couldn't ask too much of you."

"I knew those words would come back to haunt me."

She got on her knees and began to rub his back. "Don't worry, I have your back." Then she placed her arms around his chest, and gave him a kiss on the neck, "I like your body the way it is, not twisted into a pretzel."

Getting serious, Wilkins informed him that by morning, the paparazzi would be camped outside the house. Starting that night, allegations of cheating and conspiracy would hit the major networks. Using statistical data provided by Jack Wilson, a credible, but unidentified source would make the accusation that statistically, it would be impossible for a "good old boy" from Charleston, South Carolina to come out of nowhere to win two Major tournaments, without help. Added to the assertion of Craft's cheating was the Iranian's dramatic improvement on the golf course, after becoming friends with Craft. At first, people would latch onto the allegations and begin a course of public outrage, and the veteran player who started the initial rumors of cheating would come forward to grab the media spotlight.

The citizens of Charleston would be deeply hurt, but most would come to Craft's defense because they knew his true character and athletic abilities. After sitting tight for a couple of days to let the frenzy reach its peak, the team would go on the offensive, recasting the portrayal of Craft as an extraordinary person with an exceptional combination of intellectual, physical, and character attributes; a combination so rare that his not achieving extraordinary accomplishments would be underachieving. In defense of Craft, the public would rise up in mass support, crushing the opposition and exposing any real threats to the mission. The allegations of cheating linking him and the Iranian would so outrage the Islamic community, that Craft's popularity would reach its peak before the Open Championship in Scotland.

After talking through the new approach with him, she went upstairs to change into casual clothing, and returned to the secure room where he continued to stretch his muscles. Feeling guilty for surprising him with the football diversion, she asked him to go with her to the fitness room. She helped him take off his clothes and asked him to lie down on the trainer's table. She began performing a professional massage, using oil, heated sandbags, and deep strokes. The cover for her first mission at the Agency was a massage therapist. In preparation, she learned professional massage techniques. By the end of the session, he was sound asleep on the table. She put a blanket over him, and went to the secure area to continue work.

When Craft awoke, he was amazed at how relaxed he felt. Wilkins had just finished a collaboration session with the team when he entered the secure area.

"Your mother told me something intriguing about your musical skills."

"She is a proud mother, who tends to embellish things."

"May be, but would you humor me by playing the piano?"

"After the massage you gave me, I would be a fool to refuse."

They went to the sunroom and sat down at the grand piano. Wilkins gave a voice command for the integrated entertainment system to play a piano composition recently self-authored by a student at the New England Conservatory of Music. She knew this would be the first time Craft would have heard the music. After listening to the composition, Wilkins said, "Your mother told me you are able to play a musical composition after only listening to it once."

"I can, but it will differ from the original. Actually, it will be different each time I play it." He began playing.

Wilkins couldn't believe what she was hearing. It was as good, or even better than the original composition. He played with such ease and emotion.

"How did you learn to play like that?" she asked.

"I don't know. My first few music teachers couldn't deal with it. They wanted me to play music the way it was written on the music sheets. My last teacher embraced it as a special talent."

"How do you remember all music?"

"I am not really sure; my mind just organizes it. For example, if you asked me to play a romantic song, I would play the first one that comes into my mind. If you asked me the same thing tomorrow, a different song would come to mind."

"Will you play some summer themed romantic songs for me?"

Craft began playing a medley of songs, starting with a 1959 classic, *Theme from a Summer Place* and ending with the new composition,

Summer by the Sea. As music filled the room, she found her mind relaxing. It was amazing that he could just sit down at the piano and play such beautiful music from memory.

She thought his gift was like being a musical savant with both passion and creativity. *How did one person get so many gifts?* she wondered. It was going to be easy to portray him as an extraordinary person because it was simply the truth.

Wilkins asked, "If you could play in front of a large audience with an orchestra backing you up, what music would you play?"

"As a child, I dreamed of playing *Rhapsody in Blue* at Carnegie Hall in New York City. I pretended performing it hundreds of times."

No need to ask why the song was so special. It was his tribute to his father who lost his life in service to the citizens of New York City. *Rhapsody in Blue* was a 1924 jazz concerto composed by George Gershwin. Over time, the composition became known as a portrait of New York City.

The conspiracy theories of Craft's cheating spread like wildfire across the network, taking only a few hours to reach the major media outlets. By the next morning, a large gathering of reporters and spectators were camped outside the gates of the Kiawah Island house. The two agents hunkered down in the beach house, waiting two days for the frenzy to reach its peak. Several Tour players had given interviews, indicating they suspected foul play but couldn't prove it.

After two days, they agreed to address the issue, by granting a prime-time interview with Bartholomew Higgins, the host of a top news program on the British Sports Network. Higgins would interview Craft during the first segment of the show, and then Wilkins to conclude the show. Using ultra high-resolution video teleconferencing, Higgins conducted the interviews from his London broadcast studio, with the two of them at a studio in the Charleston area.

After thanking Craft for accepting the invitation and recapping his recent accomplishments on the golf course, Higgins said, "A credible source claims the probability of you, a rookie, winning two Major tournaments at over a hundred million to one. Do you see why some people might suspect you have manipulated things, to get an unfair advantage?"

"It's good for people to be skeptical. It maintains the integrity of the game," answered Craft.

"I thought you might be angry, with the allegations of cheating now in the headlines of major news outlets."

"Golf is big money. A player needs thick skin to excel."

"Who do you think is behind these allegations?"

"I don't really know. Do you?" asked Craft.

"I've been told some of the Tour players have gone public with their suspicions."

"Having suspicion is easy; having proof is a different story," responded Craft.

"Let's talk about the astonishing odds you have overcome, to become the number one ranked golfer in the world."

"I admit it, my winning two Major golf tournament is extraordinary. So what? Extraordinary events happen from time to time in every sport."

"Can you give an example?"

"Sure. I was eight years old when a journeyman golfer, Graeme McDowell, from Northern Ireland, came from behind on a Sunday to win the U.S. Open. To those who didn't know of McDowell, his winning a Major seemed pretty unbelievable. Since that time, McDowell has established himself as one of the best players in the world."

"As well as McDowell played in his early years, he didn't win two Majors in a row as a rookie," said Higgins.

"You are correct, but the next year another golfer from Northern Ireland, a place at the time not known as a golf powerhouse, entered the Tour as a rookie. Rory McIlroy dominated the first three days at the Masters, going into Sunday with a big lead. Rory didn't win, but he could have. After his devastating loss at the Masters, he rebounded strong, to win the U.S. Open Championship that same year."

"You have given excellent examples," commented Higgins. "Being British, I say this with true conviction, the odds of two golfers from Northern Ireland winning back-to-back U.S. Opens was astronomical. Also, McIlroy, as a rookie, did come very close to winning two Major tournaments in 2012. I don't remember anyone suggesting the Irishman was cheating based on statistical evidence."

"My point is that, on the surface, the accomplishments of these gentlemen appeared extraordinary, but after closer examination of the individuals, it became evident that Graeme and Rory are exceptional players who were destined for great professional achievement," Craft said.

"I think your recent friendship with Kamran Turani, from Iran, has fueled suspicions because his performance on the golf course improving dramatically after meeting you. Will you discuss your relationship?"

"We were paired together on Sunday at the Masters, and discovered we both have mutual interests outside of golf, especially motorcycle racing. While I am a novice at best, Kamran is a professional level racer. I guess you could say we conspired to help each other. In fact, we cut a deal."

"What kind of deal?" Higgins asked.

"I agreed to help Kamran improve his concentration on the golf course, and he agreed to help me improve my performance on the race track."

Higgins laughed. "Given Kamran's exceptional play at the Players and U.S. Open, I would have to say he received the better end of the deal."

"The deal was good for both of us. Kamran has agreed to co-sponsor the First Light program, so you could say the children have benefited from the deal also."

"Do you have any idea of how to satisfy those making the accusations?"

"I am not sure I can, but I am willing to do anything reasonable for the sake of the game."

"The allegations continue to be centered around your equipment."

"My grandfather once told me if people are going to fixate on a conspiracy, then make it a big one. Right now, the conspiracy involves the Charleston-Tehran connection. Let's get the Tour in on the action. If the commissioner agrees, I am willing to play the Open in Scotland, using equipment provided by the Tour. My equipment specifications are a matter of public record. There is one stipulation. Following the tournament, the equipment will be sold at public auction and the proceeds donated to the First Light program. If I am fortunate enough to win, then the people promoting the conspiracy theory will have to include the Tour."

"I see where your proposal could dispel the notion of a conspiracy. On the other hand, golf is supposed to give all competitors a fair chance to win. Your proposal gives your competition an unfair advantage."

Referencing an old saying around Charleston, Craft said, *"It's not the hammer, it's the carpenter that gets the house built."*

"I am supposed to be objective, but I'll just say it. If it were me, I would tell them all to pound sand," said Higgins.

"That's one way to deal with the problem. Another way is to keep performing on the golf course. Soon, the allegations will become so outrageous even the conspiracy folks won't believe them themselves."

Higgins thanked his guest, and announced the next segment would interview Craft's business manager.

To begin the next segment, he asked Jennifer Wilkins to explain her important role on Craft's golf team.

Jokingly, Wilkins answered, "Craft plays golf, Jefferson carries the clubs, and I do everything else."

To give viewers a firsthand look at her in action, Higgins played a short video of Wilkins addressing the media at the U.S. Open. "I think it's accurate to say, you have a personal interest in your job."

"I have both a professional and personal interest in Mr. Craft's success on and off the golf course."

"Could you elaborate on your personal interest in Mr. Craft off the golf course?"

"I don't think our personal relationship is relevant to this discussion."

Agreeing, Higgins discussed the great traditions and high ethical standards of golf, and then asked Ms. Wilkins to share her thoughts regarding the allegations of cheating.

Wilkins responded, "I would be lying if I said the allegations don't concern me. They hit at the core of a man I have come to know well."

"What would you like the world to know about Mr. Craft?"

"Peter Craft is an unassuming person, so it is easy to portray him as a country boy who came out of nowhere to win two Majors. The good people of Charleston, South Carolina know that image is far from the truth. Starting as a young child, Peter Craft achieved an extraordinary list of record-breaking accomplishments. The notion he would cheat at golf for personal gain is simply absurd. My God, he gives most of his winnings to support youth golf around the world."

She took a moment to calm herself. "If I put my emotions aside and look at things objectively, the allegations of cheating are predictable."

"You seem to have shifted gears," Higgins commented, "I am not sure the audience is following you."

"It's no secret the men on the Tour have big egos, competing for millions of dollars. Something out of the ordinary has occurred. A young man comes out of nowhere, to win the first two Majors of the year, and they want answers."

"So how do you explain this unusual situation?"

"I believe Ms. Charlotte Bates, a reporter for the *Charleston News*, said it best in an article she wrote last March, when Craft received an invitation to his first Tour event. I would like to read a short quote from the article: *Professional golf will start a new era when Peter Craft steps to the first tee at this year's Orlando Open—an era in which world-class athletes choose to compete against athletically challenged golfers, hardly a fair competition."*

"Do you consider Tiger Woods in his prime a world-class athlete?"

"In his prime, he was a good athlete, in better physical condition than most of the players on Tour, but never in the category of a world-class athlete."

"Let's assume for the moment your assertion is true. So what?" asked Higgins.

"The combination of strength and physical endurance required to perform at a world-class level is far beyond what is required to compete at golf. I am talking about having speed and endurance comparable to Olympic athletes, and those exceptional athletes who excel at physically strenuous sports like professional football, soccer, and hockey."

"So you believe Craft's extraordinary golf achievements are the result of his exceptional athletic abilities."

"Absolutely. What you saw in the first three tournaments was a superior athlete playing golf at full strength. Unfortunately, at the U.S. Open, you saw a superior athlete playing golf in a weakened condition, but still with the endurance to prevail. Being a humble man, Craft would never say what the people of Charleston already know. *Peter Craft is the best all-around athlete to ever play on the Tour."*

"Again, why is this important?"

"This distinction is important because the other Tour players are trying to explain something they have never encountered; playing golf against a competitor who has the speed, strength, and endurance of a professional athlete."

"Would you be so kind as to enlighten us with facts to support your accusation?"

"Talk is cheap. Next Tuesday, Peter Craft is scheduled to play a practice round at Saint Andrews. It just happens that two members of the British national track team, who will be competing in this year's Olympic games, have agree to put on a demonstration event with Peter Craft on Wednesday morning at the London Track Club. All proceeds will be donated to charity, half going to support the British Olympic team, and the other half to the First Light program. The demonstration will involve a 100-meter race showcasing speed, and a 1500-meter race demonstrating both speed and endurance. For a modest donation, other Tour players are welcome to participate. Kamran Turani has already agreed to compete in the 1500-meter."

Higgins expressed interest in attending the event. He challenged the veteran Tour players to step up, and disprove Ms. Wilkins' bold assertion.

Wilkins continued. "In the early evening, three swimmers from the British swim team who will be competing in the Olympics, have agreed to do a competitive race against Craft in short, medium, and long range events. Did I forget to mention that four years ago Craft qualified to be on the U.S. Olympic swim team? Unfortunately, a family illness kept him from competing at the games."

"What do you recommend people do, who want to support Craft and Turani's battle against their accusers?" asked Higgins.

"Since both players are committed to promoting youth golf around the world, I suggest those who would like to make a statement, donate to the First Light program. One hundred percent of the funds will go to the children. Mr. Craft and Mr. Turani have already made generous donations to pay for the program's administrative costs."

Higgins concluded the interview by asking everyone to come out and support the charity event, and observe Peter Craft's exceptional athletic abilities firsthand.

CHAPTER 32

EDINBURGH, SCOTLAND

Craft made a late night entry into the Scotsman Hotel using a private entrance reserved for dignitaries, caught a couple hours of sleep, and then reviewed the day's agenda with Wilkins. He would start the day, eating breakfast with Kamran followed by running in the Edinburgh 10K charity run to benefit the local Fire Brigade. Later in the afternoon, he would play a practice round at St. Andrews. She reminded him to keep his personal feelings in check with the Iranian, and cautioned him not to get caught up in the competitive spirit of the 10K race. She knew some of the best runners in Scotland would be there to challenge him. She reminded him they came to Britain to make allies, not enemies.

He sat in a private dining room looking out the window at the Edinburgh shop owners below. Soon their stores would be filled with tourists, many whom had come to the Scottish heartland, seeking relief from the dog days of summer heat. Edinburgh was located in the coastal area of the North Sea where summer temperatures seldom rose above the mid sixties. Only the hearty dared to shed their jackets and sweaters for shorts and T-shirts, even during the warmest periods of the day.

When the Iranian arrived for breakfast, he gave a warm embrace. "I want to register a complaint," Kamram joked, "Jennifer Wilkins has hurt my business prospects by telling the world how good an athlete you are. Now, finding players to bet is next to impossible, and the guys we beat in the relay race at the Players want their money back."

"What money? The way you explained the bet, it was about cleaning golf shoes."

"Don't worry. I donated your share to the First Light program."

"I wanted to meet with you to apologize for any hardship the allegations of misconduct have caused you and your family," Craft explained,

"Hardship?" Kamran laughed. "Things couldn't have worked out better. The media attack on us triggered a spontaneous rally of support among my people. The family business is flourishing, with new clients wanting to show support to counter the grave injustice being inflicted upon their noble Persian prince."

"I am glad things are working out." Craft reviewed the First Light finances with him, highlighting that millions of dollars in donations had been received in the last few days. They discussed using the money to accelerate the building of the public golf course in south Tehran and scheduling the opening ceremony to coincide with the Asian Open.

Kamran admitted links style golf with the blistering North Sea winds did not suit his game. He cautioned his friend to stay out of the impossible fairway bunkers, and recommended it would be wise to just hack it out and not try to go for the green. He told the story of attempting to hit out of a bunker to the green only 100 yards away. The ball flew into tall grass about five feet in front of the bunker. The ball had only travelled a total of ten feet, but he could not find the ball. To make things worse, the very next hole, a par three, he hit a tee shot to ten feet above the hole. After marking his ball and fixing the ball mark on the green, he replaced the ball and picked up the ball marker. Getting ready to strike the ball, he felt a big gust of wind, and then the ball started rolling down hill past the hole, nearly going in, and then rolled off the green, coming to rest on the edge of a greenside bunker where he would have to stand in the bunker to hit the ball. To make things worse, the bunker was several feet below the ball. So, instead of putting from ten feet, he was now facing an unplayable lie or trying to hit the ball with a baseball swing. He decided to get creative, turning his seven-iron backwards and hitting the ball with a left-handed swing. He shanked the ball into bunker wall. He walked off the par three with a score of six. He couldn't believe how his game had deteriorated so quickly.

Craft was no stranger to Scotland type weather conditions, having lots of experience playing winter golf in the Carolina coastal areas, navigating treacherous bunkers in cold, windy weather. A player could be aggressive when the wind was quiet but when the wind howled, conservative play with sound course management was necessary. Also, he would keep rain gear at the ready and wear layers of clothing to adapt to the changing weather conditions, which could vary as much as forty degrees during the course of a single round. After eating breakfast and catching up on the scuttlebutt among the Tour players, Kamran raised the delicate subject of Craft doing business with his father's archrival.

"I really don't care why you've chosen to do business with Baahir," Kamran said. "You need to know this guy is bad news. His business associates conveniently disappeared when it suited his purposes. Investors know he's unscrupulous, but they stay with his firm because he delivers attractive long-term financial returns, and that's all they care about."

"He has the connections needed to get the First Light program off the ground in Riyadh."

"Hey, I don't really care if you end up in a body bag," Kamran said sarcastically, "but my sister would never forgive me if her favorite American becomes another Baahir casualty."

"Speaking of your sister, our last conversation didn't go so well."

"Daria underestimates the true danger leading up to the Asian Open in Tehran. She relies too much on my uncle keeping her safe."

Craft agreed to proceed with caution, because the threats were only going to get worse, especially if he won at St. Andrews. At the same time, this was a great time to raise funds for the children of the world.

•

A large gathering of runners and volunteers waited at Hollyrood Park in the center of Edinburgh, for the start of the 10K charity run. It was a cool summer morning with temperature in the forties. Dressed in warm running attire—hats, sweat shirts, sweat pants—the patrons tried to keep warm. The Road Warriors led by Martin McKinney, the best long distance runner in the Scottish highlands, waited at the starting line. The Road Warrior, having seen news headlines of Craft's athletic prowess, decided to be the first to test the bold statement of his being the best athlete in professional golf.

The Lord Provost of Edinburgh, using a loudspeaker, thanked the citizens of Edinburgh for supporting the charity event. Behind the scenes, Wilkins had to entice the Lord Provost to host the charity event, with a generous donation to the Edinburgh Fire Brigade. While he gave a short speech on the importance of maintaining the city common areas, Craft and Kamran, dressed in hooded sweatshirts, moved unnoticed into position alongside the Road Warriors.

The horn sounded, and the Road Warriors moved out at a fast pace, quickly separating from the other runners. Approaching the 1K-mark, they settled back into a comfortable long distance pace. Looking around,

McKinney realized the Tour players were running along with the pack. They began chatting with the guys. Over the course of the next few kilometers the conversation covered a variety of topics to include championship soccer, American football, and, of course, professional golf. At the 7K-mark, McKinney picked up the pace, leaving the others behind.

At the 8K-mark, McKinney glanced back to see Craft matching him stride for stride. Much taller than the Scotsman, Craft leveraged his long stride to keep pace. If he were trying to win, this would be the point when he would kick in to high gear and force McKinney to keep up or lose. But this was not about winning; it was image building.

When McKinney realized he was not going to separate from the American, he began to slow his pace, expecting him to pass but the American stayed a stride behind. McKinney knew Craft was running with ease, and could pass at anytime if his objective was winning the race. Seeing the finish line, McKinney and Craft broke into a championship sprint, with the Scotsman crossing the finish line a half-stride ahead.

Being a proud man and knowing the American could have won, but chose not to embarrass him in front of his local townsmen, McKinney grabbed Craft's hand and raised it high into the air, symbolizing that, today Edinburgh had two champions cross the finish line. Locked arm-to-arm, the Road Warriors surrounded the professional golfers, and began singing songs of cheer acknowledging the courage shown by their new friends. The Edinburgh 10K turned into an impromptu Tuesday morning block party.

While waiting at the Edinburgh International Airport to pick up a team member, Wilkins watched the video highlights of the Scotsman and Craft crossing the finish line, and the euphoric celebration that followed.

Enroute to the town of St. Andrews, in the Scottish county of Fife, Craft relaxed in the back seat of the BMW sedan reading the message from Wilkins.

Peter, The video of McKinney and you racing to the finish is awesome. With regard to the Open, I've made arrangements with top equipment manufacturers to provide a full set of equipment designed to your specifications. You will use different equipment each day of the Open. Also, Vaughn is needed at headquarters. Your new caddy, Lenard McKnight, is waiting at the clubhouse. Running late, please wait for me before teeing off. JW

At the age of forty-two, Lenard McKnight had two decades of caddying and playing golf in the county of Fife. A large man, well over six feet tall and two hundred and fifty pounds, McKnight was in good physical condition.

Craft walked into the caddy area, with two glasses of beer. He slid a beer across the table to his new caddy and suggested they talk. The exchange of ideas was easy and covered many topics, such as playing golf under a microscope, the crazy crowd behavior to be expected during a Major, and the challenges of playing St. Andrews. Craft asked his new caddy to give a self-assessment of his strengths and weaknesses. After mentioning many strengths, including having played the old course at St. Andrews many times in all weather conditions, Lenard suggested that sometimes he became frustrated when caddying, trying to explain the right shot to hit and wishing he could just hit the shot to demonstrate.

After talking for a while, Craft asked, "How confident are you that we can win?"

Known for being a pessimist, McKnight pondered the question, and then responded, "I would say our odds are better than the rest of the field."

Not sure what he really meant, Craft pushed for a stronger commitment. "Would you rather have ten percent of any winnings or twenty-five percent of the 1st place winnings, but only if we win?"

"Twenty-five percent," answered McKnight without hesitation.

"Did I mention my plan to play each round with a different set of golf clubs?"

"It's not the hammer, it's the carpenter that gets the house built," responded the caddy having listened to Craft's interview with Higgins on the British Sports Network.

Shaking his hands with his new caddie, Craft responded, "I like a man who's willing to back up his talk."

With bodyguards close by, Craft stood in front of the Royal and Ancient Clubhouse, to greet the people who had come to watch him play a practice round. He dressed stylishly, wearing a colorful pullover sweater and a flat cap hat, as a tribute to the Scottish journeymen who came before him to forge the great traditions of golf. It was a grand summer afternoon, with cool sixty-degree temperatures and a steady shore breeze gusting to twenty miles per hour, over the treeless links course. A scholar of past Open tournaments, Craft knew the North Sea could roar like a lion, testing both player and spectators with forty-degree temperatures, gale force winds, and bone-chilling rain. Still more than a week away, it was too early to accurately forecast the weather conditions for the Open.

A female reporter for the British Sports Network, accompanied by two young children made her way through the crowd to the front. After complimenting his stylish golf attire, congratulating him on his superb 10K run and offering to write his biography, she asked, "What do you have to say to your fellow players, who question the integrity of your achievements on the golf course?"

"Before I answer your question, I want to ask a favor. When this goes to print will you please thank the people of Edinburgh for hosting this morning's 10K event, and especially Martin McKinney and the rest of the Road Warriors for their gracious hospitality and good sportsmanship?" asked Craft.

Eager to continue the interview, the reporter agreed. Before continuing, Craft signed autographs on golf gloves, and gave them to the reporter's two children.

"Now to answer your question, I think the players making these allegations should focus on playing better golf. In a twisted way, I should be thanking them. Given the recent increase in contributions to First Light program, we plan to move up the completion of the public golf course being built in south Tehran."

"Why does First Light mean so much to you?" the reporter asked.

"Well, the idea started many years ago. When I was a young child, my late grandfather would tell me that life without passion wasn't fulfilling. He encouraged me to discover my passions in life. At the time, I didn't understand, so I asked, how would I find my passion? Grandfather told me it was hard to explain, but when you want to do something badly enough that you are willing to get up early in the morning to do it, you would know. On my tenth birthday, I stood with my grandfather on the first tee of the local golf course, waiting with great excitement for the first light to come over the horizon, so I could see well enough to hit the golf ball. At that moment it occurred to me my life would be filled with passion. It's my intent to help as many children as possible find their passions in life, and what a better way to start than on the golf course?"

After acknowledging the worthiness of the First Light program, she asked, "Are you going to play the Open with Tour provided equipment?"

"No. I intend to use a different set of equipment each day of the Open provided by top golf manufacturers. After the tournament, the equipment will be auctioned off, with the proceeds going to First Light. This way the program gets four times more money than my playing with Tour equipment."

"Are you seriously considering playing professional football?"

"I plan to play here at St. Andrews in the Open and then I'll reevaluate my options."

Needing to killing time until Wilkins arrived, he began chatting with spectators. He asked some of the locals for their advice on how to tackle the Old Course. Recommendations came forth: *keep the ball on the short grass, stay out of the bunkers, keep the ball as low as possible, dress warm, bring lots of brandy...*

After acknowledging the excellent recommendations, Craft said, "There's a rule against a player seeking advice from other than his caddy on the course, so I have decided to do the next best thing."

Asking the new caddy to join him, Craft continued, "I have acquired the services of a local man who knows St. Andrews inside and out. My critics might say we have conspired to win the Open."

To loud applause, Craft introduced Lenard McKnight. Everyone knew Lenard. He was one of the few remaining truly professional caddies in the county of Fife. He was also one of the best amateur golfers in the area, with a plus-two handicap. Being the sole caregiver of a sickly mother and unable to travel, Lenard had turned down many offers from British Tour players to be their full-time caddy.

A young man sent by the starter to summon them to the 1st tee approached. Craft began walking toward the tee area when an automobile driven by Wilkins stopped on the side next to the 18th fairway. Kalani jumped out of the car, grabbed his golf clubs out of the trunk, and began walking swiftly across the 18th fairway toward the 1st tee. At the old course, the 1st and 18th fairways ran alongside each other forming one large green space of mowed short grass.

Craft jogged across the 18th fairway to meet his mentor, the man who a few weeks earlier had saved his life. Giving a long heartfelt handshake and hug, Craft said, "This is truly a pleasant surprise."

"It's fate my friend; it just took time to convince the right people."

Shaking hands with Craft's caddy, Kalani said, "It's good to see you again. No holding back. If anyone knows how to play this course, it's you."

"I thought you were banned from playing golf around here, for sand-bagging," replied Lenard.

Craft said, "I guess there is no need to introduce you two."

"We're old buddies," responded Kalani.

"You mean business partners," replied McKnight.

Stationed in Great Britain, following the 2005 attacks on the London public transportation system by suicide bombers, Kalani had spent many summer weekends playing golf in the county of Fife. He'd befriended Lenard McKnight years before, when they teamed up to win a few bucks from unsuspecting golfers looking for the old country golf experience.

The starter signaled the caddy master to request a second caddy. Craft suggested playing as if the first round of the Open, no practice shots until the hole was completed. After finishing the hole, Craft would take practice putts and chips to see how the ball rolled from different locations. Craft established the rules of engagement with his new caddie. They were going to play as a real team. He expected Lenard to tell him where to aim, how far to hit the ball and how to shape the shot. A few spectators volunteered to keep score.

Before teeing off, McKnight gave general advice to always error left on driving holes. The sea guarded the right side of the golf course going out and road coming in. Teeing off on the 1st hole, Craft did his best to follow Lenard's instructions. At first, there were some misfires, when he misunderstood what the caddy was telling him to do. Seeing that Lenard was beginning to get frustrated, Kalani handed the caddy a ball and recommended he show him. Without hesitation, Lenard grabbed a five-iron, played the ball back, and hit a low fade into the front of the green, with the ball rolling to within a few feet of the pin.

Kalani volunteered to caddy and let Lenard demonstrate the right shots to hit. After a few holes of watching Lenard play, Craft understood his thinking and his communication techniques. It was evident McKnight had a masterful understanding of the Old Course at St. Andrews, and the challenge would be getting him to explain it in a constructive way.

When they walked over the 700-year-old stone bridge on the 18th hole, Craft stopped to take pictures with spectators. At the end of the round, Craft asked the people who agreed to be his scorekeepers for the final score. Four of the scorekeepers indicated he shot a sixty-five, seven-under par. The fifth scorekeeper had Craft's score at over a hundred assessing him a two-stroke penalty in accordance with rule 8-1 for each time Craft received advice, once McKnight transitioned from caddy to player. Craft thanked them all and gave each an authentic Masters ball-marker, only obtainable by someone who had won the tournament.

Wilkins waited by the 18th fairway ready to take them to Edinburgh so they could catch a flight to London for an important planning session for the Riyadh operation. Unable to resist an opportunity to have some fun at the expense of a fellow agent, she shot a video of Kalani lugging Craft's massive golf bag up the fairway while the caddy demonstrated various shots.

After the round, Craft offered to pay ten thousand pounds if McKnight would write down his thoughts on how to play each hole under differing conditions. The caddy handed his new boss a golf diary, with hand drawn and detailed notes on every hole.

Craft reached into his golf bag, pulled out his wallet and handed him five hundred pounds, and said, "You will have the remaining funds soon."

McKnight returned to the caddy area, threw the five hundred pounds on the table, and suggested his fellow Scotsmen wager on Craft's winning the Open. The other caddies couldn't believe their ears. The most pessimistic person they ever knew was predicting a Craft win at the Open.

CHAPTER 33

Fatigued by his one day in London, Craft waited at Heathrow to board a flight to Rome, with a one-day stopover, and then on to Riyadh. Wilkins handed him coffee and then pointed to a news article in the *London Times* with a close-up picture of him crossing the finish line of the hundred-meter dash, half of a stride behind the fastest sprinter on the British Olympic team. He scanned the article.

"World-Class Athlete"
Understatement for American Golf Champion
Peter Craft took the Kingdom by storm, posting a near record-setting time in the Edinburgh 10K race, finishing his first round on St. Andrews with an impressive sixty-five, breaking ten seconds in the hundred meter dash, finishing the fifteen hundred meter race within five seconds of the current world record and swimming the two hundred meter freestyle in a time that would have won a metal at the 2024 Olympics. To put icing on the cake, Craft played a moving rendition of Rhapsody in Blue to a standing ovation at Kings Palace. Limiting this man's extraordinary talent to athletics is simply an understatement.

RIYADH, SAUDI ARABIA

The Minister of the Interior waited at the gate for the two Americans, ready to escort them through Customs and ensure they made it safely to Baahir's compound. Even though the Saudi government had grown more liberal over the past decade, appropriate dress was still an important part of the Islamic culture. Some considered conservative dress a decree from Allah. Others considered it a matter of cultural respect.

Bandar greeted the American guests, relieved they had the wisdom to dress modestly. Craft wore business casual, a long-sleeved pinstriped shirt and creased dark pants. Wilkins' stylish abaya sunglasses and silk headscarf, made her look like one of the women of the royal family.

As they walked through the public area of King Khalid International Airport, men stood in a row with their sons in front of them, pointing at the golf champion. Craft asked Bandar to wait while he walked down the row of men and children, politely shaking hands. Looking close, he noticed some of the children were girls dressed as boys, so they could see him, without drawing undue attention to themselves. Although progress had been made in some areas regarding women's rights, in Saudi Arabia only the boys were allowed to participate in golf.

The hot temperature was stifling as they exited the airport to step into a three-car motorcade. One hour later, they arrived at Baahir's estate. The marketing VP and support staff stood in front of the compound, ready to welcome the American celebrity. The government Minister voiced his disappointment, annoyed that the Saudi business tycoon was not there to greet them in person. While shaking hands with the staff, the agents listened attentively to the conversation between Bandar and the VP, spoken in their native language.

Bandar asked, "What business could be so important for Mr. Baahir to not be here in person to greet our American guests?"

"Mr. Baahir is out of town, attending to urgent business," the man replied.

"Does he not consider the children of Riyadh important?" asked the Minister.

"I assure you, Mr. Baahir believes the children of Riyadh are very important."

"I look forward to talking with Mr. Baahir at this evening's reception," said Bandar, giving the VP an opportunity to speak up now if his boss did not plan to be present this evening.

"Would you like to talk with him in private this evening?" asked the VP.

"No need," responded Bandar.

A member of the staff showed the American guests to their lodging. Wilkins would be staying in the north wing of the compound in the single women's quarters, and Craft in the south wing of the compound with the other men.

While looking at the exquisite Islamic décor of the lavish three-bedroom suite, it occurred to Craft that a man could have multiple women, one in each bedroom, if married. For a split second, he wondered what it might be like having Wilkins and Daria as wives. He quickly concluded, *while marriage with either could be divine, marriage with both would surely be hell!*

Wilkins prepared for her assignment. Later that evening she would casually walk through the compound, releasing the biosensors while pretending to admire Baahir's vast collection of priceless treasures. With light finger pressure in the right place, Wilkins could open the small compartments containing the biosensors built into the sleeves of the abaya garment. A knock on the door interrupted her thoughts.

At the door was a lady dressed in equestrian clothing, holding a garment bag. Talking with a British accent, Zahra introduced herself as the horse trainer and stable manager.

"I understand we share a love of horses," Zahra commented.

"Are you Emeril Knight's trainer?" asked Wilkins.

"You've heard of our Arabian prince?"

"He's only the finest equestrian horse in the world."

"I came to ask you if you might be interested in riding him?"

"It would be the thrill of a lifetime."

Taking a chic equestrian outfit from the bag, Zahra said, "Hope this suites your taste."

"It's beautiful. Thank you so much."

"When you are ready, I will meet you and Mr. Craft in garden area," Zahra said, as she walked out the door.

Wilkins was truly pleased. She had hoped while at the compound to get a look at Emeril Knight, but the chance to ride the beauty was spectacular. She had ridden many championship horses, but Emeril Knight was the best of the best. She called Craft with the exciting news, and to arrange a time to meet.

•

He watched Wilkins walk down the brick path into the garden with a cowgirl's confidence, wearing the tight fitting equestrian outfit, which highlighted her attractive curves. They strolled on the path through the massive gardens, admiring the brilliant collection of exotic plants and wildlife.

Zahra pulled up behind them in an electric cart. The daughter of the Saudi Minister of Finance, she had been educated in Britain and taught by the best equestrian trainers in the world.

She was older, probably pushing forty, but Craft found her unusual combination of British mannerisms and delicate dark Saudi Arabian features attractive.

Holding out her hand and using a sophisticated old English accent, Zahra said, "Mr. Craft, I presume."

Bowing at the waist and gently shaking her petite, callused hand, Craft responded, "At your service, madam."

"I've heard so much about you. You're quite famous and a bit mysterious, if you don't mind me saying so," said Zahra, talking to him as if Wilkins was not there.

"I am surprised you have time to pay attention to such trivia, given your responsibilities as trainer of the great Emeril Knight," Craft responded.

Wilkins could hardly contain herself. *Baahir's mistress was shamelessly hitting on Craft, and he was eating it up. Did he think it was his job to charm every woman in the Middle East?*

The agent realized her personal feelings were becoming a problem. She excused herself to visit the restroom. Staring at the person in the mirror, she heard Dr. Page telling her, *"Get your act together, and do your job. It's not about you. It's about the mission."*

The stables were located in a huge building, large enough to house over fifty horses and a large indoor riding arena. Eager to show off the horses and world-class training complex, Zahra stopped to pet and talk with some of the horses along the way. She had a special relationship with every one of them. At the end, in an oversized stall, was Emeril Knight.

Zahra treated the stallion to an apple, and then introduced the gentle beast to her American guests. The horse appeared to be friendly, and craved the attention and affection. Already saddled by her assistant, Emeril Knight knew it was show time. The trainer took the reins, and led the horse into the ring with the Americans walking alongside.

Now thinking clearly, Wilkins believed she was being tested to see if the intelligence Baahir had on her was accurate. Although interested in horses, the bio on Jennifer Wilkins indicated she was a novice at riding. In reality, she had exceptional skills, developed while in boarding school, winning many different championships under different names. She wanted to show Craft her advanced riding skills, but that would have to wait for another time. Today, she would play the enthusiastic novice.

Although easily able to mount the horse, she asked Craft to assist her with a lift. With Zahra watching, she rode the horse around, bouncing high in the saddle instead of moving synchronized with the horse's movement. Zahra gave mild instruction. Wilkins asked the trainer if she would mind demonstrating how to ride more smoothly. With some coaxing, Zahra agreed. The two women changed positions.

Zahra rode Emeril Knight in a big circle, moving in sync with the animal. Even Wilkins had to admit the two moved as one. She positioned the horse in the center of the ring. As she gave signals, the horse moved to the right, and then back to the left. Now, it was Zahra who had let her pride get the best of her.

With Zahra concentrating on showing riding skills, Craft took Wilkins' hand and whispered into her ear, "Someday, I want to see you ride a horse 'Godiva style'."

Hearing his mischievous musings, she punched his arm, as if he was a child misbehaving in the schoolyard when the teacher wasn't looking.

As rider and horse charged toward a simulated fence in the middle of the arena, he bumped her with his hip, to signal her to pay attention, because Zahra was trying to impress him. Emeril Knight leaped into the air, easily clearing the high hurdle. After landing on the soft sand, Zahra gave the horse a pat of approval on the back of the neck. As she gave the command, the horse stopped at a safe distance, and reared on his hind legs to show his size and strength. Zahra looked to see her guests giving polite applause. After thanking Zahra, they returned to their rooms to get ready for the evening reception.

Looking at herself in the full-length mirror wearing the abaya, she thought, with a few adjustments, the garment could become a stunning evening gown. She had a mission to perform, and male attention was the last thing she needed. It was Craft's job to draw the attention, and give her time to wander unnoticed through the halls of the compound.

At 6:50PM, Zahra knocked on the door to escort Wilkins to the reception area. The horse trainer was dressed in an abaya, modified to resemble a designer evening gown. After exchanging pleasantries, the two left together for the evening events.

As the guest of honor, Craft waited in the hallway, outside a private room where Mr. Baahir and a small group of dignitaries waited to receive him. Later they would move to the main reception area with over two hundred guests. Dressed in the same black tuxedo he wore two nights prior, when he performed at Kings Palace in London, Craft stood outside the door with Wilkins.

When the two Americans were ready, Zahra opened the doors, and announced in her formal English accent, "Please, if I may have your attention. It is time to greet our guest of honor."

As the guests in the room formed a reception line, with Mr. Baahir in the middle, Zahra continued, saying, "It is with great pleasure Mr. Baahir welcomes this year's winner of the Masters and United States Open Championships, founder of the First Light Program, and a truly marvelous athlete from the United States of America, the honorable Mr. Peter Craft. Accompanying our guest of honor is Ms. Jennifer Wilkins."

After meeting Baahir and thanking him for being their gracious host and sponsoring the First Light program in Riyadh, Wilkins blended into the background.

With Craft surrounded by guests and Wilkins standing off to the side, a young lady approached. It was Baahir's daughter, Sara. After introducing herself, Sara mentioned these affairs tended to be a gathering of the men's club. She found Sara, the daughter of one of the richest men in the world, to be down-to-earth and unassuming.

The reception moved into the main area. Several of the Tour players, without their wives, were also in attendance. They had volunteered to donate their time to provide lessons to the many children attending the First Light kick-off the next day. Feeling that Sara was set on making sure she had at least one friend at the event, Wilkins decided to involve her in the operation. She mentioned her interest in Middle Eastern artifacts to Sara. Baahir's daughter offered to give her a tour right then, taking her into areas off limits to general guests.

Thankful that Sara was there to provide a distraction, she systematically released the micro-sensors. Both were about the same age and had been educated in boarding schools throughout Europe, so they had much in common to talk about as they walked through the compound. With security watching and listening to them, Wilkins made sure their conversation did not draw any unwanted attention.

Toward the end of the tour, the subject of her relationship with Craft came up. Swearing her to secrecy, she admitted to Sara her relationship with the golf superstar was more than just a professional interest. Wilkins returned the favor by asking about Sara's romantic interests. Before answering Sara suggested they freshen up, knowing lady's restroom would not have security cameras and sensors. In the restroom, Sara implied the walls had ears. She whispered that her father would probably kill her if he found out about her affections for Kamran Turani.

Wilkins ended the conversation quickly, knowing it was too dangerous to talk about such things inside the compound. Before leaving the bathroom, Sara insisted she share one more thing with her newfound friend. Kamran had told her he was concerned that his sister had strong feelings for the American golfer.

After finishing the task of releasing the micro-sensors, Wilkins returned to the main reception area in time for dinner and the formal ceremony. They sat at the head table with Baahir, his daughter, Bandar, and other Saudi governmental dignitaries.

After dining, Baahir stood in the center of the room with a miniature microphone clipped to his lapel. He thanked his guests for their support of the First Light program in Riyadh. He emphasized the important partnership between private business and the government in building a strong future for the city by giving the children greater opportunity to develop physically, mentally, and spiritually. After a short speech, Baahir turned the floor over to the Saudi Minister of the Interior.

Bandar gave a short speech, reinforcing the partnership between private business and government, and the need to reach out to friends around the world. He talked about the American who had devoted his life to helping children in troubled areas of the world, letting his golf clubs become the tools of choice.

To a standing ovation, Craft moved to the center of the room. He talked passionately about the mission of the First Light program, and his desire to give children the opportunity to channel their energy toward positive endeavors. He talked about the progress made in the last decade of meeting children's basic needs such as food, shelter, and security, but much still remained to be done. His objective was giving children something to live for. Although golf was the initial focus of the First Light program, it wouldn't end there. He was working to build relationships around the world. He talked about his experience in Edinburgh, Scotland with the Road Warriors, and expanding the program to offer a broader range of healthy opportunities.

Craft ended his speech saying, "Ultimately, my desire is to create a vigorous environment where children are so tired from exciting activities that falling asleep is a matter of necessity, and waking at first light a matter of passion for the day ahead."

•

At 6:45AM, the motorcade pulled up in front of the Palms driving range. The First Light program, in partnership with the corporation owning the Palms, had bought the surrounding land to build a public golf course with the agreed upon intention of promoting youth golf. In addition to giving golf lessons to the children, the event would include a dedication ceremony for the new public golf course. Part of the deal was Craft's ability to provide some of the staff required to run the operation, providing a covert base from time to time to support Agency operations.

The Saudi government had registered five hundred children to receive lessons. Given the heightened threat against the golf superstar, access to the event was tightly controlled by the government and Baahir's security forces.

The program provided each child at registration a golf hat, light long sleeve athletic shirt, long pair of shorts, and high socks, similar to the uniform of the Saudi soccer team. The hats and shirts had First Light's trademark insignia on it, the letters "FL" shaped to resemble a flagstick and golf club.

Soon after the start of the First Light event, the commercial filming team of Vaughn and Kalani pulled their van over to the side of the road near the compound. The biosensors indicated thirteen people still remained in the compound, only one in the area of Baahir's office. Looking at their locations and movements, they surmised that only one of the people in the compound was a member of the security force.

Vaughn drove the van to the entrance used for deliveries. Looking at the camera and speaking into the microphone, he explained they were here to set up for filming the commercials featuring Craft. When the gate opened, Vaughn proceeded to a parking area where a man waited. In English, Vaughn explained that he wanted to prepare for the afternoon filming while the day was still cool. Not wanting to escort them during the heat of the day, the security guard agreed to let them have an early start.

The security guard led them to the garden area, where the filming would take place. Before returning to the security control center, the guard handed Vaughn a radio and told him if he needed anything, to call, and warned him not to leave the area without being escorted. Everything was going according to plan. For the first twenty-five minutes, Kalani moved around the area, setting up the equipment in different positions. His movements were being recorded using special technology built into a camera. He varied his movement, the way they had practiced in Rome, so when it came time to replace his actual presence with a 3-D holographic image, his absence would be undetected to the vigilant security people and passers-by, as long as they didn't get too close.

After thirty minutes, Vaughn called the security guard on the radio, and told him they needed to visit the restroom. After returning from the restroom with them and a few minutes of casual conversation, the security guard returned to the control center. As the security guard walked with his back turned, the holographic image appeared and Kalani slipped behind the camera. At the same time, the camera shot a spread-spectrum light beam that projected the image of an invisible wall between where Kalani was located and the entrance to the office.

In a flash, Kalani moved from the garden area to the office entrance. The biosensor monitor indicated there was only one person in the control center, so Vaughn called again on the radio, indicating he needed to go to his van to get another piece of equipment. Vaughn signaled Kalani as soon as the guard had left the control area. Within seconds, he turned the alarm off and entered Baahir's office.

Vaughn waited for the guard over by the parking lot entrance, so the guard could stand and watch Vaughn getting equipment from the van, and at the same time, see in the distance Kalani's image in the filming area.

Kalani's specialty was stealing the contents of supposedly secure computing and communications networks. Verifiable intelligence indicated Baahir's technology staff had recently installed the state-of-the-art Russian-made security system. Its vulnerability was the encrypted low-power wireless transmission between the human interface and the network. Kalani overlaid the manufacturer part number on the human interface device with an identical label containing the nano intercept device.

The next time Baahir logged into his private network, the nano-device would send a super low-power undetected transmission to the filming equipment in the garden area. As soon as the guard turned to walk back to the control center, Kalani slipped out of the office, turned the alarm back on, shutdown the holographic image, and took position operating the filming equipment as if he had been there the whole time.

The Red Crescent team had arranged for a contact in the Saudi government to call Baahir with an immediate need for financial information requiring him to access the private network from his office space. The nano-device would activate, resulting in the copying of his data files to the technology in the film equipment. They would have to keep the commercial shoot going long enough to copy all the data over the low-power transmission, which tended to be slow, to avoid detection. It would require two to three hours to copy all the data.

Soon after Vaughn and Kalani resumed their roles, unexpectedly, the sprinkler system in the garden turned on and began spraying water on to the film equipment. Vaughn picked up the radio and began yelling to tell the security guard to turn off the sprinkler system while helping Kalani move the equipment to a dry area.

Just as the security guard arrived to turn the water off, into the garden walked Baahir, Craft, and Wilkins, returning from the First Light event. Seeing the two men and equipment off to the side, soaked in water, there were a few tense seconds, and then Baahir broke into loud laughter. Playing the role of director, Vaughn acted upset, but soon they were all laughing about the unfortunate incident.

The agents hoped the equipment wasn't damaged, and would continue to work after being soaked in water. The temperature was well over a hundred. In the garden were misters spraying thin streams of water, which evaporated in the heat, reducing the temperature in the garden a few degrees. While Wilkins and Craft ate lunch with Baahir and his daughter, Kalani and Vaughn worked to set up the equipment so it would be ready when Baahir accessed his private network.

Vaughn informed Wilkins the equipment was ready to screen test. Wilkins sent a secure message to her contact in the Saudi government. Soon, one of Baahir's assistants was whispering in his ear. He excused himself and headed for his office. Ten minutes later, the equipment was recording information from the private network.

While the equipment was recording the data in Baahir's network, the agents met with the marketing VP and other staff members, to go over the script and setting the scenes. Vaughn was convincing in his role directing the commercial walk-through. Later in the afternoon, a makeup artist and costume technician arrived to assist with the filming.

Kalani passed the microchip containing the recorded data to the makeup artist. It would be transmitted back to Langley, from a secure facility in Riyadh within the next hour. The commercial filming required several takes, with the director insisting on perfection.

CHAPTER 34

CHARLESTON, SC

The team met at the secure facility in Charleston to review the results of the Riyadh operation. Vaughn congratulated the team for making the operation a success and then turned the meeting over to the Iran Ops Director.

Gul pointed to a picture of a middle-aged man dressed in Islamic cleric clothing. "This is Gilani, a cleric who was next in line to be Iran's leader before the moderates took over. Needless to say, he wants to turn back the clock. For the past several years, he's worked behind the scenes building an opposition coalition. Iran's hosting the Asian Open has been a rallying call for him, to ignite his followers. Until recently, he lacked financial resources to be much of a problem. Thanks to the Riyadh operation, we now know Gilani's in bed with the Saudi billionaire Baahir. Using funds from the Saudi, Gilani hired some Islamic mercenaries to hijack the nuclear waste. We're not sure where he's hiding it, but we think he's using his connections with Taliban leaders to hide it in the mountains of Afghanistan. Iranian leadership is attempting to resolve the problem in secrecy."

"Assuming it's in the mountains of Afghanistan," Wilkins asked, "how do we plan to recover thousands of pounds of nuclear waste?"

"We're going to assemble a small Special Ops team and go get it."

"Why not tell General Shirazi where it is and let him get it?"

"The Taliban hate Iran's current leaders for their cozy relationship with the United States. Also, Iran does not have the infrastructure to pull this off. Don't worry, we'll be nice guys and return the stolen material," Vaughn responded.

Gul continued the briefing, "Apparently, Baahir is paying Gilani to take down the Turani family. It's no longer a business vendetta, it's personal, but why is still a mystery. For a large sum of money, Gilani is making arrangements to assassinate the Turani family and undermine Iran's political stability."

"I think I know why," Wilkins interrupted.

"Then please enlighten us?" asked Gul.

"Baahir's daughter, Sara, is having a secret affair with Kamran Turani."

"How would you know this?"

"She told me."

Visibly annoyed this important information had been withheld, Gul reminded everyone to post all relevant intelligence to the All Source Intelligence System. He then concluded the briefing by casually mentioning that Gilani had infiltrated General Shirazi's security force, and enticed Ahmad Reza to head the assassination of the Turani family.

Before dismissing the team, Vaughn stated, "The President has drawn a line in the sand. If the nuclear waste threat is not resolved by the end of August, then an Executive Order will be issued to stop Americans participation in the Asian Open."

After dismissing the team, Wilkins continued to sit there, in disbelief.

Vaughn sat down across the table. "What's on your mind?"

"Are you kidding me?" she responded. "As an afterthought, Gul mentions there is contract to kill the Turani family, and you want to know what's on my mind? Does the man have ice water running through his veins? Or is he one of those human robots you hear about in the news?"

"He's an analyst, just doing his job."

"Maybe the man needs some field experience," declared Wilkins. "We're dealing with real people, not chess pieces."

"In our business people get hurt. You know that," Vaughn shot back.

"Don't give me that bullshit, Jason," shouted Wilkins. "These are good people. We used them. Now, we have a responsibility to protect them. Are you telling me our team is going to stand on the sideline and let them die?"

"The Saudi's desire to kill the Turanis has nothing to do with us. You're not thinking clearly. This has become personal for you, and that's dangerous. We have a critical timeline and any distraction could jeopardize the mission. How many innocent people will die if we drop the ball?" replied Vaughn, reaching across the table to hold her hand.

Pulling her hand away, and looked at him with dagger eyes, she insisted, "You're the leader of this team. *Goddammit... do the right thing!*"

"The decision's been made. We all have a boss, and don't forget; right now I am yours."

Wilkins left the secure facility, disabled the power source to her HuAID so she couldn't be reached, and threw it into her handbag. Exasperated by the situation, she drove through Charleston, questioning the secret life she had undertaken. With the car windows up so no one could hear her, she yelled at the top of her lungs, *"Take this job and shove it."*

On the way to Kiawah Island, she caught a glimpse of Jacksons, the tavern where she first met Peter Craft. She pulled into the parking lot thinking a strong drink was desperately needed.

A weekday afternoon, the tavern had only a few patrons. When she walked in, the three men sitting at the bar socializing with the bartender, turned their heads in unison. While looking at the gawking excuses for manhood, she thought, *now I know where the three stooges hang out in real life.*

The men giggled like little kids when they heard the young lady order a shot of Jack with a beer chaser.

After toasting the men as she drank the whiskey, Wilkins asked, "Did you hear the news about beer having female hormones?"

The men looked at her, wondering what she was going to say.

"It's a fact," Wilkins declared. "After a few pints of beer, men started talking nonsense and can't drive worth crap."

It didn't take long before Wilkins and the boys were trading jokes and buying each other's drinks.

While his partner searched for comfort at the bottom of a bottle, Craft was at Charleston Manor preparing for the British Open. Finding it hard to keep up with Craft's busy day, the paparazzi had lost interest. He started the day with a five-mile run, followed by an hour swim, then on to the golf course for several hours of practice.

Returning to the Kiawah Island house, he expected to find his partner back from the Ops meeting and ready to get to work. Wilkins was nowhere to be found, and his HuAID indicated no messages, so he proceeded to bathe and put on casual clothes, hoping to put work aside and have a relaxing evening together. He prepared dinner, got the steaks ready for the grill, and waited.

Concerned, Craft activated the team tracking capability, only to find her tracking signal was deactivated. He thought *something must have happened.* Just as he was about to contact the team inquiring into her whereabouts, he received an incoming call.

"Hey, can you get me Dolphin tickets?" asked Chris Davis.

"Don't believe everything you read," replied Craft.

"Miami would be lucky to have you as quarterback."

"By the way, congratulations on your engagement."

"Thanks. Doreen's been acting a bit mysterious lately, so I thought it was time to make a commitment."

"I'll be looking for an invite."

"Give me a break. You're going to be my best man, unless you're too busy winning Majors."

"I'd be honored to be your best man."

"I can't believe people have accused you of cheating at golf. There's a greater chance of the Pope streaking through the Vatican than that."

"No worries. They can say anything they want about me as long as it raises money for the kids."

"Hey, you might want to drop by Jacksons. My friend the bartender mentioned that Jennifer is doing some hardcore partying and was in no shape to drive."

"Chris, I really appreciate your calling. Please let your friend at Jacksons know I am on my way."

•

Although quite drunk, Wilkins continued to direct the conversation toward nothing of consequence. She was just having a good time. She and the three stooges were now challenging each other to barroom tricks. When it came her turn, she asked the bartender to place a shot of whiskey at the end of the bar, about twenty feet away.

Slowly, she tucked her fitted shirt tightly into her pants, and stretching to get limber, she waited, to let the suspense build. In a flash, she turned upside down, doing a handstand on the seat of the tall barstool. With her feet pointed straight into the air, she maintained her balance as she did a handstand on the curved wooden backrest of the chair. Only two of the four legs of the stool were now touching the floor. Still balancing on her hands, she moved over to the bar countertop. By now, the stooges were clapping and yelling, "go, go, go..." Balancing upside down on her hands, she walked the full length of the bar, picked the shot glass up with her teeth, and drank the whiskey as she flipped back on to her feet without spilling a drop, and slammed the empty shot glass on to the countertop. She took a bow to the loud cheers of the stooges, who were now her drinking mates.

By the time Craft reached Jacksons, the evening crowd had arrived. Wilkins was leading the patrons in telling funny stories. Chris' friend, the bartender, let him in the back door. He stood in back, watching Wilkins flaunt her artificial southern charm. He thought, *even drunk she's incredible.*

Noticing him standing in the back of the tavern, she motioned for Craft to come join the fun. She insisted on introducing him to all her new friends, whom she knew by their first names, by now. After socializing for a while, he suggested they return to the Kiawah Island home for dinner.

She sat with him at the bar while she contemplated what to do next. Her favorite song started to play. "Come on, *we're having fun tonight.*" She took his hand, and led him to the dance floor, saying, "I love this song." With her head firmly against his chest as they danced to a slow song, she whispered, "On top of everything else, you're a good dancer."

After finishing their dance and saying goodbye, they left the tavern. Once in the car, she began rambling about everything and anything. *She knew he would come. They needed to go on a real vacation. She trusted he wouldn't take advantage in her weakened condition but it would be okay if he did* ... And then fell soundly asleep.

He gently lifted her out of the car, carried her into the house, and tucked her comfortably into bed, wondering what could have provoked such erratic behavior. He checked periodically through the night, to make sure all was well. In the middle of the night, he helped her to the bathroom, comforted her as much as possible while she threw up several times, until there was nothing left in her stomach. After cleaning her with a wet washcloth and helping her put on a clean nightgown, he helped her back to bed.

In the morning, he brought her water, coffee, toast, and fruit, and then acted as if nothing had happened the previous evening. He figured the hangover was going to keep her in bed for a good part of the day, but other than that, she would be fine in a few hours. After whispering thank you, she rolled over on her side and went back to sleep.

Craft continued with his routine of running, swimming, and practicing his golf game. Today, he would practice at an oceanfront Kiawah Island course. A storm out at sea generated wind gusts and periods of rain similar to playing at St. Andrews. After completing the day's routine, he returned home to see Wilkins dressed and working in the secure area.

"Do you want to talk about yesterday?"

"No, but I guess we have to," she replied.

She filled him in on the Ops meeting and the exchange with Vaughn.

He listened, but more than anything, discovered her true character. She was not going to sit on the sidelines and let a family go to its death. Although she didn't say it, she was asking for his help.

Craft immediately sent a secure message requesting a team meeting as soon as possible. Disguised as Jefferson the caddy, Vaughn dropped by the Kiawah Island house. In the secure room, they established a virtual connection with Kalani at a remote location.

"Preventing the assassination of Turani family is a personal responsibility that cannot be ignored. Rather than go it alone, we are here to ask for your help," Craft declared.

Vaughn interrupted, "We have a responsibility to eliminate a known terrorist threat."

"Mr. Vaughn, I believe you once said what kept you up at night were the things you could have done but failed to take action on. For us, this is one of those times."

Kalani spoke up. "Have we considered all the options?"

"This is real world, we don't have time to consider all the options," scoffed Vaughn.

Kalani persisted, "Who's in the best position to eliminate the threat and has the most at stake?"

Thinking for a moment, all three answered at once, "General Shirazi."

"Exactly," said Kalani. "So, why don't we deliver the intel and let him finish the job? We'll keep it off the radar. Come on Jason, it's not as if we haven't done it before."

Weighing the options and knowing they were not going to let this rest, Vaughn said, "Okay, but we do it quick."

Everyone agreed.

Vaughn asked, "Do you think you could be convincing, speaking in Farsi with a German accent?"

Craft began speaking Farsi with a convincing German accent.

"Here's the deal," Vaughn said. "Wilkins will make it appear that you're still in town. A professional make-up artist will meet you at Kiawah Island. You will board a commercial aircraft for Germany, then after a short layover, on to Tehran. While you're in flight to Germany, we'll be working out the details of your engagement with the General. One of our guys will meet you in Germany to give you the operation details. You deliver the intel and get your ass out of there. At that point, it's in the General's hands. Is everyone on board?"

Wilkins said, "Jason, I promise you won't regret this."

"Get out of here; the clock's ticking."

CHAPTER 35

FRANKFURT, GERMANY

He sat at a small table in a coffee shop a few miles from the airport disguised as a middle-aged German businessman. Craft enjoyed the warm coffee, looking out the window at the rain, hoping his contact would show up soon. A man dressed in a rain jacket with a hood pulled tightly over his head walked into the coffee shop, scanned the few people inside, and then walked to Craft's table.

In German, the man said, "I hear it's quite warm in Seattle."

"I prefer sunshine over rain," responded Craft.

The man sat down, carried on a short conversation, talking about the traffic and cold weather. Then he walked out of the shop, leaving behind a newspaper on the table. After finishing his coffee, Craft exited the shop, carrying the newspaper. In the taxi back to the airport, he examined the contents wrapped inside the newspaper. It contained an older model handheld, airline tickets, a passport and bio for Erwin Klein, sanitized intelligence regarding the hit on the Turani family and General Shirazi's itinerary. In addition, there were several notes from Wilkins, helping him to prepare for the operation. The notes were written on paper that could be easily destroyed by flushing it in the aircraft toilet.

While on the flight to Tehran, Craft prepared for the off-the-record operation. If all went smoothly, he would be in Iran only a few hours, landing at 4:15AM local time, and departing on a 12:15PM flight to London. If his identity was discovered, there was a good chance he would never leave.

TEHRAN, IRAN

Erwin Klein stood in line at the airport, waiting to clear immigration. Heavily armed immigration security personnel were stationed throughout the area. There would be no VIP treatment this time. After a long wait, he reached the immigration station. The officer searched his carry-on bag, asked him to take off his business jacket, and then gave a signal. Two security officers with machine guns strapped across their chests approached.

Speaking Farsi with a German accent, Craft asked, "Is there a problem?"

Ignoring his question, the approaching officers were told, "Please take this man for questioning."

Craft was taken to a private area, and asked to sit at the desk. He waited for several minutes, while he was being monitored. He did all the normal things that a typical person would do. He acted mildly nervous, and pulled out his passport ready to show the interrogating officer.

When the officer assigned to conduct interrogation entered the room, Craft could not get any indication if he was Iranian Intelligence. The officer began a casual conversation, complimenting how well Klein spoke Farsi. Asking the typical questions concerning the intent of his visit, Craft thought it was a random interrogation, until the officer asked to see his handheld. He requested that Craft tell him the code to get access and then started scrolling through the contact list and messages.

The officer asked a series of questions regarding the information on the handheld. Craft's intense training in preparation for the Red Crescent program kicked in. He responded to the questions, pretending to be intimately familiar with the contacts and messages. In reality, he had only glanced at the information on the aircraft. Then, the officer asked to see his airline tickets.

Speaking German, the officer said, "You've come a long way to only be here a few hours."

"Some business deals are best done face-to-face," Klein answered, speaking German.

"What is the nature of this big business deal?" asked the officer.

"I am not at liberty to say. You could ask Amir Turani, but he probably won't tell you either," replied Klein.

"I wouldn't want to keep Mr. Turani waiting."

When he exited the airport, there was just enough time to get to the teahouse where the General would be having breakfast. The intel report indicated Reza would drop the General off at approximately 6:30AM, and then Reza would continue on to the local mosque for morning prayer.

While in Tehran, the General sat at the same table each morning, so he could see anyone coming through the front door. Shirazi would be armed with a handgun strapped to his side, within easy reach if needed. The agent positioned himself so his back would be to the General, but he had a microphone on the back of his shirt collar, so he could talk softly and the

General could hear him without looking directly at him. It was important for the agent to maintain a non-threatening posture. The middle-aged German pretended to be reading a book with his hands visible, and the book covering his mouth so no one noticed his talking.

Reza walked into the teahouse, looked around and then returned to car parked outside, opening the car door for General Shirazi. The General walked through the teahouse to his reserved table, where breakfast was served within a few seconds of his sitting down. The owner rushed over to welcome him, and to ensure everything was satisfactory. Observing the General had settled in and the staff had returned to serving other patrons, Klein took action to engage him.

Speaking in Farsi with a German accent, Klein spoke. "General Shirazi, please listen to me and do not acknowledge my presence. My nation has evidence regarding a deadly threat to you and your family. Someone close to you is the enemy, so please use caution. When I walk out of here, the information will be in an envelope under my table. Please acknowledge you have heard my words."

General Shirazi asked, "Why should I believe you?"

"The facts are verifiable."

"Let's talk face-to-face."

"It wouldn't be wise. I repeat, someone close to you is the enemy; trust no one until you have analyzed the information."

Craft stood, and placing the book under his arm, walked out of the teahouse, hoping the General would not overreact.

Shirazi calmly retrieved the envelope from under the table, and requested another cup of tea. Leaving the teahouse, the General asked Reza to drive him to the Turani estate. Ready to open the envelope, it occurred to him the office could be bugged by his own security. He then informed Reza he would travel alone by helicopter to the Supreme Leader's mountain home. Arriving at the mountain home, he went to a room reserved for private prayer and scripture reading. He opened the envelope. After reading it carefully, he requested a private meeting with the Supreme Leader.

Within a few hours, the Supreme Leader's personal security officer had validated the money transfer. Shirazi was devastated by the news but felt Reza, a loyal comrade, deserved a chance to prove his innocence. Rather than being a traitor, Reza might be involved in a secret operation to expose a true threat. The General needed to know if his trusted friend would go through with the assassination. And if so, who else might be involved?

LONDON, ENGLAND

Wilkins waited at Heathrow for his flight from Tehran to arrive. She could only imagine his discomfort, having been in disguise for over 48 hours. To expedite his passing through British immigration, she had placed his cover identity, Erwin Klein, on the special access list. It was a list set up between U.S. and British Intelligence organizations, to speed friendly agents clearing immigration.

She pulled the car up in front of the airport exit, with the window down and motioned to the middle-aged man standing in the passenger pickup area. He stepped into the car and pushed the seat back to get maximum legroom.

He asked, "Can we talk?"

"The car's clean," she said.

"I can't wait to get out of this disguise, it's driving me crazy."

"I left a bottle of cream in the hotel room. Trust me, it will stop the itching."

"Trusting you is easy, your notes saved my butt."

"How did Shirazi take the news?" she asked.

"Okay I guess, given he didn't put a bullet in the back of my head."

"After meeting with you, Reza drove the General to the Turani estate, where he took a helicopter to the Supreme Leader's mountain home, leaving Reza behind. We assume he was looking for a safe place to look at the intel we gave him."

"How did we do keeping the operation off the radar?"

"Walker hasn't fired us yet, so she probably doesn't know."

"How are you feeling these days?" he asked.

"Well, I probably won't be drinking much alcohol for a while."

"Callie sent a message saying your performance at Jacksons has become legendary."

"Hey, thanks for looking after me. Now that you've seen me at my worst..."

Still dressed as a middle age German spy, Craft asked, "Are you coming on to a man who's old enough to be your father?"

She gave him a "you must be dreaming" look and then reached for the magazine on the side of the door, and handed it to him. The magazine was the current issue of the *London Review* with "VINDICATED" printed across the cover in big letters and below, a picture of them walking hand-and-hand on the beach in Charleston. He thumbed through the magazine, to see several tasteful pictures of them showing each other modest affection. While the article left the perception that the two had an intimate relationship, it still left wiggle room for redefining it as friendship as opposed to romance.

She passed him a package with personal items and a note with the room number.

"Are you going someplace? He asked. "I was looking forward to us spending the evening together."

"Well, that's not going to happen. For some ungodly reason, I've been assigned to the Special Ops team responsible for recovering the nuclear waste."

"That's crazy. You're not combat-trained."

"Someone thinks I am," she responded. "Since I am not going to be at the Open, I created an 'Ask Jen' application you can access with your HuAID. Told you I was good at computer stuff."

He thought she was joking but thanked her anyway. "Just when I was getting to know the real you, you drop me like a hot potato to go off in the woods with some Neanderthals," he complained.

"You old guys will say anything to get a young babe between the sheets."

"Maybe when I get out of this disguise, I won't feel so vulnerable," he confessed.

"Seriously, I am going to drop you off at the hotel and keep going. They need me to help analyze new intelligence."

"When will I see you again?"

"I am not sure, but we'll stay connected."

"So what you're really saying is, go have fun playing golf while you do the real work," he said sarcastically.

"What I am really saying is you need to take care of business at the Open and keep an eye on the Reza situation."

She dropped him off at the Savoy London Hotel. Once in the room, he locked the door, and looked into the mirror, ready to turn the aging process back a couple of decades. He worked fast, but with delicate precision, to remove the disguise, placing fake flesh and artificial inserts in a bag to be destroyed. After bathing and then rubbing the cream all over his body to relieve the itching, he had a new appreciation for actors who lived a life in costume.

CHAPTER 36

COUNTY OF FIFE, SCOTLAND

Lenard McKnight checked the four sets of golf equipment that Craft would be playing with during the tournament against the inventory list. With media and manufacturing representatives watching, the caddy asked the equipment engineer to sign a legal document asserting the golf gear passed testing. Lenard announced to the equipment representatives that he would determine the order in which equipment would be used the same way golfers determined the order of play on the 1st tee. He place the four sets of equipment at the corners of an imaginary square and then, standing in the middle, tossed a golf tee into the air. Looking at the direction in which the tee pointed, Lenard picked up the Callaway golf equipment and walked out of the building headed for the practice range.

The day was unusually mild, with soft winds and afternoon temperatures in the mid seventies. The leader board showed a cluster of players between even and three under par. When Craft entered the practice area, the crowd erupted with applause. Seeing Lenard waiting at the assigned practice space, he pulled the diary of golf notes from his pocket. After greeting McKnight with a hearty handshake, he handed back the book and thanked him for sharing the invaluable information.

Craft reminded his caddy they were partners. Lenard smiled and began rattling off commands. Craft hit shots in response to the commands, quickly adjusting to the feel of the Callaway golf clubs. He asked Lenard what a realistic target score for the day's round should be. The caddy responded by flashing both hands indicating the target should be ten under par, a score of 62. Knowing the course record was nine under par and his caddy was one of the most conservative men in county of Fife, Craft left the practice area thinking that if he met his caddy's expectation, then it would be a very good day.

After hitting a few putts at the practice green, Craft walked to the 1st tee with Lenard following closely behind. As some spectators reached out to shake hands to wish him good luck, others made comments mocking him. A young man, wearing a traditional Scottish green plaid kilt, threw an egg at Craft, yelling, "Yankee, go home!" The egg hit Craft in the back and splattered on to a nearby child. Lenard dropped the golf clubs and reached over the ropes to grab the egg thrower by his jacket, knocking him to the ground. Security personnel restrained the man, who was yelling profanities as they dragged him away. Observing he was shaken but unhurt, the caddy watched as Craft made a joke, used a golf towel to help clean the egg off the child and himself, and then gave the child a silver dollar ball marker.

Craft knew it was instinctive for the 250-pound Scotsman to react by grabbing the egg thrower, but it was an unnecessary diversion. At the 1st tee area away from the crowd, he talked with the Lenard, emphasizing the need to stay cool and let the security people do their job.

Regaining his composure, McKnight noticed the massive crowd lining the 1st hole. He gave a big smile when he realized for the next four days, they would have the advantage of a human barrier surrounding every hole to stop any wayward shots.

After greeting his playing partners, Craft waited for Lenard to hand him a club and give instructions. Craft would be first on the tee. After being announced by the starter, he stood behind the teed ball, visualizing the ball's flight. Pointing to the small gorse bush at the edge of the burn, Lenard told him to hit a three-wood left of center. Just as Craft began his back swing, a spectator standing approximately thirty feet from the tee area pulled a handgun out of his coat pocket and yelled, *"You're a disgrace to the game."*

Reacting to the gun, Craft let go of the club, sending it flying down the fairway and dove onto the ground as bullets passed by. After a few moments of confusion, he could see the gunman was secure on the ground. Lenard fell to his knees, holding his shoulder with blood gushing. Before Craft could get up, security personnel around the tee area were calling on the radio for the medical team. Craft grabbed the towel used to wipe the clubs from the golf bag and pressed it on Lenard's shoulder to stop the bleeding. Lenard sat on the ground, in shock from the pain and blood loss. The ambulance, with player and caddy aboard, sped off to the local medical center.

Wilkins observed her new look in the hotel bathroom mirror. The short hair and cosmetic enhancements would help her pass as a female soldier on the Special Ops team. With an hour remaining before leaving to catch the flight to Kuwait, she watched a delayed broadcast of Craft playing at the Open.

Showing a picture of him being hit with an egg walking to the 1st tee, the announcer said, "I guess not everyone loves the Yank."

Reacting to the announcer's statement, she yelled at the FVTV display, *"You're an idiot."*

As the camera zoomed in on Craft standing at the 1st tee, she was amazed at how good he looked, even with egg on his shirt. She played with the control unit zooming in on different parts of his body. The HuAID placed on the desk began flashing with a high priority alert. Distracted for a moment by the alert, she turned her attention away from the broadcast. When she looked back at the display, she saw Craft lying on the ground and pandemonium at the 1st tee.

Trying to remain calm, she activated the secure circuit to hear Vaughn's voice on the other end, "There's been a shooting at the Open. Craft not hurt but his caddy took a bullet in the shoulder."

"How is Lenard doing?" she asked.

"Not sure yet. Craft is at medical center with him," Vaughn answered.

"Who was the shooter?" she asked.

"The initial report indicates the shooter is a local fanatic known around Saint Andrews to be a bit crazy. Apparently, the man felt obligated to avenge the injustice that Craft's cheating has inflicted on the integrity of the game of golf. He supposedly hid the weapon onsite sometime earlier in the week, before the secure perimeter was established for the tournament. Tournament play has been cancelled for the day, while they assess the threat and re-establish security."

COUNTY OF FIFE, SCOTLAND

She was standing by the 14th hole watching her brother become increasing frustrated as he missed another short birdie putt, to remain two over par. Without warning, the foghorns sounded to stop tournament play. With no sign of bad weather, the players appeared puzzled by the action.

With the sounds of sirens in the background getting louder, the word of shooting at the 1st tee resonated through the crowd. Daria Turani ran to her brother standing by the 14th green. Kamran spent a few moments comforting his sister before flagging down a tournament official who informed him that Peter Craft and his caddy had been taken by ambulance to the local medical center. Overhearing the conversation, Daria began running for the exit.

Craft sat in a private room, talking with Wilkins, still in London. After making sure he was okay, she informed him that Reza was on his way to London, apparently to make security preparations for a special event being held by the Turani family. Although the shooter was no longer a threat, Reza being in Britain was alarming.

While he tried to assure her that the situation was under control, she secretly contemplated options for getting him help. Figuring the assassin would not act until all the family members were together, they agreed he had to stay close to Daria Turani as long as Reza posed a threat.

Anxiously waiting word of McKnight's condition, he received notification the tournament would restart the next day at 11:00AM. Following Lenard's surgery, the doctor stopped by to deliver the good news. No permanent damage. Lenard would fully recover in a few weeks. When Craft went into the room, Lenard was sitting up in good spirits.

The caddy asked, "Did you break the course record today?"

"Your inability to dodge a bullet resulted in the tournament being cancelled for the day."

"If the guy could shoot straight, you'd be the one in this bed. Now, go out there and crush those bastards."

"You're not getting off so easy," said Craft.

"You call taking a bullet in the shoulder getting off easy?"

"Hey, we have a deal. I need you out on the golf course tomorrow. If you can muster enough strength to walk the course, I'll carry the golf clubs. If you agree, then I will notify the equipment manufacturers to provide easy to carry golf bags."

"I'll be waiting for you to pick me up in the morning," responded the caddy.

"We tee off at 11AM. What's important now is you get rest and get off the meds as soon as possible so your head is clear."

When Craft walked out of the medical center, a mob of reporters tried to surround him. Embarrassed by the lapse in security, the Tour Commissioner had assigned a security detail to protect him. The security team formed a perimeter, keeping media personnel at a distance as they shouted questions.

He made a short statement, apologizing for the distraction, the impact on his fellow competitors and the major inconvenience to golf fans. His plan was to put this harmful event behind and get ready to give his best effort going forward. When asked about Lenard McKnight, he stated the doctors would be more qualified to give an update on his medical condition, but the news was good.

While answering questions, a young lady wearing sunglasses, a long coat, and a colorful scarf covering her head caught his eye. Knowing she had his attention, Daria walked up the stairs into the building. After responding to more questions, he excused himself and walked back into the medical center.

Seeing Daria waiting in the gift shop, he hurried across the lobby to meet her. He gently lifted the sunglasses covering her eyes, to see a face consumed with worry. After consoling his friend for a few tender moments, Craft asked, "Do you have a car?"

"Javid is waiting."

"Wait at the back of the Sailor's Tavern in the middle of town. I will meet you in fifteen minutes."

Although relieved that Daria traveled with security, he questioned the young man's loyalties. Was Javid a pawn in Reza's dangerous game, or General Shirazi's trusted agent? Only time would tell.

The security force cleared the way for Craft to make his way to the waiting vehicle. Instructing the driver to stop, Craft, along with the security team, entered the tavern. After ordering a beer, he proceeded down the hall toward the restroom but passed through the maintenance room instead and out the back door.

Craft said hello to Javid as he slid into the back seat of the waiting sedan to join Daria. Once out of the town, he sent a message to inform his driver he would be having dinner at an undisclosed location. The driver, working under an agency contract, knew to not ask questions. The driver went into the tavern to let the security team know they wouldn't be needed.

Javid turned off the main road onto a gravel road, waving to the guard as he passed through the gate, and drove up the road to the sea cottage on top of the bluff overlooking the North Sea.

Daria said, "I rented a place away from the crowds and cameras, hoping we might have some time together without the paparazzi."

"Is your brother staying here?"

"Just me. My uncle has people watching the place, so you should assume he already knows you're here."

"Is that a problem?"

Still shaken from the day's events, she tried to muster a joke saying, "Not for me, but my gentlemen friends seem to mysteriously disappear."

"Great, I feel real secure now."

"Don't worry, my uncle is quite fond of you. He's already sent a message inquiring about your health following the shooting."

With the evening chill setting in, Craft started a fire in the stone fireplace. While sitting together on the old English sofa in the warmth of the fire, Daria began to ramble, "They told me you were shot. You tried to warm me of the dangers. I didn't listen, evil people mired in the past want to hurt us..."

Pulling her close, he said, "I am not hurt. Lenard will be as good as new in a few weeks, and the crazy guy who did this will be locked up for a long time."

They sat by the fire in silence, holding each other. Exhausted and relieved, she dozed off in his arms. Craft placed her head gently on the sofa and covered her body with a nearby blanket. He went to the kitchen in search of food. When he bent down to look into a lower cabinet, he felt a sharp pain on the left side of his upper back. Feeling dried blood on his shirt, he went looking for a mirror to survey the damage. The pain increased as he slowly removed his shirt.

Twisting his body so he could see his injured back in the bathroom mirror, he discovered a large bruise with deep cuts. He recalled falling on something when he dropped to the ground in reaction to the gunshots. He thought a sharp metal tee marker must have caused the bruising.

Now awake and looking through the open bathroom door, Daria watched as he tried to examine his injury. She picked up a light chair from the bedroom and walked into the bathroom. "Please sit. You need medical attention."

"What are your qualifications?" he asked.

"I have a brother who crashes motorcycles."

As she examined the wound, he asked, "I hope you're not holding a grudge."

Affectionately kissing his shoulder, she responded, "Do you really think I am a spiteful person? Wait here, I'll be right back."

While he waited, she searched the cottage for the needed materials, returning to the bathroom with antiseptic, a washcloth, soap, lotion, cotton, tape, and a clean shirt. Soaking the washcloth in warm water and then she gently cleaned the bruise and removed the dirt embedded in the cuts. She thought it adorable when he closed his eyes like a child in anticipation of the pain that would come when she sprayed the antiseptic on the cuts. After rubbing lotion on his back and covering the bruise with a bandage, she help him get dressed, tenderly buttoning his shirt.

He couldn't help thinking about all the time his mother lovingly patched him up after a hard-hitting football games. As much as he delighted in capturing the full attention of a woman who could pass for a Persian goddess, he knew time was running out. He had to figure out what Reza was planning, and why General Shirazi hadn't taken action. The General had all the information necessary to verify Reza's guilt, so why take the risk. Current intelligence indicated Shirazi had a meeting scheduled in London in four days. If he could keep Kamran and Daria at St. Andrews, then Reza would not have the opportunity to strike with a single attack until the family gathered in London.

Shutting the bathroom door, Craft checked the semi-automatic pistol strapped to his leg, thinking the next person who took a shot at him would not be so lucky. Unsure about his true feelings, protecting Daria was instinctive and to do so meant he would have to find a way to stay close and be in position, if necessary, to stop the assault.

Daria warmed up seafood bisque she'd purchased at the local market the previous day. They ate at the table, talked like old friends, and let the stress of the day flow out of their bodies. After dinner, they again lounged by the fireplace. She rested with her petite body curled up on the sofa. Craft sat on the thick rug in front of the sofa where he could extend his long legs. He turned his head, so he could give Daria his full attention, looking directly into her stunning dark eyes.

Holding her hand with one hand and slowly caressing her leg with his other hand, he confided, "I knew you would come find me today."

"How did you know?" she asked.

"I just knew," Craft answered. "When I was struggling at the U.S. Open, just seeing you gave me the will to focus. You might think I don't know what's going on around me, but I remember the spot our paths crossed during Sunday's round. In fact, while my energy was draining and the heat had scrambled my brain, I waited on the 16th hole to see you before teeing off."

She wanted to believe him, but his relationship with Wilkins was unsettling. "You were destined to win; I was there to be a witness."

Sensing her skepticism, Craft decided to take a more direct approach. "Will you help me win the Open Championship?"

She laughed, "Are you asking me to be your caddy?"

Pretending to feel the muscles in her right arm of her hundred pound body, he said, "Although you're in excellent condition, lugging a golf bag that probably weighs more than you is not going to be much help."

"We could make your bag lighter. How many clubs do you really need? I won the ladies championship at our golf club carrying only eight clubs. Fourteen clubs seem a bit much, if you ask me."

"Oh, so it's not going to be hard enough that I am playing with different clubs each day, you want me to play with fewer clubs, too?"

"Okay, if you don't want me to be your caddy, then how can I help you win?"

In a more serious tone, he answered, "Think about what you have already done. By caring, you've already helped me dispel the negative energy of today's violence. You kept me physically strong by tending to my hurt body..."

As he talked, Daria leaned over the sofa, putting her face closer and closer to his until their lips were close enough to touch.

"What I am saying is, *we have a connection,*" Craft stated.

Overcome by his urgent appeal, deep blue eyes and boyish smile, she gave him a series of short kisses, as he continued trying to make his point. He responded with a longer, more intense kiss. Lost in the moment of his lingering and seductive caress, she resisted the impulse to further engage in titillating behavior, sensing their sexual desires were nearing the point of no return. Gathering herself, she thought, although tremendously tempting, adding the complexity of a sexual relationship was not the way to help him win the Open. For now, being a friend would have to suffice. Being lovers would have to wait.

Regaining her composure, Daria commented, "As you have pointed out in the past, our being together in public could be dangerous."

Getting up to add wood and stoke the fire, Craft replied, "We need a good reason to be together, that's all."

The words flew out of her mouth before she could think. "You mean, a reason like being your business manager?"

"Exactly. If Jennifer was here, then people would expect to see us together because she's my business manager."

"Since we're talking about her, why isn't she here?"

"The success of the First Light program has become time consuming."

"So what would be the reason for our being together?"

"You are a professional writer and owner of a major publication. You could be working on a story of my quest to win 'The Grand Slam of Golf' potentially culminating in the great Persian city of Tehran. Of course I have to win here in Scotland first and I need you by my side to do that."

"Are you volunteering to be a cover story for *Persian Woman*?"

"You know the market. Do you think it makes sense?"

"Yes it makes sense. A few months ago, you were unknown outside of Charleston and now you're world famous. It would be a great honor to tell the world about the real Peter Craft."

She shifted her body to a sitting position on the sofa and pulled Craft's hands, helping him slide up from the floor to the sofa next to her.

"You have to know my interest in you has never been business motivated. Yes, I once said my interest in you was to sell magazines, but that was never true. I was trying to be clever when you put me on the spot."

"Let's just say our being together is good business for both of us."

After shoveling ash from the fire into a metal box by the fireplace, adding wood, and stoking the flames, he sat back down on the sofa.

She snuggled close, so he could feel her feminine curves and she could rest comfortably against his large muscular body.

"We have a mutual interest to make the world a better place," Craft continued, "I can feel it, and by the look in your eyes today, you do, too. Anyway, the last time we talked you made the point that you didn't want to be left standing on the sidelines. Figuratively speaking, this plan gets you into the game and us playing on the same team."

"I plan to tell the world about the real you, not a manufactured image.

I think the real you is much more interesting." Thrilled with the idea, she sent a message to the *Persian Woman* team in New York City. Not wanting to derail the evening, she decided not to press him further regarding his relationship with Jennifer Wilkins. In her heart, she knew he was a man worth fighting for, but now was neither the time nor the place.

Fatigued from the long day, Craft asked, "Would you mind if I stayed tonight in the guestroom?"

"Of course not," she responded. Wondering if the guestroom was really where he wanted to stay, but knowing tonight it would have to do.

He asked, "How is Kamran doing?"

"He struggled today. A links course doesn't suit his game," she answered.

"When I stopped by Saint Andrews a couple of weeks ago for a practice round, we had a chance to talk."

She retrieved a piece of paper from her handbag and handing it to him, saying, "You did more than talk."

It was the newspaper article from the *London Times*, highlighting his short visit in Great Britain where he engaged in running and swimming demonstrations with the British Olympians.

"Is your brother seeing anyone?" Craft asked.

She hesitated for a moment to contemplate the potential dangers of sharing her secret, and then said, "What I am going to tell you could put you in danger. Do you still want to know?"

"Apparently, I could already be in danger by association, so facing the danger together is better than not knowing."

Relieved that finely she was going to share the knowledge of her brother secret romance with a trusted friend, she confided, "My brother has entered into a modern day Romeo and Juliet relationship. He is seeing Sara Baahir."

He acted shocked at the news. "Is he nuts? He lectured me on the dangers of getting involved with Baahir. What is he thinking?"

After a short tempting kiss, Daria seductively whispered, "Romance can affect a man's judgment."

"That's a fact," Craft replied. "I am having difficulty thinking clearly right now."

"At first, I was livid about my brother getting involved with the Saudi monster's daughter. Then I met Sara. She is a really nice."

"You have to know that Baahir will rain vengeance against all involved. What are you doing to protect yourself?"

"I am building a trusting relationship with a strong man who's going to protect me."

"I am flattered that you think so much of me, but you need to keep professional security. Does your uncle Shirazi know about the situation?"

"I am sure Reza knows; his people provide security when we travel abroad."

"I am sure he does," Craft said, wanting to tell her that Reza was not to be trusted but now was not the time.

The grandfather clock in the corner of the room sounded eleven gongs. He stood and easily lifting the young lady off the sofa and holding her in his arms, he said, "If we trust each other, we will get through this, but right now it's important we face this together."

"I am so sorry my brother's friendship has put you in danger," she said.

"No need to apologize. Your brother's friendship with me has brought us together."

Overcome by the events of the day, Daria escorted him to the guest room and then left him with a good night kiss.

CHAPTER 37

She reviewed the "Eyes Only" message for one last time, trying not to let her feelings trump sound judgment. After sending the message, she sat back in the chair contemplating the consequences of what she had done. She regretted not being there to help take down Reza but the recovery operation took priority. Although the decision to seek assistance from a highly trusted source was rational, she believed Craft would consider her actions an unnecessary betrayal. With time running out she would have to accept the consequences.

When the Special Ops team assembled for the first time in the briefing room, it was obvious to Wilkins the other team members were highly skilled soldiers, the best of the best. She resisted the temptation to scream, "*Why am I here?*"

She listened attentively as Kalani, the team leader, started the operations briefing. "Some of you have asked about the composition of the team, so let's deal with it up front. The secrecy and dynamic nature of the operation required a small team with a collective, broad set of skills, who could be ready to execute within a week. Trust me, every team member has a diverse set of skills but every team member excels at one critical skill needed for this operation. *We are all horsemen.*"

COUNTY OF FIFE, SCOTLAND

Awakened by the early morning light, Daria rolled out of bed, enjoyed a hot morning shower and then navigated through the full closet of clothes, carefully selecting her attire for the day. She marveled at Maurice's unique fashion designs, blending warm wool Scottish styles with the flowing Arabian garment designs. Dressed in cheery plaid colors, she left the bedroom refreshed and ready to face the day ahead.

Daria walked into the kitchen, eager to coax her guest out of seclusion with the smell of fresh coffee and breakfast cooking. Disappointment consumed her when she saw the guestroom door open and no sight of Craft. She felt like a discarded woman, who, after a wonderful intimate evening, awakens to a note left on the pillow by a remorseful man who bolts in the middle of the night.

In a daze, she looked out through the sunroom window to the beach below. Struggling to see through the morning fog, the image of a man came into focus. Realizing her American friend awoke early to appreciate the sea breezes of a grand Scottish morning, her feelings of being a scorned woman vanished. Her heart pulsed like a young girl in anticipation of going on a first date. She took deep breaths, trying to bring her emotions under control.

Craft sat at the bottom of the steps leading down to the beach reading the "Eyes Only" message from Wilkins.

Peter, The situation is dangerous. You need help! I feel terrible not being able to tell you this in person, but here it goes. Your mother is a CIA operative working under non-official cover. She has worked for the Agency for years. I discovered this during our trip to Australia. I hope you understand my dilemma but your mother asked me to keep her secret. She contacted me following the shooting and wanted to know everything. I have briefed her regarding the threat to the Turani family. In response to my personal request, she is on her way to St. Andrews to help. Before doing anything you'll come to regret, please consider protecting your mother's secret. JW

•

With two cups of coffee, Daria walked downstairs to sit and share the morning tranquility with her American friend. Seeing the unfamiliar look of worry on his face, she handed him a cup of coffee, put her hand on his back, leaned her head against his shoulder and lovingly asked, "What's captured your mind so early in the morning?"

"My mother is en route from Australia."

"Can't blame her. A crazy man tried to shoot her son. She wants to be there for you and make sure you're safe."

"Will you help keep my mother occupied?" he asked.

"I would love to spend time with your mother. How long has it been since you've seen her?"

"The week after the U.S. Open when I filmed the public service announcements in Brisbane, Australia."

Reading in between the lines, she figured he didn't go to Australia alone. *So where do I fit into the picture,* she wondered. "What are you going to tell your mother about us?"

"The truth," he answered.

"The truth is good. So, what's the truth?"

"You're a friend, who's writing a story about a Tour rookie's quest to win the Grand Slam."

"As friends, how close are we?"

"That's for you to decide."

"What are you going to say when she asks if we have a romantic relationship?"

He tried to change the subject. "Did I mention how beautiful you look today in your stylish Scottish clothes? Did Maurice design them?"

"You know your mother is going to ask. What are you going to tell her about us?"

He looked at his watch. "Can we talk about this another time? I need to pickup Lenard and get to Saint Andrews soon."

Wanting to do her part in helping him win, she dropped the inquiry, and instead insisted he have a hot breakfast before leaving for the golf course.

•

In response to the previous day's shooting, the Scottish authorities had requested security force volunteers from across the island. Enough security volunteers showed up to create a human barrier between the players and the spectators. Every one of the eighteen holes was lined with security personnel, each standing approximately twenty feet apart, facing the crowd of spectators so they would be in position to apprehend anyone posing a threat.

The tournament director and head of security asked Craft if he approved of the security steps, and if he had any special requests. He received special permission for Daria to walk along with the rules official inside the security perimeter.

Lenard, with his arm in a sling, and Craft, with a golf bag across his back, approached the 1st tee, to thunderous applause and Scottish bagpipers playing *Scotland the Brave* in celebration of their willingness to continue playing. After conferring with McKnight, Craft stepped to the tee and hit a three-wood into perfect position a hundred yards from the green.

The temperature was in the low sixties, ten degrees cooler than the previous day. The roaring winds of the North Sea swept across the course with short bouts of rain passing through, causing Craft to put on and take off rain clothes three times in the first nine holes. The leader board showed several players between three under and even par, all three having finished the previous day. The players on the course today were fighting to break par. The conditions favored Craft, who had developed excellent course management skills playing in severe winter conditions along the Carolina coast.

He arrived at 17th hole with a two-stroke lead at five under par. The 17th hole at St. Andrews—affectionately referred to as the "The Road Hole"—was one of the world's most famous golf holes. The long 495-yard par-4 began with an unusual tee shot requiring the player to take aim over a corner of The Old Course Hotel, in order to have a reasonable length approach shot. The green, guarded by a deep greenside bunker and gravel road, presented a formidable challenge for the best of golfers.

Craft enjoyed the spectacular view of the 17th hole while patiently waiting for the group ahead to clear the fairway. He noticed Daria was no longer within the secure area. Looking around, he caught a glimpse of her having an intense conversation with her brother. On the verge of leaving the teeing area to confront Kamran, a familiar voice called out. He turned to see his mother standing outside the secure area accompanied by the Tour Commissioner.

Normally, Amanda Craft would never have distracted her son during the course of play, but she could see the situation was about to get out of control. Her son redirected his focus away from the inappropriate behavior of Kamran, who should not be disrupting other players on the course. Acting surprised, Craft welcomed his mother and then turned his attention back to Daria. A tournament official intervened, demanding Kamran immediately leave the area or be disqualified from the tournament.

Figuratively speaking, Lenard was about to have a heart attack on the spot, seeing all the distractions taking place on the 17th tee. The pain in his shoulder made it difficult to find the energy to keep his player focused on the task at hand. Seeing the red-faced Scotsman with one arm in a sling and the other arm waving a red towel like a football official ready to throw a personal foul penalty, Craft quickly pulled his driver out of the bag, tossed the head cover on the ground, put the ball and tee in the ground, and before Lenard could give guidance, struck the ball.

The launch angle of the tee shot was too low to clear the corner of the hotel. The ball ricocheted off the side of the building, landing in the high rough, 230 yards from the green. A marshal ran into the rough and held up a hand to indicate the ball was found.

Observing that Lenard was struggling to finish the round, Craft joked with the Scotsman, hoping to take his mind off the pain. The ball was buried in the tall grass, leaving a long, difficult approach to the green. Craft's approach shot drifted off-line, landing in the deep greenside bunker. After surveying the lie of the ball, he climbed out of the bunker, and as Lenard held the bag upright with one hand, he selected the 64-degree wedge. He hit the ball with a hard steep blast into the sand. The ball hit the bunker wall a couple of inches from the top, shot straight up into the air, and then rolled back into the bunker a few inches from where he last hit. The loud sound of disappointment radiated throughout the crowd in reaction to the failed bunker shot.

He stepped out of the bunker to wipe the sand off the golf club. Seeing the exasperated look on the Scotsman's face, He said jokingly, "Looks like I'll be doing a Hitler."

"What in the hell is a Hitler?" the Scotsman bellowed.

"Taking two shots in a bunker," Craft responded, referring to the way Hitler supposedly died at the end of World War II.

With Lenard laughing loudly, Craft climbed back down into the deep bunker, positioning the ball slightly more forward in his stance, and blasted into the sand. The ball flew out of the sand, landing next to the flagstick for a tap-in bogey five. The Craft-McKnight team went on to par the 18th hole, finishing the first round with a one-stroke lead at four under par. After posting his score and thanking Lenard for his heroic efforts, it was time to face the media. A large collection of reporters assembled in the media area, waiting for his arrival.

Responding to question after question regarding the shooting, Craft asked, "Does anyone want to talk about today's golf round?"

Amanda could see her son getting frustrated with the line of questioning. She stepped forward to take control of the interview. Surprised by his mother's willingness to step into the fray, the reporters eagerly sought Amanda Craft's perspective on the recent events. A reporter herself, she had researched the bios of many of the assembled media representatives. She talked as though she was an insider, using first names and asking them the questions, turning the session into a conversation, as opposed to an interview. She cited the attempt on her son's life and then made a personal appeal for each of them to take personal responsibility for their role in fueling the rising tension.

Craft's emotions began to take over as he coped with the knowledge his mother was a CIA operative. He recalled times as a child, when his mother would leave on short notice for places around the world. He rationalized her frequent absences to her job as a freelance news reporter. Although he missed his mother when she was away, he never felt neglected because his grandfather was always there to be the caregiver at home. He thought it now made sense why his mother never remarried. She probably didn't want to lie to her partner about her secret life. Being in Naval Intelligence, his grandfather must have known. After thinking through the situation, he began to empathize with his mother's life choices. He felt both relieved and foolish that his mother had known all the time he was being deceptive about his motivation for playing on the Tour. She had taken an oath, just as he had, to serve the nation and keep secret her involvement with the Agency.

After responding to several questions, someone asked about her son's relationship with the Iranian model. Suggesting it would be better for Ms. Turani to answer the question herself, Amanda gave her a gracious introduction and then welcomed the young lady to the podium.

Daria talked enthusiastically about her plans to write a cover story for *Persian Woman* featuring the man from Charleston's quest to win the Grand Slam. With Craft having the first day's lead at the Open, the chance of his winning a third Major tournament in a row had become a real possibility in the collective minds of the media. Skillfully sidestepping questions concerning their personal relationship, she kept the focus on their common goal of strengthening East-West relations.

Seeing the reporters captivated by the Iranian woman who had taken center stage, he slipped away, headed for the player's locker room, in hopes of smoothing things over with Kamran.

The Iranian was waiting in the locker room, and before Craft could say a word, pushed him up against the wall of wooden lockers, holding him by the collar of his shirt. "You have put my sister in danger."

With a quick defensive move, Craft broke the Iranian's grip, twisted him around, and slammed his face against the lockers, pinning his right arm behind his back. "You're wrong. Your secret romance has put everyone in danger."

Surprised by the turn of events, Kamran appealed, "Please, let's talk."

"That's why I am here." Sitting down at a table in the player's lounge, Craft ordered two shots of single malt scotch. "If I know about your love interest, then you should assume Sara's father also knows," Craft said.

"You know about Sara because my sister told you," responded the Iranian.

"You're wrong again. I know because Sara told Jennifer Wilkins, when we were in Riyadh. Please listen to me. I am a friend trying to help."

After apologizing for his rash behavior, Kaman asked, "Why are you getting involved in matters that don't concern you?"

"The matter does concern me. The road to 'The Grand Slam of Golf' ends in Tehran on your home turf. I can't win if the tournament is cancelled."

"You will have to beat me to win."

"Neither of us can win the tournament if it gets cancelled. Believe me, I know you are going to be tough to beat on your home course."

"How will you feel, if I am the one to stop your winning?"

"Probably no worse than you felt after losing the U.S. Open. Anyway, Baahir has a financial interest in stopping your father, and you have raised the stakes, by giving him a personal reason to take vengeance on your family and me by association. He sees an opportunity to kill two birds with one stone, stopping the Asian Open and destroy the family of his business competitor at the same time."

"My uncle will take care of Baahir."

"If I remember correctly, you were the one telling me Baahir is a dangerous man, and I believed you. After doing some research, you may be underestimating his potential to strike. Your uncle is not invincible. Powerful people with strong religious convictions could give Baahir the tools he needs to strike a devastating blow."

"So why involve Daria?"

"I want to make sure your sister is not a causality of our risky behavior."

"Just yesterday, someone tried to kill you on the 1st tee. How do you keep my sister out of the line of fire?"

"Golf fanatics are not the real threat. The real threat are people like Baahir who stand to lose money and power from a changing Iran."

"I don't want to see my sister hurt."

"Then you need to trust me."

"My sister has become infatuated with a man she cannot have."

"Who are you to say who your sister can or cannot have?"

"Look in the mirror; you're not Persian."

"Is that what you tell Sara? She doesn't look Persian either."

"It's different."

"You're the one who needs to look in the mirror. Imposing rules on your sister that you refuse to follow seems repressive to me."

"It doesn't matter. My sister is going to follow her heart anyway."

After apologizing for his bad behavior, Kamran left the locker room, comforted in the knowledge his American friend cared about his sister and would fight to protect her, if challenged. Surprised at Craft's martial arts skills, Kamran contemplated ways to win a few bucks from some of the self-proclaimed tough guys on Tour.

TOP SECRET BASE, KUWAIT

The Geronimo test was a combined measurement of speed, agility, and shooting accuracy. The participant had to ride a horse through an obstacle course while shooting at moving targets and reloading the gun only twice. After a few hours of practice, each team member executed the test three times with three different horses. The final test score was a calculation based on the scores of the three individual tests.

With the Geronimo test results on the large display, Kalani said, "Read it and weep, gentlemen. It appears we have a real Annie Oakley on the team. Our lady member of the team has posted the highest score."

After a few minutes of adulation from the adoring male members of the team, Wilkins checked the day's events at the Open and then sat down with team members to enjoy a cold drink and listen to the next stage of the Ops briefing.

Kalani pointed to picture of a mountainous installation somewhere in

Afghanistan. "The Intel folks believe Gilani's men are hiding the stolen nuclear waste here. We plan to spook him, so he has to move the material. We believe he will move it during the day, because he knows our special forces own the night. Gilani is well aware of America's aversion to civilian casualties, so we expect him to move the material to a heavily populated area. There is only one way out of the mountainous region for the first twenty miles, but then there's a three-way fork in the road and we do not know which direction will be taken. The plan is to have a team along each of the three roads. Once the vehicle commits to one of the three routes, the two teams on the untraveled routes will ride horses across rough terrain to reach the intersecting point before the vehicle arrives. We have to take control of the truck without inflicting damage, so it can be moved to a location where the night fliers are able to pick it up. We may have to defend for several hours until it's dark enough for the heavy lift helicopter to get us out of there. That's all for now. Please eat dinner and get a good night's sleep; the operational tempo is going to pick-up tomorrow."

COUNTY OF FIFE, SCOTLAND

Craft prepared for the difficult night ahead trying to keep it together while having dinner with his mother at the Richardson Hotel. One innocent inquiry by his mother could set him off. He reached for the bottle of pills that Dr. Page had given him, for when his focus was lost and emotions out of control. The thought of having to redefine his relationship with his mother scared him. Not for a single moment had he ever considered the possibility of her working for the Agency.

His nerves began to settle when he realized his mother was the same person, the person who made great sacrifices to give him a good life, the person who still loved his father years after his death and the person who flew from Australia to be there for her son. He walked into the Richardson Hotel, determined to not let anything ever come between them.

He found the conversation easy because he no longer felt the need to protect his cover. As always, the focus of her questions were all about how he was doing and what was going on in his personal life. Amanda did not really care much whether he was winning or losing at golf. What she cared about was how he was handling life in the public eye, and was he taking appropriate actions to stay safe.

After dinner, Craft was off to check on Daria. The driver turned the car off the country road into the sea cottage driveway. The gate was open and unguarded. Craft asked the driver to hurry. At the top of the hill in front of the house, he jumped out of the car and raced to the front door, knocking loudly.

In a panic, Daria opened the front door and pointed to the sunroom, "A man was looking in the window."

Bending down to pull the gun from the holster strapped to his leg, Craft ran out the door. He could see a man's form dressed in black at the bottom of the stairs beginning to run up the beach. Craft moved quickly and carefully down the stairs, and then sprinted at full speed up the beach. He tackled the man from behind.

With the gun pointed at the man's chest, Craft instructed him to get up and take off the black ski mask. It was Christopher Reed from the *London Review,* shaking like someone fearing death was soon to come.

"Mr. Reed, you nearly got yourself shot," Craft said.

"We have gun laws in Britain."

"Stalking laws, too, I believe. Do you want to settle this in the courts?"

"No."

"Then get your sorry ass out of here before I pull the trigger."

Not surprised to learn that Reed was the man snooping around the cottage, Daria said as she placed the shotgun back in the gun cabinet, "I am so glad you arrived when you did. I freaked out seeing that pervert peeking through the window."

"Where is Javid, and why was the gate left open?"

"Reza needed Javid in London, and I had him leave the gate open because I knew you were coming and it's a manual gate."

"If you don't mind, I want my security team to provide protection. The Tour has given me a small army. Thank goodness it was only Reed. Next time, we may not be so lucky."

"Thank you. I am not feeling real safe right now."

"Kamran and I got into it today. I think it's under control, but we need to talk."

They sat back down at the kitchen table. She poured them each a glass of wine, and said, "Whatever you have to say, it doesn't matter."

"I came to the Open, intending to be with you. It just so happened you found me first."

"I am glad you want to be with me," she said.

"There is more to it than that. When we were in Riyadh meeting with Baahir, Sara told Jennifer about her relationship with your brother. When she mentioned it to me, I knew you were not safe. I figured if I knew, then Sara's father also knew and my being in Riyadh was somehow part of his plan to strike back at your family."

"So you came to the Open, armed and ready to protect me?"

"Yes. And when your brother confronted me in the locker room, he was angry that I had put you in danger. I told him I knew about Sara before you told me."

"Why concern yourself in such matters?"

"That's what your brother asked. Somehow I knew this is all happening because of my friendship with Kamran, but it's more than that. I believe together we can bring our nations closer, but if Baahir has his way, we may never have the chance."

Daria had him take off his shirt so she could see how the bruised back was healing. She changed the bandage, and then led him to the guest room. She asked him to put some athletic shorts on and lie on his stomach on the edge of the bed. She soon returned from the other bedroom with body lotion and proceeded to give him a massage. The exhausted man fell asleep. She covered him, turned off the light, and then retired to her bedroom for the evening.

TEHRAN, IRAN

Years earlier, Asadi had anticipated the need for secure communications. He studied the big data analysis techniques used by Iranian and foreign intelligence organizations to detect patterns that could be used to identify covert activities. To eliminate the possibility of leaving a traceable pattern, he used commercially available computing services, so his small amount of data was stored in the same computing environment as millions of other people. For the intelligence organizations, it would be the equivalent of looking for a needle in a haystack. To make it more difficult to find, the data was encrypted and stored in a different location each time, using a new identity and new access codes.

Once the operation began, he intended to keep a buffer between his physical location and those with whom he communicated. He replicated in the cyber world the equivalent of the way handlers and spies communicated using drop locations. A key was that in the cyber world, there was a different drop location would be used for each information exchange, and that drop could be located anyplace in the world.

The CEO had access to the company's corporate security system containing years of employee personal identity information. This gave him a unique identity to use each time he accessed the public network to activate a virtual server. The actual physical location of the virtual server could be in any one of the commercial data centers in the world. A courier would be used to distribute access codes and keep Asadi's physical location unknown. No one other than he ever possessed more than one active access code, and it only worked for a short period of time.

CHAPTER 38

TOP SECRET BASE, KUWAIT

The practice site was set up to replicate the operational terrain in Afghanistan. The team broke up into three groups of two people each. Each group would take up their positions and wait along one of the three potential transport routes. As soon as the team received notice of the actual route, the two groups out of position would have to ride horses carrying equipment several miles to reach the intercept point, prior to the arrival of the vehicles transporting the nuclear material.

Although the team along the chosen route, could, if necessary, take action to slow the vehicles, the full team needed to reach the intercept point in least three minutes before the vehicle transporting the nuclear waste. The highly synchronized operation required meticulous execution. Taking out the hostiles, without rendering the vehicle carrying the nuclear waste inoperable, would be difficult and dangerous.

Wilkins' assignment, being the fastest rider on the team, was to catch the transport vehicle and bring it to a stop before it left the road and crashed. It would be a team effort, with other members shooting anyone presenting a threat in the heat of the battle. If all went well, the hostiles would be dead in a matter of seconds. If not, the team would have to improvise to find a way to take control of the nuclear material. Once they had control of the truck, they could drive to a location where they could defend the position until heavy lift extraction.

The men in the vehicles tried various techniques to mimic the expected behavior of the hijackers. Twice, Wilkins was hit by a rubber bullet with enough force to knock her off the horse traveling at a full gallop. After hours of intense training, feeling physically defeated, she struggled to mount her horse. The other team members quickly provided the needed assistance and encouragement to continue the training. She appreciated the toughness and determination of the other team members, realizing this brutal training was just another day for them. She found comfort in knowing whatever happened during the operation, the team would be there for her.

Craft finished his second round with a five-stroke lead and then went to a near by fitness center to do a hard cardiovascular workout. While he worked out, Daria stood in line at the market, checking the items on the counter against her shopping list. She had invited Peter and Amanda Craft to the cottage for dinner. Ready to load the groceries into the back of the SUV, she stopped to read a message on her HuAID. The message was an apology that his mother would not be coming to dinner. The excuse given was that his mother was needed in London to make script changes so filming in Australia could continue. The real reason was to get a head start figuring out what Reza was up to. After finishing loading the groceries into the back of the car, she slammed the door loud enough to draw the attention of others nearby.

The previous day's meeting with Amanda Craft was friendly, but a bit strained. The contentious scene with her brother on the 17th hole made for a rocky start. She had hoped to have a chance to smooth things over at the golf course today, but Ms. Craft, tired from the previous day's long journey, decided to have a day of rest. Now, she was heading to London. She had been a bit nervous about spending the whole evening with Craft's mother anyway, so now she could have a quiet evening alone with the man who was on track to win his third Major golf tournament.

At the cottage, Daria moved around the kitchen with grace, like a professional chef putting the finishing touches on a gourmet meal. The tomato and cucumber salad sat in the middle of the table, ready to serve. The Persian lamb stew warmed in the oven. The saffron and rose ice cream chilled in the refrigerator.

The tempting kitchen aromas relived warm memories of her childhood growing up in Tehran, learning to cook as the apprentice of Mama Shirazi. She recalled how her grandmother, an expert at cooking traditional Persian foods, loved being in the kitchen. Daria didn't remember much about her mother, who died giving birth to her brother, but she was told her mother also had an interest in cooking as well. Devastated by the loss of her daughter, Mama Shirazi found great comfort in teaching her granddaughter how to cook the secret family recipes passed down through generations of Persian royalty.

She stretched out on the bunk in the compound, physically beaten during the daytime training, trying to regain her strength for the long night ahead. As if chasing an escaping vehicle on a horse wasn't challenging enough, tonight the team would conduct a late night exercise to protect the captured nuclear waste from attacking hostiles, until the material and forces could be extracted by helicopter. She had already grown attached to the horses and dreaded having to release the wonderful animals to the local population at the completion of the operation. She hoped to make a special appeal to Vaughn to reconsider the plan to leave the horses behind.

Wilkins scanned through Amanda's intelligence summary and was stunned at how fast Craft's mother had comprehended the details of the time, place, and nature of the threat. Now confident that she had made the right decision to involve Craft's mother in the operation she remembered Vaughn saying every agent needed a mentor. She thought, *maybe Amanda Craft could be mine.*

While resting, Wilkins tried to catch up on the previous day's events. She watched video of the interviews following the 1st round, listening to the Iranian girl tell the world of her plan to write a cover story for *Persian Woman.* After listening to the interview, Wilkins thought, *You may be able to write a puff piece that the public will eat up, but you will never know the real Peter Craft.*

With feelings of jealousy beginning to take root Wilkins decided to limit her thoughts to ensuring Craft had sufficient information regarding the threat against the Turani family. She scanned the sports headlines to see he held a five-stroke lead going into the third round at the Open, and was on pace to break the record for the lowest tournament score in the Open Champion. *Wow,* she thought, *he really is good enough to be the best player in the world.*

Her HuAID flashed with a high priority message. The message read: *Jen, are you okay? No one will tell me anything about the operation. I am going to kick Gul's ass the next time I see him. No one is responding to my messages. If I don't hear something soon, I am going to walk off the course and come find you. PC*

His willingness to drop everything to make sure she was all right filled her with renewed energy and determination. She remembered those long hours of uncertainty during the VIPER I mission, when just knowing he was alive meant everything. She responded to his message, and then jumped off the bunk and ran out the door, re-energized to brave the night.

COUNTY OF FIFE, SCOTLAND

Craft read the message from Wilkins in response to his inquiry.

Peter, I am fine and Gul is just doing his job. It's standard procedure to shutdown all outside communications regarding the operation. I now know there's a good reason for me to be here. Please don't let my absence distract you. With regard to Reza, here is what I know. General Shirazi and Amir Turani will be arriving in London on Sunday evening. The Turani family will be attending a celebration Tuesday night at the Kensington Hotel in London for Amir Turani's 60th birthday. After dinner, the Turani family will be transported by Reza's security to a country inn outside of London, owned by long-time Iranian family friends. Reza has made arrangements to acquire a shoulder-fired missile on the black market. Will take possession on Tuesday morning. The most likely target is the car transporting the family to the country inn. Reza has filed a flight plan departing London at 11:15PM Tuesday evening. Potential attack positions along the route are being assessed. Can't wait to tell you about my horseplay with the guys. JW

Craft was relieved to know she was vital to the operation and not being subjected to an act of retribution for insubordination. He suspected whatever she was doing had something to do with horses, given the reference to horseplay in her message.

When he arrived at the sea cottage, Daria had dinner ready. They sat in the sunroom enjoying a bottle of wine before dinner. During dinner, Craft complimented her on the exquisite meal and asked if she would be willing to teach him how to cook authentic Persian cuisine. She volunteered to show him but tonight his help cleaning up after dinner would have to do.

Craft proposed they take an evening walk on the beach. He asked Daria to sit on the bottom step where he slipped off her shoes and rolled up her pants legs. After kicking off his shoes and rolling up his pants, he took her hand and led her into the water.

As Daria stepped into the water, she said, "My God, this water is cold; do they put ice cubes in it?"

"Don't worry, you'll get used to it," he replied.

They walked along the beach, relishing the quiet and the saltwater rolling over their feet. After a few minutes of silence, Daria approached the subject of their relationship saying, "I dream about you sometimes."

With the moonlight reflecting off the water and the steady wind at their backs, Craft said, "So, tell me about your dreams."

"All I will say is you're in my dreams a lot. And those dreams are quite pleasant dreams," she replied.

"I do want to be with you, but I must also be respectful of the differences in our cultures."

"We're people like everyone else," Daria responded.

"In my culture, a consenting sexual relationship between two single adults is an accepted norm, but not in yours. To make things more complicated, your uncle Shirazi is a powerful and protective man. How has he dealt with other men in your life?"

"I don't know."

"You don't know," he repeated. "Okay, I will ask it another way. Are they still alive?"

She stopped. Hesitating for a moment, visibly uncomfortable about what she was going to say, she timidly answered, "I don't know, because there's never been any other man in my life."

Was it possible that one of the most attractive women in the world had never been with a man? He knew the answer. It was true. She was waiting for the right man, and he fit the profile. "Let's enjoy our time together and see where things go."

"Okay then, would you consider spending a day with me in London after the Open? We are having a birthday celebration for my father's 60th birthday, and it would be special if you could attend. I would like your mother to attend also, since she was unable to make it to dinner tonight."

"I would enjoy spending time with you in London. Who knows, maybe I will have a chance to bond with your uncle Shirazi before he decides to kill me."

"In all seriousness, I love my uncle dearly, but he is old school. I never actually thought of what he might do to someone if he disapproved."

"Let's hope we'll never have to cross that bridge."

"My uncle probably thinks we have already crossed that bridge, given that you have been staying here at the cottage."

"I suggest we spend the day together, just you and me, driving through the beautiful Scottish countryside. I hear there are beautiful sights along the way."

"First, you need to get the job done on the course; then we can talk about a long ride through the countryside."

"Unlike the U.S. Open, I couldn't be more confident about winning *because Lenard won't let us lose!*"

CHAPTER 39

COUNTY OF FIFE, SCOTLAND

Craft hoisted the Claret Jug high in the air to the sound of booming cheers in front of the Royal and Ancient Clubhouse at St. Andrews. Craft insisted on having names Craft-McKnight engraved on the ancient trophy to acknowledge the Scotsman's critical role in winning the Open Championship. The Royal and Ancient Golf Club initially resisted but caved to public protest, given that Lenard had taken a bullet at the 1st tee.

Even though he won the prestigious tournament without Smartball, he struggled mentally to stay in the moment because soon Wilkins would deploy to the wilderness of Afghanistan. Uncharacteristic of a confident champion, he began to question himself. *Was his focus on Reza misguided? Were his feelings for Daria affecting his judgment? Would he be there if Wilkins needed him? Was his mother's involvement necessary?*

Then out of the blue, a reporter yelled, "Mr. Craft, are you going to accept the Cyber Golf challenge?"

Craft had no idea of what the reporter was talking about. After asking for clarification it became apparent that the Cyber Golf Association had made a public offer to donate thirty million dollars to the charity of his choice if he beat the Cyber Golf Champion, Kai Peng, in a single eighteen hole match held at a traditional golf course. Craft figured playing the match was a way to keep golf in the headlines leading up to Asian Open and raise funds for the First Light program.

Craft responded, "I accept."

TOP SECRET BASE, KUWAIT

The team performed final equipment checks getting ready for their evening deployment. Confident the team was ready, Kalani made last minute preparations to lead the team through the Afghan wilderness. He worked out operational details with Vaughn, who would stay behind to man the command center. Vaughn's job would be to monitor activities, keep the executives informed, and coordinate any requirements that might arise during execution, such as satellite feeds or emergency airdrops. In the dark of night, the Special Ops team would be airlifted into the operational zone, approximately two hundred miles from the location of the stolen nuclear waste. Over the next few days, they would gradually move into position to execute the operation. Fluent in the Pashto and Dari, the languages of the local tribesmen, and disguised as Afghan drug smugglers, the team would blend in with the indigenous population. The locals had built an economy based on drug trafficking through their villages, by providing basic services for cash.

Wilkins relaxed alone in the stable, brushing and washing the horses. In two hours, the team would be required to surrender all electronic equipment not explicitly issued for the operation. For a person who typically worked several hours each day interacting on the network, the thought of spending several days in an undeveloped country, disguised as an Afghan man, disconnected from all modern communication was terrifying.

Unsettled by the thought of Craft with the Iranian girl, Wilkins brushed the big stallion harder and faster until, in protest, the animal kicked at the wall behind. In a soft calming voice, she apologized to the loyal companion for causing him discomfort. She patted the horse on the nose and feed him an apple. Thoughts of Craft again occupied her mind. Of course, making sure no harm came to the Turani family was the right thing to do, but at what cost? *Had she offered him up without a fight? Did she deliver Sampson into the hands of Delilah? Was Craft willing to give up his life as an agent to pursue a foreign love?*

She sat on the ground in the corner of the stable rocking softly back and forth, trying to rationalize the choices she had made in life. Given there were times when she had engaged in intimate behavior for the sake of a mission, she wondered how far Craft would go with the Iranian girl.

Vaughn walked into the stable with a cold drink in his hand. Seeing Wilkins sitting in the corner of the stable, deep in thought, he offered her the cold drink, a real luxury in the heat of the desert, and then sat down next to her.

"I thought you would want to know. Craft just won the British Open. Without any assistance, he broke the goddamn record," Vaughn declared.

"What's next for him?" she asked.

"He just accepted a thirty million dollar offer to play the Cyber Golf

Champion in a winner-take-all match sometime before the Asia Open."

"Why would he do that?"

"You're the media expert. Passing on an opportunity to win millions for the First Light program would demonstrate a lack of commitment. Also, using the cyber golf connection to engage the Chinese is a great opportunity. Maybe Craft could win next year's Cyber Golf Championship. If he knows how to catch the Chinese cheating, he probably knows how to beat them."

Wanting to be alone, Wilkins responded, "Jason, you're a busy man, so cut to the chase. Why are you here?"

"I want to talk and see if we can't patch things up. Let me be the first to tell you, your performance during training has been fantastic. But more than that, you've really stepped up your game."

"Coming from you, it means a lot."

Holding her hand, Vaughn said, "I have a confession. When I asked you to take on this mission, I never expected you to be going into the backcountry of Afghanistan with those cowboys. I thought Kalani was nuts when he told me you were vital to the operation. I objected, but he made his case. How did you get so damn good on a horse?"

"When you take a Nebraskan girl off the farm and put her in 'million dollar a year' boarding schools, she looks for loyal companionship. I found it with horses."

"You and Craft are special. You're the only people I have ever talked into accepting a mission solely for the good of the nation."

"I am feeling a bit stressed at the moment," Wilkins responded, shaking like a daughter ready to confess a wrongdoing to her father.

"I would be concerned if you weren't. My God, I was an absolute basket case before my first Special Ops deployment."

"I find it hard to visualize you curled up in the corner of a stable, scared you're headed into the valley of death."

"Ask Kalani. I cleaned the barrel of my gun so much the metal was wearing thin. Being scared keeps you alive; it's losing focus that gets you killed. I will tell you one thing, Kalani is still the best leader, and if I had any equestrian skills, which I don't, I would take your place."

Her lips turned up with a slight smile.

"We have work to do. Can't have you leave tonight with worries on the home front." He assured her anything she said was in confidence, without retribution and asked for her trust. "I need to know what's going on in your head, so I can help."

She hesitated for a moment and then said, "I am not sure where to start."

"Then let me start," Vaughn responded. "You were right. We do have a responsibility to protect people we get involved in our operations."

With time running short, Wilkins told him everything, except her feelings for Craft and her fear of losing him to the Iranian girl.

After carefully listen to her concerns, he assured her that the Turani family's safety was a top priority. He was fully aware of Reza's devious plan and was confident that the situation would soon be resolved. "How do you think Craft is handling the operation at the Open without you?"

"He is doing his job," she responded, in defense of her partner.

"You're both great agents, but together you're much better than alone. It's encouraging to know the nation will be left in good hands when we old dogs head out to pasture."

"You'll never give this up; you love it."

"You're so wrong," Vaughn replied. He pulled out his HuAID and began scrolling through family pictures. "I would give this job up in a *New York minute* if I knew we had the right people committed to keep our nation safe. I will be honest, agents like you two are hard to find and difficult to keep. Both of you could be doing anything you want in life and you chose to serve the nation. Most of the people I know are doing this because their choices are limited."

Wilkins said, "Your grandchildren are precious."

He pulled a flask from his pocket filled with Jack Daniels Whiskey, offered her a drink, and then said, "When this is all over, I want us to go to Jacksons in Charleston so you can show me the barroom trick that has everyone talking."

When she realized he had been looking after her as a protective father who wanted to make sure his daughter was safe without interfering, she decided to answer his question directly. "I am pissed Craft is falling for the Iranian girl," she said.

"Has he really? Or, as you said, is he just doing his job?"

"Have you seen her? She's beautiful. What man wouldn't want to come home to Daria?"

"You're beautiful. What man wouldn't want to come home to you?

Peter is well grounded in southern values; he will make the right decision."

"What's the right decision?" she asked.

"He will choose family."

LONDON, ENGLAND

When they reached the Kensington Hotel, security personnel waited at the underground entrance so they could enter the hotel out of public view. Amanda Craft, having arrived in London two days earlier, arranged for adjoining rooms where Peter and Daria could rest and dress before the evening's event.

As far as Amanda could detect, Reza's plan remained unchanged. Her job was to stay out of the way, but be prepared to take Reza out if necessary. She tapped into the hotel reservations system and observed that an unidentified person had recently reserved a block of rooms. Determined to know who was behind the transaction, she activated an Agency tracer program. To avoid detection, the original transaction had moved through several firewalls in the global network. After discovering the anonymous reservations had originated in Iran, she contacted an associate at U.S. Cyber Command who was able to determine the reservation originated from the bureau of the Supreme Leader.

Amanda analyzed the facts. General Shirazi had met the previous day with British Intelligence. The mysterious hotel room reservations made by the Supreme Leader. Reza was still left in charge of security. That evening the whole family would be attending Amir Turani's birthday celebration.

She asked herself, *What does it all mean?* Then the fuzzy notion of the General's plan became more apparent. She raced through the scenario of things that could go wrong. She wondered, *What if Reza also discovered the General's plan?*

With time running short, she sent an emergency alert message to Catherine Walker, asking for immediate approval to use a precious Agency application with the ability to determine if anyone else had attempted to trace the origin of anonymous room reservations. After receiving the Director's approval, Amanda ran the scan. The report came back negative. Reza had not traced the hotel reservation.

•

As the security personnel unloaded the luggage from the vehicle, Daria regretted their day alone together had come to an end. She enjoyed having his full attention, viewing the beautiful sights, listening to elegant piano compositions and lots of conversation. Glancing at her watch, she was pleased they still had almost four hours to rest and get ready for the evening.

Craft tried to appear undistracted while his mind busily formulated a plan to make sure Reza's plot failed. He wished he had received from Wilkins an update on his mother's status but he didn't, so he would have to proceed on gut instinct. The consequences of failing to act were unthinkable. He had to make sure Reza never had a chance to fire the missile. The head of hotel security handed Craft a note.

Peter, I arranged for you and Daria to have hotel rooms so you can rest before this evening's festivities. Looking forward to hearing about your victory at the Open and trip through the English countryside. I will meet you in the Lobby at 6:45PM. Love, Mom

•

Daria was delighted to have a hotel room separate from his mother to rest, dress, and continue the day's conversation with her American friend. She observed that Craft's mood had changed since their arrival in London. She wondered if the pressure of their two families coming together might be weighing on his mind.

Craft needed time alone to put into action his plan to engage Reza. To buy time, he suggested they go to a nearby health center to work out, expecting her to decline the offer. As expected, Daria indicated the team back in New York was feeling the pressure of the next week's *Persian Woman* issue deadline. They needed her, the boss, to make a few decisions.

Just as Craft was about to go into his room to pack an exercise bag, Daria asked, "Do you think your mother and my father might connect with each other?"

"Your father is a charming man, but my mother is in a serious relationship with a man back in Australia," he replied.

Annoyed by his callous response, Daria responded, "That's not what I meant."

With his mind on Reza, he responded, "I see my mother and your father connecting on many levels, which are you referring to?"

"You seem pre-occupied. Let's talk another time."

He needed Daria in a cooperative mood for the evening, so he continued the conversation, "We should talk now, given our parents will be meeting in a few hours."

"Both our parents have spent their lifetime trying to move past the tragic event of losing a lover," she responded.

Before he could say a word, Daria began telling stories of times as a child when she would find her father sitting in his office in a trance, starring at the picture of her mother on the wall and talking to the picture, as if her mother was still alive.

"It's your father's birthday, so bringing up such difficult subject is not wise," Craft cautioned.

Seeing he was struggling to focus on what she was saying, Daria sat down next to him and gave him the look. In their short time together, they had developed their own body language as a form of communication. She was giving him the look of opportunity where, if he chose, he could look through her eyes to touch the woman inside. It was an opportunity he would not want to overlook too often, or it would be the demise of their promising relationship.

Daria continued, "It's not about talking. When people have a common experience as traumatic as losing a lover, it is how that experience shaped their lives that become the connection."

With the conversation getting deep and time running out, he needed to bring the dialogue to an end without dampening her spirit. She was reaching out, but the timing was not good. "I get it. We both lost parents at a young age. We've never really talked about it, but the connection is there, it has to be. That traumatic experience has shaped who we are and what we strive to be."

Satisfied that he had taken the opportunity to look through her eyes and into her soul, she kissed him and then announced he would be on his own, because she had scheduled a working meeting with the *Persian Woman* team, who had traveled from New York City for the celebration.

Overcome by gloom, he sat in the living room area, reflecting on their relationship, knowing he would never be able to share with Daria the profound impact his father's tragic death had on his life. He wondered if he could ever have a fulfilling relationship with a person from whom he must keep such secrets.

In her room, Amanda looked down at the notes on the table. Although General Shirazi's strategy of deception had crystallized in her mind, she still had questions to be answered. *Was Reza in this alone or did he have help? If Reza was managing onsite security at the Kensington, who was going to be firing the missile?*

A skilled agent, Amanda tapped into the hotel's security system and began scanning through the hotel common areas. It wasn't long before she had located Reza. He met with hotel security, and then walked through the parking garage. At the end of the garage, Reza stopped to talk to someone. Zooming in on the person, the face of Javid came into focus. She zoomed in on their faces, and began video recording the speech. Unable to pick up the actual audio, she transmitted the recorded video to the Agency for processing. The Agency had a capability to process video images, effectively reading lips in any language, and translate them into English audio. The audio wasn't perfect, but it was good enough.

She read the transcript of the audio translation. Reza would be leaving the Kensington early, to perform an onsite security walk through of the country inn before General Shirazi's arrival. After the event concluded, Javid would drive General Shirazi and his family to the country inn. He reminded the young man to call on the secure radio link, to let him know when they left the Kensington. Reza concluded the conversation, telling Javid it was important all Turani family members returned to the country inn in the limo because General Shirazi had prepared a family surprise. After asking Javid to swear on his mother's grave to keep the secret, Reza told him of the General's plan to give Amir Turani a family portrait.

Why had Shirazi let this deadly plot go so far? she wondered. Given the verifiable intelligence provided to Shirazi and his pattern of dealing with traitors in the past, Reza should be deceased. She suspected the General wanted to be certain Reza had gone to the dark side before taking action. *I would not want to be in Reza's shoes if he pulls the trigger on the missile,* she thought.

TOP SECRET BASE, KUWAIT

He leaned back in a chair with his feet up on the desk with a Cuban cigar in his hand. Vaughn blew smoke rings as he tracked the progress of the Special Ops team, now in the wildness of Afghanistan. The team was slowly making its way toward the location of the stolen nuclear waste. He expected the pace of the operation to accelerate, following the conclusion of events in London. Unknown to Craft, his rogue operation to save the Turani family had now become vital to national security. The team decided to leverage Shirazi's takedown of Reza to force Gilani to move the stolen nuclear waste.

Given the interdependency between the Turani family assassination and Afghanistan operation, Vaughn decided it was time to teach the young agent from Charleston a lesson about the consequences of working outside the system. It was inevitable that up and coming agents at some time in their career would find themselves going native. From personal experience, Vaughn knew being disconnected from the people and resources that keep you informed and safe was the loneliest feeling in the world. Seasoned agents had learned to build a virtual family, a network of people they could always trust.

Reminiscent of his young days, he began laughing as he recalled some of the bonehead mistakes he made trying to go it alone. He had to learn the hard way and had the scars to prove it. Vaughn saw some of his own characteristics in Craft. He knew the young agent would not sit on the sidelines hoping all would turn out well. Vaughn retrieved Wilkins' HuAID from the safe. Using a piece of tape to lift her fingerprints from the bottle, he bypassed the biometric scan. Posing as Wilkins, he sent a message to Craft.

LONDON, ENGLAND

Craft received the message that was supposedly sent by Wilkins.

Peter, Sorry for not contacting you sooner, but training is grueling. Your winning the Open was awesome. You better rest because Vaughn said you're going to be needed for the Afghanistan operation in a couple of days. Please be careful in London and remember, sometimes doing nothing is the right decision. Ops security is about to shut down all nonessential communication, so I will be out of contact for a while. JW

He thought the tone was unusual, observing a lack of urgency and a failure to provide an update on his mother's activities. Something was not right, but with only a few hours until Reza's attack on the Turani family, he needed to take action. He needed special equipment fast. Remembering

Wilkins had created the *Ask Jen* application, he assumed she would have anticipated his need for special equipment. Craft began navigating through the list of *Ask Jen* topics.

Her resourcefulness was remarkable. Wilkins had covered everything he might need, to include mission needs such as obtaining untraceable money, tracing bank transactions, and bypassing security systems as well as pleasurable things such as the best nightclubs, restaurants, and pubs. In addition, the application had a long list of personal contacts to be used if necessary for special purposes, such as obtaining a forged passport or accessing government records.

Craft activated the *Need Special Equipment* video clip. A recording of Wilkins began to play, giving personal instructions on how to obtain the equipment quickly. She gave a tribute to her grandfather, for much of his fortune was being used to establish a vast international network providing special services for friendly agents throughout the world. The network hid under the cover of private for-profit businesses. Although the agency knew of the capability and frequently used it, Wilkins had a special high authentication code set up by her grandfather. Requests using the special code would be treated as ultra-high priority, and kept off-the-record.

Uncertain about where and how to deliver the needed equipment, he left the hotel dressed in running clothes, to survey the surrounding area. The paparazzi waited outside the hotel in hopes of snapping a few pictures of the golf superstar. The media vultures gave up trying to keep up with him and returned to the hotel stakeout. After circling the local area, cutting through narrow alleyways and through crowded areas, Craft returned to the hotel to complete the equipment request. Within a few seconds of submitting the request, he received confirmation along with the code to get into the requested vehicle.

Craft sent a message to his mother and Daria, saying he needed to meet another Tour player to discuss a business opportunity and might be a few minutes late for the evening's event. He would meet them at the reception as soon as possible. Craft waited in the nearby public parking garage a few blocks from the hotel, until the van parked and the person driving exited the parking lot. Craft approached the van, and entered the access code. He inspected the equipment, making sure everything needed was accounted for and he knew how to operate each item.

Craft's mother waited in the lobby of the hotel wearing a bright formal summer dress purchased from the *Persian Woman* catalog, diamond earrings, and a gold choker, highlighting her petite features. She gasped in surprise, as Daria arrived wearing a nearly identical dress and jewelry. After laughing and complimenting each other on their exquisite taste, Ms. Craft volunteered to return to her room and change. Daria insisted the shoes they wore made them distinctively different and the rules of fashion remained unbroken.

The two ladies were about to leave for the birthday celebration, when Peter walked into the lobby. Like throwing fresh meat to a pack of lions, the paparazzi pushed to get around hotel security to take pictures. Observing the escalating situation, Craft, with a lady on each arm, moved to an area where they posed for pictures.

Whispering so only the ladies could hear, Craft commented, "I hope you have plenty of these beautiful dresses in stock, because the world is going to want all of them after seeing pictures of you."

While Craft and the ladies posed for pictures, Kamran Turani arrived in the lobby with his father and uncle, with Reza close at hand. After a few moments of introductions, the whole group posed for pictures, before moving to the ballroom where the birthday celebration would be held.

Craft stopped to greet and talk with Reza and Javid standing at the entrance to the ballroom. During the conversation, he handed each of them an official ball-marker coin commemorating this year's U.S. Open Championship. Attached to each coin was a biosensor that would attach to their bodies, and allow them both to be tracked for 48 hours even if the coins were removed.

Several people made the trip from Iran to London for Amir's birthday celebration. Craft moved through the room, introducing his mother to several of the people he had already met during his visit to Tehran. He minimized his direct contact with General Shirazi by engaging in vigorous conversation with his mother and the guests.

Daria took him by the hand and began introducing him to the *Persian Woman* team. Excited about the cover story, the team members talked about their strategy for making him the most interesting man in the world. Although he listened politely, Daria knew the last thing he wanted was for the women across the world to be fighting for his affections.

Amir Turani mingled among the crowd, while General Shirazi surrounded himself with a small group off to the side. Amir positioned himself where he could have some time alone with Amanda Craft, the radiant American journalist. They engaged in pleasant conversation about the special qualities and accomplishments of their children. Amir mentioned the challenges of raising the children as a single parent. Amanda kept the conversation centered on his journey through life, asking soft questions to give him an opportunity to keep talking.

With the early reception coming to an end, the room lights dimmed indicating it was time for guests to proceed to the room where dinner would be served. As special guests, Peter and Amanda Craft were seated at the head table. Initially, the conversation was polite and formal, but with time, tight lips began to loosen.

At the dinner table, Peter took control of the conversation, turning the attention to the First Light program. Kamran and Peter talked about plans to open the first public golf course in south Tehran and asked for name suggestions. Attempting to break the ice with General Shirazi, Craft thanked the General for his hospitality, and extended an invitation for all to visit Charleston.

While the guests were being served dessert, Daria and some of the girls on the *Persian Woman* team disappeared from the dining room. A few minutes later, General Shirazi excused himself and also left the room. The element of surprise began to build as a group with eastern musical instruments setup in a corner of the room.

With a microphone in hand, General Shirazi entered the room and announced that Amir's daughter was committed to returning the great art of Persian dance to Iran. To the rhythm of a drumbeat and sitar, the young women, dressed in colorful flowing silk costumes, entered the room. The girls had practiced the dance routines for months at a dance studio back in New York City.

The men's eyes were transfixed on the motions of the young ladies, moving in unison around the center of the room. After completing the first dance, Daria took her father's hand and led him to the center of the room. With Amir standing in the center, the girls began dancing in a circle. Daria then went over to the band area and pulled a sword from under a cloth, and returned to hand it to her father. The band began playing. While the girls danced slowly in a circle, Amir performed a traditional warrior's dance. Soon General Shirazi and Kamran joined Amir in the center of the room. The men spun in a circle with their hands on their hips, kicking their legs to the beat of the music.

The girls danced around the room, inviting all the ladies to join in, forming a line dance. The men in the room formed a circle, lightly clapping to the rhythms and watched the ladies dance in a circle, in traditional dances passed on for many generations.

While the ladies continued to dance, Javid informed Craft of the General's desire to talk with him in private. The General waited on a balcony of the ballroom, with Reza standing at the doorway to ensure they had privacy. Surprised to see the General smoking a cigar, Craft graciously accepted the invitation to join him. They both stood on the balcony, enjoying their cigars and waiting for the other one to begin the conversation. A big man, rugged from years of living outdoors during military operations, the General was now looking to enjoy the finer things in life, like a good cigar.

Anticipating this was the moment when the General was going to tell him to stay away from his niece or suffer the consequences, he began planning his response.

Speaking English with a difficult accent, Shirazi said, "Mr. Craft, I have a favor to ask."

"How can I be of service?" Craft replied.

"Daria tells me you're a remarkable pianist, able to play anything from memory. Would you be so gracious to play Amir's favorite piano composition, Beethoven's Moonlight Sonata?" the General asked.

Quickly considering his options, Craft determined it would be easier to agree than to run the risk of disappointing the man. "It would be a pleasure," Craft answered.

When they returned to the ballroom, the lights were lower, with a large grand piano in the middle of the room and a spotlight on the bench. With everyone waiting in anticipation, Craft sat at the piano positioned in the center of the room. He looked lovingly at his mother as he began playing. His hands moved gracefully across the keyboard as the sound from the beautiful sonata radiated throughout the room. Amir closed his eyes as he listened intensely to each beautifully shaped note. Although Craft had not heard the composition in many years, each note was etched in his memory. But he could not resist improvising as he played. He didn't know why; he just did. When the song ended, you could have hear a pin drop in the silence, then the room erupted into applause and then, led by Amir and

General Shirazi, the room gave him a standing ovation.

In unison, Daria and Amanda pulled tissues from their small bags to wipe the tears from their eyes. With tears still rolling down his cheeks, Amir thanked everyone for making his 60th birthday a day he would cherish forever. He had heard the song played hundreds of times over, but never with the feeling the American had blended into each and every note.

With the main part of the evening coming to the close, Craft gave his mother a look, signaling it was time to leave. Amanda thanked everyone for the wonderful evening, and asked her son to escort her back to the room. He told Daria he would be back to say goodbye before she left with the family to go to the country inn.

Amanda walked slowly, trying to delay, hoping he would decide to abort whatever plan he had to engage Reza. He insisted on returning to say a proper goodbye to the Turani family. Before she could say a word, he was gone.

Along with other guests at the celebration, Craft stood waving goodbye as the limo, driven by Javid, pulled out of the hotel lot. He waited until the limo was out of sight, then walked out of the parking garage and began running. He reached the van parked two blocks away, entered the door code, started the engine and pulled out. The tracking device codes for Javid and Reza were already programmed into the navigation system. He moved quickly through the back streets, catching up with the limo just before it went into the short underground tunnel.

Craft turned off the expressway, and pulled the van over to the side of the road. He activated the van's remote door and ramp. Out of the back of the van he drove a high performance motorcycle and began racing through side streets, with an equipment bag on his back. He looked at the HuAID on his wrist to see Reza already located at the intercept point, and Javid and the Turani family in route. At the current pace, he estimated he would reach the intercept point just in time.

Nearing the intercept point, Craft pulled the motorcycle off to the side of the road and began running up the hill between him and Reza. At the top of the hill, Craft reached for the binoculars around his neck and scanned the intercept site. He located the assassin a hundred yards away, waiting behind a small storage building with the shoulder-fired missile ready to launch.

Craft pulled the bag off his back, quickly assembled and loaded the sniper rifle. Taking a position out of sight, leaning against a pile of rocks, he peered through the riflescope. To get a clean shot, he would have to wait for Reza to move away from the storage building. As the limo approached, Craft was about to fire his weapon when he felt a sharp pain in his back. Unable to move, he watched helplessly as Reza moved away from the building, and fired the missile. *The limousine carrying the Turani family exploded into flames.*

CHAPTER 40

LONDON, ENGLAND

A private jet waited at the Luton Airport, thirty miles north of London. The pilot was thankful for his good fortune. Two days earlier, an unidentified client had paid ten thousand pounds in advance to book a short flight to the Azores. He waited anxiously for the client to arrive relieved the aircraft mechanics were able to complete the overdue maintenance on time.

Reza was on his way to meet face-to-face with Baahir in the Azores to discuss other potential business arrangements. With the Turani family and General Shirazi out of the way, business opportunities in Iran for Baahir would increase, although some obstacles might arise from time-to-time. Reza was positioning himself to be Baahir's enforcer in Iran.

Shortly after Reza arrived, the pilot had the jet in the air. Reza scanned through digital pictures taken following the explosion, to show proof of his success. Given the bodies were consumed in the explosion, there was an element of faith required. He figured by the time they met, the news of the Turani family's demise would be broadcast on the major media networks.

UNDISCLOSED LOCATION

Lying naked on a cold floor, in total darkness, he transitioned in and out of consciousness. With a massive headache, barely able to think, he pulled himself up to a sitting position, leaning against the cold wall. Still disoriented, anger consumed him, as the violent explosion replayed in his mind. He vowed to hunt down and kill whoever prevented him from stopping Reza. As his mind began to clear, he still had many nagging questions. *Why had General Shirazi gone to his execution, with the knowledge of Reza's planned treachery? Why had his mother not stopped Reza? Who had stopped him from taking the shot? Who had imprisoned him?*

In the cold and dark, Craft fought back his emotions, trying to think through the situation. He replayed the scene in his mind. *The Turani family left in the limo, someone stopped him before he could kill Reza, Reza fired the missile, the limo exploded, someone kidnapped him, although emotionally bruised, he was uninjured...*

At the top of his lungs, Craft yelled, "Vaughn, get me out of here."

The door opened, the light turned on, and in walked Jason Vaughn.

Looking at the younger agent, Vaughn said, "You look like crap."

"You better have good news," Craft demanded.

"Good news. You almost single handedly screwed-up a British Intelligence operation," declared Vaughn.

"Who was in the limo?" asked the naked agent.

"The limo was on auto pilot, with stage props resembling the Turani family members. I assure you the family is unharmed. Please get cleaned up and for heaven sakes take a shower. You stink."

"Oh, by the way Shirazi is a cleaver man, killing two birds with one stone," Vaughn said, handing him a copy of the *London Times* with the headline *"Saudi Billionaire Dies in Plane Crash"* written in bold letters.

After reading the article, Craft concluded both Reza and Baahir died in the crash.

LONDON, ENGLAND

The aircraft accelerated down the runway at Heathrow Airport, bound for Brisbane, Australia. As the flight was ready to lift off into the air, Amanda reached across the armrest to take the hand of the man sitting next to her. He tenderly took her hand and gave a confident smile, signaling job well done.

When the flight reached cruising altitude and the engine noise softened, making it easier to talk, Amanda asked, "Do you think he is going to be all right?"

"Other than a bruised ego, he'll be fine," answered Jeremy West.

AFGHANISTAN

Summer night starlight filled the sky. Wilkins took her turn with two other men, guarding the camp while the others slept. She walked slowly around the camp, looking for anomalies. While checking the horses, she noticed a dim light radiating from Kalani's tent. Then the tent flap flew open. As he walked closer, she could see his eyes getting big as golf balls.

"Vaughn wanted me to deliver the good news," Kalani said.

"I could use some good news," she responded.

"The Turani family is doing fine. Can't say the same for Reza and Baahir. They perished in a mid air collision a few hours ago."

"How is Craft doing?"

"He's physically fine, but his spirits are in the gutter."

"What happened?"

"Craft was about the take Reza out, when he was immobilized with a fast-acting tranquilizer dart in the back. He went down seeing the limo explode into flames believing the Turani family had been killed, but the Brits had pulled a bait and switch. He is with Vaughn now, getting his head back on straight."

"Thanks for telling me. Craft is tough; he'll recover fast."

"By the way, he has sent numerous messages asking me to confirm you're okay. Would you do me a favor and talk with him, so I can have some peace."

Kalani pushed the connect button on his radio, handed it to the agent and said, "You have five minutes."

Craft answered the call with urgency. Hearing the concern in his voice, Wilkins assured him the operation was progressing as planned and not to worry. She made an appeal to go easy on Vaughn, because the old man really was looking out for them. Although he wouldn't talk about his ordeal in London, she could tell his confidence had been shaken. As she ended the call, she took comfort in knowing he eagerly awaited her return.

TOP SECRET BASE, KUWAIT

Vaughn sat at a table, reading intelligence updates when Craft entered the Command Center. Expecting a confrontation, Vaughn was ready to let the young agent blow off some steam. After fixing a cup of coffee, Craft sat down at the table.

Vaughn looked up from the papers and asked, "What's on your mind?"

In a contrite tone, Craft asked, "How can I help?"

"Are you ready to be there in case Wilkins needs backup?" Vaughn asked.

"Absolutely!"

On the move all day, the Special Ops team finally rested around the campfire at dusk, eating rations and telling stories. Tired of hanging out with the machismo soldiers who thrived on the Spartan life, Wilkins craved a warm bath and a steak. She didn't mind the warm days, but the cold nights were miserable. One night, she actually considered asking one of the men if she could climb into his sleeping bag just to absorb some of his body warmth. It wasn't sexual. It was survival.

Over the years, the men had amassed a large arsenal of stories and jokes to pass the time waiting for things to happen. It was their way of bonding and releasing the stress of the day. Some of the men used discretion, choosing their words in mixed company. Other treated Wilkins as one of the boys, and just said whatever crossed their minds. Although the men could be rather crude, these were the warriors she wanted on her side when life was on the line.

A miniature unmanned air vehicle circled the sky, with the ability to detect movement in the local area. Kalani was relieved because so far, the operation had been uneventful. Since arriving in Afghanistan, the team had trekked through the countryside during the day and camped at night with minimal contact from the locals.

To simplify things, the team referred to the three potential intercept locations for capturing the stolen nuclear waste as "Derby," "Preakness," and "Belmont," after the triple-crown horse races. When the time came to transition into the next phase of the operation, the team would divide into groups, with each group traveling to one of the intercept locations. Once the actual intercept location was known, the horses at that location would get to rest while the other horses rode hard, carrying equipment and riders across the rugged terrain to the intercept location in time to engage the hijackers.

The team was under no illusion that recovering the stolen materials would be easy. Gilani had hired jihadists who left the Iranian Revolutionary Guard in opposition to the new Iranian leadership. Although the hijackers were well trained and committed to the cause, they did not have the backing of a strong military force. The Special Ops team held the advantage of surprise and a powerful access to the most capable military in the world.

Signaling everyone to huddle up, Kalani informed the team it was time to move into the next phase of the operation. Without a word, the team packed up, saddled the horses, and broke camp in pairs. Kalani and Wilkins began the all night trek across rough terrain to Derby while the other teams headed for Preakness and Belmont.

•

The stealth transport streamed across the sky. The light in the cargo area flashed red, indicating the aircraft was nearing the drop zone. Craft did a last minute equipment check and gave the flight chief the thumbs-up signal. The crew pushed the large cargo box to the door. The engines changed pitch as the aircraft slowed, the door opened and the gusting wind whirled through the cargo area, making it nearly impossible to hear. The light started flashing yellow and then green.

The crew pushed the cargo box out of the aircraft. Struggling against the wind, Craft moved to the open door and jumped, following the cargo box to the ground. Jumping from 8,000 feet, he listened as the audio altimeter counted down. At 3,000 feet, the parachute inflated. Thankful for the professional instructors while in Kuwait, he prepared for a safe night landing. With an automatic weapon strapped to his side, he scanned the ground with a narrow beam flashlight, looking for a safe place to land. Within a few feet of the ground, Craft pulled hard on the ropes, drifting to a soft landing.

•

With dawn upon them and still more than two hours from their destination, Kalani decided to take the risk and cut through a narrow mountain pass, with a steep rocky mountain wall on one side and a narrow deep stream on the other. They moved slowly, their weapons in easy reach. They dismounted and walked, using the horses as shields, sensing they were being watched, and easy targets for hostiles who might be located in the bush on the other side of the stream.

Two men appear from the dark shadows a hundred yards ahead. Dressed in traditional clothing, loose pajama-like trousers, turbans, and mid length jackets, the tribesmen walked towards them. Kalani recognized the imprint of the concealed weapons and their military grade boots. He signaled Wilkins, indicating the approaching men were hostiles. Kalani casually raised his arm to acknowledge the approaching tribesmen. With a small mirror in the palm of his hand, he caught a glimpse of four hostiles approaching slowly from behind with rifles drawn.

Kalani made a quick move, pulling a flare gun from the saddlebag and sent a blazing flame into the ground in front of the horses, causing the animals to rear up on their hind legs, destabilizing the riders. As two men attempted to pull weapons hidden under their jackets, Wilkins pulled a Beretta M9 pistol and fired two shots, dropping both of the approaching men.

Riding the horses, Kalani and Wilkins dashed down the trail. After regaining control of their horses, the hostiles gave chase, shooting their guns wildly hoping to hit something. Bullets ricocheting off the rocks sent sparks flying in every direction. Unsure of what might be waiting ahead, they rode the horses across a shallow part of the stream, pulled their automatic rifles from the saddlebags and took up position on high ground, where they could defend against the hostiles. An expert marksman, Kalani fired a shot, nicking the ear of the man who appeared to be in charge, sending the message that the next shot would be through the heart. The hostiles turned to retreat.

A whirlwind of thoughts entered her mind. *Were the men she killed bandits trying to provide for their families? Did they have children? Would someone bury them? Did she really have to kill them?...*

Seeing the young girl had lost her focus, Kalani said, "Those were professional militants, not local tribesmen."

"How do you know?" she snapped back.

Wincing from the pain in his side, he answered, "Both wore military issued boots."

About to challenge his statement, she saw blood oozing from his side. "You've been shot," Wilkins proclaimed.

She examined the wound while he kept a lookout for the hostiles. Apparently, a bullet fragment had ricocheted off the rocks, piercing his side. Rummaging through the supplies in the saddlebags, she located medical supplies, including bandages, painkillers, a scalpel, and other items.

Starting to treat the wound, she said, "Nothing vital is damaged. It's a bullet fragment. I'll patch you up."

"Do you know what you are doing?"

"I've watched videos. How hard could it be?" She administered the sedative, removed the fragment, cleaned the wound, closed the laceration with stitching tape and applied a bandage. Although the injury was not life threatening, the blood loss would surely weaken him. Looking at her watch, she realized they had lost valuable time in reaching Derby. After helping him onto his horse, they continued their journey.

Relieved when they reached Derby before the transport moved, she worked fast to get the equipment off the horses. The animals needed rest and nourishment to regain their strength. While she cared for the horses, Kalani sent a message to Vaughn updating him on the situation. Lightheaded and finding it painful to move, he motioned for her to join him. She sat down next to him in the shade under a tree.

"I've lost a lot of blood, so my riding a horse to one of the other intercept points is too risky. If the intercept point is not Derby, you'll have to go on alone."

"I am not going anywhere alone. We came here together, and we are going home together."

"The success of this operation depends on knowing our limitations. If I try to make the ride, there's a good chance of my passing out on a galloping horse. I barely made it here and we were going slowly."

"We don't have to make that decision yet," replied Wilkins.

"We don't have time. The horses are trained to follow each other, so you should rebalance the weight across the horses to make up for my weight and you'll be able to travel faster."

"What do you mean, we don't have time? We could be here for hours, maybe days, so you could get your strength back."

He showed her the alert indicating the transport was on the move, he said, "We have thirty minutes until the intercept location is determined."

"I am not leaving you here."

"Listen to me. I'm the one getting off easy. Vaughn has a contingency plan to get me to the pickup site. We are going to leave here together with the nuclear waste. I don't want to understate my value to the mission, but you are the essential asset. You're the only one on the team who can ride a horse fast enough to catch the truck when it tries to accelerate to escape the attack. Every one of the other guys could perform my role."

"Do I have a choice?"

"No. It's an order!"

"Okay, but if you're not at the pickup location tonight, we're coming to get you."

"I'll be there. Now, get ready to ride."

With the horses packed and ready to go, Wilkins waited anxiously, praying for the transport to be in route to Derby.

"BELMONT," Kalani yelled.

CHAPTER 41

Vaughn sent an urgent message to the Belmont team, designating the senior man onsite as the team leader. The new team leader welcomed the news of a replacement for Kalani being in route. Now there would be no need to change team assignments with only a few minutes remaining before the transport reached the intercept point.

Craft rode through the rough terrain on motorcycle, equipped with a cover identity, dressed in combat gear, and disguised with a few cosmetic changes. He stopped, quickly concealed the motorcycle in order not to draw unnecessary attention to the operation, and began running the last two miles on foot.

Upon arrival, Craft conferred for a moment with the two onsite team members, and then hustled down the road to take a position where he would have a clear line-of-sight to the back of the transport vehicle as it tried to escape. With the intercept plan committed to memory, he now knew the importance of Wilkins to the operation's success. The window of opportunity to take control of the transport vehicle without inflicting damage was short. The several tons of nuclear waste would delay the vehicle's ability to accelerate to a speed fast enough to outpace a galloping horse. Wilkins' equestrian skills and light weight gave her a speed advantage on a well-conditioned horse. The horse would be able to run side-by-side with the vehicle for a short period of time. The tall stature of the horse would enable the rider to make a quick entrance into the vehicle cab.

While Craft took position at the Belmont site, Wilkins rode swiftly across the rugged terrain. Gasping, snorting, and profusely sweating, the horses were racing to the point of total exhaustion. After nearly falling off the lead horse when it stumbled, she gently pulled back to slow the pace, sensing the stallions were pushing their limits. Trained to go hard and long as the rider demanded, it was her job to balance the risks. Counting down the seconds, she was on pace to arrive at Belmont three minutes before the transport. To ease her mind of the animals' harsh treatment, she promised the horses she would get them to a ranch, where they could run and graze all day long.

Wilkins arrived at Belmont with horses and equipment intact. With only seconds to spare, she mounted a fresh horse, did a weapons check, and took up position. Thankful for the grueling physical and mental training, she took several deep breaths, hoping to calm her nerves and regain her focus for the next phase of the operation. She ticked down the seconds as the smaller lead vehicle passed by—five… four… three… two… one.

The lead vehicle was hit with a perfectly angled missile, exploding with an upward thrust, lifting the vehicle off the road into the air. The vehicle landed in flames several feet from the road. In a coordinated attack, three seconds later a missile hit the trailing vehicle. It burst into flames, blocking the road from behind.

As expected, the transport vehicle ground its gears hard, trying to accelerate. Wilkins rode the horse up the bank and charged down the highway, closing fast on the vehicle as it strained to pick up speed. She leaned forward clinging tight to the horse's neck to reduce the wind drag with a gun in one hand and the other holding onto the horse, she watched for hostiles. Two rifles appeared from the back of the vehicle. Before she could fire her weapon, bullets whizzed by her and the two hostiles fell to the ground.

As Wilkins approached the back of the transport vehicle, the horse strained to keep pace as the vehicle continued to accelerate. Looking at the reflection in the side view mirror, she could see the hostile who had cracked open the door, attempting to be in position to shoot when she pulled out from behind the truck. With the horse running hard, it was time to make a move. She shifted the gun from one hand to the other to get a better angle. As she charged out from behind the vehicle, the hostile opened the door, exposing his body. With an automatic reflex, she fired, but the horse stumbled, sending the shots high. Now vulnerable for a fatal blow, she prepared to dive off the horse. Before the hostile could fire, a bullet whizzed by and the hostile's body exploded, covering rider and horse in blood and human tissue.

The hostile's body fell to the ground, causing the animal to jump, losing valuable time. Wiping the man's blood from her face, Wilkins kicked the horse, demanding all the horse had. She pulled alongside of the vehicle.

With the door wide open, she pointed the gun at the driver's head, and yelled in Farsi, "Stop the vehicle now."

The driver's eyes bulging with fear, as he yelled, "Don't shoot!" in English. She grabbed the door, keeping the gun pointed at him and shifted her feet on to the sideboard of the vehicle cab. With Wilkins now fully supported by the vehicle, the horse slowed down. The driver, a large man with a full beard and a turban, began to slow the vehicle, begging her not to shoot.

As she tried to reassure the man she would not shoot, a bullet crashed through the windshield, leaving a headless body and the vehicle out of control. With broken glass, bodily fluids and human remains filling the vehicle cab, Wilkins fought desperately to reach the steering wheel. When she pulled hard on the steering column to avoid going off the side of the road, the wheels on one side of the vehicle left the road for a moment. Not strong enough to push the driver's headless body out of the way, she slipped in between the dead man and steering wheel. While guiding the truck straight down the road, she brought the truck to a stop.

When Craft reached the transport vehicle, the gore was indescribable, and the trauma to Wilkins severe. She had lost consciousness. He quickly but gently removed her from cab. As he walked away with her in his arms, a soldier pulled the dead man from the vehicle, jumped in the driver's seat, and began driving down the road. Another soldier rode up on a horse and tossed Craft the medical bag.

There was no time for modesty. He removed his shirt and pants, leaving him topless in athletic shorts. He cut off her clothes and worked fast, cleaning the dead man's blood and brains off her body with bandages and disinfectant. As he cared for her, he talked softly, saying things he hoped would inspire her to respond, but the ordeal had been too much. He administered a strong sedative, and then lifted her into the arms of the last soldier, who waited anxiously, knowing more hostiles were soon to follow. With Wilkins securely between his strong arms, the soldier galloped down the road toward the pickup site. The shirtless Craft disappeared into the brush.

When Wilkins arrived at the pickup sight, the medical specialist placed her in the safe location and continued giving her a strong sedative. She had done her job; it was now time for the others to do what they did best, decimate the enemy.

Using tracking devices, the team located equipment dropped during previous night. The pickup location was perfect for the operation. It had rough mountainous terrain behind, high open ground in front, and a small hill to protect the transport vehicle from a direct line of fire. The open high ground provided an accessible landing area for the heavy-lift helicopter when it arrived that evening. The hostiles would have to attack from low-lying positions, and fight uphill to reach the open area. The most important aspect of the location was its inability for the transport to be hit by a conventional line-of-sight missile.

With no air support, the biggest threat the hostiles could bring would be the use of smart weapons, having the ability to redirect the flight of the missile in mid-air. Anticipating the threat, the Special Ops team was ready to test the new smart weapon intercept, the same capability that was being tested during the U.S. Open Championship. The men dug in, expecting a fight to be coming soon.

They observed a small force moving quickly across the terrain, about eight miles out. The Special Ops team waited for the hostiles to move closer and then fired two missiles, taking out two small all-terrain vehicles. The hostiles stopped immediately and took cover.

As expected, the hostiles fired a smart weapon. The intercept capability engaged, keeping the missile on its original course, exploding high on the mountainside. Relieved the intercept worked, the Special Ops leader gave the order to take a defensive posture, and most of all, do not do anything unless necessary, to avoid risking injury.

At this point, the hostiles' only threat was to wait until dark and hope to take down the helicopter when it arrived. As night approached, the team sent flares into the sky and systematically fired to keep the hostiles from attempting to advance. At 9:35PM local time, the team leader gave the signal to pull back, leaving a small time of vulnerability when the hostiles could advance, potentially reaching the higher ground without taking heavy fire.

A soft high-pitched sound filled the air. The team looked at each other, knowing if the hostiles had any sense, they would be in full retreat because their worst nightmare had just arrived. Two massive floodlights lit the ground below, followed by thousands of rounds of gunfire. Within seconds, the hostiles that had not retreated were eliminated. The gunship circled the area one last time and disappeared into the night. The Special Ops team had surgically embedded electronic identification chips so the men flying air cover could identify the good guys. Using high-resolution heat sensors, any human-sized organic object outside the perimeter not wearing a good guy ID was destroyed.

The team moved quickly to gather the equipment and horses. At 9:56PM, the heavy-lift helicopter landed. The transport vehicle drove up the ramp into the aircraft. The team loaded the horses, equipment and then strapped in for takeoff. The crew waited for the team leader to give the signal to lift off. Looking at his watch, he waited.

The flight crew chief said, "Sir, I have orders to lift off in 90 seconds."

Just as the crew manning the door was about to hit the lever to close the door, the team let out a cheer, as the sound of a motorcycle grew louder and louder. The motorcycle, with shirtless Craft driving and Kalani hanging on for dear life, drove up the ramp and came to an abrupt stop. The door closed as the helicopter lifted into the sky.

CHAPTER 42

TOP SECRET BASE, KUWAIT

Craft waited to be debriefed, a standard procedure used by the CIA to get everyone's firsthand account of what went down during an operation. However, after being subjected to hours of physical and mental evaluation, he became impatient and slipped away to find Wilkins. When he was discovered in a restricted area of the medical building, Vaughn ordered him detained by base security.

Craft thought the armed jarhead guarding the door might welcome a physical confrontation just to break up the day's boredom, so he decided to engage him in psychological warfare. He removed the HuAID from his wrist, unfolded it, forming a large touch-sensitive display, and began searching the network for information regarding the upcoming college football season.

To annoy the marine, he pretended to be a sports analyst critiquing each college football team's strengths and weaknesses. To make it appear interactive, Craft would ask the marine his opinion and then mimicked the soldier's answer, trying to strike a nerve. The guard did not take the bait; he stood confidently by the door showing no reaction to the verbal barbs. After talking two hour straight without getting a reaction, Craft applauded the man's self-control and then stood up from behind the desk and started to leave the room. The marine upholstered his M45 pistol and Craft sat back down.

When the door to the office opened, Vaughn walked in. With the pistol in his left hand pointed at Craft, the marine saluted Vaughn. As the marine holstered his gun and prepared to leave the room, he turned his attention back to the prisoner sitting at the commander's desk. With a big ear-to-ear smile and a slow southern draw, the marine said, "Roll Tide."

Craft fell back in the chair with both hands held over his heart and said, "It would have hurt less if you had shot me."

Figuratively speaking, the two words uttered by the marine felt like a dagger thrust into his heart. Five years earlier, the Alabama Crimson Tide football team had beat Clemson by 35 points in a national championship game. To make matters worse, Craft had incurred a separated shoulder early in the 1st quarter from a cheap blindside hit long after throwing a touchdown pass to take a seven point lead. To acknowledge the marine's psychological victory, Craft gave the man a "one-finger" solute.

Watching the macho exchange between the two gladiators, Vaughn said, "It's good to see you're working hard to bond with the troops."

"I should've kicked his ass," Craft grumbled as the marine left the room.

"My money is on the marine," said Vaughn.

Craft started to complain but backed-off when he noticed the blood-shot eyes of a man who had not slept in many hours.

After pouring coffee and handing a cup to the young agent, Vaughn said, "This coffee sucks but it's the best they have at this oasis."

Sipping the drink, Craft responded, "You're right. This stuff is toxic."

"If you're looking for an ass to kick, I'm the one who ordered you be given a full examination."

"Now why would you do that?"

"To keep you busy so you didn't interfere," answered Vaughn.

"I had no intension of interfering."

"Couldn't take the change of another rogue operation."

"So that's why you've had me locked up in this office for hours?"

"You were found in a restricted area."

"So how are they doing?"

"I'm not going to sugarcoat it," answered Vaughn. "Kalani incurred severe blood loss. It was touch and go for a while."

"How's he now?"

"He's on those fast healing drugs you enjoyed so much. Should be back in action in a few days."

"That's great news. When can I see him?"

"We'll stop by before heading back to the states."

After hearing the good news, Craft asked to go to the restroom. Vaughn told him if he didn't return within five minutes, he would send the marine to find him.

When Craft returned, he asked, "How is she?"

With a big sigh, Vaughn answered, "Physically Jennifer is fine but mentally fragile. It's not just the trauma of the operation, she's has other stuff that has to be dealt with."

He knew exactly what Vaughn was implying. The tragic death of her father and having to live under different identities most of her life would take its toll on anyone's mental state. With the horrific images of Wilkins in the transport vehicle covered in blood and guts still fresh in his mind, Craft asked, "Can I see her?"

"I am afraid not," responded Vaughn.

"I won't interfere, just want to help."

"She's already on her way to Virginia."

"Why Virginia?"

"So Page can attend to her treatment."

Visibly shaken by the news, Craft confided, "If you could have seen the emptiness in her eyes. It was frightening. She didn't recognize me. She just stared. I need to see life back in her eyes or that look will haunt me forever."

"I know you're taking this hard… We all are. We had a heart-to-heart talk before the Afghanistan operation. I hope this does not come as a surprise but she has feelings for you."

"This mission has us both on an emotional rollercoaster," Craft confessed.

"As a man who wants the best for both of you," Vaughn said, "I recommend you take time to sort out your feelings and then be straight with her. She deserves it."

"I understand sir," he replied, finding Vaughn's candor uncomfortable but at the same time genuine.

In a consoling tone, Vaughn said, "We have to keep perspective. The team recovered the nuclear waste with no fatalities. Quite frankly, I consider it to be a damn near miracle!"

Glad to move on to another topic, Craft nodded his head in agreement.

Vaughn looked at the young man with as much intensity as his tired eyes could muster. "I say this in all honesty: Jennifer Wilkins is alive because you had the balls to do the right thing in a bad situation."

Then with a raised voice, Vaughn demanded, *"Now you have to let others do their jobs!"*

"I don't want to interfere, just be kept informed. Is that too much to ask?"

"In this case it is," Vaughn insisted. "Emily Page is a remarkable psychologist. She needs space to do her job. Right now, she thinks it's best for her to control communications with Wilkins. I trust her judgment. Do you?"

Reluctantly, Craft answered, "Yes."

"I have a novel idea," said Vaughn. "While Page does her job we do ours."

"What's our job?"

"To execute the mission," Vaughn declared.

"Okay," Craft repeated, "But what's the mission now the nuclear waste is recovered?"

"No change. Our mission is to ensure the safety of Americans attending the Asian Open."

"I mean operationally, what's next?"

"First, let's talk about you," Vaughn responded. "You had a rough few weeks. How are you handling things?"

Craft wanted to scream, *My world is coming apart and you want to know how I am doing? Wilkins doesn't recognize me; my mother is living a secret life; I am deceiving the world at a game I love...*

"Obviously some things are bothering you. So let's talk," Vaughn said.

"Did you know my mother works for the Agency?"

"Technically she doesn't."

"I don't understand," Craft commented, letting his frustration show.

"Unlike you, your mother was never an employee of the Agency. She worked as a self-employed contractor under non-official cover. For years, Director Walker acted as her handler. Years ago, I learned of the operative, code named, SPARROW, but never met her. I had no idea the operative was your mother until recently."

"I can't picture my mother as an agent," Craft confided.

"For what it's worth, she's a damn good one. She was a major player in locating Bin Laden in Pakistan. As a foreign reporter, she built an elaborate network of intelligence sources throughout the Middle East. I suspect she had some help from your grandfather. His work in Middle East Naval Intelligence is legendary. Looking back, it's not much of a stretch to think that you both joined the Agency's fight to end terrorism. Philosophically speaking, your actions are your father's legacy. As tragic as your father's death was, you and your mother have made it count for something."

Thinking about Vaughn's insightful words, he decided the dreaded conversation with his mother would have to take place soon.

"I know you want to get the debrief over with but what else is on your mind?" Vaughn asked.

Craft was ready to change topic again. "Why are we going forward with the cyber golf challenge?"

"Don't you want to kick the cheating bastard's ass?" Vaughn asked, referring to Cyber Golf Champion, Kai Peng.

"Kai is not a bad guy. And calling someone a cheating bastard seems a bit two-faced given what we've been doing," Craft responded.

"Good point. I'll rephrase the question. Don't you want to win millions of dollars for the First Light program while at the same time finding out what the Chinese are up to?"

"What do the Chinese have to do with ensuring the safety of Americans attending the Asian Open?" Craft asked.

"Nothing at all," Vaughn replied. "But sometimes opportunity knocks."

"So, what about Iran?"

Vaughn pulled out a flask filled with whiskey, took a drink, and handed it to Craft, saying, "I am sick of coffee. How about something a bit stronger?"

Craft took a swig and handed it back.

"Once you get some rest back home, you'll be spending plenty of time in Iran," Vaughn continued, "Dignitaries across the Middle East are making generous offers to the First Light program contingent on having a face-to-face meeting with the Grand Slam contender."

"I am looking forward to a few days back home," Craft commented.

"Rodger that. I've rented a lake house in Western Maryland for a family vacation," Vaughn responded.

Since Vaughn had brought up the subject of family, Craft seized the opportunity to discover more of his personal life. With some coaxing, Vaughn flipped through pictures and played short videos of his family. Craft concluded his team leader was living proof an agent could also have a good family life.

Vaughn began the debrief by telling him he had a good idea of what occurred during the operation and wanted to start at the point when the team engaged the hostiles transporting the nuclear waste.

"What do you want to know?" asked Craft.

"When Wilkins chased after the transport vehicle, you shot two hostiles in the back of the vehicle who were preparing to fire their weapons."

"That's correct."

"Do you still consider those shots to have been necessary?"

"Yes sir."

"Why?"

"If I didn't take out the hostiles, then at minimum, it would have been a diversion potentially slowing Wilkins from reaching the transport."

"Did your shots put Wilkins in danger."

"No."

"Why not?"

"I had clean shots at the hostiles. She was never in danger."

"Remember, this is non-attribution, we're simply trying to get your version of the facts for the record and capture lessons learned. Let's turn the clock forward. When Wilkins pulled alongside of the vehicle, what did you see and do?"

"I could see the hostile on the passenger side of the vehicle crack the door open, waiting for Wilkins to make her move. I didn't shoot initially because she was in the best position to engage the hostile, but the horse stumbled and she misfired. Then I shot."

Vaughn projected a simulated picture of the scene showing the positions of the vehicle, the hostile, Wilkins and Craft.

"Does this picture look about right?"

"Yes sir."

"It appears you had to make a near perfect shot to hit the hostile and not Wilkins."

"I didn't really think about it."

"You must have considered the possibility of delivering a lethal injury to your partner," Vaughn insisted.

"Taking the shot was the only option," Craft replied.

"Trust me. I am not questioning your judgment. At the risk of repeating myself, she is alive because you had the balls to do the right thing in a difficult situation. What intrigues me is your having the psychological strength to execute a perfect shot with everything on the line. The fear of failure would have prevented most from pulling the trigger."

"Could be genetic," Craft responded. "After all, my father did race into burning buildings to save lives. Maybe you should send me for more testing."

"Get packed. We'll visit Kalani and then catch the next flight to the states."

Director Walker offered her colleague and friend a cold drink. After commiserating about the punishing summer heat, the conversation took a serious tone. The Director wanted Dr. Page's professional opinion regarding Ms. Beach's (aka Jennifer Wilkins) psychological condition. They discussed the horrific experience haunting the young agent. Neither of them thought they would have had the emotional strength to survive the ordeal without mental scaring.

Dr. Page said, "We have to keep in mind, the operation was a remarkable success."

"Yes, but at what cost?" Walker responded.

Dr. Page countered, "Catherine, I am confused. Have we reversed roles? I believe it's your job to advocate for the mission and mine for the person."

"Emily, we've been friends for a long time. Right now my conscience is on shaky ground. I promised James Crawford to look after his granddaughter. I've let the pressures of the job cloud my judgment, and now his granddaughter has paid the price."

"I'm not going to sugarcoat it because you're feeling guilty. She's suffered severe emotional trauma, but with appropriate treatment, she could recover."

"What do you really think is causing the memory loss?" asked the Director.

"I suspect it's the toxic combination of guilt, mortality, helplessness, and failure. The guilt from having to kill two hostiles and then leave an injured team member to fend for himself started the decline. When the horse stumbled, leaving her vulnerable to attack, the reality of death flashed in her mind. The real culprit was the final scene with the vehicle driver. I am guessing the driver pleaded for his life. She believed the situation was under control, and then felt helpless when the driver was shot and the vehicle strayed out of control. Although the operation was a resounding success, she failed to honor her agreement to spare the driver's life."

"Let me know if there is anything at all you might need to treat Ms. Beach. I mean anything," the Director insisted.

Annoyed at having to undergo a psychological evaluation and being isolated from outside communications, Wilkins passed the time reading the current issue of *Persian Woman* featuring the golf superstar, Peter Craft. The crack of nearby thunder drew her attention away for the magazine. She looked out the window to see the approaching dark clouds. A severe afternoon storm rolled across the Potomac River. A spider crawling on the windowsill caught her attention. With the mindset that the only good bug was a dead bug, she rolled up the magazine and lashed at the insect, scoring a direct hit.

In preparation for Dr. Page's psychoanalysis, she looked at the picture of Craft on the cover of the magazine, holding up the Claret Jug with the bug remains splattered across his face. She jokingly reflected on how the disfigured picture made her feel. Then she rolled the magazine up again and hit the spider on the windowsill over and over just to make sure it would never bother anyone else again. They were supposed to be there for each other. *Didn't he know how much she needed him?*

In the course of hours, her role had transitioned from being center stage in a critical international mission to that of a back office lab experiment. *So what if I can't remember,* she thought, *I am not the first agent to freak out during an operation and probably won't be the last.* Extremely fatigued from sleepless nights, she fumbled through her handbag, trying to find the bottle with the amphetamines that helped her keep functioning during the day.

"Sorry to keep you waiting. The traffic getting here from Langley was horrible," said Dr. Page, while she folded up the small red umbrella.

"No problem. I don't have much to do these days."

"I know the team has come to know you as Jennifer Wilkins, but would you mind if I call you by your given name, Victoria?"

"Victoria is fine."

"You may be feeling a bit disconnected from the world these days. Well, you can blame that on me. In just a few hours, my office has been inundated with inquires regarding your status, and when they will be able to talk with you. In fact, the Director herself wanted to talk before I met with you today."

"What's on the Director's mind?" Wilkins asked.

"She regrets involving you in the operation. I am talking out of school here. But we just had the strangest conversation where we reversed roles. I was trying to ease her mind by reminding her the operation was successful, and she was reminding me of the human cost."

"What human cost? No one died."

"You're correct, but let's not understate the trauma you have experienced. When a situation escalates to the level where the mind shuts down, 'We *have a problem, Houston*', if you know what I mean."

"Isn't it better to not remember?"

"I think you know the answer, but let's talk about it anyway. How have you been sleeping?" the doctor asked.

"Okay, I suppose."

"Victoria, I am a medical doctor. I can tell when someone is taking bennies to stay alert. Not a good long term solution."

"I think the nightmares will go away over time."

"Over time if not treated, the results of severe trauma could be debilitating. I am going to be as direct with you as I possibly can. I have reviewed two decades of cases of good agents having experienced severe trauma. The ones who reached out early and dealt with the situation did much better than those who went on with life and tried to tough it out."

"Do I have a choice here?"

"Victoria, this is America; you have a choice, and the people who care about you, and the list is long, pray you make the right choice. I am here to share with you a situation that occurred eight years ago, where I believe the wrong decision was made and the nation and a young girl paid the price. Anticipating that you might want to go back to work and try to tough this out on your own, I received special approval from the Director to share this file with you. Before we start, I want to give you a chance to object. I plan to talk with you about your grandfather and the great trauma resulting from your father's death. If you think this is too much or would rather not know, I will understand. You take some time to decide what you want to do and I will find us cold drinks."

Returning with two bottles of water, Dr. Page said, "If we go down this path, it's going to be interactive, because it's crucial for you to validate my observations. Are you willing to do this?"

"Yes."

Dr. Page gave the young lady a chance to describe her grandfather, growing up in Nebraska prior to her father's death. After listening to Victoria's lengthy and accurate description of her grandfather, Dr. Page provided the Agency's assessment. They both agreed James Crawford was extremely intelligent, committed to the national defense, and passionate about defending the nation against terrorism throughout the world. He lived a balanced life, finding time for family, friends, and civic causes.

Dr. Page said, "You already know this; your grandfather took your father's death very personally. As stated in the file, I met with him to offer treatment, but he thought psychological therapy was for weak people. The data shows nothing could be farther from the truth. The therapy I am offering is a hard road but the alternative can be much harder."

"Tell me what changes you observed in your grandfather after your father's death, and we'll compare notes," said Dr. Page.

"I was at boarding schools most the time, but granddad was going full out all the time. He never stopped to smell the roses. Before my father's death, we spent days together riding horses, fishing, and just enjoying each other." She began to sob.

"Sorry for putting you through this, but I have to make my point," declared the doctor. "Read the file; your grandfather was consumed by guilt for putting you and your father in danger. Then, guilt led to revenge. Then, revenge turned into a life of living on the edge. Of course, we are shaped by the events in our lives, good and bad, but untreated severe trauma can drive our existence. Your grandfather died in a reckless boating accident, traveling much too fast."

"You made your point. What do we have to do?" Wilkins asked.

"It's straight forward and at the same time, it's going to be extremely difficult. The memory of what happened during the operation is repressed, but not lost. We have to bring it out of your subconscious into your conscious, and then we have to get a balanced perspective, examining the good and bad."

"Other than recovering the stolen nuclear waste, what possibly could be good?"

"You're alive," Dr. Page answered.

CHAPTER 43

CIA HEADQUARTERS
MCLEAN, VA

The Director of Clandestine Service expressed his delight that young agent, Wilkins, would be rejoining the Red Crescent team. In a sympathetic tone, he admired the professional manner in which she had executed her unique role in the Afghanistan operation and regretted the trauma she had experienced. Surprised by the DCS's display of compassion, Vaughn wondered if the Frenchman was voicing genuine concern or executing a page out of the CIA leadership guide. He didn't know the man very well but empathy for others didn't fit his bulldog reputation. Still, his words seemed sincere.

With the executive team assembled, Beaumont began the meeting by insisting the team remain vigilant with the Asian Open only weeks away. After covering a few administrative topics—retirements, budget cuts, and organizational changes—he asked Vaughn to stand up. From his wine cellar, stocked with the best French wine, he held up two bottles of Champagne, Louis Roederer 2005, and said, "When our citizens return safely from the Asian Open please share this champagne with your team. In just a few weeks, your team has eliminated a major terrorist threat and installed Intel collection devices throughout the Middle East."

The DCS joked that the National Security Agency had asked for additional budget to keep up with the growth in new sources of intelligence. Craft had traveled to fourteen high priority locations installing Wilson's power outlets at all of them. With some prodding, the Middle East Chief offered a half-hearted compliment, admitting the intelligence collection in his area had improved. Vaughn graciously accepted the champagne for the team.

Beaumont mentioned the White House was pissed that despite improved Iranian intelligence, Director Walker continued to tell Congress that *significant uncertainty* remained regarding Iran's security posture. At the same time, the President was giving campaign speeches encouraging westerners to attend the Asian Open in Tehran. He laughed as he read out loud the recommendation from the White House staff to use the words *"some uncertainty"* instead of *"significant uncertainty"* in the assessment summary.

"What in the hell does *'some uncertainty'* mean?" he bellowed, "We don't live in a perfect world. There's always some uncertainty. Those idiots want to dismantle an assessment structure that's taken years to build because they don't like reality. Well, you can take this to the bank. As long as the whereabouts of some Al Qaeda leaders are unknown, we have *significant uncertainty* regarding the security of Americans in Iran."

After taking a drink from the large water bottle he brought to the meeting, the DCS asked, "So, what's up with the Chinese? Why would they bankroll a golf tournament for thirty million?"

Vaughn responded, "The Chinese government is a big investor in the cyber golf market. They want to gain credibility by taking on the man who has won three Majors."

The DCS held up the *Washington Post* sports page and pointed to an article showing Craft being a fifty-to-one favorite to beat the Chinese contender, Kai Peng. "If the odds makers are right, then their guy is going to get crushed. We all know the Chinese government doesn't like to lose, so what's going on?"

"We know they helped Peng win the Cyber Golf Championship. Why not give him an edge in this tournament also?" said Vaughn.

"How?" Beaumont asked. "Computer magic isn't going to work."

"We have satellite video of Peng. He scored in the low 60's his last five rounds playing on a traditional golf course. He's an excellent athlete and appears to have some assistance," replied Vaughn.

Surprised by his answer, the DCS asked, "What kind of assistance? Do they have Smartball? Has the Red Crescent program been compromised?"

"Wilson is dissecting one of Peng's golf balls right now. If they have a Smartball capability, I suspect they discovered it on their own," answered Vaughn.

"So let's assume they have something similar to Smartball. How should we handle the situation?" asked Beaumont.

The executive team discussed options then agreed the best course of action would be to neutralize the capability and let the match continue on a level playing field.

General Shirazi returned to his morning routine of having breakfast at his favorite teahouse in Tehran, feeling the situation was back under control with the assassin Reza dead, Gilani locked up, and the stolen nuclear waste in a safe place. His new head of security, Javid, guarded the teahouse entrance ensuring only expected visitors were allowed inside.

With the Grand Slam of Golf title on the line, projections for attendance at the Asian Open in Tehran had tripled. While local business owners welcome the additional commerce, many residence were concerned about the influx of foreigners and the associated dangers. The Supreme Leader made a public statement that it was the duty of all citizens to welcome foreigners as invited guests. He encouraged the nation to take the opportunity to show the world Iran's beauty and uniqueness. In private, the nation's spiritual leader made it clear to his inner circle that it was General Shirazi's job to build public confidence by ensuring the local community that law and order would prevail throughout the streets of Tehran.

Today, the General's calendar was filled with meetings, mostly government and civilian executives wanting his assurance that appropriate security was in place to handle the influx of people coming to the tournament. There was no shortage of ridiculous recommendations being offered. The previous day a shop owner recommended making foreigners wear armbands so they could be easily identified. He tried to listen politely while bringing each meeting to a quick end.

The General was both thankful and alarmed that in the dead of night the U.S. had dropped off the transport vehicle filled with stolen nuclear waste at his estate undetected by his security force. If the U.S. could do that, he wondered, what other covert capabilities might they have? *How did they know where Gilani hid the stolen material? Was the Asian Open a diversion to get U.S. agents into Iran? Was it really U.S., and not German Intelligence, that had discovered Reza's assassination plot?*

After considering some of the possibilities, he asked himself...*was his family's friendship with the American golfer contrived? If yes, why?*

After reviewing his schedule, he thought it unusual the CEO of a chemical company in Hamedan would want to meet. Other than a few tourists, Hamedan should be unaffected by Iran hosting a golf tournament. His staff accepted the meeting as a goodwill gesture to the city's mayor, a close friend of his brother-in-law Amir Turani.

When the CEO arrived at the teahouse, Javid searched the man for hidden weapons before introducing him to the General. About the same age, the two men sat in silence for a moment, sizing each other up. The General immediately inquired to why the man wanted to meet.

After politely thanking the General for accepting his meeting request, the CEO began praising the magnificent landscape of Shirazi's desert estate in Qom. Seeing the puzzled look on the General's face, the CEO made a quick pitch that his company could save him money by providing high quality fertilizer and pesticide chemicals at low prices.

Suspicious that the man might have a hidden agenda, the General began asking pointed questions about him and his company. When the CEO mentioned his British education, the General started talking in English.

"Did you really come here to sell me chemicals?"

"Sir, I would like your endorsement to sell my products to the Iranian government," the CEO said.

"The government has a competitive process for acquiring products... use it."

"I understand," the CEO responded, placing a small gift bag on the table.

Glancing inside the bag to see the box of Excluivos Cuban cigars, the General smiled to show his approval of the gift and then said, *"Masha Allah."*

"Salaam," Asadi responded before leaving the teahouse.

Having done his research, Asadi knew the General cherished fine Cuban cigars and would have one in his mouth by evening.

CHAPTER 44

CIA HEADQUARTERS
MCLEAN, VA

With the Grand Slam title at stake, media coverage of the superstar golfer from Charleston hit peak levels. Now entering a critical period when Americans would soon be on-site in Iran, the CIA's Intel analysts vigorously monitored Middle East activities, looking for anything out of the ordinary. The Middle East listening devices installed by Craft were delivering valuable intelligence but none directed at the Asian Open.

The President received a boost in the polls by touting "American exceptionalism" and using Craft's winning Major Tour events to make his point. He encouraged U.S. citizens to show up in force to experience the most extraordinary golf tournament in decades. It wasn't his promotion of the Asian Open that Director Walker objected to; in fact, she agreed with it. What Walker took issue with was the President characterizing the security risk to Americans as minimal. With the election a few weeks away, she believed the White House was maneuvering to setup the Agency to take the blame if something went wrong in Tehran. With a locked Top Secret briefcase handcuffed to her arm, she raced out of the room, headed for another 1600 Pennsylvania Avenue meeting.

As usual, the President stressed the importance of having a complete and accurate Iranian intelligence assessment. Ordinarily, she wouldn't have hesitated to speak her mind, but now was not the time. His reelection campaign had turned ugly, and his opponent was hammering his pro big business foreign policy. As the President continued to talk, Walker recalled the day she promised to always give him a truthful assessment of the intelligence situation, both good and bad.

After completing an Iran intelligence update, Director Walker once again concluded the briefing by saying, "Although no actionable threat is known at this time, *significant uncertainty remains.*"

When she arrived back at Langley headquarters, an "Eyes Only" folder rested on her desk. A statistically significant number of intercepts, having searched and correlated massive amounts of voice and data communications across the Middle East, detected the phrase, *"Soon all will know Allah's power to enact vengeance upon the earth."*

"Catherine, you have to see this right now," The DCS shouted from his office.

Catherine Walker watched the video of a man—masked by a turban and scarf so only his eyes were visible—rant Islamic scripture, calling for jihad and threatening, *"Soon all will know Allah's power to enact vengeance upon the earth."*

Having heard it many times as a young intelligence analyst, the voice was familiar, but she wanted the DCS to confirm her suspicions.

"Who's the speaker?" Walker asked.

"The voice scan, adjusted for age, matches the al-Qaeda leader, Malek Asadi," the DCS answered.

"I recognize the voice... It's Asadi," the Director agreed. "Where do you think he's hiding?"

"The video is clean, but odds are he's somewhere in Iran," the DCS answered.

"Asadi was born in Tehran. I tracked him after 9/11. I always suspected he escaped death in Iraq by hiding in Iran, but we had no proof," said Walker.

"Do you think he's a real threat?" asked the DCS.

"He's an absolute monster and well educated. A product of Britain education, he tested an explosive device by blowing up his home with his parents in it," the CIA Director replied.

A motorcade, transporting Director Walker, raced through the streets of D.C to Andrews Air Force base, where the President waited on Air Force One, ready to depart for a four state campaign swing. After listening to the Director's concern and scanning the updated intelligence assessment, the President initiated an urgent virtual meeting with Rahimi, the President of the Republic of Iran.

Aware of the Asadi video, President Rahimi insisted Iranian Intelligence was aggressively investigating the matter. Rahimi portrayed the video as an empty threat, vehemently denied his nation having given safe harbor to al-Qaeda terrorists, and agreed to continue sharing intelligence. To make his point that appropriate security was in place, the Iranian President declared his intent to attend the Asian Open and invited the U.S. President to be his guest.

The President graciously declined the invitation, and ended the conversation. Following a heated discussion regarding the potential implications of the threat on national security, the President and Walker agreed to move forward to aggressively mitigate the threat by conducting an operation inside Iran.

By the time the Director returned from the White House, the DCS was waiting to give an update.

"I think we found the needle in the haystack," Beaumont said. "With over eighty percent certainty, the city of Hamedan is the origin of the Asadi phrase flooding the net."

KAULA LUMPUR, MALAYSIA

With the Asian Open on the horizon and the Grand Slam of Golf on the line, Craft's iconic fame made him easily recognizable around the world. To get him into Kuala Lumpur undetected, the team arranged a series of alleged sightings, misdirecting public attention away from his actual location. Once in the city, he spent the early morning at a private residence a few miles from the golf course where his match against the Cyber Golf Champion, Kai Peng, would begin at 10AM. Deep in thought, Craft sat on the terrace sipping orange juice. With the fingers on his left hand, he rolled the miniature pencil, used to record golf scores, back and forth on the tabletop to the rhythm of the Chinese piano composition, *Eastern Winds*.

Still troubled by the memory of her despondent stare and deflated spirit, a full night of sleep was a rarity, even after exhausting workouts and endless travel through the Middle East. Resenting Dr. Page's decision to have Wilkins go through treatment without him, he once again found himself trapped in circular thoughts. *Why shutdown communications? Why let her go through treatment alone? Why didn't he insist on seeing her? Why, why, why...*

With a quick flick of his fingers the pencil launched across the terrace hitting the wall and tumbled to the floor. He stood abruptly and left the patio area determined that, with or without Page's okay, he would see her soon. Then a disturbing thought crossed his mind. *What if to get well she had to put the past behind, including him?*

As the car transporting him moved slowly through heavy traffic to the golf course, he struggled mentally to turn his attention to the mission. Initially he thought his match against Peng was an unnecessary distraction.

Now it served the purpose of drawing media attention away from the growing calls for jihad by Islamic clerics. What Craft found ironic was replacing one movement by extremists with another. To many, golf was similar to a religious experience, capturing a person's mind, body, and soul. A place where real miracles occurred like the most improbable "double eagle"—a score of three under par on a single hole—that only a few people had ever experienced in a century of golf. Today's match was symbolic of a holy crusade in which the true believers of traditional golf would rise up to fight the cyber infidels, those incredulous people intent on destroying centuries of great golf tradition.

Born in Hong Kong, Peng was the product of an intense Chinese-British education and physical training program. An exceptional athlete, Peng gave up an opportunity to play professional basketball so he could join his father in building the cyber golf market. To obtain the needed power and financial resources, they partnered with officials in the Chinese government. Peng adopted a raw, edgy style, that would appeal to the "gamer" community.

Even though Peng had a reasonable chance of winning the match on his own, the Chinese operatives wanted to leave nothing to chance. A covert organization within the Chinese Military—the same organization that penetrated the cyber golf network to help Peng win the Cyber Golf Championship—invented a Smartball capability. What they didn't know was they were not the first to invent it.

Craft received a high priority message while in route to the golf course. Vaughn, along with other team members, were ordered to report immediately to the Top Secret Base in Kuwait. Craft's assignment was to improvise as necessary to end the match without damaging his public image and then board a private aircraft in two hours to join the other team members. He had to assume that Peng's Smartball capability was still operational, given he had not received a confirmation from Vaughn that it had been disabled. Craft quickly worked the timeline. To make the flight in two hours he would have to bring the match to conclusion within the first few holes. His mind raced through options trying to come up with a plan where the media would not trashing him for walking off the golf course before the match was finished.

As they approached the golf course, Craft asked the driver to stay with the vehicle and be ready to leave at anytime during the match. As the car passed through the front gate and proceeded up the road to the clubhouse, Craft observed that fan loyalties were obvious by the way people dressed. The fans supporting traditional golf dressed in typical golf attire—collared shirts, neatly pressed paints or shorts, and classic golf hats. The cyber golf fans dressed as if they were going to a heavy metal rock concert— tattoos, body piercings, and t-shirts with bold statements splashed across the front and back.

Craft was ready to improvise. Before getting out of the car, he accessed a video clip of Peng being interviewed following the Cyber Golf Championship. Then he stepped out of the car, retrieved his golf clubs, and with the golf bag strapped across his back walked though the clubhouse.

When he entered the media area, a reporter shouted, "Where's Jefferson?"

"Why would I have a caddy?" Craft responded while activating the Peng video clip on the large display in the media area. The video showed Peng responding to the question, "Should cyber golfers be allowed to use a caddy to obtain advice?"

With his edgy style, Kai Peng responded, "Caddies are for wimps."

As Craft started to walk out of the media area a reporter yelled, "Peng is on the range right now with his caddy."

Craft stopped to sign autographs, expecting the news of his not using a caddy to reach Peng before his arrival at the practice range. As Craft walked into the practice area, the traditional golf fans began cheering loudly and then started a soft chant, "Caddies are for wimps, caddies are for wimps..." that grew louder and louder.

In retaliation, the cyber golf fans went on a counter offensive, yelling as loud as they could, "Kai Peng, Kai Peng ..."

Visibly annoyed by the unexpected confrontation, the Chinese team huddled together with Peng to discuss options. If Peng used a caddy, the media would be relentless at attacking his tough guy image. Alternatively, if he chose to play without a caddy then his technical advantage would be gone because the equipment to manipulate ball flight was hidden in the bottom of the golf bag. To make things worse, Peng would have to carry a golf bag twenty-five pounds heavier than a typical golf bag because of the extra equipment. The team was forced to choose, protect Peng's macho image or have the technology advantage.

Craft stood on the 1st tee watching the Chinese team conduct what appeared to be a board meeting giving each member a chance to voice an opinion.

With only two minutes remaining before the match was scheduled to begin, the match official asked, "Is there anything you would like me to tell Mr. Peng?"

"You can tell him to... *shut up, step up, and tee up*," responded Craft.

After a short conversation with the official, Peng picked up his golf bag and started walking toward the 1st tee. Other than different ethnicities, the two players appeared nearly identical, standing six-foot, six-inches tall and weighing 220 pounds. With Craft's dark hair and Peng's bleached blond hair, there would be no mistaking the two players on the course. As expected, by the time Peng reached the tee he had mentally accepted the challenge of having to play Craft straight up. What he didn't know was his technology advantage was now a liability that Craft intended to exploit.

In setting up the match, Peng explicitly requested the rules be amended to preclude "give me" putts. In match play, one player may choose to give the other play a putt rather than slow the pace of play by waiting for the player to execute a short putt that he is certain to make. Consistent with Peng's tough guy image, he wanted all putts to be made or the hole forfeited.

Both players hit solid drives and conservative approach shots to the 1st green leaving long birdie putts. With an aggressive stroke, Peng's putt hit the edge of the hole causing a lip out, leaving a four-foot par putt. Craft lagged his putt, going past the hole a few inches. Instead of tapping the short putt in for par, Craft retrieved a ball marker from his pocket and placed it on the ground behind where his ball had come to rest. Peng gave his opponent the putt but the official reminded him that "give me" putts were prohibited.

Visible annoyed, Peng rolled his eyes, as Craft placed his ball-marker six inches from the hole and picked up his ball. He could have asked Craft to move the marker but he didn't want to give the arrogant American that satisfaction. Under normal circumstances, Peng's chance of making the routine putt was nearly certain but today he was playing with a golf ball made with a ferrite plasma core.

Unbeknown to Peng, the ball-marker placed near the line of his putt had a strong magnetic field. Wilson had given Craft a magnetic ball-marker so he would be able to tell which balls in his bag had ferrite plasma cores because their metallic properties would be attracted to magnetic field. As Peng's short putt passed by the ball-marker, the magnetic field pulled the golf ball off line missing the hole. Some traditional golf fans erupted with cheers, while Peng stared at the line wondering what just happened?

Craft tapped his short putt in the hole to go 1-up in the match. He then bent over and used his repair tool to fix an imaginary bump in the green where Peng's ball had veered off line. Walking off the 1st green, Craft said just loud enough for his opponent to hear, "I guess you don't need to worry about repairing ball marks in the cyber world."

Before hitting his tee shot, Craft called over to the match official and expressed his concern that tournament security was insufficient to maintain crowd control giving the back and forth taunting between spectator groups.

Overhearing the conversation, Peng said loud enough for spectators to hear, "You would think a major champion could handle a little crowd noise."

The par-three 2nd hole required a 204-yard carry over water to reach the green. Craft hit his tee shot short, leaving an uphill eleven-foot putt. Peng's hit his tee shot hole high, leaving a slippery five-footer from above the hole.

Being the furthest from the hole, Craft would putt first. While Craft squatted to look at the line of his putt, Peng stood directly in Craft's line-of-sight, practicing his putting stroke. A flagrant violation of golf etiquette, Peng's behavior infuriated traditional golf fans. On the Tour, golf etiquette was a true measure of one's character. In fact, golf etiquette was so important, it was the first section in the *Rules of Golf.*

As Craft began to take his stance to putt, someone yelled, "Get out of his line you uncouth son of a bitch."

Ignoring the outburst, Peng continued to practice his putting stroke. With a smooth stroke, Craft rolled the ball on line into the hole for a birdie.

Just as Peng was about to strike his downhill five-footer, someone yelled, "Golf etiquette is not optional." The putt hit the edge of the cup with too much speed, rolling several feet past the hole. With time running out, Craft walked over and picked up his opponent's golf ball and handed back to him. Attached to the side of the golf ball was his magnetic ball-marker.

"Kai, could we talk in private?" Craft asked.

Realizing Craft had discovered his ball's magnet properties, he thought it would be unwise to refuse. They walked to an area away from spectators.

"I am ending the match right now before people get hurt. We can go our separate ways and let the media spin machines have a field day or we can be united and take the competition to another level."

"What are you proposing?" Peng humbly asked.

"Together, we promote a world golf championship requiring the players to compete in both golf environments."

"I like your imagination," Peng replied.

The men shook hands and then announced their intent to end the match to the event organizers. Together, they approached the spectators to explain their safety concerns and the agreement for them to compete in both traditional and cyber matches in the future. Although spectators were disappointed, the image of two golf icons standing together communicated the expectation of something new in the world of golf.

TOP SECRET BASE, KUWAIT

Craft reclined in the plush leather seat, as the Citation VII jet moved through the sky at near supersonic speed. Other than the message telling him to report to the Top Secret Base in Kuwait, he was unaware of the developing situation because the program's OPSEC manager had shutdown mission-related communications during the flight. He closed his eyes hoping to catch a few minutes of sleep before reconnecting with the team.

Half asleep, he reminisced about the first time he met Wilkins at Jacksons Tavern in Charleston and then his mood turned melancholy. The memory of pulling her out of the truck in Afghanistan entered his mind again. He attempted to rationalize that, like many other patriots, she was a causality of a successful operation. Unsatisfied with his computer-like thought process, he began questioning if the personal price of fighting terrorists was too high. To remain sharp, his mental-focus had to stay in the present but thoughts of the past now consumed him.

Once on the ground, the jet taxied into a large maintenance hangar where he could exit the aircraft undetected from "eyes in the sky" cameras. When Craft appeared at the door, she anxiously waited at the bottom of the staircase to see his reaction. Overcome by seeing the vibrant color in her face and passion in her eyes, he tried to speak but the words wouldn't come out.

"You look as if you have seen a ghost," Wilkins said, reaching out to hold his hands.

With teary eyes, he said, "I thought..." unable to finish the sentence.

"You can say it," she confided. "I was really messed up."

"Are you okay? I mean really okay?" he asked with urgency.

"I am much better but I still have a lot of baggage to deal with... It's going to take time," she answered.

"I wanted to be there to help," he said, whipping tears from his eyes.

"You mean saving my life wasn't enough to feed your big ego," she said, while tenderly squeezing his hands.

"That's not what I meant."

"Look, I needed help but not the kind you could've given me."

"I could've handle your being angry," Craft insisted. "What I couldn't deal with was your broken spirit."

While his caring words were sincere, she couldn't help think his feelings for the Iranian girl might be just as strong. With a serious terrorist threat on the horizon, now was not the time to test the strength of his affections. In fact, she was not really sure about her own feelings.

"It's time we get down to business," she said.

"So, what's going on?"

"The sleeper terrorist, Asadi, is active after twenty-five years of hiding in Iran. This guy is bad news. Educated in Britain, Asadi justified killing his own parents because they succumbed to the temptations of Western life."

"Sounds like a calculating psychopath."

"He is and we have to take him out fast, before the President shut things down."

Just then a soldier drove up in a hydrogen-fueled vehicle resembling a modified golf cart with dark windows. The soldier motioned for them to get in and proceeded to drive them to the main base complex to join the other team members.

When they walked into the SCIF, the team was assembled at the conference table with Vaughn at the head. After each team member read and signed the new Operational Order, Vaughn began. "This is the first-ever Priority One operation. The threat is real and immediate. American lives are in grave danger. As indicated in the Ops Order, we have the go ahead to eliminate the threat imposed by Malek Asadi *by any means necessary!*"

The team knew exactly what Vaughn meant. For years, the agency had been forced to fight terrorists using a complex set of rules *when the terrorists had no rules.* Repeatedly, Director Walker went to Capitol Hill, to plead for special authorization to engage terrorists. In exchange for quietly accepting budget cuts, Congress recently enacted the Top Secret "Priority One" provision. This legislation gave the CIA special authority when American civilians were in immediate danger. Given Americans were already in route to Iran to attend the Asian Open, the Director had enacted the special provision.

CHAPTER 45

TOP SECRET BASE, KUWAIT

Gul began the Ops briefing, with a series of pictures, video clips, and documents profiling the stealth terrorist, Malek Asadi. He presented a time sequence starting with Asadi in the mid 1990s as a university student in Britain studying Biochemical Engineering. Then the clock turned forward a decade to show Asadi as an al-Qaeda leader. The last segment of the briefing showed computer-generated images of Asadi in his 50's, projecting the effects of aging.

To communicate the serious threat imposed by the stealth terrorist, Gul said, "Asadi has managed to hide in the shadows for twenty-five years, waiting for the right opportunity to strike. At five-foot, nine-inches tall with a projected weight of 150 pounds, Asadi fits the physical profile of most Iranian men, so picking him out in a crowd will not be easy. What makes him extremely dangerous is his rare mental composition—high intellect, extreme patience, bioengineering education, strategic thinker, ruthless behavior, totally committed to jihad…"

At the conclusion of the briefing, the team acknowledged it would take an extraordinary effort to take out Asadi on Iranian soil. To ease rising tensions in the room, Vaughn joked, "No need to worry because if this operation goes south, we have a teammate who can arrange for us to spend the rest of our days grazing in the pastures of Montana."

"No problem. I can make it happen if you don't mind sleeping in a barn and eating oats," Wilkins replied.

The team knew the boss was needling Wilkins about the horses from the Afghanistan operation relocated to a ranch in Montana.

Ready to move forward, Vaughn said, "We have no time to be running down rat holes. We need a good plan, fast. Let's take some time to think through this together."

Craft spoke up, "Someone had to have helped Asadi obtain a new identity."

"So, you think the Iranian leadership was involved?" asked Vaughn.

"Maybe not top leadership… more likely an unsanctioned activity sympathetic to al-Qaeda," answered Craft.

"Khamenei would never have risked a war with the United States, after seeing how fast the U.S. took down Saddam Hussein," Wilkins commented, referring to Khamenei, the Supreme Leader of Iran during the time when Asadi went into hiding.

"She's right," Kalani commented. "I saw the transcript of President Bush telling Khamenei if Iran was found harboring al-Qaeda, he would order a 20-ton 'bunker buster' on the Supreme Leader's precious mountain estate with him in it."

"If Craft is right," Vaughn asked, "then how could we narrow the field of possibilities?"

"General Shirazi's rise to power was attributed to his success at purging extremists from government positions," Craft responded, "Let's run a search to identify Iranian government personnel, both military and intelligence, having transitioned to inactive status since the new leadership took office. Then filter out those attributed to normal reasons, such as retirement, medical, and natural deaths."

While back at Langley analysts searched for operatives linked to Asadi, Wilkins informed the team that with the Asian Open only a week away, media coverage would soon turn negative if Craft remained out of the public eye. She planned to make media coverage an operational advantage. Since the Asadi threat originated in the city of Hamedan, Wilkins had arranged for a publicity meeting with Hamedan's mayor on Sunday morning to discuss the city's participation in the First Light program. Soon, a press release of the meeting would be issued. She expected the meeting would draw the attention of American golf fans in Iran. With hordes of Americans roving the city of Hamedan, she believed the team's undercover activities would go unnoticed.

"We have three days to complete the operation," Vaughn bellowed, scanning the Director's message, "or the President will authorize a State Department travel directive requiring all Americans to leave Iran immediately."

Wilkins tried to keep the focus on operational success. "The meeting with the mayor of Hamedan makes a good transitioning point," she said, "By then, we should know what Asadi is up to and we'll still have twenty-four hours to finish the job; just in time for Craft to attend the dedication ceremony for the south Tehran Public Golf Course."

"After checking my schedule, I am available to takedown Asadi after lunch on Sunday," Craft joked, "provided the mayor doesn't demand golf lessons in the afternoon."

"No worries. The mayor has no interest in golf. He's hosting Sunday's meeting as a good will gesture to Amir Turani in hopes of attracting investment funds for the city," Wilkins replied.

The eternal optimist, Kalani, said, "We have a whole seventy-two hours! Hell, I've got time for a power nap."

"Enough sarcasm," Vaughn declared. "Now let's get back to work."

Analysts at Agency headquarters generated a list of five operatives that previously worked for internal affairs within the Iranian Intelligence. Three of the five men had died recently from respiratory failure.

After scanning the data, Kalani spoke up, "I believe Asadi is severing ties with those who can connect him with his al-Qaeda past. We better move fast before all the operatives are dead."

"I am sure it's not a coincidence they died of respiratory failure. He must be using a biochemical agent to kill them," Vaughn surmised.

"You're not going to believe this," Wilkins declared. "One of the operatives had a second career working for British Intelligence. He died in a London hotel room five weeks ago."

One of the few people at the CIA with the Director's home phone number, Vaughn used a secure line to call Walker at home in Reston, Virginia. After briefing her on the situation, she immediately called the Head of British Intelligence to request a postmortem analysis of the dead operative, looking for traces of known biochemical agents.

After searching the database used to track foreign agents, Wilkins said, "The whereabouts of the two living operatives are unknown. We should assume they know the others are dead, and are either working with Asadi or in hiding trying to stay alive."

Vaughn acknowledged the plan going forward made sense, thanked everyone for contributing, and encouraged the team to get a couple hours of rest, because the pace of the next three days would be grueling.

They fought to steady their balance, after a rough flight from Kuwait to the small fishing boat waiting in the rough seas. The rocking motion and dead fish smell had the team leader wishing the queasy feeling in his gut would soon pass. With morning's first light on the horizon, the vessel motored through the fog along the coastline.

Craft was an experienced sailor, having grown up in the Carolina coastal areas. His equilibrium was unaffected by the turbulent sea conditions. Fixated on the phrase *"by any means necessary"* in the Operational Order, his mind began to confront its true meaning. Of course there were limits to what they would do, especially if it involved harm to innocent people. *Otherwise, what separated them from the terrorists they fought?*

Now consumed by a growing swell of concern, he considered approaching the topic, hoping for reassurance. With Vaughn clinging to the side of the boat, ready to throw up at any moment, Craft decided to trust his moral compasses would stop him from going too far.

As the boat turned toward shore, Craft put his head back, closed his eyes, and felt the refreshing sea breeze hit against his face. The fishing boat slowed as it pulled up to a private dock on the southern coast of the Caspian Sea, a few miles from the city of Babol.

Vaughn, an effective interrogator, was notorious for extracting essential information from unwilling participants. Although fluent in Farsi, Vaughn found the mystique of having an intermediary performing the role of an interpreter—a variation of the good cop/bad-cop interrogation technique—an effective method to get information from a related party that was not actually the person of interest. As an intermediary, the interpreter could soften or harden responses to questions depending on how the interrogation proceeded. Vaughn's burly physical appearance was enough to intimidate most.

Moein, one of the two living operatives linked to Asadi, had family living in the city. In the dark of night, they made their way to a nearby garage where an old faded blue Ford Edge waited, a car selected to easily blend in with local traffic. Craft maneuvered through the back streets, parking near where Moein's youngest brother lived. The brother was a devout Muslim who regularly attended morning prayers at the neighbor mosque. With a picture of the man displayed on his HuAID, Vaughn waited in the car, with a small handgun in one hand and a miniature hypodermic needle in the other. Looking through binoculars, Vaughn watched the front door of the house, hoping today was not the day that Moein's brother decided to sleep in.

Still faced with an unsettled stomach, Vaughn tried to keep it together when the house door opened. Moein's youngest brother walked down the street alone toward the mosque. Craft pulled the car to the side of the road a few feet in front of the target. Within seconds, Vaughn had the man in the car, sleeping like a baby from the drug he had administered. With the unconscious man in the back seat, Craft drove to the home of the older brother, who lived alone, worked nights, and was known to sleep late in the morning.

Before going into the house, Vaughn gave the unconscious man a shot in the arm that would revive him in seven minutes. Checking his watch, Vaughn entered the house. Just as the younger brother began to wake, Vaughn gave the signal. Craft assisted the man, who was now conscious but still woozy from the drugs, out of the car. Unable to resist Craft's over-powering strength, the man accompanied him into the house. The older brother sat, with his arms and legs strapped to a wooden kitchen chair.

Bending down to look at the restrained man in the face, speaking in Farsi, Craft asked, "Where is your brother Moein?"

Spitting at Craft, the man replied, "You're a disgusting pig."

Vaughn held a gun against the younger brother's head, and told Craft to ask him again. Craft repeated the question. The man in chair turned his head away. Vaughn fired the gun and the younger brother fell to the ground, with blood pouring on the floor. Then he put the gun to the older brother's head and told Craft to ask him again. Craft repeated the question. In a state of panic, the man screamed the address of the rented apartment in Tehran where his brother Moein stayed.

After taking pictures of the two brothers, Vaughn lifted the younger brother off the floor and wiped the fake blood off his head. When fired at close range, the soft weapon designed by Jack Wilson would knock a person unconscious while exploding a fake blood packet. At the proper angle, the shot to the head looked very real. Vaughn injected a drug into the brothers that would keep them unconscious for twelve hours leaving them a window of time to detain Moein.

After being airlifted to Turkmenistan on the border of Iran, Kalani made his way to Mashad, traveling by motorcycle to track down the other living operative. Kalani had minimal information regarding the operative's whereabouts so he mingled with men at the local mosque after morning prayers. Familiar with the local customs and fluent in Farsi, Kalani engaged in the normal conversation that followed prayers.

The local people, living in a remote city far from Tehran, were not onboard with Iran's new direction. When Allah's time for reckoning came, the people of Mashad wanted to make sure they were seen as the true followers of his word, as decreed by the holy prophet Mohammad. Kalani engaged in dialogue with a few of the local men sympathetic to the calls for jihad. He used the Asadi video as a conversation piece.

By mid morning, Kalani had gathered information to know the operative was staying at a house in a remote area outside of town. The men at the mosque suspected that the operative was travelling, because he had not attended prayers for several days.

As Kalani approached the operative's country home quietly, on foot, the dogs barked viciously, having gone without food for days. He removed slices of beef jerky from his backpack and tossed it to the dogs to distract them. He pushed open the only door to the house and the smell of death filled the air. Slowly working his way to the back bedroom, he found a decomposed body lying on the bed. He put his backpack on the floor, removed tools and materials, and went to work. As if a skilled surgeon, he removed tissue samples of key body parts, carefully packaging them in small airtight bags.

TOP SECRET BASE, KUWAIT

At Vaughn's direction, the CIA station chief in Tehran had assets watching a small one-room home in north Tehran. Public records indicated the place was rented to Vahid Salehi, an employee at the Sabz Pardes Country Club. The surveillance team captured video of a man entering the home and sent it for processing. Soon, they received confirmation the man inside was operative Moein.

Mortified by the incompetence of British Intelligence, Wilkins couldn't believe the body of the dead operative in Britain had been cremated without an autopsy. Thinking that the only chance of discovering the kind of biochemical agent Asadi possessed had literally, gone up in smoke, she resorted to eating a day-old pastry left in the pantry area of the SCIF. "Thank you Kalani," she yelled to the empty room when she learned he had specimens from the dead operative in Mashad. Within the hour, a medical examiner working for the Agency stationed in Rome was in route to Kuwait. By late afternoon, the core team had returned.

Vaughn thought it was time to get the Iranians involved. He did not want to antagonize General Shirazi by conducting a covert CIA operation under his nose. He planned to have Erwin Klein, the invented German intelligence officer played by Peter Craft in disguise, pay the General another visit. Again Klein would deliver Shirazi valuable intelligence of great interest to his security operation. As Vaughn was about to coordinate his plan with DCS, he received an urgent update from the Chief of Middle East Operations. General Shirazi had taken ill with respiratory issues. As a result, the General's security organization was in turmoil. With Reza gone and young Javid not ready to assume command, an internal power struggle had ensued. With Iranian security in chaos, he expected the President would throw the 'red flag' stopping the Asian Open. *At this point it really didn't matter. As long as the bioweapon was destroyed and Asadi stopped, preferably by putting a stake through the evil bastard's heart, then the President could do whatever,* Vaughn thought.

Instead of notifying Iranian authorities, Vaughn authorized CIA field agents to apprehend Moein, and take him to a covert facility in Tehran. With time running out, Vaughn and Kalani boarded a covert flight to Tehran while the others stayed behind to piece together Asadi's evil plot.

Craft rested on a cot in the briefing room waiting for the medical examiner's report. Having dozed off, he woke to Wilkins' shout, "Oh my God. Asadi has *BlueBlood*!"

Trying to focus his waking eyes, Craft asked, "How bad is it?"

"Real bad," she answered. "BlueBlood is a synthetic virus manufactured in the 1990s by a microbiologist dubbed Dr. Germ, who worked for Saddam Hussein. We thought Hussein had stockpiled biochemical weapons, but we never found them."

"The name BlueBlood must mean something."

"Correct. When exposed to the virus, a person's body turns blue from the lack of oxygen in the blood when the lungs collapse. BlueBlood is extremely hard to detect. Two days after being infected, you develop flu-like symptoms. Then the flu progresses into pneumonia. Five days after being infected, the lungs collapse. Although not contagious, anyone who comes in contact with the virus will perish. Transmission is by touch or ingestion," she explained.

"Do you think Asadi can produce it?" Craft asked.

"Not likely. It's too complex to manufacture, but with the right equipment, he could keep it active," Wilkins answered.

Drawing a timeline on an electronic whiteboard, starting in 1990 and ending in 2028, Craft said, "Let's map it out."

Attaching electronic note cards along the timeline, the team began connecting related events, or as some might say, "connecting the dots."

After putting all the information on the wall, they could see Asadi's evil plot begin to reveal itself.

"Let's work the Asadi thread," Craft suggested. "He goes into hiding in 2003, and shows up in Iran in 2028. Let's assume the operatives from Iranian Intelligence gave Asadi a new identity in 2003."

"What would be the motive?" she asked.

"He had an Iranian heritage, they share a common cause, and Asadi had valuable biochemical skills," Craft responded.

"Let's work the BlueBlood thread," suggested Wilkins. "The virus was created in Iraq in the 1990s. Over the last few weeks, the virus was used to kill four operatives, with the last one having been killed a few days ago. He also probably used it to infect Shirazi."

Scanning his HuAID, Craft said, "The General is dead. I just received a message from Daria that her uncle unexpectedly passed away. She thinks it's from his new found love for smoking cigars."

"Maybe a BlueBlood cigar?" Wilkins responded, taken back by the naivety of the Iranian girl's thinking.

"Let's continue with the BlueBlood thread," Craft said, wanting to get the conversation off Daria and back on track.

"Okay, during the fall of Saddam Hussein in Iraq in early 2000s, let's assume Syria stashed Saddam's biochemical weapons. So what?" she asked.

"Ten years later, Syria was engulfed in a long civil war. Assad might have cut a deal with the Iranian operatives to hide the biochemical weapons in

Iran. Given the centuries of conflict between Sunnis and Shias, it's probably a stretch," he said.

"Not necessarily," Wilkins replied. "Although much of Syria is Sunni, Bashar al-Assad was Alawite, a prominent minority religious group who describe themselves as a sect of Shi'a Islam. Anyway, he probably didn't have many options, so maybe he cut a deal with the Iranian operatives... you know... the lesser of the evils. On the other hand, why not just cut the deal with the Supreme Leader, Khamenei?"

"In 2012, Iran's leadership was committed to a nuclear program, resulting in severe trade sanctions imposed by Western nations. Probably wasn't a priority," he responded. "It's reasonable to assume if Asadi was in Iran beginning in 2003, and the operatives were looking in 2012 to hide the BlueBlood virus, they would turn to Asadi, but only if he could keep it active."

"Given that Asadi recently used the virus to kill people, he must be in a position where he could have kept it active," she declared.

"If Asadi's secret life is in the Hamedan area, then what kind of business do you think could sustain the virus?"

"That's a good question for the analysts to research."

"If Asadi has had the virus for more than a decade, then why hadn't he used it before?" Craft asked.

"Let's assume that for many years the operatives kept Asadi on a short leash, but that all changed with the power shifted in 2021, when General Shirazi purged the operatives from the government. Also, covertly transporting biochemicals to foreign lands would require extensive logistics. In a sense, Western infidels coming to Iran, by the thousands, is the equivalent of *the mountain coming to Mohammad*," Wilkins inferred.

Agreeing the theory was plausible they asked the team to continue the analysis and begin searching for companies that met the profile.

CHAPTER 46

Sitting with arms and feet strapped to the chair, the operative struggled to free himself as he regained consciousness.

Speaking Farsi in a calm tone, Kalani asked, "What's your name?"

"Vahid Salehi," the man replied.

Showing the man a picture of Moein's younger brother, on the floor in a pool of blood, Kalani said, "We're serious men."

Trying not to show his emotions, the man looked away.

Showing the man a picture of his older brother strapped into a chair, Kalani said, "This man is a wise man. He's alive because he knew where to find you."

"These men are strangers," the man replied.

Shaking his head, Kalani said, "Denying your own family is despicable. But then, that's what you have been trained to do."

"I am Vahid Salehi," insisted the man.

"We know you are involved in a plot to kill the people attending the Asian Open," Kalani responded.

Seeing the operative looking at the clock on the wall, Kalani said, "No need to worry about the time. This will be over quickly. Trust me, we are going to find out what you know in the next few minutes."

Kalani could see in the man's steely look that he was prepared for the traditional rough treatment that might follow. He thought to himself that the operative had probably read U.S interrogation guidelines, and knew exactly what the limits were. Prior to the recent Priority One legislation, the operative would have been correct.

"I am going to tell you what we know about your relationship with Asadi," Kalani continued, "Then you're going to tell us what you know. Don't worry; we're not going to kill you. That would make you a martyr, but you'll probably wish we had."

Kalani could see his eyes begin to show anxiety, fearing the unknown. This introduction period was an important part of the process. They needed his mind in hyper-drive, trying to imagine the possibilities of what the next steps might be.

"You are Moein Tehrani, operating under the cover identity of Vahid Salehi. You worked for a small cell within Iranian Intelligence that hid the al-Qaeda leader, Malek Asadi. The other men you worked with are now dead, at the hands of Asadi. You are involved in a plot to bring harm to those attending the Asian Open at the golf course where you work."

"I am Vahid Salehi, a maintenance worker for the Sabz Pardes Country Club."

"Being experienced yourself in conducting interrogations, you probably think we are going to do something barbaric, such as water-boarding because cutting off body parts like the Iranian Intelligence is known to do, is forbidden by our laws. With Asadi on the loose, we do not have time for a lengthy interrogation or a test of wills."

With Kalani holding the man's head so he had to look, Vaughn placed a clear glass canister on a small table in front of the operative. Vaughn slowly emptied the contents of the canister onto the table. The bug-like devices lined up in a row, resembling a legion of ants.

"These bug-looking things are synthetic devices made of nanotechnology," Kalani said.

Seeing both curiosity and fear in the operative's eyes, Kalani continued, "To be honest, I don't know much about this nanotechnology stuff, but this man is an expert," pointing to Vaughn, who was dressed like a computer geek wearing big rim glasses and a wrinkled button down shirt.

"My associate invented this new technology and really wants to test its full capabilities," said Kalani.

Vaughn tapped his HuAID and the nano-bugs began moving in unison, like a marching band of ants. He tapped the HuAID again and the nano-bugs began boring holes in the table.

"Being a bit old fashioned, I would rather you tell us what you know, and we could save the experiment for another day. On the other hand, he loves this technology stuff and hopes you choose to say nothing. He wants to demonstrate the nano-bugs can take control of your body. Then we can control your mind forever, but if you ask me it all looks painful."

Regaining confidence, the operative proudly said, "Allah will have his revenge."

With a quick motion, Kalani pulled out a knife and cut the operative's shirt off. He turned to Vaughn and said, in Farsi so the operative could understand, "He's not going to talk, so let the bugs get the information."

Vaughn started hitting the HuAID touch display. The bugs began to crawl off the table and slowly up the operative's arms, and then began to spread out across his chest.

The operative frantically fidgeted, as the bugs spread across his upper body. Then, all the nano-bugs stopped.

"You can tell us what you know, or we'll let the bugs go into your brain and get the information. What is your name?" Kalani asked again.

"Vahid Salehi," the operative answered.

As he walked toward the door, Kalani said, "We are wasting time; let the bugs loose."

Smiling like a mad scientist, Vaughn hit buttons on HuAID display, and the bugs began racing around his body.

Just as the bugs were about to go into his ears and nose, the operative screamed, "Stop, stop, stop... I tell you..."

Vaughn stopped the bugs.

Kalani came back into the room, and looked into the eyes of the operative. The fear of the nano-bugs entering his body had nearly sent him into shock.

"What is your name?" Kalani asked.

"Moein," the operative responded.

"What is your whole name?"

"Moein Tehrani," the operative answered.

The nano-bugs moved off the operative's body, and back onto the table. Large beads of sweat fell off the operative body, forming a puddle on the floor. Kalani freed one of the operative's hands, and gave him a bottle of water.

Consumed by the fear of the nano-bugs taking control of his body, Moein decided to confess. He was not a friend of Asadi. He cooperated, because Asadi threatened to kill his family with the virus. Moein told them what he knew. Vaughn sent a message to the team; his story checked out.

After they had all the information he was able to give, Kalani told him his brothers were both banged up, but otherwise unharmed. Kalani placed a call to Moein's younger brother, and let them talk for a while.

After the short conversation with his brother, Moein said, "Thank you for sparing my family."

Looking eye-to-eye with the operative, Kalani responded, "We are serious people, but we do not kill innocent people to achieve our goals. *That's what makes us different.*"

CIA HEADQUARTERS
MCLEAN, VA

Director Walker requested a meeting with the President, National Security Advisor, and the Director of National Intelligence, to discuss the developing Iranian situation. To kick-off the meeting, she said, "We have an important decision to make. I thought it better to discuss it face-to-face. We have uncovered the details regarding the Asadi threat. For maximum effect, the evil bastard intends to infect Asian Open attendees with the deadly BlueBlood virus."

"Does he have the means to pull it off?" the President asked.

"Up to a few hours ago, the answer would have been yes. We believe that Asadi has enough BlueBlood to kill thousands of people. When infected, a person develops flu-like symptoms leading to respiratory failure in five days. We know the virus is active, because he used it to terminate other operatives who could connect him to his al-Qaeda past. Also, we believe he used the virus to kill General Shirazi sending Iran's security operations into chaos. Until a few hours ago, Asadi had an inside man working on the maintenance crew at the golf course, hosting the Asian Open."

"Wouldn't a person have to come into direct contact with the virus to be infected?" asked the Director of National Intelligence.

"Yes. But Asadi is educated in biochemical engineering. He knows the virus and its limitations. We believe he has kept the virus active for several years. Knowing the virus would stay active in water for several hours, he intended to put it into the golf course's irrigation system. When the pumps turned on during the early morning hours to irrigate the golf course, the virus would be disbursed to all the green areas in a matter of minutes. The probability of tournament attendees being infected was over 99 percent."

"What's the risk now?" asked the President.

"Given that we now know what we are looking for, the risk is low. But

Asadi could make a run for it with the virus and leave us searching for another twenty-five years."

Pausing to let the executives ponder the gravity of the situation, Director Walker continued, "I don't need to tell you, but I am going to anyway. This is the first time a terrorist organization has acquired a weapon of mass destruction, along with the capability to use it. You might say that *today begins a new era of terrorism in the world.*"

Shaking his head in disgust, the National Security Advisor commented, "We all knew this time would come. How it's handled is going to be a benchmark for those who wish to follow in Asadi's footsteps."

Clenching his fist, the President said, "I will tell you how we are going to handle it. We are going to cut the head off the viper and show it to the world."

"Mr. President, the window of opportunity for taking down Asadi is closing fast. Current intelligence has indicated Asadi is the CEO of Hamedan Chemie and has been keeping the BlueBlood virus at the company site for years."

"Do we physically know where Asadi is right now?" asked the President.

"No. He's been using the ruse of corporate travel and an advance communications scheme to hide his actual location," Walker answered.

"What options do we have?" asked the President.

"Killing Asadi will not go unnoticed. One option is to get the Iranian government involved. The other is to go it alone," Walker answered.

The President replied, "You said, Shirazi is dead and Iranian security is dysfunctional. So, getting the Iranian government involved seems risky. Especially, since Asadi has operated under their nose for a quarter of a century."

"Sir, I have to be honest. Going it alone has a higher probability of success, but the consequences could be severe. Executing a major operation in Iran could get complicated, not to mention setting our relationship with the country back years."

Rhetorically speaking, the President asked, "How many years would our relationship with Iran be setback, if Asadi succeeded in killing thousands of Westerners, including the best Tour players in the world?"

After discussing the advantages and disadvantages of taking out Asadi, the Director felt obligated to remind everyone that retreat was still an option.

Walker said, "We have sufficient evidence to justify the State Department issuing a directive, requiring all Americans to leave Iran immediately."

Ignoring the Director's comment, the President said, "If we took control of the building, how would we handle the biochemical material?"

"We'd have to destroy it. The seals on the containers must be broken immediately, followed by high intensity incineration."

"How do we know he doesn't have the material stored in other places?" the Director of National Intelligence asked.

"We don't. But Hamedan Chemie is a small company with only one building. We think the odds are good the material resides there," Walker answered.

"I want Asadi terminated and his bioweapon neutralized," demanded the President.

"If this operation is discovered, and it most likely will be, irreparable damage to your reelection could result," commented the National Security Advisor.

"I was elected to do a job. Ridding the world of this monster is right now my number one priority," declared the President.

The President sent a secure message to Director Walker, with instructions on how to reach him directly. After disconnecting from the meeting, she took a moment to reflect on the situation. A few days earlier, the burdens of the campaign seem to have consumed the President, but now he was willing to roll the dice politically to rid the world of a dangerous man. Knowing history was filled with leaders who bent to political pressures, she thought it was a true privilege to work for a person who placed *the good of the nation first*.

CHAPTER 47

Craft and Wilkins arrived in Tehran on a private aircraft at 1am local time. The on duty immigration officer, an Agency asset, allowed them to pass through the immigration checkpoint with minimum inspection. They drove to Hamedan, reaching the Parisian Hotel just before sunrise. The agents, already having the entry code, slipped unnoticed into a room on the top-floor of the hotel. Peering through binoculars at Hamedan Chemie, Craft analyzed drawings and pictures of the building looking for weak points that could be exploited.

Wilkins tapped into the company's payroll system to obtain workforce data. The company had four hundred active employees, most working during daylight hours. Based on job titles, she assumed only members of the security worked during the evening hours. She estimated a small force of ten, or less, would be onsite once the day shift ended.

The large one-level concrete building, surrounded by an electrified fence, sat on high ground. To enter the building, employees walked up an access road from the parking area below and passed through an entrance next to the front gate. The front gate opened and closed electronically to let authorized vehicles pass through. Satellite pictures showed a loading dock on the left side of the building. While discussing options, they agreed that minimizing damage to the facility, if possible, was the right thing to do. Destroying a company that employed people from the local community would only make enemies, and after all, they were certain that most of the employees were unaware of Asadi's illegal activities.

After completing the initial surveillance work, Wilkins moved to another room several floors below. At 9AM, the agents met with Hamedan's mayor and his assistant in the hotel's dining room for breakfast. When the exhausted agents walked into the dining room, people applauded. The room was filled with reporters and tourists who had travelled to the city to see the famous American golfer who, with a win at the Asian Open would become the only person, other than Bobby Jones in 1930, to achieve the Grand Slam of Golf by winning all four Major Championships in a single year.

During breakfast, the mayor admitted he knew nothing about the game of golf. Two weeks earlier, Amir Turani personally visited Hamedan to educate him regarding the First Light program and its potential contribution to the economic development of the city. Having been elected on a platform of economic development, the mayor was not about to let the opportunity to have a First Light program pass by without trying to make it work.

They talked about Hamedan's rich traditions and the needs of the city's youth. After breakfast, they travelled to the mayor's office to meet with his staff, and other city officials. They talked about funding, potential sites, timing, and other considerations, and then agreed in principle to go forward with the initiative, based on the development of a detailed plan.

Craft stood with the mayor, in front of the office building where they had just met, to answer questions regarding the city's First Light initiative. To put reporters who wanted to talk golf at ease, Wilkins let them know that the Grand Slam contender would be available back at the hotel to answer questions regarding the upcoming tournament.

Once back at the Parisian Hotel, the agents acted casually, like time was not an issue. Craft sat in the hotel garden, drinking lemonade so no one would suspect anything out of the ordinary. He talked with reporters and tourists for nearly two hours, until some started excusing themselves to leave. While both agents' outside appearances fit the roles of golf superstar and Business Manager, inside both agents were restless, knowing soon the mission would come to an end.

Questions about security and his being shot at during the Open in Scotland still continued. Craft responded in a sincere manner, acknowledging there were always going to be risks when you were in the public eye. He turned the questions around, indicating he did not really know what was going on in the heads of the people asking questions.

When asked why he wasn't in Tehran practicing to win the Asian Open, Craft answered, "For me, balance is what life is about. Many of you have travelled long distances to come here to enjoy this wonderful city and have a chance to talk with me. That means a lot. There will be plenty of time for practice. Today is about spending time with you."

Wilkins marveled at how mentally compartmentalized Craft could be. That evening, he would be performing a dangerous intelligence operation, but he was still able to give reporters his undivided attention. In reality, she knew he had to be fully aware of the time but it didn't show. At one point, she used her HuAID to access Craft's biometrics. Amazingly, his heart rate ran comfortably low, hardly fatigued from the stress.

After two hours of answering questions and with only a few reporters remaining, Craft invited everyone to join him in the hotel for lunch, at his expense. Following lunch, he announced it was time for him to return to Tehran. The agents went to the local airport, to board a private aircraft to Tehran.

When the aircraft departed, the agents, in disguise, drove away in a van left by a local agent working for the Iran station chief. The exact plan for neutralizing the biochemical material was still developing. Instantaneously, Craft shifted from superstar golfer to CIA agent. He reviewed the checklist of things that needed to be done to prepare for the operation. With the van covertly hidden near the Hamedan Chemie site, Craft assembled a miniature-stealth unmanned air vehicle, MS-UAV, and loaded packets of biosensors into the vehicle's small cargo area. The biosensors were the same technology used in Riyadh, to track people in Baahir's compound. Using a HuAID application to control its flight, Craft directed the MS-UAV to make a quick pass over the building, dropping biosensors near the air intake for the ventilation system. Designed to penetrate through the air filter, soon the biosensors would distribute themselves throughout the building. Once the daytime employees left, the biosensors would provide critical tactical information, showing the positions of the remaining people in the building.

When the MS-UAV returned, Craft loaded the V-Bee into the cargo area of the vehicle. Also, made of nano-bio technology, the V-Bee mimicked a large flying insect. Designed for both autonomous and remote control, the device resembled an insect. The V-Bee could maneuver through the building, providing live video and audio.

Controlling the flight of the vehicle, the MS-UAV dropped the V-Bee near the loading dock at the back of the building. The V-Bee waited for the door to open, and then flew into the building and hid quietly in a dark area. The V-Bee was designed to go into inactive mode, to conserve power until activated.

As long as the other agents were in Tehran tracking down Asadi, the specific details of the operation would remain fluid. Knowing that to neutralize the biochemical materials required breaking the seals on the canisters, followed by high intensity incineration, the two agents went into the city in search of critical equipment.

TEHRAN, IRAN

Unable to locate Asadi's physical location, the CIA agents would use the operative to draw the al-Qaeda leader out of hiding. Moein returned to work at the golf course as normal, hoping the few hours he was captive would go unnoticed. While out on the golf course cutting the grass, the anonymous courier placed instructions for contacting Asadi in his locker. Following the instructions, Moein accessed the virtual server, and then entered the security code. At 2PM local time, he sent a message to Asadi, expressing concern that suspicious activity at the golf course placed them in jeopardy and requested a face-to-face to discuss the situation further. Moein received a short response, indicating a car would pick him up at 6PM at a location near his north Tehran residence.

Given the complexity of the method that Asadi implemented to keep his physical location hidden, Vaughn assumed that the vehicle sent to pick up Moein would have the ability to detect and neutralize typical tracking methods. After discussing tracking options with Wilson back at CIA Headquarters, they decided to use a modified version of the florescent lotion used during the VIPER I operation. The lotion would remain inactive, until exposed to a laser light at a specific frequency. This feature was necessary to avoid multiple trails being created by other vehicles, driving through the lotion prior to the target vehicle's arrival. Vaughn would discretely apply an invisible lotion on the roadside, where the target vehicle would have to stop to pickup Moein. When the target vehicle pulled away, the tires would roll through the lotion, leaving a glowing florescent trail that could be tracked by special sensing equipment, and displayed on Vaughn's HuAID. He made arrangement to get the needed materials from the local CIA station.

At 5:55PM, Moein waited at the designated place to be picked up. Vaughn sat at a nearby outdoor café, in view of the pickup location. At 6PM, a Ford pickup truck with a Hamedan Chemie logo on the driver-side door stopped at the designated location. The driver motioned for Moein to get in. The operative looked at the man driving through the window and then gave a signal, making the palm of his left hand visible to Vaughn, while stepping into the vehicle that Asadi was the driver.

Vaughn flashed the laser light, activating the florescent lotion while Kalani took pictures of the person driving. Leaving money on the café table, the two agents casually walked around the corner and stepped into the waiting Toyota sedan. After delaying a few minutes to give the pickup vehicle some distance, they began to follow the florescent trail. Watching the display on his HuAID, Vaughn gave directions as Kalani maneuvered through the streets of Tehran. The florescent trail led to a highway connecting Tehran with Hamedan.

Vaughn said, "We may be in luck. I think he is headed to the Hamedan Chemie site."

"We could use some pomaika'i," responded Kalani, meaning good luck in Hawaiian.

Vaughn gave an update to the team in Hamedan.

Making conversation, Kalani asked, "Tonight we are going to engage Asadi on his home field, being outnumbered, outgunned, and probably without the element of surprise. Why do you think this is going to work?"

"Because he doesn't know our plan," Vaughn responded.

"How do you know he doesn't know our plan?" Kalani replied.

"Because we are improvising and don't have a plan," Vaughn answered. "Let's hope the young guns have something figured out by the time we get there."

"Man, I am getting too old for this stuff," Kalani said. "I am ready to find a golf course back in the Aloha State and spend my time teaching the grandchildren how to break par."

"I've been having similar thoughts," said Vaughn.

As Vaughn dozed off, Kalani continued driving. Now in a remote area between Tehran and Hamedan, the florescent trail showed the truck had pulled off to the side of the road. He stopped the car.

Wading into the brush near the area where Asadi had stopped the truck, Vaughn declared, "We have trouble."

Lying in tall grass, a few feet from the road, was a body. With his eyes wide open, Moein laid in the grass, dead with a bullet wound to the head and another to his heart.

"Well, he knows we're coming, and he is going there to move the BlueBlood canisters," Vaughn pronounced.

"This guy is serious. Do you think we are ready or should we stand down?" asked Kalani.

"No standing down! We have this viper in our crosshairs and he is going down tonight."

HAMDAM, IRAN

Expecting Asadi to arrive at the Hamedan Chemie site soon, Craft activated the V-Bee to begin the live audio-video feed from inside the building. With the agents watching, the pickup truck with Asadi driving came around the corner, with tires squealing, and raced up the access road. Before the electronic gate had time to fully open, the truck smashed through, and came to an abrupt stop alongside the loading dock.

Asadi sprinted into the building, as the Toyota sedan, with Kalani driving, reached the coordination point. The agents watched audio-video feed from inside the building. The high ceilings enabled the V-Bee to move freely, keeping a safe distance and avoiding detection. The team watched and listened intensely to Asadi's movements and orders.

Barking orders in Farsi to three men, Asadi demanded, "Get the canisters into the truck."

When one of men mentioned putting hazardous protective clothing on, Asadi pulled out a gun and shouted, "We don't have time. Get the canisters into the truck now."

Knowing that Asadi was going to try to escape with the BlueBlood virus, Vaughn turned to the young agents and asked, "So, what's the plan?"

Craft spoke up. "If you provide cover, we'll take care of this."

Shaking his head, Vaughn looked at Kalani and said, "They're worried we'll get in their way. Maybe we should go have coffee or something."

Entering a code into the cypher-lock and putting his hand on the bio-sensor, Asadi pulled the handle and the door opened. In the middle of the room were four large 90-pound canisters. Each of the men picked up a canister and carried it out of the room.

Anticipating Asadi would be departing soon, Wilkins sent a message to the Red Crescent team. Soon, sirens began to sound throughout the city. The Hamedan police and fire departments were flooded with false alarms that would delay them from responding to activities at the Hamedan

Chemie site. While Vaughn and Kalani prepared their weapons to give cover, the other agents raced to get into position.

Asadi and one of the men stepped into the pickup truck, with the four canisters in the back. The other two men boarded a nearby SUV that led the way down the access road with the pickup truck following closely behind.

Just as the SUV passed a side road, Wilkins drove the Toyota sedan out from behind a small building and slammed into the SUV, sending it into a spin. To avoid crashing, Asadi pulled hard on the steering wheel, turning left onto the side road. The men tried to escape but were quickly terminated.

Before Asadi could react, bright headlights blinded him. The pickup truck crashed into the large, long steel bars of a garbage truck that were lowered as if to pick up a heavy trash container. The steel bars ripped through the front of the pickup truck, with such force the airbags did not have time to inflate, killing both men.

Craft pulled on the lever and the steel bars lifted the pickup truck. The canisters containing the BlueBlood virus fell out of the back of the truck into the big compartment, through a door on top of the garbage truck. Then he lowered the pickup truck to a 45-degree angle and began recording video through the windshield of the bloody Asadi looking at him in horror, with the steel bar sticking through his body. He then climbed onto of the top of the garbage truck, captured video of the four canisters, and then activated the powerful cylinders used to compress garbage. He yelled, "Start count down." And then began sprinting away from the truck. Using voice recognition, the HuAID began the three-second count down. The garbage truck, packed with explosives, detonated as Craft took shelter behind a nearby rock wall. The intense heat from a passing fireball singed his hair. The other agent raced down the road to Craft's aid. Knocked out by the explosion, he struggled to regain his bearings.

Looking up at three agents frantically trying to revive him, Craft said, "Coach, I'm okay."

While laughing at Craft thinking he got knocked out playing a football game, the two men got him into the van. With Wilkins driving, the team raced away from the site. Twenty minutes later, they were on a covert flight back to the base in Kuwait. With mission communications shut down by OPSEC during the flight, the two older agents stretched out in the sleeper lounge chairs. Not having slept for over 48 hours, they were both sound asleep within minutes of lift off.

Having recovered with no damage other than some charred hair, Craft enjoyed a celebratory drink. After toasting the destruction of the virus and Asadi going to meet his maker, the young agents sat in silence wondering where their relationship would go from here. Each time one broached the topic the other changed the conversation to something related to the mission. Both of them knew they were better together as agents than they were alone; but neither was sure that the same held true for other parts of their life. *Had they gone too far? Could they work together and not be intimately involved? Could they be intimately involved and continue to work together? Could they have a family together and live the life of CIA agents?*

WASHINGTON, D.C.

Ducking his head through the door into the oval office, The White House Chief of Staff said, "Mr. President, he's on the phone, demanding to speak to you."

"President Rahimi, I assume you're calling to thank my country for assisting you in averting a mass murder of foreigners on Iranian soil," said the President.

"The United States has no authority to conduct unsanctioned operations in my country. It's an act of war," declared Rahimi.

"So let me get this straight. You're declaring an act of war based on the unauthorized killing of an al-Qaeda terrorist ready to unleash a bioweapon strong enough to kill everyone in Tehran?" asked the President.

"Don't put words in my mouth," yelled President Rahimi. "You have broken our agreement to share intelligence."

"You mean the way you shared intelligence regarding the hijacking of nuclear waste from the nuclear program that you don't have. Was our recovering the stolen material and returning it to you also an act of war?" asked the President.

"Iran is a sovereign nation. All Americans must leave Iran immediately," threatened Iran's President.

"You will get no apology from my nation for saving your ass. Good day," said the President of the United States, hitting the disconnect button on the secure phone.

CHAPTER 48

MANHATTAN, N.Y.

"John Sullivan at your service," said the man standing at fire station entrance.

Shaking hands, Craft thanked the fire chief for taking time out of his day to give him a tour of the fire station. Overcome by the excitement of meeting his uncle, Craft explained that his intent was to meet the firefighters and pay tribute to the brave men who had given their lives on September 11, 2001. As they walked down the memorial hallway with pictures of the fallen men on the wall, he sensed his uncle's sadness and personal loss. Stopping for a moment to show respect, Craft softly ran his fingers over the name Peter James Sullivan engraved on a gold plate under his father's picture.

After greeting the on-duty firefighters and giving them a chance to express their disappointment about the Asian Open being cancelled, Craft shifted the conversation to their important and dangerous job, protecting the citizens of New York. The firefighters were more interested in what it was like to play golf on the Tour than anything else. By now many of them had played cyber golf in golf studios, now located all over the city. He spent an hour giving golf tips and telling jokes.

Once in the chief's office, John Sullivan pointed to a picture of a young man on his desk, and proudly announced his son, Peter, was the fourth generation of Sullivans to serve in the NY City Fire Department. The chief said proudly that his son was named after his older brother, a firefighter who had given his life during the 9/11 attacks. Craft asked a few questions about his son but didn't want to appear overly interested. He left the fire station, feeling a missing piece of his life had been found. At the same time, the need to foster a family bond with the Sullivans was overwhelming.

Craft zipped up his warm jacket and pulled a ski hat over his cold ears. He walked through the streets of lower Manhattan, wondering what it must have been like twenty-eight years earlier when his mother attended graduate school at New York University. Still mid morning, he stopped at a pastry shop for a cup of coffee. Attempting to keep warm, he sat at a table in back, away from the door. Soon, a familiar face walked in.

The large man stopped to ordering coffee, and then proceeded to sit down at the table with him.

"What brings you to New York?" asked Vaughn.

"I was about to ask you the same question?" responded Craft.

Removing a gold medal from his pocket and placing it on the table, Vaughn announced, "Congratulations. I am here to give you the Intelligence Star."

In a moment of sincerity, Vaughn read the commendation, signed by the President and Director Walker, listing his important contributions to the Red Crescent program. It was the Intelligence Community's medal for personal acts of valor. After giving Craft time to look at the medal and reflect on the honor, Vaughn retrieved the medal and put it back into his pocket. The medal would reside at Agency headquarters attributed to an anonymous member of the clandestine service. Craft knew he would never see the medal again, but appreciated the recognition.

"So, what brings you to New York," Vaughn asked again.

"If you haven't noticed, I am a sentimental guy," Craft replied. "Twenty-eight years ago today, my parents had their first date here in Manhattan. It's my intention to experience that first date."

"A date takes another person," commented Vaughn.

"Yes it does and I don't plan to be late," responded Craft.

Pulling out a flask and pouring a touch of whiskey into each of their coffee cups, Vaughn made a toast, "I pray you come back to work with special memories."

After touching cups and taking a drink, Craft asked, "Speaking of work, what's next for me?"

"Continue playing golf, winning golf tournaments, growing the First Light program and waiting to be contacted," replied Vaughn.

"Will the team stay together?" Craft asked.

"Afraid not. You're on your own for a while. The team has been reassigned. The truth be told, I was disappointed the Asian Open was cancelled. Caddying on the Tour was my dream assignment."

"If my job is to play golf then I still need a caddy," Craft commented.

"Yes but not me. I'm going to retire at the end of the year."

"Congratulations, if that's what you really want to do. You certainly deserve it," said Craft, acknowledging his years of devotion to the nation.

"It's time," Vaughn replied.

"Maybe we'll see you on the old men's tour?" Craft said, referring to the tour for men over fifty years old.

"I am content to stay right at home in my four bedroom Virginia estate."

"How are things in the front office? I have to admit, it took some big ones for the President to tell Rahimi to go pound sand," commented Craft.

"It almost cost him the election, but that's politics. Quite frankly, I am more concerned about you. How are you sleeping these days?"

"No guilt, just vacillation on my part. And that's going to be fixed," responded Craft.

Watching the silhouette of the young man from Charleston disappear out of the coffee shop, Vaughn had the ironic thought, *it was by breaking the rules, that the game of golf was saved.*

As his father did, Craft arrived ten minutes early and stood at the entrance to the New York University library. When she arrived, he thanked her for agreeing to celebrate the anniversary of his parents first date. They start downtown with a brisk ride on the Staten Island Ferry and worked their way uptown. After a short subway ride, they boarded the ferry and made their way to the forward deck just as the voyage began across the harbor to Staten Island. The cold gusting winds made standing difficult as the boat rocked cutting through rough harbor waves. They snuggled together to keep warm. The five miles, twenty-five minute ride had them craving a cup of coffee. On the return trip, they sat inside the boat cabin where they could talk, protected from the cold wind. After the ferry ride, they walked toward mid-town to see the Christmas decorations and then stopped for lunch at one of the many sandwich shops along the way. Craft commented that being a southern boy, he had only seen people skating outdoors on television. They walked several blocks up 5th Avenue to Rockefeller Center and waited in line to give skating a try. Both being novice ice skaters, they attempted a couple of laps around the rink while hanging on to the side-walls for dear life. Cold and sore, both decided to hang the skates up before someone got hurt.

It was late in the day; the tall buildings to the southwest blocked the sunlight. Approaching Central Park, he asked, "Will you join me in a horse and carriage ride around Central Park?"

She said, "Only if I can pick the horse."

They walked along the sidewalk looking for a friendly horse and driver, as well as a warm swathe. She chose a beautiful white horse snacking on carrots. As Craft paid the driver, he also bought a red rose. He presented the rose while helping her into the carriage. They cuddled with the blanket across their legs as the horse slowly trotted down the street with the driver whistling "White Christmas."

Feeling the warmth of his strong body and reflecting on the wonderful day, she wondered if this was more than just experiencing his parents' first date. Something had changed. They had given each other their full attention from the moment they set eyes on each other that morning.

Comfortable wrapped in his arms, she asked, "Peter Craft, what is it that you want from me?"

"I want us to be together... I mean as a couple," he said.

"Are you telling me you're ready to make a commitment?" she asked.

Opening a box with a beautiful diamond ring, the same ring his father had given his mother, he answered, "Yes I am." He then asked, "Will you marry me?"

Looking at the beautiful ring and love in his eyes, she answered, "Yes, I will marry you, but..."

"But what?" he asked with a quizzical look on his face.

"Aren't you afraid it will hurt our careers?" she asked, looking at the beautiful ring on her finger.

Pulling her close, he whispered in her ear, *"Motivated people find a way."*

ACKNOWLEDGEMENTS

First and foremost, I thank my father, an avid reader of novels, for inspiring me to write this book. I thank my colleagues, friends, and family for encouraging me to persevere when it would have been easy to give up. I would like to offer a special thanks to Cindy, Judy, Lindsay, Maryam, Eric, Steve, Kalani, Peter, and Vance for their unselfish contributions to this novel. My deepest thanks goes to Frank Bevacqua, Diane Dale, and Linda Cashdan for their exceptional help editing and critiquing the content. I also want to thank Kate Weisel for cover design and book production support. Most of all, I would like to thank my wife Janice for her love and support and the many hours of patient listening as the plot developed.

DENNIS BRODERICK grew up in Fort Edward, New York and attended Northeastern University in Boston, Massachusetts. His career, built upon an electrical engineering education, spans over thirty years of professional experience to include Executive Vice President of a systems engineering consulting company. He and his wife Janice are proud parents of six children. In addition, Dennis is an avid amateur golfer with many golf friends and a single-digit handicap. He is a member of the 1757 Golf Club in Dulles, Virginia.

Made in the USA
Charleston, SC
14 May 2015